Disturb
Not the
Dream

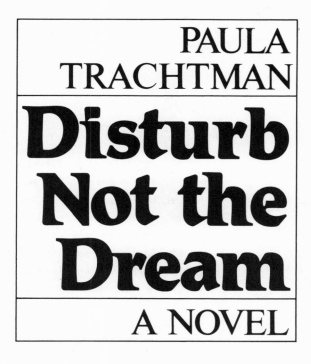

PAULA
TRACHTMAN

Disturb Not the Dream

A NOVEL

CROWN PUBLISHERS, INC.
NEW YORK

Printed in the United States of America
Published simultaneously in Canada
by General Publishing Company Limited
Library of Congress Cataloging in Publication Data
Trachtman, Paula.
Disturb not the dream.
I. Title.
PS3570.R24D5 1981   813'.54   80-24463
ISBN: 0-517-543222
Design by Camilla Filancia
10 9 8 7 6 5 4 3 2 1
First Edition

For PEGGY O'SHEA—*who made it all happen*

Flow gently sweet Afton
Among thy green braes
Flow gently I'll sing thee
A song in thy praise
My Mary's asleep by
Thy murmuring stream
Flow gently sweet Afton—
Disturb not her dream.

ROBERT BURNS

Disturb
Not the
Dream

PROLOGUE 1938

The house defended itself well, thanks to the meticulous care with which it had been built. Thick plaster walls muffled the screams of the storm, while heavy shutters over the windows and doors protected them from the incredible power of the wind, which sent roofs, trees, and living things tumbling through the gathering darkness like toys. Even the huge sheets of water heaved against the house by the raging ocean splashed to nothing when confronted by its sturdy hand-hewn shingles.

Inside, the light of myriad candles and hurricane lamps bathed the labyrinth of interconnected rooms in a soft golden glow that was almost romantic. The large, squarish parlor, dominated by a massive brick fireplace, looked comfortable, Victorian—remote as a Christmas card illustration from the chaos outside. Its stern family portraits stared down upon the clutter of overstuffed sofas and chairs with Puritanical stoicism.

The eerie figure materializing from the odd little door next to the fireplace hesitated but a moment, oil lamp in hand, before continuing on about its business.

First through the cheerful, oak-paneled dining room with its graceful French chandelier and glowing sconces, then into the spacious, whitewashed country kitchen, past the hearth in the exposed brick wall. A quick glance up the back stairs showed them to be empty, as was the warren of of nearby maids' rooms and the larger studio beyond. The cavernous library proved equally vacant when probed by the impatient lamp.

Firmly, steadily, the figure walked its globe of light up the broad central staircase, pausing briefly at the window landing to try to peer through the octagon of stained glass. Once on the second-floor landing, the shadowy form hesitated, studied the long hallway and its series of solid doors, all of them closed. A grunt seemed to signify some quick decision, and it was moving again, gliding across the lush carpet from one door to another. The first was locked, or jammed, and could not be forced, but the next yielded easily. The bedroom behind it was empty, and so was the next and the one after that. Impatience had given way to a whimpering frenzy. Doors swung open with a crash, the light thrust inside in a savage swing of arm.

The last door alone rewarded its frantic search, and for a few brief moments light met light.

Its work done, the figure emerged and shut the door with a care approaching love, breathing hard. The first door remained a challenge, had to be breeched, but from above came human sounds, a mouselike squeal followed by nervous laughter, and the globe of light was deflected, sought out the door leading to the attic stairway. It opened with efficient silence; the lamp was left behind to hold it ajar as the hunched figure began climbing to the darkness above, a different kind of light flashing in its free hand.

Meanwhile, in the first bedroom, door bolted to secure her against the storm's suggestion of God-like threats, five-year-old Jessica remained outwardly calm. Despite the fear that made her lungs feel hollow, she was determined to prove that she was "a big girl" now. She had remained bravely alone in her pink-and-white room since late afternoon, waiting to be called down to supper. Perched on the edge of her canopied bed, her sole external concession to the fear was the desperate manner in which she clutched Missy Boo, a calico kitten, to her chest, laughing aloud when the kitten squeezed free and commenced diving at the shifting shadows cast by the hurricane lamp her mother had given her after the electricity had gone off.

2

At that instant, as if frozen behind museum glass, Jessica's delicate beauty was a cameo of childhood's curves and planes, the lamp's sensual rays fingering her tilted profile and flowery pinafore with longing.

Suddenly tired of being brave and alone, she decided to visit Nancy in her attic rooms. Tucking Missy Boo under her arm, she unbolted the door and stepped into the hall. Almost unconsciously, she became aware at once of another sound besides the blurred shrieks of the storm, a strange but insistent tapping and dragging sound above her, a counterpoint of sorts that whispered through her tense body without echo. She walked past the lamp on the floor and mounted the narrow stairway with cautious slowness, using the pine wall as a guide. Soon she was in the attic sitting area, confronting the closed door to the maid's bedroom from which liquid candlelight spilled around the door frame.

The storm was much louder up here, separated from her only by the thin skin of the roof boards. It seemed as if fists were about to burst through and crush her on the spot. Jessica hurried to throw open Nancy's door, anticipating her laughing, soothing welcome.

There, on the threshold of pleasure, her fear found human form.

She screamed, screamed from the pit of her being, but her tiny, panic-stricken voice was as nothing against the howling wind. the bedroom was a mass of writhing shadows, a vague, black figure leaned over the bed and blotted out the candlelight, its arm rising and falling with furious speed, the glinting object in its hand slashing at the two naked bodies entwined on the bed.

"Here! Here! Here!" a muffled voice grunted. "You wanted it, have it!"

Jessica could not see or would not see what happened next, not clearly. The hand with the knife had reached for the unseen ceiling, the knife now holding aloft a dripping

3

cylinder of flesh, like a pipe, like a melted pipe. "Eat it! Eat it, whore!" the figure's grunts were explosive, hysterical, shoving the length of darkness into Nancy's pale face, a face made alien by wide-eyed terror, incomprehension.

Run, Nancy! Please run! Jessica mouthed the words, but sensed that it was too late. The knife had shed its grisly burden and was once more in flight, was descending, was burying its silver-bird sleekness deep inside Nancy's pearl stomach, ripping upward, ripping. The other body had slid to the floor into a pool of its own blood and was still, arms and legs twisted beneath it.

Now the figure was turning, its features in shadow, obviously startled to discover the little girl and her kitten framed in the doorway. It was moving toward her, a familiar stranger, smiling falsely, hiding the stained knife; but Jessica had already turned and was racing for the stairway. Some innate common sense prevented her from tumbling headlong down the stairs as she retraced her steps with deliberate coolness, trembling and sweaty, but refusing to risk a missed step.

Once safe on the second-floor landing, she grasped the kitten tighter to her chest, unaware of its tiny claws pecking at her dress front. She ran first to Garrick's room, but it was dark and empty. Panic was about to overwhelm her. The dragging and tapping sound had returned to penetrate the storm's distant noises. She headed for the puddle of light seeping from under Diedre's door and was ready to weep in relief when she burst inside and found her sister at her dressing table as usual, flanked by two tall candles. But instead of staring intently at her flawless reflection in search of treacherous pimples, Diedre had apparently fallen asleep in the middle of combing her hair, her pretty head and its swirls of raven curls resting lightly on her arm. "Diedre!" Jessica shouted in annoyance and terror, rushing over to shake her sister awake.

It was a mistake that would haunt her years later.

4

In slow motion, Diedre's body began to slide away from her touch, tumbled to the floor. Diedre's head remained on the dressing table, however, blood pouring from the smashed, tangled network of muscle and bone that had once been her neck.

The tapping and dragging sound was closer, but she did not hear it, her stare transfixed by the head of her sister lying so quietly, so naturally on the table. What saved her was the mirror. In the corner of its horrible tableau, the black figure loomed, grew larger, knife raised. She spun around and dodged past its falling arc in one swift, instinctive thrust of energy, the blade humming near her ear like a scythe.

At the end of the hallway, Jessica ran down the rear staircase. The storm's fury was increasing, shutters rattling in protest under its repeated blows, but Jessica was again in the grip of a strange serenity. Mommy and Daddy would rescue her. She knew that in her heart, and the thought brought a measure of peace, the habitual certainty of an adult world that could defeat any menace at will. They would hug and tease her, convince her that it was all a dream, just another bad dream.

The whitish spaces of the kitchen were empty, a single candle on the table throwing a weak light at its vast expanse. As she crossed the tiled floor she began to slip, almost fell. Glancing down, she realized that the dream was not finished. Blood was everywhere in thickish, sticky puddles, and amid the puddles lay several indistinct forms, forms that took shape under her horrified gaze. Tandy, the mother cat, and her four kittens had been cut open and thrown aside like broken dolls, their heads severed.

But these deaths, perhaps death itself, could no longer touch or move her. Pretending to be a lady, she tiptoed daintily around the small corpses, sensing that she must hurry but no longer quite sure why. Only the sound urged her on, that tapping and dragging sound that continued to haunt her during lulls in the storm's relentless clatter. Her mind whispered to her, warned her that there was nowhere left to hide but in the pantry closet, in her secret place. She stooped over and crept inside pulling the doors shut behind her. The kitten was asleep or dazed, and she petted it without stop until she fell asleep in the cubby Nancy had showed her behind the shelves.

Time and space lost meaning. It was snug, womb-dark, and the hours elapsed into dreamless sleep. The storm abated. Morning sunlight poked under the doors of the pantry and tickled her awake. Aching and cramped, Jessica clutched the kitten, which did not stir, and emerged, blinking, into the light. She did not see the blood splattered on the floor and walls, the heads of the cats. It was morning, and the nightmare had ended at last. She walked into the parlor and was not surprised to find the bulky body of her father sprawled near the cellar door, a knife protruding from his chest.

She shuffled past him without hesitation, drawn by the open door near the fireplace, the one she had always been warned against. A small voice struggled to be heard. She glanced down the shaft that led to the storm cellar and saw her mother crumpled in a heap near the foot of the ladderlike stair. Her mother's head jutted out at a peculiar angle, but she managed to smile up at her, whispering, "My baby, my poor baby."

Jessica climbed down carefully and lay the kitten by her mother's head, running her fingers through her mother's long, graying hair, crooning to her the same lullaby she used to croon to Jessica when the little girl was afraid of the dark and could not sleep. Her mother finally stopped crying, but the daughter continued to croon over her until her voice was hoarse and cracking. It grew dark in a while, and then light again, before voices clawed at the edges of her vision, before firm but kind hands led her away, soldiers of the prince—come to save his princess. She had left reality behind her.

Part 1

Mulberry stands on Dune Road in Southampton, quite close to the Shinnecock Inlet formed by the 1938 hurricane. Built by their parents as a wedding gift for Slade and Irene Desmond in 1888, the house had survived everything, even its reputation.

A typical Victorian cottage of weathered shingle, replete with towers and turrets, porches and gazebos, it sits back rather complacently amid its three acres, commanding an impressive view of the Atlantic. In pristine condition, the grounds beautifully treed, tended, and flowered, it is difficult to give credence to the tales of horror that the locals insist took place within its walls. The stories become more lurid and exaggerated, surely, from years of telling.

The young Desmonds had been a strikingly handsome couple, tall, golden, with identical deep blue eyes. Since they were first cousins, their parents had been hesitant about allowing them to marry each other, but Irene's pregnancy had quickly overcome the objections. Evan, their only child, was, despite his grandparents' fears of consanguinity, perfect. Except for the railroad accident that took the lives of both sets of grandparents in 1892, the young Desmonds' lives were idyllic. They had everything anyone could dream of wanting: money, looks, health. And as if that weren't enough, they adored one another. Everyone commented on how devoted the child was to his parents; he stayed close to them and rarely took his eyes off them. Truly a household to be envied.

One August evening Irene stood at the bay window watching the moon riding the sea it had silvered. The light played over her nude body, and Slade, from the depths of their four-poster bed, admired its perfection. After ten years of marriage, he was still impressed with his wife's beauty. He smiled, thinking of how much pleasure they had taken in each other over the years. As if reading his thoughts, Irene turned toward him with an answering smile.

"Darling, let's go get Evan. We've been so busy all week, we've hardly seen him." She pulled him out of bed and the parents padded down the carpeted hall to their son's room. Slade pulled back the curtains, waiting as Irene coaxed the boy awake.

"Come on, dear, it's time to get up and have a nice party with Mummy and Daddy." The handsome child, heavy with sleep, felt the familiar sense of dread flood over him as he felt himself lifted in his father's strong arms. Placed gently on the marriage bed, he trembled at the touch of his mother's cool, practiced hands on his body, while his father watched, eyes glittering, eager for his turn in the game. Evan lay back passively. Experience had taught him that neither tears nor struggles would be of any use. He could only hope (for experience had also taught him that prayers were of no avail) that they wouldn't hurt him too much and that the "party" would not last too long.

After what seemed to him an eternity, and they were satisfied, he was allowed to creep back to his bed. The household finally slept.

He awoke in a pool of sweat, trembling and choking. He knew it hadn't been a wish-fulfillment dream, nor a fantasy, nor a corruption of the primal scene—as that asshole Freud had tried to tell him. Goddamn it! It *had* happened. That and all the other things that Viennese fakir had assured him were due to the workings of his id, Oedipal conflicts, fixations, and the rest of that jargon. He would have been better off if he'd come right back to the States after the war instead of wasting a good part of a year in analysis in

8

Austria. Musingly he thought that Freud was just too much of a middle-class Jew to believe that such things as Evan Desmond described could possibly have reality.

Wrenching his thoughts back to so-called sanity, he contemplated the day ahead of him. It was the annual Independence Day celebration at the club—bound to be the usual bore, but there was always the chance that someone's houseguest might prove to be an amusing conquest. Of making a conquest he had not a doubt. Even out of his cavalry uniform, loaded with its war-hero medals, Evan was a striking figure. "Greek god" was the phrase most often used to describe the perfection of his golden looks and tall, broad-shouldered, lithe body. He was impeccably groomed, exquisitely mannered, perfectly tailored, Princeton educated, and filthy rich. His parents had gone down together on the *Titanic,* leaving him their vast fortune as a birthday gift when he was twenty-one years old. Unfortunately their deaths had been too easy, he often brooded; for years he had plotted to ensure their dying in a slow and lingeringly painful way, preferably at his own hands. The anniversary of their drowning always filled him with an enormous sense of frustrated rage.

As he dressed for the club's luncheon buffet, he practiced his gleaming smile in the mirror. Grimacing, he laughed to himself at the thought that upon his death, he'd probably look like the last portrait in *The Picture of Dorian Gray.* Convinced he had nowhere left to go but to hell, he intended to go with great distinction. Approaching the age of thirty, he was determined to accelerate his rate of debauchery. Perhaps it was part of what Dr. Freud had described as his death wish. He considered it revenge for his past.

2

At the club, a brilliant sun sparked diamonds off the dark blue of the Atlantic. Members and their guests strolled about the manicured grounds that stretched from the cavernous Tudor mansion, which served as the clubhouse, to the dunes, which kept the sea at bay. It was a perfect day, all agreed, a symbol that this postwar world was going to be splendid indeed.

Traditionally, this fête was the summer "slave-mart," a time for parents to display nubile daughters available for the great marriage auction. Carefully arranged in a canvas lounge chair, Evalynn Ambrose tried dutifully to display her charms, as per instructions.

She felt they were of dubious distinctions. She was small and slender, with regular features in an oval face made heavy looking by thick eyebrows detracting from the long lashes framing large brown eyes. Her hair was pulled back in an unbecoming bun, since her parents didn't approve of either short hair or long flowing tresses, while the voluminous white organdy dress with its pink sash gave her the look of a dumpy child. Her parents had made it abundantly clear that if she didn't make a "catch" this season, it would be their last summer in the Hamptons. They would have to live in poverty, a condition they had minutely described as approximating the sixth circle of hell.

Marjorie Ambrose, a handsome woman of forty, sat at a nearby table with her dowager cronies of many summers, gaily discussing the season's charity functions. Grimly she wondered what they'd think if they knew of her true financial straits. Harry's fortune had unexpectedly fallen, rather than risen due to the war. At age sixty he was too old for a comeback, and she had little jewelry left to sell. As she animatedly chatted with the "girls," she was inwardly filled with dread at the thought of losing the only way of life she had ever known. How their friends would revel in the gossip of their downfall! It was all up to Evalynn now, but could her only child pull it off? Surreptitiously glancing in her daughter's direction, she was doubtful. She now realized that it had been an error to have had her convent-schooled from first through twelfth grades. Her daughter was just too quiet and genteel for this postwar generation; sweet and demure as she was, her mother could see nothing about her that would help her compete with brash girls who flirted outrageously and flaunted their charms.

Evalynn sipped her lemonade and inwardly sighed over her family problems, wondering if she could attract any of the eligible men. When she had told her parents she never wanted to marry but would rather devote herself to church work, their outrage had stunned her. After all they had done for her, her mother had ranted, the least she could do would be to help them in their old age, and surround them with adorable grandchildren, sired by a wealthy husband. Always dutiful ("Honor thy father and mother"), she had finally given in; the Sisters had told her that being a good wife and mother was a great blessing in the eyes of Our Lord. Picturing herself, Madonna-like, with a child, she smiled, a secret, wistful smile. It caught the eye of Evan Desmond on his way to the bar. That Mona Lisa-like quality drew his attention to a girl he'd normally never notice. No—not his type at all—too refined for his tastes. But his interest was piqued. What was behind that beautiful, enigmatic expression? He'd never bothered to seduce a correct young virgin. It might be a challenge worthy of his talents to corrupt this gentle little creature. Immediately he felt cheered; he had a project for summer 1919.

As he sat at the bar, he started making discreet inquiries

about the brunette in the white dress. *That* was Evalynn Ambrose? Before he had enlisted in 1914, she'd been a scrawny child. While others might see her as rather plain, his connoisseur's eye had noted her potential. A good haircut, some makeup, a thinner eyebrow, and clothes to bring out the fullness of her body would make her look ravishing. He'd enjoy playing Pygmalion. Casually he sought out her parents, feigning interest in their vapid conversation and insincere concern about his well-being during the war. Politely accepting their commiseration for his hardships, he thought what fools people were. War was the ultimate experience of his life—when else could it be lived so intensely? He'd enjoyed the licensed killing. They'd made him a hero for the greatest pleasure he'd ever had.

The Ambroses were surprised and delighted when he asked after their daughter, and brought him over for a reintroduction. He was almost thirteen years older, and with his reputation as a rake, Evalynn was the last girl in the world in whom they'd expect him to express any interest. The conversation was brief and cordial, with mutual agreement to meet again "very soon." Evan strolled off, leaving the Ambrose family to wonder if his notice had any significance.

Desmond plotted his campaign with all the care and lavish attention to detail that had marked his brilliance as an officer in battle. Each time he arranged to "bump into" the girl, he spoke to her a bit longer than the time before. The times between meetings grew shorter and soon he was calling at the Ambrose home on Captain's Neck. With parental consent, he escorted her to club functions in the evenings; during the day he took her motoring, yachting, or out to play tennis or golf.

The would-be in-laws were ecstatic. "Harry, can you believe that Desmond is truly interested in our little mouse?"

"Well, he's certainly doing a good imitation of a young man come courting, Marjorie. What do you think he sees in Evalynn? Of course she's a darling child, but not the type you'd think a man like Desmond would pursue."

"I've given that a great deal of thought," his wife rejoined. "I think he's sick and tired of the wild life he's led, and wants to settle down with a respectable, well-bred young lady from a good family. I'm sure he wants an heir to carry on his name—and to inherit that fortune. He couldn't find a better girl than ours. All these loud girls today shamelessly pursuing him, no better than they should be, I'm sure. Why shouldn't he turn to someone like our daughter? He'd change all those wicked ways people gossip about, for the love of a good woman. And I'm sure that gossip is just malicious—everyone is simply jealous of his looks and money."

And so the Ambroses spun the fantasy they so desperately wanted to believe—and tried to bring Evalynn into it to live there with them.

Their daughter, on her part, was totally bewildered by this handsome man's attentions. He was charming and a perfect companion, but she was never comfortable with him. He smelled of whiskey and tobacco and always seemed to be touching her "accidentally." Even though he accompanied her to church on Sundays, she had a feeling he mocked her and her faith. She tried to explain her unease to her mother, to no avail.

"Don't be a goose, Evalynn, you simply do not have enough experience of the world to know what you're talking about. Evan Desmond is probably the catch of the century, and you'd best set your cap for him while he's showing such interest."

"What am I supposed to do, Mother? I just always feel that he's laughing at all of us."

"Just be sweet and pleasant and never contradict him, dear. Of course should he make improper advances, you must refuse. Anything more than a brief kiss on the cheek at this stage will never do. If a girl permits any intimacies, how will a man know she is virtuous? No man wants damaged goods, I can assure you of that, my girl."

"But, Mother, what does that mean? How does a man know if a woman is damaged? How does it show?"

"Evalynn Ambrose, hush right now," her mother replied, "this is no fit conversation for a young girl. When you're married your husband will teach you all you have to know about IT. And if you're a very lucky lady, Evan Desmond might be your husband."

To that end, all of Mr. Desmond's casual suggestions were followed. Her hair was cut and styled, her eyebrows tweezed, makeup permitted, and a new wardrobe purchased by the sale of a lovely pearl ring. Secretly, the girl had to admit she had never looked so well—why she was actually becoming popular; the boys flocked about her. Frank Harris was the one she liked best. He was kind and shared her devout faith in Jesus. Comfortable with each other, they animatedly talked about books and school and nature and God. They found a shared interest in the work of the missionaries and spoke excitedly of the glory of bringing Christ to the heathens. Amusedly Evan watched the budding romance, knowing that as long as he was in the picture, the girl's parents would never permit its flowering. Irritated that this snip of a girl would prefer the Harris boy to himself, he swung into action. The next phase was romance.

To his chagrin, Evalynn seemed totally immune to every

14

ploy or advance; she was even becoming adept at avoiding and preventing them. No matter how romantic the setting, she resisted his considerable charm. While dancing in the moonlight or sailing among the coves of Shelter Island, he tried in vain to arouse her latent sexuality. Puzzled, he tried to think it through. Could it be that she was as she seemed? Pure, good, devout, and innocent. Did such qualities actually exist? Almost dazed by the thought, he realized that he might be forced to admit that virtue did exist, and right here in the person of this lovely young girl.

Evan took two weeks off to think seriously about his "project," and neither called nor visited the Ambrose home. Relieved, Evalynn saw more and more of Frank Harris, and hoped the tension with her suitor was at an end. Her parents kept questioning her about what she had done "to drive Desmond off," refusing to believe her response that she had honestly done nothing.

"How could you, Evalynn, how could you have destroyed your future and ours by letting him slip through your fingers? What have you done?" was her mother's constant refrain. Her father sighed a lot and seemed to shrink into himself. Twenty years older than his wife, he just seemed defeated. Her heart went out to her parents in their disappointment, but she was happy spinning daydreams of a future life with Frank, whom she now saw daily.

Evan's return with a huge bouquet of roses for her mother, and a lavish box of chocolates for herself, shattered her hopes. What *did* this man want of her? It was all so confusing. The confusion was cleared within a few days when her parents, beaming, called her into the drawing room to announce that Mr. Evan Desmond had asked for her hand in marriage, and they had assured him of her acceptance. Craftily he had then left, certain they would ensure her assent. To their utter amazement Evalynn blazed with anger.

"How could you give your consent! I will *not* marry that

man—not ever! I don't love him, he frightens me. I am not a slave to be sold to suit your needs," and bursting into tears, she ran to lock herself in her room.

Stunned by her vehemence, the Ambroses looked at each other aghast. "Are we doing the right thing, Marjorie? After all, she's not even eighteen—she's just a child. Perhaps we should let her have her way."

"Don't be stupid, Harry. I was her age when I married you at my parents' arrangements. Girls simply cannot be trusted to make suitable marriages. They're forever thinking of romance—a lot of good *that* will do when she has to scrub floors. We've done everything for her all of her life—it's now time she thought of us. If this match falls through, we'll have to spend the rest of our lives in a tiny flat somewhere in Queens, hoping none of our friends find out what we've come to. I'll have none of that!"

And putting on her most dulcet tones, Marjorie Ambrose called her future son-in-law to tell him that of course Evalynn was thrilled by the news, but too overcome by the honor to speak to him at once. She'd write in a few days when her shyness had worn off.

It took three days of coaxing, pleading, and cajoling to get the girl to come out of her room, and another three days to get her to change her mind. Trained from birth to obedience, it was impossible for her to hold out in her defiance. Her mother was relentless, "Do you want to see your father a broken man? Do you want to see me on my knees cleaning floors? Have you forgotten your faith? Do you not honor your parents? What would the Sisters think of your sins of pride and disobedience?"

Desperately, the girl clutched at straws, "But, Mother, he's not a Catholic, how can I marry him in my church?"

"Mr. Desmond is a magnanimous gentleman. He has agreed to be married in our faith, and to bring up your children as practicing Catholics. What more could you ask, you wilfull child! Do you realize the awesome responsibility

16

you have? You can bring him to Jesus. You can reform him from his past errors and show him the Truth." This was the mother's clinching argument.

By the end of the week, Evan Desmond received a stiff, but proper, note thanking him for the honor, and accepting his proposal of marriage. Frank Harris received a tear-stained note that sent him away—some said into the priesthood.

Indian summer weather held for the October wedding at St. Peter's Church. The summer community motored out and stayed at their forty-room "cottages" for the event of the year. The others were put up at the Irving Hotel on Hill Street. Imagine that chit of a girl getting the catch of the century, socially and financially! The community was agog at the lavish arrangements, and at the refurbishing Desmond had made in Mulberry, his house on Dune Road, in honor of his bride. In addition, he purportedly had given her a king's ransom in jewels as a wedding gift. Who would have believed that the dissolute playboy could have fallen head over heels in love? Rumor had it that he had "advanced" his in-laws enough to make them comfortable for the rest of their lives, and had paid for the trousseau and reception as well. What a lucky girl that Evalynn was. And who would have thought she'd turn out such a beauty? A swan indeed!

The lobster-and-champagne reception was held in white silk Arabian-style tents on the lush grounds of the Ambrose estate. The bride seemed nervous, as was fitting, and the groom was resplendent. At 5 P.M., in a shower of rice, they left to spend their wedding night at Mulberry. Their honeymoon—a crossing on the *Queen Mary* for a year's tour of the Continent—was to start in three days.

Evalynn had prayed for guidance daily and had taken her marriage vows sincerely determined to keep them. She would be an exemplary wife and mother, and, by doing so, would bring Desmond to the True Church. In this way she would serve God and make her sacrifices all worthwhile. Her parents were happy, and Evan seemed to be; this gave her hope for the future.

On his part, Evan was astounded to realize he had actually fallen in love with this gentle young girl. He even thought seriously of becoming a Catholic. He could truly begin life anew and perhaps the blackness and nightmares would leave him forever when he had been forgiven his sins and transgressions. For the first time in his life, Evan Desmond was looking forward to the future. Could the Church succeed where Freud had failed?

The bridegroom had to laugh to himself. Here he was in his own dressing room, nervous as a virgin as he slipped into maroon silk pajamas and matching robe. With every consideration he had read of, he gave his bride time to change into her night clothes and get under the covers to protect her modesty. The brocade curtains had been drawn in the flower-filled master bedroom and a fire was glowing in the graceful wood-carved fireplace. He was going to be such a gentle and considerate lover that his wife—he quivered at the thought—would have to fall in love with him. How his former friends would sneer at him now.

Quietly, he entered the bedroom, closing the door behind him. His wife looked so lovely, and so frightened, that he had to smile. Her dark hair was soft and full about the oval of her face, and her brown eyes were large and soft, trembling brightly with unshed tears. Her lips were small and full and as he leaned over to kiss them gently, he put his hand on her bare shoulder. Evalynn stiffened immediately.

18

"Don't worry so, darling, I promise I won't hurt you. Just try to relax." At his most charming, Evan sat on the edge of the great four-poster and talked of the wonderful honeymoon trip they'd take. As he saw her start to relax, he continued to chat amiably as he walked about to his side of the bed and removed his robe and pajama top. Sliding under the covers, he held her gently in his arms for a long time, stroking her hair, murmuring of how much he loved her.

When the tension left her eyes, he slowly started to kiss her with greater passion and to stroke her body with his warm, practiced hands. As she started to respond, he slid out of his pajama bottoms and pushed her nightgown up to her waist to stroke her thighs and rounded belly. "Come now, you don't need this lacy business all over you," he coaxed.

She was embarrassed, but, docile as always, sat up and pulled her wedding nightdress over her head. He took it from her hands and dropped it on the floor. As she lay back on the pillow he gazed upon her naked body with delight. It was just as he knew it would be—perfect. Her legs were long and shapely, the breasts pear shaped, curved and full, her waist tiny.

"You are truly lovely—no, don't try to cover your body. Let me teach you to take joy and pleasure in it"—and he bent his head to kiss her breasts. Evalynn could not believe how beautiful this married love was, and as her body responded to her husband's expert manipulations, she wondered at how glorious physical sensation could be. He gently forced her thighs apart, and satisfied that her body was taking on the rhythm he was orchestrating, he slowly but firmly started to press into her. Holding her tight, he murmured, "Now, darling, it's only going to hurt for a brief second, and then we'll truly be man and wife."

Her moan of pleasure reassured him, and he thrust home

19

quickly. For a second he froze, then pulled out with a cry of rage and, to his wife's horror, started to shout as he smacked her head from side to side.

"You rotten cunt, you whore, scum of Babylon," were just a few of the kinder epithets Evan hurled at his wife as he dragged her out of their marriage bed and flung her on the floor in front of the fireplace. She lay there trembling and gazing at him in speechless horror as tears poured down her face, which was streaked with his fingermarks. Evan towered over her in maniacal rage, a poker in his hand. "All right now, bitch! Who was it? Was it your father? Or your priest? Or that mewling boy you were laying? Or was it all three at once?"

Terrified by the mad gleam in his eyes the girl was frozen, staring up at him. Afraid he'd kill her, he dropped the poker and struggled for control. He put on his robe, switched on the lights, and pulled her to her feet. Wordlessly he examined her body, inch by inch. "Why you goddamned whore—you've not only been fucking, you've had a bastard! These nipples are brown, not pink, and these are stretch marks, tiny, but here on your breasts and stomach. Are you going to tell me another story of the virgin birth? I never believed the first one, I warn you. The truth, and all of it—now—or I'll throw you into the fire."

The cold detachment with which he said this was somehow worse than his rage. He pushed her to the rug and settled back in the large velvet wing chair by the fire. Crouched at his feet, face averted, she haltingly told him her story.

It started the summer before she was sixteen. The Rudder's houseguest was a boy named John Soles; he had just completed his freshman year at Yale and he paid a lot of attention to her. She had never been popular and was thrilled that a college man was interested. He was tall and heavy, and not really good looking, but in her eyes he became a Prince Charming as he escorted her to all the

20

functions. Mousy Evalynn Ambrose had a boyfriend! Her parents thought he was a nice enough boy and were delighted that she was doing something other than reading or going to church. Near the end of August, they gave them permission to go to the club's young people's dance, provided she was home no later than 11 P.M. She was having a marvelous time and thought John was too, so she was surprised when about 9 o'clock he suggested that they leave. As usual, she was sure she'd done something wrong and that he was tired of being with her.

He didn't seem angry, and when on the way home he suggested pulling over to park behind the town beach pavilion to look at the ocean, she gladly agreed. There was plenty of time before her curfew, and she was eager to find out about this romance business her friends were always giggling about. She was hoping John would kiss her—she was so eager to know what that was like. When he suggested getting out of the car to sit on the deck in front of the pavilion to be more comfortable, she nodded. He took the lap robe along and spread it for her. She felt like a princess as she settled her skirts about her, he was behaving like such a Galahad. She heard him moving behind her as she watched the moon on the waves, then he sat down, put his arm around her, and took her hand.

Evan grinned lewdly as she choked out, "He put his—his 'thing' in my hand. I screamed, but he placed his hand across my mouth and held me down." The girl then repeated John Soles' words as if they had been indelibly imprinted upon her memory.

"Listen to me, Evie, and listen carefully," said John Soles. "Don't you play games with me! Who do you think you are? I'm not going home with blue balls for a girl like you. If you're going to be a cock-teaser, you have to pay the price. I've invested time and money in you, and tonight is the return on my investment. Don't try that innocent young virgin stuff with me. You know the score. Didn't you always squeeze back when I squeezed your hand? Just nod—right. Did you move away when I put my arm around you when we drove? Did you let me hold you close when we danced when no one was looking? Did you come here of your own free will? O.K., case closed, so come across now, and no more games."

Cautiously, John had removed his hand; she looked too stunned to speak, but when she took breath to scream once more, he clapped his hand across her mouth again and easily pressed her small body down on the blanket with his bulk. Numbly she noted that he had carefully hung his white flannel trousers and his drawers across the rail of the deck, along with his jacket. She tried to struggle, but his weight was crushing, suffocating. "O.K., Evie," he said. "If you promise not to scream I'll let up on you. Promise?" At her nod, he shifted his body and removed his hand. He moved quickly and reached for something from his jacket pocket. Before she could scramble to her feet he was holding her down again, while stuffing his handkerchief into her mouth.

In a low rapid tone, he lectured her. "Now, girl, hear this. I'm going to be a lawyer, like my dad. I can tell you now that no jury in the world would convict a young gentleman like myself of rape when a girl admits that she left a chaperoned dance early, agrees to a joyride, sits down on a blanket at a deserted beach—all of her own free will. Even your parents wouldn't believe you—you wouldn't want them to know what you're doing now, would you?"

Wide-eyed with terror, she shook her head at the thought of her parents knowing of her disgrace—all of her own doing. She closed her eyes and prayed for a miracle. There weren't any that night.

He easily pinned her hands behind her body by the weight of his torso on hers, and his hands busily pushed her skirts above her waist. Deftly he slid her underpants off, jeering as she vainly kicked her legs to fight him off. "Don't

22

worry, sweetheart, you'll get what you want in a minute. Now I'm going to shove your pants under your sweet little ass so we don't muss up this nice blanket."

His heavy hands pinched and roughly fondled her. He pushed her legs apart with his and forced her knees up, laughing at her squirming and muffled cries.

"Just move like that when I get this inside you, and we'll both have a great ole time, my girl—keep it up. How do you like the feel of this?" He placed his member on her belly and grinned at the fright in her eyes.

John played his fingers between her legs, then started to rub hard.

"Boy are you ready," he murmured. "You're all hot and slippery."

It was that time of the month when she got the discharge that embarrassed her as much as did her monthly periods, but no one had ever explained either one to her. The girl lay in rigid terror as she felt him guide himself into the opening between her legs. The pain made her struggle anew and the tears streamed down her face, the gag muffling her screams.

"Don't worry, baby, we'll be there soon. Daddy'll take good care of you," he panted. "Here's what you want, what all you bitches want." A savage thrust tore into her. The pain was excruciating, but he didn't stop, he kept pushing and rubbing and grunting until she started to lose consciousness. With a cry, he finally stopped and lay atop her for a while—catching his breath.

"Boy, you really were a virgin. Lucky you had a demolition expert like me on the job. Look at all the trouble I've saved the next guy."

With a laugh he pulled away and lay beside her on the blanket, one heavy arm still flung over her body. She lay like a rag doll—too exhausted and broken to move.

Companionably he pulled the handkerchief out of her mouth and gave it to her to "mop up with." John got up

23

and, whistling cheerfully, was busily getting dressed. As he did so, she noticed dully that he hadn't even removed his shoes—nor even kissed her once.

"Come on now, Evie, better get up and pull yourself together. I know I'm great, but I don't think we have time for another round tonight—unless you insist."

When he moved toward her, she scrambled to her feet and stared at him helplessly, too stunned to cry anymore.

"Now clean yourself up so you don't mess up the car seat on the way home. Sometimes I think virgins are more trouble than they're worth—nothing personal, Evie."

She followed his directions, moving painfully, humiliated beyond speech. On the way home, John talked gaily of all the good times they could have now, ignoring her silence. Escorting her into the house, he stood close behind her as she called "good-night" to her parents, and ran upstairs. It was a few minutes to 11.

Evalynn heard him explaining that she had developed a severe headache. After exchanging pleasantries, he left the house, whistling loudly. She wept until dawn, then stayed in her darkened room for three days, telling her mother it was "that time." She never saw John Soles again.

Two weeks later she returned to her beloved convent school upstate, and as the peace and routine worked its magic, she refused to think of what had been. She was barely aware that her period had stopped coming.

Busily she made plans for the year. After the New Year, her parents were leaving on a six-month cruise of the Caribbean and South America; the war prevented their annual pilgrimage to the Continent. They had agreed she might stay with the nuns, instead of with their friends, during her school vacation. How she looked forward to the peace of the cloistered life!

It was just before the November recess that Sister Mary Joseffa called her favorite pupil into her office for a brief conference.

24

"Evalynn, I wonder if there is something troubling you. You are quieter than ever, and I couldn't help but notice you looked heavier when I was supervising bath night last week."

The Sister's gentle concern threw Evalynn into a fit of weeping, and into facing the reality she had been denying. In broken gasps, she poured out her story of terror and humiliation, and of her fear for the future.

"My child, we must tell your parents at once."

At this, the girl went into greater paroxysms of weeping. On her knees she pleaded with the Sister to find an alternative.

"This will destroy them, Sister Mary. I'm all that they have. They'll never see me or speak to me again. It would be like being dead. Oh, please, please!"

The young Sister was tender and compassionate, and just a few years older than her charge. Her heart bled for the wounded innocent.

"My child, please compose yourself. I promise I will pray tonight for Divine Guidance. If I can find an answer, I will tell you tomorrow."

The gleam of hope in the girl's eyes was almost harder for Sister Mary to bear than had been her tears. They both spent most of the night praying.

In the morning, Evie went into the meeting with great apprehension. Sister Mary was pale and exhausted and spoke quietly.

"I am going to enter into a great deception, for which I believe God will forgive me. Your child can bring great joy and happiness to a good family who will adopt and raise it as their own. Your life and that of your family will not be destroyed. God has shown me the way." So the two young women knelt once more and prayed their thanks to the Savior.

The Ambroses were so busy during the Christmas recess that they barely had time for their daughter. Their ship sailed on January 1, and there were a million last-minute details to attend to. Evie was grateful for their distraction and kept to herself as much as possible. Fortunately, the dress style covered her thickening waist. Her parents had agreed to let their child spend the winter at Retreat with Sister Mary, since she was so persistent about it. They knew she'd be in good hands.

Sister Mary, in the meantime, claiming poor health, had received permission to spend several months at her family's home in Vermont. The school authorities were pleased that Evie could go with her to help her, and felt it would determine the girl's choosing to join their order. They all felt she really had the calling. Sister Mary, sick at the deception, kept reminding herself that protecting a violated young girl, her innocent parents, and, most of all, an innocent baby, could not be an abomination in the eyes of the Lord. The tension showed in her face, and her colleagues were glad she was going to get a rest.

Once in the mountain cabin, they laid in all their food and supplies and bundled up against the Vermont winter; no one could tell the girl was pregnant the few times they ventured into town. Sister Mary had all the items necessary for the birth and they assiduously studied the midwife manuals. So it was that in April, a few weeks early, a child of sixteen and a half years was delivered of a child. It was washed, clothed, wrapped immediately, and taken by Sister Mary to someone who had arranged for the adoption. She wouldn't let Evie (groggy from chloroform) see the child, nor did she even tell her its sex. She had decided that the baby must be put out of her mind immediately. They prayed together for forgiveness and talked of God's mercy and compassion. Later they both went to confession and received absolution for their sins. By the time Evie rejoined her parents in early June, she looked her old self again.

5

Evan Desmond had listened to every word stonily, prodding her with his foot when she halted too long. He looked at her carefully. It was all probably true, but what did that matter to him? His hopes for redemption had vanished with her virginity. There was no Truth, no virtue, just as he'd always known.

"Your whoremongering parents have passed you off on me, and you are scum for not telling me the truth—is this not so, my lovely bride?"

Trembling and weeping afresh the girl tried to explain. "I thought if God had forgiven me, He would see that everything would be well. I promise you, Evan, that if you'll only forgive me, I will be a perfect wife to you until the day I die. I will do all you ask of me forever."

"Do you really mean that?"

"Oh, yes, Evan. Please give me a chance."

"Will you swear it by the crucifix around your neck?"

"Most humbly and willingly." It was the one given her by Sister Mary Joseffa.

"Then get down on your knees before me, take your crucifix in your hand. Swear."

"I hereby swear by Almighty God that I will be unto you a perfect wife and obey your every wish."

He smiled at her, with a pang, for she *was* beautiful and touching in the sincerity of her despair. But his life had been shattered. Never again would he allow himself the pain of hope. Better to go back to the old ways of certain damnation. Darkness was an old friend. "Now I shall make a vow in return for yours. You have taken from me the last hope for my soul's redemption, and you'll pay for this sin for the rest of your life."

His assault upon her body stunned her. She never could have believed that such cruelties and degradation were possible. When he was through, he pulled her to her feet with exaggerated courtesy, recommending a hot bath to relieve her tortured muscles. He laughed as she stumbled to the bathroom, then stood in the doorway to remind her that suicide was a sin.

"Imagine having a night like this for eternity?" She whirled toward him—he could even read her mind!

"Then please kill me or let me go away. I promise that you'll never see me or hear from me again," she wept.

"The only way I'd kill you is, perhaps, by fucking you to death. As for letting you go," he continued gravely, "you are my wife according to the law and your church. Would you break the laws of both man *and* God?"

The next two days, and most of their time on the *Queen Mary,* was spent in bed, where Evan seemed determined to carry out his threat. Stupefied by his relentless violations of her body, Evalynn thought she was in hell, doing penance for her deceptions. Ceaselessly she prayed for deliverance from Evan and his savage demands, and after a few weeks that seemed like years, they were answered. Her husband finally must have decided to forgive her, because he was a model of devotion for the time of their stay abroad—tender, solicitous, showering her with lovely gifts. Evalynn wept with gratitude. His lovemaking became so gentle and skillful that she quickly learned to look forward to his sexual advances, and he encouraged her to make her own now that he had "freed her from her sexual prison." By the time they got back to New York in April, she was a picture of a glowing, happily married woman.

At the receptions they gave in their exquisite town house in Murray Hill, Evan was first amused then annoyed to find

28

his wife the center of male attention. It was not only her beauty and elegance that attracted the men, but like dogs they seemed to sense she was sexually ready. Even an expert like Evan was hard pressed to decide whether the innocence enhancing that strong sexuality was real or feigned. In their bedroom she had become a good match for him, although any attempts at anything other than the "missionary" position brought instant frigidity. Yet, Evan plotted the next part of his punishment with enormous care, for he never had and never would forgive her deception in their marriage.

The first step was to move to their estate on Dune Road, ostensibly for the summer; but he had no intention of bringing his wife back to the social whirl of New York City, where she might pull away from his total domination of her life. The next step was her pregnancy. Eve was overjoyed to find she was to be a mother of a child she could keep and love. Wistfully she thought of that first baby, but tried to push the thought of it out of her consciousness with the plans for Evan's child. The father-to-be insisted upon making all the arrangements, over the objections of Mrs. Ambrose. Strangely, he chose an old country doctor, insisting that he was the best man for a country birthing.

"Evan, you know how much I respect you," said his mother-in-law, "but are you sure Dr. Hedges is the right man? He's terribly old-fashioned, as well as past his prime, and I don't know if he'll come to the city for the birth."

"That's all nonsense," came the rebuttal, "he's a splendid doctor, and the baby will be born right here—I've decided to give up town life and become a country squire. It's a sacrifice I gladly make for the health of my wife and future children." He enjoyed the startled look on the women's faces. *No one* but the natives lived in the Hamptons off-season! Eve was sure her husband knew best and was flattered that he seemed to want her all to himself—except in "that way." Evan said that Dr. Hedges had warned against sexual activity, explaining that it would be "bad for the baby."

"You wouldn't want anything to happen to him now, would you, ducky?"

"Of course not, Evan, we can wait until after he's born, and then we can have those wonderful times together again."

She waited, but according to rumors, Evan didn't. When she asked him he was angry.

"Aren't you above listening to local fishwife gossip, Eve? Are you going to believe some nag rather than your husband? And even if I do have a lark now and then, isn't it only natural for a man like me? I do it only out of consideration for you, and for our child, and here you are becoming a shrew."

Frightened and guilty at his anger, Eve was subdued. Dutifully she followed all of his directives. She must eat enormous quantities of food and get lots of rest with her feet up; she was to go out as little as possible. When she demurred she was sharply reminded that she was too young and inexperienced to make her own decisions when it came to her welfare and that of the child she was carrying. Dr. Hedges's orders were to be followed to the letter. They were; and it was, as Eve reluctantly complained to her mother on one of the latter's rare visits, like being imprisoned. Both women agreed, however, that Evan was the most concerned of all prospective fathers. Eve dutifully followed his orders, and by the end of her ninth month, she could barely move about her bedroom.

The birth was long, and the servants, if they hadn't known what a devoted husband Mr. Desmond was, would have thought that was a look of satisfaction on his face as he heard his wife screaming in labor. At his insistence, she had natural childbirth, for he claimed that the anesthetic would harm the child and the mother.

As she looked at her newborn son, Eve thought her husband must have been right all along, for the boy was beautiful and well-formed and healthily howling. Happy, but exhausted by the birth, she waited for someone to take the baby to feed him. In a semistupor she heard Evan and Dr. Hedges discussing her breasts.

"Oh, yes, Mr. Desmond, there's plenty of nourishment there for your son, and her breasts are in fine condition. Let's put the young lad to nurse before he howls himself into a fit."

Humiliated by being discussed this way, she tried to remonstrate. "But no one I know ever nursed their babies, Dr. Hedges. They all had nursemaids and bottles and things."

"Well, young mother, your husband agrees with me that the old ways are best. Don't you love your baby?"

Cuddling him closer she replied. "Of course I do, I love him dearly already. I only thought—"

It *was* a nice feeling she realized drowsily, as the baby sucked contentedly. Evan, as always, was right.

As the baby grew, Evan refused to allow her to use a bottle at all; she was tied to her son for twenty-four hours a day. The father would not hear of a baby crying; so he was nursed at the slightest whimper for almost a year. As much as she loved Garrick, she wished for some time for herself away from the house, some time for Evan and her to be together as they had been. He never seemed to look at her now—she admitted to herself she was a mess. She had to eat a lot if she was to keep nursing and her figure was a wreck. She wore loose wrappers all day to fit her spread girth and to be ready to nurse the ever-hungry baby. There was no time for beauty parlors or makeup. She couldn't wait to start dieting and get back to her old self. Each week she asked, "Evan, don't you think Garrick can go onto a bottle now? He's so healthy I'm sure he'll do fine."

The response was always the same, "He's healthy because

he's being fed nature's way. Give the poor baby some more time. There's no hurry."

Once he lashed out at her importunings with, "You gave your firstborn away—do you want to do the same to my son?"

Deeply wounded, she wept, and never asked again. Garrick was a year old when she stopped nursing him, but Evan insisted he would not allow a maid to take care of his child, so she rarely got out of the house. During the summer there were at least acquaintances who dropped by, and doting grandparents to visit, but in September she was alone again in the beautiful house by the sea. Evan was much away "on business," the nature of which he refused to discuss. She made the best of her time by enjoying her son's progress.

When she stopped nursing, she eagerly awaited Evan's advances. He had told her they couldn't have relations until then because it would harm the flow of her milk. She brushed her hair, put on some makeup, got into a lovely pink French lace nightgown, and waited for him to come to bed. When he did, he smelled of liquor, and roughly told her to remove her gown. When she hesitantly did so, he pushed her in front of the mirror and they both gazed at her body. It was puffy, with rolls of fat and pendulous breasts. Dark veins marred her skin, she looked away, humiliated by her nakedness.

"Oh, Evan, I'll go on a diet and exercise. You'll see, I'll be beautiful again and then you'll want me."

"A mother shouldn't think of lust, my dear, but about her children," he chided. "Our honeymoon is over. It's hardly seemly for people in our position to be at each other all the time. I'll do my husbandly duty by you. You have to put away your depraved sexual appetite—it's neither normal nor healthy."

Stung by his words, Eve started to cry as she futilely tried to cover her body with her hands. What was wrong with her? Evan must be right—he always was. Why did she have this terrible craving for the feeling of his mouth, his hands, his sex? She must ask God to help her overcome these bad feelings and desires.

As if moved by her tears, Evan led her back to bed. "Now, my dear, don't weep. Just spread your legs apart— so."

Clambering on top of her, he pushed into her without prelude and was done before she even realized what was happening. Kissing her on the forehead, her husband left her bed and went back into his bedroom, leaving his wife totally bewildered.

The performance was repeated on a weekly basis in this exact fashion, leaving her with a terrible craving for more of him—a feeling she prayed to God to help her overcome. When she shyly announced she was pregnant again, he stopped coming to her room. The pattern of the first pregnancy and birth was repeated, and their daughter Diedre was also nursed. Evan returned to her bed when the baby was six months old and in four "husbandly duties" impregnated her again. The cycle continued so that in five years she had borne Evan Desmond four healthy children, all by natural childbirth and all breast-fed. She was twenty-five years old, and looked forty.

Evan bought all of Evalynn's clothing, since she had so little time to shop. If she complained about their dowdiness, his retort was that there was precious little choice in her size. He encouraged her to pull her hair back in a bun, "sensible and proper" he called it. He bought her oxford shoes and lisle stockings—to cover the veins in her legs caused by the successive pregnancies. Always the devoted husband, he plied her with chocolate and cakes, and, at dinner, heaped her plate with potatoes. "A mother has to eat to keep up her strength."

Every Sunday he punctiliously drove his wife and children to church; though he himself had never converted, he kept his promises—he always did. Eve found consolation in her religion, praying daily for relief from her depraved cravings for her husband's body. She went to confession, where the priest assured her that God would forgive her sin of lust, if she was sincere in repentance. The children took most of her time and energy; she tried to go to bed exhausted so that sleep would come quickly. Embarrassed by her looks, she avoided going out or having guests. It was hard to accept the look of shock in their eyes when they realized this frump of a woman had been, just a few years ago, the lovely Eve Desmond. Even harder to accept was the admiration in their eyes for Evan, handsomer than ever, and a proud father.

He spoiled the children dreadfully and they adored him, sharing his tolerance for their fat, anxious mother who was always worried about their being so overindulged, especially Diedre, the only daughter. Her father and brothers treated her like a princess, and she basked in their admiration and attention, totally ignoring her mother—an attitude Evan seemed to encourage.

"After all, Eve, you wouldn't want this lovely child to grow up to be like you," he laughed.

She cringed at his laugh. He had never set foot in her bedroom since the birth of Edward five years ago. Rumors reached her that he had been seen with glamorous women, but she didn't have the courage to reproach him. Who could blame him? He had a wife who was repellent to bed with, except for breeding purposes, she thought bitterly. Each day she prayed for strength to accept her lot.

Mrs. Ambrose was embarrassed by her daughter's looks. "Really, Evie, it's a wonder Evan comes home at all. Have you no pride? How *could* you let yourself go like this? Diet, fix your hair, do your face, get nice clothes! It's lucky you have those children, or your husband would leave you and you'd have no one to blame but yourself."

Eve sighed wearily. How could she tell her mother of

Evan's insistence that she overeat, that he chose her clothes and hairstyle, and, most shameful, that he only came to her bed to impregnate her?

Desperately she tried. She lost weight, followed her mother's directives, and prayed that her husband would notice and desire her once more. One night she left her bedroom door open, waiting for him to come home from an evening out. As he passed the door, she called to him. He entered, smiling blandly.

"Well, my dear, you've got yourself all prettied up—makeup, perfume, filmy negligee. What have you in mind?"

"Evan, couldn't you—we—couldn't we be like husband and wife to each other again—like the old days? I know I've let myself go, but I'll try so hard to be right for you again. Please, Evan?"

She was flushed with the embarrassment of pleading, and he was slightly tipsy. Wordlessly he started to strip, closing the bedroom door behind him. It was time for the next phase of his leisurely descent into hell.

Tears of gratitude welled up in his wife's eyes as she looked at his perfect physique—he would come back to her at last. All of her patience would have proved worthwhile. She trembled as she felt his long hard fingers touch her breasts, his mouth nuzzling at her neck. Skillfully he brought her to a passion greater than she had ever experienced. As he rubbed between her legs she begged him to enter her.

"Now, Evan, please now."

"Don't be so greedy, my love, we have plenty of time. Don't you remember the old days when I'd make love to you for hours? Now, how badly do you want me, darling?"

"Evan, please, I want it so badly."

"All right then, let's see if you remember your old lessons. If you don't it's your last chance to have me back in your bed."

Obediently she followed his directions, and as a reward

he entered her and brought her to climax three times before telling her to roll over for another "old-time game." She was ashamed at how happy she felt when he finally left her bed at dawn. For weeks he came to her every night, and humbly grateful to have her husband back, she did everything he asked, afraid to complain about "unnatural acts." He brought a book of sex illustrations and had her practice the positions in the pictures before the mirror. Vastly amused, he complimented her upon her proficiency.

"Once a whore, always a whore, eh, Evie?"

Startled, she stared up at him as she knelt at his feet, waiting for his pleasure. Cruelly and carefully he reminded her of the "good old days," enjoying the shock in her eyes as she remembered all those dreadful things that had happened on their wedding night and honeymoon.

"Now you'll never have to worry again, my dear. I've indulged you for old times' sake. No man will ever look at you or desire you again. You're pathetic—with your drooping breasts and sagging ass and stretch marks all over your body, let alone those varicose veins all over your legs. Your chin is drooping and your eyes are starting to get wrinkled. You're thirty-two years old and you're going to be an old woman for the rest of your life. Good-night, Eve. Sweet dreams." He smiled at her as he left the room—never to enter again.

"Pregnant again? Well at least we know it's the last one, don't we, dear wife? Unless of course you get raped again, which is doubtful. I often wonder where your bastard is— don't you?"

With this response to her announcement, Eve Desmond abandoned all hope and devoted all her energies to being a mother and housewife. She went out only to go to church with her children. When Jessica was born, people gossiped that the mother looked more like a grandmother, but the child was exquisite. As she grew, she captivated everyone who knew her. Evan absolutely doted upon her, with what seemed to be the only sincere passion of his life. At age eleven Diedre was resentful and became sulky at having a rival in the family, but quickly learned to hide her resentment to avoid her father's displeasure.

A loving father all day to his children, the evenings were for his pleasure, and the old rumors about Evan Desmond grew rife. According to local stories, he was a prodigious drinker and lover, with no woman safe from his attentions if he decided he wanted her. Many did not blame him—after all, his wife was an old bag, but then ugly gossip started about his predilection for young girls as he approached his fiftieth birthday, still handsome and debonair.

Increasingly disturbed by the talk that reached her, Eve finally got up enough courage to confront her husband. She waited in the living room one Saturday night and when he came home at 3 A.M. asked him about his purported affairs with young girls.

"I can't see where it's any of your affair. Be glad I'm not doing it at home with the children," he muttered drunkenly.

As she stared at him in disbelief, she gasped, "You wouldn't, you couldn't." He laughed at the terror in her face, "You've forgotten all the lovely stories I told you on our honeymoon, my dear. Why, when I was Garrick's age, my parents were playing sandwich with me in their marriage bed. It was great family fun. Wouldn't you like to play with Garrick?"

With an unearthly howl Eve sprang at her husband, trying to claw his face. He easily held her hands.

"If you're not quiet you'll wake the children. You wouldn't want them to know what's happening now, would you? I'm warning you to behave yourself, or I'll have you locked up as insane and you'll never see your children again. I'll have them all to myself. No one would believe your demented tales and I could practice raising my children as my parents raised me. We could have marvelous times together that you could only enjoy imagining in your padded cell."

The enormity of what he said stunned her. She couldn't believe what he was saying, but he seemed capable of any cruelty. His own children? Could he? He was right—everyone thought she was queer, Evan had seen to that. No one would believe her.

"You've warned me, Evan. Now let me warn you. If I see the slightest sign of your making an attempt to corrupt our children—I will kill you. I swear this by Almighty God." Quietly, and with dignity, she left the room to the sound of his amused laughter.

Half-crazed by Evan's warning, Eve watched her children constantly. Every sign of affection he showed them seemed sexual to her now. She tried to make sure he was never alone with them. Outwardly, she was quieter and more restrained than ever, while her inner tensions mounted unbearably. How long could this nightmare last?

As always in times of stress, her thoughts turned to Sister Mary Joseffa. What would she advise? What would she do in this intolerable situation?

It had been twenty years since they had parted, after Eve's graduation. Sister had joined a cloistered order in her beloved New England, a move that had left Eve with yet another burden of guilt, knowing how much the nun had loved teaching. Somehow she knew it had been done as a form of penance, to expiate the guilt Sister had felt for the lies she had told and the deception she had practiced—all for Eve's sake. At the birth of each of her children, Eve thought of Sister Mary midwifing her firstborn with love and compassion. Every April twenty-first she said a birthday prayer for that child, fervently wishing for it the love and happiness missing in her own life. Often she wished she at least knew its sex, so that she might better picture her child growing up, but Sister had been adamant. She believed the less Eve knew, the less the memories would haunt her. Perhaps she was right.

Each year, Eve wrote Sister Mary a letter to tell her news of her family and to thank her for having taught her to go on, no matter what. The nun was not permitted to communicate, but Eve felt sure that Mary Joseffa would always pray for her, and for all of her children. Mystically she drew strength and comfort from the thought.

"Oh, Sister," she murmured, "when will God have punished me enough for my sins? Remember me in your prayers!" and she fingered the crucifix her teacher had given her, with a blessing, as a parting gift.

So the months dribbled past in fear and anxiety; but Evan played the model husband and father, and the children were happy and healthy. Once again Eve began to feel she could relax a little. Her husband seemed to love his children. Surely his threats were only made to punish her for the sin he could never forgive. She had learned to accept and live with this knowledge; as long as her children were well, nothing else on earth mattered.

Evalynn went to church frequently to pray for Divine Guidance, finding solace in familiar rituals. The demands of her growing family had prevented her from extensive participation in church work, but the Sisters always stopped to chat with her and appreciated the obvious sincerity of her devotion. Among themselves they sometimes gently gossiped about whether Mrs. Desmond would not have been happier in their vocation. The novice, Sister Immaculata, often asked questions about her, as if sympathizing with the strain under which the woman seemed to be living. The young nun often found reasons to stop and talk to Eve, fixing her with burning eyes, the sole redeeming feature in an otherwise truly homely face.

Eve tried to be friendly with the girl, but she was repelled by her looks, her hulking body, and her clumsy, shambling gait. Discomfitted and guilty over such an un-Christian attitude, the woman redoubled her efforts to be kind to this grotesque creature of God. One day, as they were arranging altar flowers, Eve shyly confessed that she envied Sister Immaculata her calling.

"I had always felt it was mine," she ventured, "but our Lord had other ideas for me. My teacher, Sister Mary Joseffa, always said that obedience was the road to God."

"I knew a Sister Mary Joseffa during my novitiate in Vermont. I took care of her during my medical studies program," the nun volunteered.

Eagerly, Eve plied the girl with questions, only to be informed that her good teacher had died of cancer the year before.

The woman wept openly in her grief, yet when the girl reached out as if to comfort her, she instinctively shrank from her touch, feeling guilty again as the girl's eyes blazed at the rejection. She wordlessly shuffled off, head buried in her hands.

In susbsequent visits to the church, Eve often caught Sister Immaculata studying her with a haunted look on her face, but she was too hesitant to approach and ask forgiveness for her rebuff of the offered comfort. Some things, she believed, were better left unsaid. For a long time, her sorrow at Sister Mary Joseffa's untimely passing was simply overwhelming. It took the entire summer for her to come out of the depression weighing upon her.

7

It was September of 1938. Eve went through the routine of checking the hurricane supplies always kept in the storm cellar. The living-room entrance to the basement was a unique feature designed so one would not have to be inconvenienced to get down there in emergencies. It was always kept locked, with the key out of reach of little hands. Eve was afraid that one of the children would fall down the ladderlike stairs. Now there was only Jessica to worry about, the others were old enough to be careful, but she was afraid one of them might forget to lock the door, and so checked it every time she walked through the room.

Jessica had started school that September and loved her kindergarten class. Garrick was starting his senior year at the high school and discussing colleges. Eve had urged all of them to go to boarding school, but their father had insisted that he wanted his family near him, and of course he'd won. The children were surprised that their mother would want them away, but attributed it to her eccentric nature. They were a handsome family—Garrick a man at seventeen, Diedre a beauty of sixteen, Drew at fourteen was studious, while Edward was a mischievious scamp of twelve. Eve looked at them with fierce love, they were the only reason for her existence; she would gladly die for them—it would be easier than living, she thought.

Life was even more difficult since Evan, over her objections, had hired a new housemaid, a pretty little local girl of sixteen. He insisted that Nancy live in, so that breakfast could be served early. She was given the attic bedroom, which had its own sitting room with fireplace. His wife was sure that Evan was sleeping with the girl, since she often heard footsteps creeping up the attic stairs very late at night. Grimly she watched over her own brood, hoping Nancy could satisfy his appetite for young flesh, and kept silent about the affair. She was surprised that the Chesters would allow their daugher to stay in the house, Evan's reputation being as it was, but since the Depression jobs were scarcer than ever and the local families needed every cent to survive. Evan had been hurt by the 1929 Crash, but how badly he refused to disclose. The household help was now down to Nancy and a "daily," meaning more drudgery for Evalynn. Her parents had also been affected by the Crash and had been forced to sell their summer estate. They now rented a small cottage near the beach, for the season, planning to stay there until the end of September to help celebrate Jessica's fifth birthday on the thirtieth.

September 20 was a gray, heavy day, which had the barometer dropping steadily. Between having her period and being susceptible to moods influenced by the weather, Eve felt miserable and went to bed early. The thunderstorm woke her late at night, from a sleep that seemed drugged. Guiltily she went to Jessica's room—her baby was terrified of storms—but the little bed was empty. The light drew her down the wide staircase to the living room where she found Evan holding Jessica on his lap, kissing away her tears and stroking her hair. Controlling her panic, she carried Jessica back to bed, singing her favorite lullaby, "Sweet Afton," to soothe her. The music box was left to continue the melody as the mother closed the door behind her and went downstairs to confront the father.

The latter was standing with his back to the fireplace and smiled sardonically as his obviously distraught wife came into the room. Anticipating her attack, he took the offensive.

"I know what your sick mind has made of my comforting

a baby terrified of a storm. You are insane with your Puritan repressions and sexual fantasies. I can see by your eyes you're determined to kill me someday; rather than leave these poor children to be raised by a madwoman, I'd kill them first!"

His wife flinched and recoiled from the mad gleam in his eyes as his fingers tightened around the poker. His maniacal laughter followed her up the stairs and intruded into her nightmares for the few hours before a sullen dawn awakened her.

Trying to imitate her customary bustle as she and Nancy got the children off to school, her mind tried to find a plan to save her children from a father close to the edge of total dissolution into madness. Grasping at straws, she told Drew and Edward to go to their grandparents directly from school—they were to have dinner there. She would pick Jessica up at noon, as usual, and the two older children had play rehearsal after school. A plan started to form.

Driving Jessica home from kindergarten for lunch, Eve tried to listen to her child's usual happy chatter as the scheme for release took shape. It was hard to concentrate, especially with the peculiar weather. The day was abnormally oppressive and still, an ominous gray everywhere suffusing the normal greens and blues of sea meeting land along Dune Road. The surge of the tide was louder than she could ever remember it. She felt depressed as an overwhelming sense of malaise swept over her. She *must* fight it off to save her children!

Nancy was bringing up hurricane supplies from the cellar.

"Feels like a big blow coming up, Mrs. Desmond," she called out cheerfully. "Better have everything ready."

"Just remember to lock that door and get about your business," snapped the lady of the house.

Nancy grimaced behind her back as she went into the kitchen, followed by Jessica, who was eager to see the latest batch of kittens in the pantry closet and to have lunch with Nancy, who always seemed to return the child's love and devotion wholeheartedly.

As Eve hurriedly tried to pack a few things for each child and for herself, the phone rang. Children were to be sent home from school if there was someone home—did she authorize their leaving?

"Of course—but why?"

"There are storm warnings, Mrs. Desmond—looks like a heavy one."

Eve hung up and carefully put the suitcase in the hidden cubby in her closet. Sighing, she had to abandon her plan until the next day.

At 2 P.M. Garrick and Diedre came in excitedly talking of the approaching storm. Drew and Edward had gone to the Ambroses, as directed, and would probably have to spend the night there; the rains were getting worse. The two older children were in high spirits, excited at the prospect of a new experience, and ran about the house with Nancy and Jessica to view the storm from different vantage points. Evan struggled in after 3 P.M., drenched from the rain in the short walk from the driveway. As the children crowded about him lovingly, he shot Eve a look that made her shudder, then smiled sweetly at his children. He seemed upset that his younger sons were at the Ambroses, but Garrick assured him they'd be fine.

"Besides, they'll be a help getting the house safe against the storm. The old folks can use a hand—Grandfather is almost eighty now. We'd better start closing up here. Let's go gang!"

They laughed as they got soaked struggling to close shutters and storm doors, and let the pets into the kitchen. At 4 P.M. the children cheered as the electricity and phone failed. It was really an adventure now! The candles and hurricane lamps were lighted, and they amused themselves making shadow figures on the walls. It seemed less like fun, however, when the sound of the storm overwhelmed them. There was the bass pounding of the sea, the shriek of the wind, and over all a terrifying, unearthly sound that sobered and frightened them out of their high spirits. When they looked out of the shutter crescents they saw trees snap without hearing the sound they made in breaking, and watched them sail past the house.

Only Evan seemed to grow livelier as the hurricane, incredibly, intensified. His eyes bright, his cheeks flushed, he ran from window to window describing the carnage. At 5 P.M., with no sign of the fury abating, they all went to their rooms to get ready for what Mr. Desmond described as a "fine picnic supper" he offered to prepare—their "daily" having left early to get home to her own family. In her room Eve heard footsteps creaking on the attic stairs.

"That monster," she muttered, "even in this warning sent by God he must molest that poor child in his own home."

SOUTHAMPTON PRESS
September 28, 1938

On September 23, rescuers forcing entry into the Desmond home on Dune Road were met with a terrifying sight. Garrick, age 17 and his sister Diedre, 16, were found horribly murdered, as was their housemaid Nancy Chester, also age 16. It would appear, according to reports by Chief of Police Tom Doyle, that Mr. Desmond had killed them, then his wife, and finally had taken his own life, hara-kari style by his knife.

The sole survivor, Jessica Desmond, age 5, was found in the cellar, sitting close to her mother's body, where it had apparently been thrown after the stabbing. The chief wept openly as he described the child's singing a lullaby to the body, a dead kitten clutched to her chest.

As far as can be determined, her brothers Andrew, 14, and Edward, 12, were at their grandparents' home when the hurricane struck. The Ambrose cottage was totally demolished when the ocean broke through this section of Dune Road, joining Shinnecock Bay and forming an inlet. None of the bodies has been recovered thus far.

SOUTHAMPTON PRESS
October 30, 1938

The terrible tragedy that struck the Desmond family has claimed yet another victim. Little Jessica Desmond, age 5, has been sent to a mental clinic in NYC. The doctors at Southampton Hospital, after a one-month study, have concluded that she will never speak or react normally again. Her condition is called severe, irreversible catatonia.

One of the psychiatrists called in from NYC as a consultant, who prefers to remain anonymous, says that it is probably just as well, for if she was to regain her senses, her memories would send her back into yet another form of insanity. Intensive searches have thus far failed to turn up any relatives. The bodies of her two missing brothers, and grandparents, have not yet been found.

SOUTHAMPTON PRESS
September 21, 1939

This reporter, checking into the anniversary events of the killer hurricane, was informed that little Jessica Desmond died in August in the Payne Whitney Mental Clinic in NYC. All that remains now of the Desmonds is their former home on Dune Road, ironically one of the few left unscathed by the storm.

Part II

The voice whined and sobbed, "Oh, Dr. Bradley, you simply can't imagine what it's like being married to that man. Why didn't I listen to my mother? She was always right—they're beasts, all beasts!"

Catching herself, Mrs. Andersen looked up at her psychiatrist through tear-swollen eyes.

Smiling reassuringly, Bert stood up to his six-feet-four-inch height and drew his patient to the office door—her fifty-minute hour was up, thank God. How Mr. Andersen tolerated this harridan, let alone paid his very high fees, was something at which he always marveled; he found it difficult to keep from strangling the woman in his office. Making proper noises, he assured his patient that she was coming along beautifully, and that all would be well.

"God bless you, doctor, if it weren't for you, I don't know what would become of me." Naked adoration was clear in her reddened eyes. Sighing heavily, she dreamed away the time until she could see her "shrink" again.

On his part, Bert sighed with profound relief when the Tuesday 4 P.M. had left. Leaving his comfortable office, he asked Sheila to lock up when she left, and wearily mounted the elegant mahogany staircase to his living quarters.

The soothing beiges and earth tones of the contemporary living room, its splashes of color provided by the modern art decorating the walls, always relaxed him. Alice really had a marvelous sense of style in decorating—as in everything. Sinking into one of the luxurious couches, he loosened his tie and consciously willed himself to unwind. It was an unwritten law in the household that he was not to be disturbed from 5 P.M. to 6 P.M.—jokingly referred to as his "save my sanity time." Looking out the floor-to-ceiling windows, he enjoyed the sight of the foliage showing in the terraced garden. Spring always made him feel restless. It seemed unnatural to be living in a city when the earth was busily greening. Wryly he thought that no matter how he was encased in Guccis and Cardins, he was still a country boy from Cape Cod. How he wished he were back there again! Analyzing his train of thought, he realized that part of the syndrome was due to the fact that he would be fifty years old in 1979—only three more years. Half a century! Catching himself, he determined not to get into self-analysis—just to concentrate on relaxing. Lighting a cigarette, mixing a drink, putting Mozart on the Fisher stereo, he gave himself up to the sounds and sights and feelings of hedonism, and quietly despised himself for it.

In the large, plant-filled, all-white kitchen-dining area, the evening meal was being prepared with practiced efficiency.

"I don't know how you do it, Miz Bradley. All these years I've been with you, and every meal you turn out is better than the one before." There was real admiration in the warm Southern voice.

"You know I couldn't do it without you, Mattie," came the fond reply. "We really have a great team here."

Stepping to the window to look down at her youngest child playing in the garden with her big brother, Alice thought of how smoothly her life was running, and of how fortunate she was. Hers was one of the few marriages she knew of still intact. Checking the clock, she took off her apron to spend her time with Bert before the children's hour.

"We'll be eating at seven o'clock, Mattie," Alice called,

and crossed the parquet hallway to the living room. She stood outside for a moment listening to the music and hoping to find her husband in a better mood than he had been in the past few weeks. He'd been increasingly irritable, not only with her, but with the children. What was worse, Bert refused to acknowledge the change in his normally pleasant personality. Opening the sliding doors, she entered to join her handsome husband, who looked up at her with frank admiration in his glance. At forty-three, his wife was still beautiful and sexy in the simple, tailored styles that suited her honey-blonde, aristocratic looks. Tonight her brown silk slacks and white blouse set off her lithe body, kept supple by daily sessions at the gym. She wore the fabulous strand of pearls he had given her for her fortieth birthday; she rarely took them off.

"Hey, how was your day? Oops, I forgot—today is Andersen day. You're going to be moody, right?"

Reaching up, Bert pulled his wife down on his lap and kissed her.

"I can always be grateful that I'm not Mr. Andersen—if nothing else!"

Her luminous brown eyes sparkled as she sensed his tension lessening.

"Come on now, is that the best you can do in the compliment department today? After I've slaved all day to make your favorite dinner, you can come up with something better than that."

"You made duck à l'orange?"

"You guessed it—I wanted you to be cheery for the party tonight."

"Oh no, not tonight," he groaned, "can't we just stay at home for once? Why must we always be part of a scene?" Unceremoniously, he moved her off his lap and stood up to prowl the large room with growing anger.

Alice sighed. Despite his protestations, Bert *was* getting to be a grouch. Sometimes she wondered if he were having an affair that was taking its toll upon his emotional equilibrium. She'd heard enough stories about doctors and their patients—but no, not Bert. He rarely spent a night away from their conjugal bed, and his days were filled with patients and professional matters—or at least so he said. Watching his lean length move about the room, it was easy to see why women would pursue him. After more than twenty years of marriage, she still felt excited by his presence. The silver just starting to show in his dark, curly hair made him look more distinguished than ever. Even his scowl was attractive in the saturnine face he turned toward her as he growled.

"Where in the hell are you dragging me tonight? A benefit for unwed orangutans? I think we've been every-where else."

"Please, Bert, be reasonable. It's to honor the outgoing director of the clinic. Don't you remember? It's been on your appointment calendar for a month."

Shamed, Bert slumped into the Eames chair.

"I *am* sorry, Alice. I don't know what's wrong with me lately. Everything seems to set me off, and you have to bear the brunt. If it's any consolation, please know I'm ashamed of myself even while I'm snarling at you. Will you forgive me—again?"

"Of course, darling. I know you've been overworked lately. Can't you cut down on your case load? Or give up some of your volunteer time at the clinic?"

"Give up the clinic hours? Good God no!" he exploded. "Don't you realize those are the only hours when I feel I'm doing what I trained for for twelve years! I spend the greater part of my waking hours acting as a toilet, being dumped on by spoiled, rich people who have the time and money to pay my exorbitant fees to feel they're 'getting it together.' Is that what my parents and I worked for—to make me into a 'golden bowl'"?

Alice was stunned by the rage that shook him as he shouted at her. She had never known there was a violent side to her husband; aside from his recent irritability, she'd never known Bert to be anything but kind and calm.

Glaring at her wildly, he continued his tirade.

"I went into psychiatry to help people. My parents slaved to put me through school. They never had a thing in their lives, and before I could even begin to repay them, or to show them my gratitude, they were dead, killed in that jalopy they couldn't afford to have new brakes on. And how do I repay their dream? Their beloved son sits in Manhattan spending more on himself in a week than they ever made in a year."

Catching himself at the sight of the bewildered look on his wife's face, Bert stopped and, obviously struggling for control, went to the bar to fix himself another drink with shaking hands, his back to Alice.

"But, darling, I never knew you felt this way—you've never said a word in all these years. How was I to know? You're not being fair to me or to yourself keeping all this bottled up in you. Why haven't you talked to me?"

"Because, Alice, you hate to talk about anything unpleasant—anything that might disturb the tenor of our lives. You were raised as a total hedonist, you're raising our children the same way, and I've let you carry me along. It was a lot easier than going into the slums and working with the people who desperately need the help I could give them. I didn't feel I had the call to be a minister, like my father, but I *did* want to spend my life doing *something* useful!"

The despairing tone in which this was said made it somehow harder to bear than his anger.

"When you started your practice you said that the rich were just as entitled to good psychiatric care as the poor. Why have you turned against everything so suddenly? Is it a sin to have beautiful things and a good life?"

"Yes it is, when others have nothing. You assuage your conscience by four hours a week of volunteer work and by giving and going to fund-raising parties for the art world."

"And you?" she flung back.

"Fair enough. I give half a day a week to a free clinic. The difference is, it doesn't satisfy *me*. I might as well tell you the whole story," he said abruptly. "George Webber and I are going to start a free psychiatric clinic on the Lower East Side in the fall."

Relief seemed to flood him as he made this announcement and sat down on the ottoman to await her reaction.

Alice, as always, kept tight control of her emotional response. "Well, if this is what has been bothering you all of these months, I suppose it's just as well to get it out into the open. It's hardly something we can discuss tonight. Dinner will be ready soon and we have to change for the party. Shall we talk about it in detail another time?"

Brooking no response, she rose in what her husband called her best "Seven Sisters" manner, and moved gracefully out of the room.

The dining room looked like a setting out of *Better Homes and Gardens*. Bright Finnish place mats on the round white table echoed the colors of the flowers in the dark-blue bowl in its center. An exposed brick wall accentuated the pool of light from the ceiling spot focused upon the attractive family sharing the day's news along with their meal. The children were too full of chatter to notice the strain between their parents.

Stacey had her father's dark good looks and would have been a beauty, were she not so overripe. There was a slight sullenness to her expression and her voice was a loud whine as she demanded the firstborn's right to be heard.

"But *why* can't I go to Europe with Jennifer and Hilary? I'm seventeen years old and *perfectly* capable of taking care of myself! Why do you persist in treating me like a baby?"

"Because you *persist* in acting like one, fatso," retorted younger-by-a-year Richard.

"Mother, are you going to allow your son to talk to me that way?"

"Richie, that's not nice," admonished five-year-old Lissie.

Bert took over. "Richard, apologize to your sister immediately or go to your room." Recognizing that tone, Richard immediately complied.

"You know I'm just teasing, Stace. Can't you take a joke? I'm sorry. O.K.?"

"No. It's not O.K. You are a miserable worm and—"

"Enough, Stacey, he apologized and we are going to have a pleasant family dinner, not a recital of recriminations," interjected her mother.

"Well, he started it; you always stick up for your darling boy! Freud is always right, isn't he, Daddy?"

"Stacey, we are not going to discuss Oedipal theory at the dinner table, nor argue about Europe. You heard your mother. We are going to have a pleasant dinner if it chokes us all."

Laughter broke the family tension as Bert asked each of his children in turn abot their progress at their respective schools. Only half-listening to their responses, he gazed at them with sincere affection—blood of his blood. Long ago, he had sworn to Alice that he would be a father and husband, rather than a psychiatrist to his family. He had succeeded to the point where he sometimes felt he was probably blind to any flaws they might have. Each an only child, the parents had been determined to have a "real" family, and were often baffled by the interacting emotions of each child claiming a full share of parental attention and affection.

Lissie was perfect—his golden girl with curly hair and the brightest, deepest blue eyes imaginable. They must have been a heritage of some great-grandparents, since everyone else in both families was brown-eyed. She was a happy child, always singing and babbling endlessly about the wonders of the world she rediscovered each day. The only shadow in her life was that she had no pets, due to her mother's aversion to animals. Richard was brilliant, like his father, Bert thought complacently, watching his son looking owlishly through horn-rimmed glasses while considering a remark addressed to him by his mother. He was just growing out of his awkward age, and in a few years would probably be quite a ladies' man. It was Stacey who concerned him most. Was her overweight due to a feeling of being unloved? Or was she on the Pill without their knowledge? Was her crowd into drugs and sex? She would never discuss her private life with them, claiming everything was great and that she and her friends never did anything "bad." He often wondered about that, but didn't know how to break through her "no trespassing" attitude. It was certainly easier to counsel other people than to deal with one's own family problems.

Lissie was claiming his attention now. "But, Daddy, what *will* we do this summer? Are we going to stay with Grandma and Grandpa?"

Bert frowned. Stacey *had* raised a problem. The older children were too old for camp this year, Lissie was too young. She loved staying with the Arlens in their gracious Colonial house in Connecticut. There were acres of trees, a pony, and a beautiful pool, but Bert felt that it was time for her to be with children her own age in the summer. He and Alice had usually traveled when he took his August vacation, but that too had seemed to pall.

"Tell you what, kiddies. Your mother and I have to go out tonight. Why don't you three sit down and have a conference? You can leave a list of suggestions on our night table in the bedroom, and we'll see if we can decide by the weekend."

This idea was met by a murmur of approval as Alice shot him an admiring glance for his expertise at extricating them from a touchy situation.

"Remember, all of you, Mattie is in charge now. Lissie, you're to be in bed by eight-thirty. Stacey and Richard, make sure all your schoolwork is done and be in bed no later than eleven o'clock. Don't open the door to anyone." Alice recited this as if it were an incantation that would keep them all safe.

"Don't worry, Mom, you keep forgetting there's a man in the house. I'm not a kid anymore," Richard reassured her.

"A *man?* Why, you twerp, you wouldn't—"

"Stacey, stop belittling your brother and get to your homework *now.*" Stacey glared in response, but flounced off to her room.

The Bradleys dressed for the party quickly and rather silently, being overly polite to each other, as couples often are when aware of potential problems surfacing. They both knew Bert's bombshell about changing jobs had to be dealt with that night.

Checking themselves in the mirror, they saw a strikingly handsome couple, and smiled in mutual recognition of that fact. It eased the tension somewhat, and they were both more cheerful as they left for the party at the Dakota.

Stacey called the meeting to order in the paneled den that served as the family room. The fireplace was filled with a vase of yellow spring flowers, which pleasantly scented the air.

"O.K., I'm the oldest and I say we should go to Europe this summer."

"I'm the number-one son and I say we should go on an African camera safari."

Both turned toward Lissie and urged her to cast her lot with one of them to make a majority decision.

Gravely, her big blue eyes looked at one, and then at the other, sensing their tensions.

"I want to go to Grandma's house," she finally said, and ran off to tell Mattie she was ready for bed.

Her siblings sat in the den glaring at each other.

"Well, we might as well leave the folks a long list so maybe we'll get a chance to do something interesting," Richard said, "but I have the feeling that Europe is out Stace."

"I haven't given up yet, baby brother. If I work on Dad long enough, he'll probably give in."

"Yeah—just to shut you up. You really know how to be obnoxious."

"Look who's talking, mamma's boy. The way you suck around Mom when you want to buy another piece of equipment for your nuclear reactor or whatever the hell you're building in your room makes me sick!" She ended the exchange by stalking out of the room.

Richard stayed behind and watched TV for a while. Remembering he'd forgotten to copy the math homework assignment, he picked up the phone to call Chip Banks to get it. Stacey was on the line. Instead of hanging up, he idly listened and his eyes widened behind the thick lenses as he heard her telling—yes, it was Jennifer—the details of what was apparently her latest sexual exploit.

". . . hung like a horse, Jen, you really have to try it with him. When he went into me I thought—wait a minute—do you have your TV on?"

At the negative response, Stacey said sweetly, "Richard, you little prick, you'd better hang up before you wet your pants."

He heard Jennifer giggle as he slammed the receiver, his face scarlet at the shame of being caught, at the idea of *his* sister doing "it" and a sudden realization of his own state of arousal.

Before he could escape to the safety of his room, Stacey cornered him.

"Going to jerk-off, Sonny-boy?"

He tried to avoid looking at her as she confronted him wearing only a see-through baby doll nightie. He couldn't help but notice that she had neglected to wear the pantie part. The gown barely covered her bottom and her heavy breasts strained the fabric so that they were clearly delineated. His breath came short as she crowded against him. All he could think of were the statues of the fertility goddesses he had seen in his anthropology book.

"You're not going to tell the parents about my conversation, are you, Richie?" she cooed as she "accidentally" brushed her hand across his bulging groin. "It's not that I'm doing anything wrong, it's just that they're such Puritans about their little children."

"But, Stacey, suppose you get pregnant—or you catch some disease. You're too young to be fooling around. Boys don't respect girls who put out," her brother blurted, trying to act manly and sophisticated.

"I don't want to be respected, you asshole, I want to be fucked!"

Laughing at the expression of total shock on his face, she pulled him into her room and pushed him onto her frilly bed.

"Listen, stupid, I've been screwing around since I was fourteen. I've been on the Pill for years and I get checked out every six months at a G-Y-N clinic downtown. I don't want Mom and Dad to know until I'm ready to tell them. Now promise you'll never tell what you heard. I can't take the chance of them grounding me, or starting to watch every move I make—or Dad starting to agonize over me and my immortal soul."

Richard tried to muster his dignity. "I can't promise, Stacey. Something might happen and I'd have to tell. No one should promise something they can't guarantee keeping." Promises were sacred in the Bradley household.

His sister's hazel eyes narrowed. "You self-righteous little bastard. You're still a virgin, aren't you?"

"That is none of your business."

"That's why you're so uptight. If you tell the old folks a word about me, I'll tell them you've been trying to make out with me."

Incredulous, he could only gape as she sweetly intoned, swaying before him, "Is that what you want to keep you quiet? Wanna play house with big sister?"

Her husky laughter followed him as he ran out of her room into the sanctuary of his own room, where his dreams were troubled all night with visions of himself toying with Stacey. Waking himself when he felt arousal troubling his sleep had become a habit; he hated the idea of his mother finding his sheet stained, it seemed an admission of having impure thoughts. Women should be respected—goddesses like his mom. He didn't want her to know that her beloved son wasn't worthy of her love. Damn Stacey! She must have noticed him peeking at her when she left her door or the bathroom door ajar; probably did it on purpose. That's what the guys at school called a cock-teaser. Only she didn't tease, she actually had been getting laid—for three years!

He pictured her nude, long hair over the pillow, voluptuous thighs spread wide, knees flexed, stretching out her arms to a faceless body, its stomach rubbing against the thrust of her own ecstatic writhings.

Jesus! His own sister, just a year older and already a sexual veteran. Exhausted, he fell asleep again.

The party for Dr. Gowan's retirement was large and elegant. Alice stood at the windows facing the park and watched the lights on the Fifth Avenue side. As much as she loved her East Side brownstone, she missed having a view, but they had the advantage of a garden, which was marvelous for the children. Perhaps now that the children were older they could buy a huge penthouse on Fifth, one with wraparound terraces. It would be fabulous to be able to decorate wide rooms with windows instead of meeting the challenge of the narrow spaces of a town house. Of course the expenses—then remembering Bert's threat of leaving private practice, she frowned and turned to look for him.

He was easy to spot; even in a swarm of beautiful people, he stood out. She noted, to her discomfort, that Astrid was coming over to chat with her.

"Your guy is really entranced by that young woman with the boobies. He didn't even answer when I greeted him."

"Probably a colleague from the hospital," she replied smoothly. "You know how dedicated Bert is to his work. He's always talking shop."

Ultra-chic Astrid Newsome had a yen for Bert and made no bones about it. Annoyed that he didn't seem to be interested in her well-displayed charms, she took every opportunity of gossiping and guessing about his extramarital life. Bert had told his wife that Astrid had been so enraged when he had refused her last offer of bedding her that she'd accused him of having come out of the closet. Bert a gay! Smiling at the memory, Alice excused herself and moved to her husband's side.

He was so engrossed in his conversation that she had to put her hand on his shoulder to capture his attention. The blank look he turned in her direction irritated her; it was almost as if he didn't know her.

"Sorry, darling, I was so absorbed in technical details I forgot where I was for a moment. I'd like you to meet Nedra Robbins. She's going to work for George and me in our new clinic."

Controlling her startle reflex at the idea that the clinic was a *fait accompli,* Alice turned her attention to her husband's new associate. Quickly, her practiced eye assessed Nedra. No, she didn't look like a threat. She was fairly tall, very dark with a sensuous face, an hourglass figure, cheap dress. Not Dr. Bradley's type at all—or had his tastes changed? The girl *was* young, no more than twenty-five.

"It's a pleasure to meet you, Mrs. Bradley. I've heard so much about you from Dr. Bradley, and of course I've read about you in the society news for years."

Alice murmured all the right things while trying to puzzle Ms. Robbins's comments. Was the warmth in the greeting sincere or was it all a put-down? Hard to tell. The admiration and envy in her eyes was real enough, and Alice basked in it, knowing full well that the backless green dress set off her body to its lean, youthful perfection.

"And what will your function be in this projected venture, Miss Robbins?" she drawled in her best Miss Porter's voice, as counterpoint to this young woman's obvious New Yorkese.

"Dr. Bradley has hired me as a psychiatric social worker, and I'm thrilled at the prospect of working with him and Dr. Webber. They're probably the best, the most dedicated people in the profession."

Bradley smiled at the sincerity and excitement in the young woman's voice. Alice looked at him sharply. Could such youthful adulation turn him on? Best to keep her eye on this situation. She had no intention of ending up as one of those women who lose their husbands to a starry-eyed young thing worshiping at the shrine. The campaign started immediately. Flashing her most dazzling smile, she avowed how lovely it had been to meet her husband's future employee, and gently drew him away to mingle with their social set. Staying close to his side, she was her most charming, amusing, and intelligent self all evening. Slowly but surely she felt Bert starting to respond to her as a woman, and a sense of triumph shot through her. She still had the power to turn him on.

60

He nodded eagerly at her whispered suggestion that they cut out early and made their good-byes, claiming early A.M. appointments.

As the sleek, brown Mercedes purred them through the park and home, Alice kept her strong artist's hand on Bert's inner thigh, moving her fingers persistently into his flesh, creeping closer to the burgeoning bulge of him and telling him in a husky voice what she'd like him to do to her once they were home. She enjoyed the power she had over him; to see his face grow eager with passion sparked her own. Already she felt that flutter and the warmth between her thighs.

Once inside their ecru-and-brown bedroom, she posed before the mirror in the dim light and unhooked the halter of her dress. The thin silk jersey slid to the floor, and she kicked it away to stand in only pantyhose and pearls. Bert stripped quickly and came to stand behind her. He watched her face in the mirror as he ran his hands over her breasts. He pulled her hose down and pushed between her thighs, as his wife pushed back against him until his engorged member forced her thighs apart. With a quick laugh she turned toward him and drew him to the thick carpet. Alice came quickly, with hard gasping breaths, but Bert must have had more to drink that she realized—he seemed ready to go all night. Kissing her passionately until she could barely breathe, he rolled her over quickly, despite her protests that he knew she never liked it "that way."

"It's O.K., sweetheart. There's no such thing as bad sex. Just relax and enjoy it," he breathed into her ear. Alice tried, pretending to enjoy and share his passion. God knew it wouldn't be the first time she'd put on *that* act.

Inadvertently, and unnoticed, Richard was a frightened witness to his parents' couplings. Having heard their voices, he had come to the bedroom door, left slightly ajar in their haste, to talk to them about his sister. Mesmerized as if by the writhings of cobras, his eyes remained glued to their entwined bodies until they broke apart and moved to the bed. The spell broken, the son went back to bed and lay staring up at the ceiling. What had been fierce love for his mother began its metamorphosis to rage, as the primal scene he'd watched replayed in his mind. Never would he forget—or forgive. *No such thing as bad sex*—O.K.!

Unaware of Richard's recent presence, the parents lay in the super-king-sized bed, Alice's head on her husband's broad, hairy chest.

"I do love you so, Bert," she murmured, "I worry when you're not happy. Maybe you've been working too hard. A good rest this summer might clear your head about this clinic business.'

"It's not work, Alice, it's doing work I loathe that makes me feel like a whore—*that's* enervating. Once I'm in the clinic, self-respect will replace this suppressed rage that caused my fatigue."

Ignoring the psychology, Alice zeroed in on the practical.

"How will we live if the clinic is free? Will you keep some private patients?"

"I was afraid you'd ask that. It's the part I dreaded having to tell you about; I guess that's why I've been so irritable and defensive, knowing that there was no other way."

Sitting up against the burled elm headboard, Bert switched on the reading light and lit a cigarette. Staring straight ahead he explained.

"In the next few years we're going to have to change our life-style, Alice. I have enough in investments to carry us for many years, *if* we cut back expenses. Your folks have trust funds for the kids, and we have their college funds all paid up, so there's no worry about them."

His wife sat bolt upright, pulling the sheet about her as she asked, "What kind of expenses do we have to cut down on?" At his hesitation, Alice looked up into her husband's face.

"First, we'll have to sell this house and move into a three-bedroom apartment, say down around Gramercy, so I can be closer to my job." Sensing her increasing tension, he continued firmly,

"Mattie can come in half a day five times a week, but we can't afford a full-time, sleep-in maid. We'll have to sell one car, and quite frankly, it would help enormously if you could get a job, even a part-time paying position."

"Anything else?" came the iciest tone he'd ever heard.

Plunging on, he concluded, "We will have to stop entertaining so lavishly and going out constantly. The kids will have to take a cut in allowance or get part-time jobs, and we have to stop all this unnecessary, impulse buying. I think we should destroy all our credit cards to resist temptation."

"Are you quite finished now?"

"Yes, Alice, I guess that's about it."

"All right, now you listen to me, Bert Bradley, while I give you some free analysis."

The venom in her tone startled him. Her normally velvety dark eyes were as cold, as hard, and as bright as diamonds as they blazed at him with total fury. Too late, he realized he had attacked the very foundation of her being: her home and hearth. Her retaliation was bound to be merciless, and it was.

"How dare you present me with a *fait accompli!* After twenty-two years of marriage don't you think I am entitled to be *asked* about what my future is to be? Do you think I'm a child to have decisions made for me—or do you think I'm mentally or emotionally incompetent?"

Recognizing the futility of trying to answer, Bert resigned

himself to letting her spew out her anger, hoping that in the calm that must inevitably follow, he'd be able to seek some semblance of accord.

"All you've *ever* thought about is *yourself,* you and your precious conscience and your sainted parents. Martyrs fighting for a cross to bear. Am I supposed to be yours?"

He watched, almost awestruck, as her face twisted with rage and spite, marveling that just a short while before he had watched that same face glow with the pleasure of the thrusts of his lovemaking.

"Where was your exquisite morality when you seduced me as a means of getting me to marry you because you'd taken my virginity? Where were all your fine ideals of ministering to the poor when you played up to my father and let him set you up in practice? I was there when you promised my parents you'd see to it that my life-style would never be less than what they'd provided—and that was a tall order, which I admit you've managed to fill. Why should my children and I now have any less than I did—or less than they've ever had?"

Answering her own string of rhetorical questions, Alice paused for breath and continued more quietly, yet in a more deadly tone of voice. "You've never gotten over your upbringing as a minister's son. As you get older you're afraid your Maker is going to punish you for all the pleasure you've had, that you'll burn forever in hellflame. You think that by spending the rest of your life expiating the sin of having enjoyed the past, you'll go right to heaven when you die and see your Mummy and Daddy. Well, I've got news for you, Sonny-boy, I'll make your life here on earth hell if you proceed with your mewling plans for goodness and mercy. As a matter of fact, hell will be a place to be eagerly entered for relief when I'm through with you!"

The silence that followed this last pronouncement was total. Bert stared at his wife as if in shock. Never in all the years he'd known her had he suspected that such a cauldron of hate and malice bubbled beneath the elegant surface of the beautiful, talented Alice Arlen Bradley. How could he, as an acknowledged expert psychiatrist, have been unaware of this facet of her psyche? Alice continued to glare at him with a malevolent expression that destroyed every semblance of charm and beauty she had. Her body was rigid and she looked as if she were about to spring for his jugular.

Automatically the doctor surfaced in the astounded husband.

"Darling," he began soothingly, "I never realized what I was doing to you—to us. It's good to have it all out in the open. I apologize for my behavior. You're absolutely right, it was a foul thing to make plans without consulting you."

Suspiciously, Alice looked at her husband, gauging his professional manners.

"Don't you try to placate me, Dr. Bradley. I'm not one of your damn patients, thank God!"

But as Bert continued to speak gently and sincerely, his practiced eye noted her muscles starting to relax. The anger and tension left her face, but the wariness in her eyes remained as he persuasively continued.

"We'll take a vacation, Alice, and try to get in touch with ourselves and each other—the people we've become over the years without noticing the metamorphosis. I hadn't realized I'd become such a selfish bastard, and a MCP to boot—if that's not being redundant."

A faint smile about her pale lips rewarded him as he coaxed her to lie down. She slumped against him as he enveloped her in his arms, and in a matter of minutes was fast asleep, apparently in a state of total exhaustion from spent rage.

Bert lay awake for a very long time, staring into the darkness, which became peopled with figures right out of Michelangelo's *The Last Judgment*—figures reaching out, crying to him to save their souls, while Alice sneeringly kept him from reaching them.

6

Breakfast the next morning seemed the usual cheerful rush of getting three children off to school—two of whom treated each other with icy disdain, rather than the normal A.M. bickering. Even Lissie seemed bewildered, especially as her parents seemed so strange behind their facade of false cheeriness.

Mattie gave the child an extra hug as she put her on the nursery school station wagon, noticing her strain.

"Don't you worry, sweetness. By the time you get back from school, the family'll be the same as always. Some days folks just don't get along as good as other days."

Nodding brightly, she stepped into the happy chatter of greetings in the wagon, "Sit here, Lissie. Sit here."

When Mattie got back to clear the kitchen, Sheila Warren was at the dining table, having her usual cup of coffee with the doctor before the day's appointments began. Five years of impeccable service had earned her the right to special privileges. Bright, loyal, and totally dedicated to her boss, Sheila had even agreed to take a cut in pay to move to the new clinic, and to keep news about it a secret from Alice. She sighed inwardly, wondering if Bradley realized she'd pay to be able to stay in his presence. He was the only glamour in her drab existence. Often as she lay in bed in her apartment in Queens, she tried to imagine what it would be like to be Mrs. Bertram Bradley. The thought of marrying any lesser a being seemed degrading, a loss of self-esteem, so she remained single, dreaming that one day by some TV twist, he'd become hers.

Alice often joked with Bert about the naked adoration in his secretary's eyes, but aside from her worth as an employee, which he truly respected, poor Sheila was too dumpy and plain to even be thought of as a sexual creature, which was the main reason she had been hired. One couldn't control the attractiveness of the patients, but one didn't have to thrust temptation in on an office situation. Still, Ms. Warren enjoyed and took pride in her role as secretary—girl (now woman) Friday, and courtesy aunt to the Bradley "brats," as she fondly referred to them.

This morning, though aware of some tension in her employer, she nevertheless briskly went through the morning routine of announcing appointments, new patients, meetings, and so forth.

". . . and Dr. Webber left a message. He wants to know if you're going to the Southampton conference on adolescent peer group maladjustment this weekend. He said to tell you he was going and would pick you up if you've registered."

"Am I registered, Sheila?"

"Yes, Dr. Bradley. You told me to send the deposit last month in case you decided to attend, so I kept your calendar clear for Friday afternoon."

She blushed at the admiring glance he sent her.

"Sheila, you're fantastic. Remind me to give you a monthly bonus. You never mess up a detail. Call Dr. Webber and tell him to pick me up at three P.M. It'll be a good chance for us to talk, and I need a change of pace. I'll be down in ten minutes."

Whistling cheerily, Bert went to the study to tell Alice of his weekend plans. He found her putting her gear together for her sculpting class at the Ninety-second Street Y.

"It's about time you started giving the classes instead of taking them, darling." There was no doubting the sincerity in his remark. Samples of Alice's work throughout the house were as good as any found in the major galleries.

"Thanks, Bert, but let's not avoid the problem. When are we going to talk it out?"

"I give you my solemn oath that will be as soon as I get back from the Southampton conference this weekend."

She looked up sharply, her voice petulant.

"What conference? We have a gallery opening on Friday, a dinner dance on Saturday, and I promised the kids we'd go riding with them on Sunday."

"Didn't Sheila tell you about it? She's had it on the calendar for a month. First time I've known her to slip up."

The consternation in his voice seemed real enough, and they finally agreed that he was to go—that she was sufficiently liberated to appear solo at the social functions.

Relief flooded Bert as he went downstairs to his office; he had managed to buy some time, and talking with Webber might help him to resolve his dilemma.

George Webber expertly steered his 1975 Oldsmobile 88 through the streets of Long Island City, already starting to jam with weekenders heading for the Long Island Expressway, their umbilical cord to the glories of the Hamptons.

"We've saved seventy-five cents by using the bridge instead of the tunnel. How's that for practicing economy? Have to start using these little tricks now that we're giving up our private practices," George grinned. Glum silence answered him.

"What is it, Bert? You haven't uttered a sound since we left Seventy-ninth Street, and you look like you need a bottle of Elavil. Care to talk about it?"

Bert looked at the driver with affection. George was not only his friend and mentor, but had also been his analyst when he was preparing for his boards. They went back almost twenty-five years together, without a serious disagreement. Though only six years older, Webber was a father surrogate. Early family responsibilities had matured him quickly, and he had always seemed wise beyond his years. Needing someone to parent, he had responded warmly when Bert had sought him out in the trauma caused by his parents' death in that fiery crash. Never having married, Bert was the closest thing he had to family now.

"Thought you'd never ask," he sighed. "It's Alice. She's absolutely, violently opposed to our project—and I have to admit that it's mostly my fault. I just sprang it on her without warning, without discussion, and in a dictatorial manner. On the one hand, I can't blame her for her reaction, but on the other hand, I almost hate her for her callous disregard of the needs of the people we want to serve. But, I love her." Bert intoned this morosely as he gazed out over the industrial sprawl enveloping both sides of the roadway.

George whistled through his teeth. "That's quite a plate of scrambled eggs you've handed me." Adopting a professional tone and manner, George deftly began to query Bert about the exact details of the confrontation. By the time they were passing the cemeteries of central Queens, he felt he could present his friend with a hypothesis.

"How badly do you want to come into this clinic with me, Bert?"

Startled, Bert looked at him sharply. "More than anything I've ever wanted since I got Alice to agree to marry me," he stated flatly.

"If that's true, then why did you present the case to your wife in a manner that you *knew* would guarantee her total rejection?"

Stunned silence greeted the quiet question.

"You know Alice well enough," the older man persisted, "to realize she would need a long, persuasive buildup before she could possibly even consider your proposal. And yet you dive-bomb her with it. Wouldn't you say, if a patient told you this story, that he *wanted* to be stopped from taking an action that subconsciously terrified him?"

Bert's outraged rebuttal called forth a grave, "Methinks he doth protest too much! Stop for a moment and sort out your thoughts, Bert. You're just overreacting."

Accepting the advice, they drove in silence as George switched over to the Grand Central Parkway to avoid the noise and crowding of the trucks. By the time they had reached the Nassau County line, Bert felt sufficiently in control to resume the discussion.

"O.K.—it wasn't a low blow. You were reacting as an analyst rather than as a friend. That's inevitable in our profession. Let me submit this counterhypothesis: that I was so wary of Alice's refusal, of her possible attempt to dissuade me, that I went right ahead with our plans without giving her the opportunity of rejecting the proposal. Will that hold water, Dr. Webber?"

"Yes, Dr. Bradley, that is a possibility. But only your subconscious knows the truth, and may never let it surface. The point is, what are you going to do?"

"That is the question I was hoping you'd help me answer, George. If I can't change Alice's mind, my choices are either to leave her and my family, and to destroy their personal lives as well as my own, or to stay as I am and destroy myself and them eventually, as my bitterness overcomes my vaunted self-control and I hate them all for my sacrifice. La Rochefoucauld was right—'Self-sacrifice *is* suicide.'"

"Talk about Hobson's choice! The only solution then is to get Alice to agree to our plan. I hate to be mercenary, but those were her funds you intended to use to bankroll the operation until we can arrange for public financing, weren't they?"

Bert nodded. "Her parents insisted that everything we

70

own be in her name. Our style of living has ensured that just about everything I earn is swallowed up. I never worried about the future because of the various bonds and trusts we have, but now without her signature, I'm absolutely stymied—and fundless. What in God's name do we do now?"

George glanced briefly at his friend's anguished expression.

"We will, as two of the finest psychiatrists in New York City, see to it that Alice changes her mind," he stated calmly. "By September our clinic will be a reality. I'll work out the details— No, that's it on the subject for now," he added firmly. "Let's concentrate on the drive and on the conference."

Brooking no argument, George turned the talk to other matters and, at exit 44, swung back onto the L.I.E.

"How do you know your way around these wilds so well? I've never been past Great Neck."

"Used to summer out here as a kid, and I manage to spend a weekend or two in the Hamptons almost every summer as a nostalgia trip. You've never been out at all?"

"Nope. You know the old saw. 'In August all psychiatrists are at the Cape while all their patients are in the Hamptons.' I figured it would be a good place to keep away from."

George laughed. "It has the same ratio of neurotics as any other playground of the rich. I'm sure you'll love it. Geologically it's identical to the Cape—formed by the same glacial moraine, matter of fact. Which reminds me, how is it you never vacation in the Cape? Afraid it would bring back painful memories?"

"No, it was just something we drifted out of. The Arlens never liked the shore, and their place was so damned attractive to summer at—then we started to 'do' Europe, take cruises, travel with the kids. I hardly realized I hadn't any roots of my own."

71

They spoke desultorily of their respective summers and assiduously avoided discussing what was foremost on their minds—the clinic.

At Westhampton, George turned the big green car off the highway and drove to Southampton via picturesque local roads, which delighted his passenger. Dune Road, with the canal on one side and the ocean on the other, had him glowing with enthusiasm for the first time in months. George explained,

"This is the same barrier beach that extends from Coney Island eastward. The big blow in 1938 broke this section off from Fire Island. Where were you during the hurricane, Bert?"

"Right on the Cape. It was the most horrendous, yet marvelous, experience of my life. I was about twelve or thirteen and the adventure of it captured my imagination. I had this weird, exhilarating feeling that I was in control of the carnage." He laughed as George peered at him quizzically, and nodded,

"I'm almost ashamed to admit it, but yes, I had a similar reaction. I was out here taking advantage of the Indian summer when the storm broke. There was absolutely no warning; my family and I were just lucky that our house held. Every other house on our strip of Dune Road in Westhampton was destroyed. I remember watching, I swear it, a *cow* fly by to land in the hedges on the other side of the canal. I was awestruck, dumbstruck, but secretly thrilled beyond words. I've felt guilty all of my life for feeling fortunate to have experienced that storm."

They rode in companionable silence, each with memories of the hurricane reinforced by the shore setting.

George drove to the end of the road, the Shinnecock Inlet on their left, the ocean on their right, en route to the Hampton Bays Ponquogue Bridge. George passed it to show Bert the inlet formed by the storm.

"Dune Road continued right into Southampton until

1938. The ocean swept it away right here, taking about a dozen houses with it."

Looking across the waters sparkling in the late afternoon spring sunshine, it was hard to imagine the sea on a wild rampage.

Bert was entranced by the setting.

"It is like the Cape, but somehow it's even better. It's absolutely idyllic—sea on one side, bay on the other, big trees, dune grass, white sands. Looks like a chamber of commerce poster."

George laughed at his enthusiasm. "I'll take you on a tour tomorrow afternoon. Right now we'd better scuttle. Cocktails at six P.M. at Southampton Hospital."

True to his word, George drove Bert around the area when their meeting adjourned at 3 P.M. the next day. It had been a fruitful discussion, and they eagerly dissected the finer points of the lecture, Bert using examples from the lives of his two older children to illustrate his viewpoint. The beauty of the scenery soon infringed upon his train of thought, however, and he fell silent as he looked, through openings in carefully trimmed, enormous hedges, upon huge mansions surrounded by stately trees and manicured acres of lawns sweeping to the ocean dunes on one side, and to Lake Agawam on the other. Windmills dotted the landscape, while here and there along the dunes were bold thrusts of modern architecture attempting to echo the feel of surf, sand, and gulls. Aware of his friend's emotional response to the beauty, George drove slowly and silently down quiet roads shaded by giant elms, enjoying Bert's appreciation of his childhood landscape.

At the venerable Atlantic Bathing Corporation, they left the car in the preseason emptiness of the parking field and walked the beach, passing the Moorish structure of the club wih its orange tiled roof.

"Membership dues are dirt cheap here, but they want your pedigree before they let you join. I think you have to prove your ancestors fought against Cromwell before you're admitted," George joked as they paced the sands, incongruous in their city attire.

His companion didn't answer, seemingly absorbed by the perfection of the ocean views and the sparkling, crisp day. As they continued to walk, Bert gazed at the houses visible from the beach and stopped abruptly.

"I've made up my mind, George. I've solved one problem at least: My family and I are going to spend the summer out here. I feel as if I've come home at last."

He laughed at the astonished look on George's face as the latter remonstrated, "How in God's name is that going to solve anything? Here you're trying to figure out how to get your wife to agree to live in relative poverty, and now you propose to start by bringing her to summer at one of the world's most expensive resorts. I really fail to follow your logic."

"There isn't any. For the first and probably last time in my life, I'm going to do something on sheer impulse. I want a summer here with my family. I have a feeling that will resolve all the problems—one way or another."

Despite all of his friend's attempts to dissuade him, Bert was adamant. His final argument was that by spending a summer together for the first time since Lissie was born, the family would become close-knit once more, and he would be able to persuade them all to back his venture and accept a new life-style come September. Nothing George said could change his mind.

Over dinner that evening, Dr. Bradley queried the local doctors about the possibility of summer rentals. The head of

74

the hospital, Dr. Courtney, was delighted with his colleague's interest. The courtly, silver-haired physician, a gentleman in his late sixties, had roots in the area that went back more than three hundred years, and was a perfect source of information.

"Most of the houses near the water are already rented, or being used by their respective owners," he told his questioner. "Rentals are usually taken by early March. Some families have rented the same houses for twenty years and more. If you can find a house this late in the season you should get a good break on the price, especially if it's after the Memorial Day weekend. The rent is usually halved by then, especially on the big ones."

At the younger man's eager request, the doctor put in a phone call to Michael Carleton, real estate agent-cum-local historian, who promised to pick Dr. Bradley up at 8 A.M. the following morning to show him what was available, before the 10 A.M. Sunday session began.

When Carleton pulled up at the inn at 7:55 A.M., Bradley was already pacing the street, awaiting his arrival. The former was a short, stocky man, apple-cheeked and balding, wearing steel-rimmed spectacles, who got out of the car to introduce himself with a firm handshake.

"Sorry to have gotten you out so early on Sunday, Mr. Carleton, but I have to get back to the city this evening, and I can't miss the seminars I came for."

"Not at all, doctor. Sunday is a major workday for people in my line and I'm an early riser. Delighted that you're so conscientious; wish more of your ilk were."

Accepting the backhanded compliment without comment, Bert asked the agent about possible rentals along the ocean front. In the stretch he most admired, there were apparently only two, one an ultra-modern place with pool and tennis court, the other an old house "with charm." As Dr. Courtney had advised, the prices were already reduced, since the following weekend was the Memorial Day holiday. Should Dr. Bradley want a house away from the ocean, there were two or three available at a lower price, but he insisted on a location on the strip off Gin Lane, which led to Dune Road.

The first house was an extravagant affair of decks and levels and acres of glass flooding the rooms with the early morning light, which fell across beautiful examples of modern art, scattered over the walls of the two-story vaulted-ceilinged rooms. It was starkly modern, reminding the prospective leasee of his own home and those of many of his friends. The grounds were geometrically laid out about the grass tennis court and the Olympic-sized pool, and the rental price, reduced, was $25,000 for the season. The second house was down a tree-shaded circular drive and commanded an impressive view of the ocean from its perfectly landscaped acres. It was gabled and porched, porticoed and turreted in the Victorian manner, its shingles gray-weathered with age, nicely setting off newly painted white trim. Bradley liked it immediately; it reminded him of houses he had known on the Cape, when he was growing up in Wellfleet. The viewing of the interior was a nostalgia trip—overstuffed furniture newly covered in brightly patterned chintzes, Oriental rugs, wainscoting, massive oak pieces, large chandeliers—it all delighted him. The square living room was dominated by a massive stone fireplace, whose proportions were skewed by a door improbably placed alongside it.

At his quizzical look, Carleton explained,

"Everyone is put off by that door—it's a unique feature. It leads to a storm cellar for emergency shelter and supplies.

It's kept locked because the stairwell is so steep. Here, have a look."

Reaching for a key under a vase on the mantel, he opened the door to show his client a ladderlike stairway leading to total blackness below. There was no electric switch, since logiclaly the cellar would only be used if the lights blew out, so one would have to descend by lantern or candlelight. Bert shuddered as the darkness seemed to rise and seep into the pleasant room. He quickly slammed the door, which the agent locked, carefully replacing the key. The rest of the house tour was pleasant—a cheerful white-washed country kitchen with a fireplace in an exposed brick wall, a nest of tiny maids' rooms apparently long unused, four huge master bedrooms, and two smaller ones, an attic sitting-bedroom suite, a baronial dining room, a paneled library—all rooms with fireplaces. When he saw the large, light-filled studio beyond the kitchen and the playhouse, surrounded by its own hedges, at the end of the garden, Bert knew the house was perfect for his family. As he explained to the agent,

"It might have been designed for us. A bedroom for each, room for guests, a studio for my wife, a playhouse for my little girl, a library for me, and an attic suite for an *au pair* girl to take care of Lissie. I know I should show a facade of reluctance to get the price down, but if it's within reason, I'll take it."

"Without your wife's approval?"

"I know she'll love it as much as I do. How much?"

Leafing through his book, Mr. Carleton quoted a price reduced to $10,000 for the season, and Bert sat down at the dining room table to write out a deposit check for $1,500. Pleased with the deal, Bert got back in plenty of time for the first seminar.

On his way into the session, he stopped to tell Dr. Courtney of his success, describing the find in lively detail.

"Oh, that's Mulberry, the old Desmond place." He looked at Bert wonderingly. "Did Michael tell you the history of the family?" Upon hearing the negative, Courtney told Bert he'd fill him in on the details over lunch. He proceeded to do so in the sun-filled doctors' dining room. Bert was intrigued and sobered as Dr. Courtney told him of the family's tragedy. He described his futile attempt to bring five-year-old Jessica Desmond out of the schizophrenic condition caused by the trauma of having witnessed the shocking murder and mutilation of her family.

"I was a young intern then, but I remember how we had to pry a dead kitten out of her fingers and give her drugs to get her eyes to shut. Until that point she just kept singing a lullaby, "Sweet Afton," over and over, in a voice totally cracked—apparently from having sung it for more than a day. After she woke from that first sleep, she never made another sound—became as rigid as a two-by-four, just staring straight ahead."

"Cataleptic?"

Courtney nodded, "Exactly."

"We realized we were limited here, so after a month we had her transferred to Payne Whitney Clinic in Manhattan. There was plenty of money in the estate, according to the attorney, so we figured, why not the best?"

He smiled as Bert nodded vigorous assent.

"I personally brought her to Dr. Barakian, who then headed the children's ward. I remember how entranced he was with her beauty, he kept saying that she was the most beautiful child he'd ever seen. He promised to do his best. I'm sure he tried."

"I remember hearing about him," Bert interjected. "No one seems to know what became of him. Just seems to have dropped from sight."

"I know, he left a few months after the Desmond child died. Perhaps he was disheartened at his failure. Happens to the best of us, and he was one of the best."

Grave silence followed his comment, as the people at the table remembered their own crises at losing a patient to death or irrevocable madness.

"If the entire family was wiped out, who owns the house? And who paid for the expensive renovations?"

"If I remember correctly, the bank controls the estate and rents the house. What the provisions of the will were, I'm not quite sure. There were two other boys, who had stayed at their maternal grandparents' cottage down the road that night. That cottage was swept away, and their bodies were never found. If you run into Tom Skidmore this summer, he can probably tell you about the house, he was the Desmond attorney."

The talk drifted to clinical matters, and then to plans for the summer. Courtney said he looked forward to meeting Mrs. Bradley.

Mrs. Bradley's reaction was one of stunned disbelief. Bert had cleverly called a family conference, knowing she wouldn't make a scene in front of the children, who were totally delighted with the news of a summer at the shore. The idea of the Hamptons pleased even Stacey, who grudgingly allowed it to be a reasonable alternative to Europe. Seeing the enthusiasm of the children, Bert felt Alice would have to temper her anger at his actions. Lissie, who had never seen the ocean, was thrilled and started chanting a song about sand and whales while hopping about the room on one foot.

"Did you see Lissie's reaction, Alice? I can't wait to see her playing on the beach."

A good offense is the best defense, thought Bert, smiling innocently at his wife.

Later, when they were alone, he half-listened to her tirade, having anticipated on the drive back home that afternoon practically everything she'd have to say. He could tell from the tenor of her remarks that she wasn't all that displeased, just furious at yet another example of his not consulting her, "his high-handed, male chauvinist ways." But this time it was a move in what she considered the "right" direction for the Bradleys.

". . . and you know how my parents hate the shore. They never let me go at all. They said I had a bad scare in a hurricane when I was a very little girl, and they'd never even let me look at *pictures* of a beach. What am I going to tell them?"

"Don't tell them anything at all. Once we're in and settled, they'll realize how foolish they've been all of these years. They'll love coming out to see the kids in that setting. It's exactly the kind of place they would have chosen for themselves."

As Bert dwelled on the attractive details of the house and grounds, he could almost feel Alice's anger dissolve.

"The studio is absolutely perfect for your sculpting. Whoever built it must have had you in mind. And the whole place was painted and cleaned this spring. All you have to do is hang the clothes in the closets. There's even a full range of gourmet cooking equipment."

By the time he had finished, Alice was starting a list of

80

people to invite for weekends, wondering aloud if they shouldn't buy a beach house. He wisely skirted *that* issue and reminded her not to tell her parents until the last possible moment. The children were told that their summer plans were secret, a surprise for the Arlens that must not be given away before the O.K. was sounded. They swore an oath to remain silent with many giggles; even the tension between Richard and Stacey seemed to fade. Alice grudgingly told Bert he had made a wise move, but that if he ever did anything like that again, she swore she'd take the kids and leave—permanently. Her husband had a feeling she meant it.

Every spring Mrs. Arlen sought out and hired an *au pair* girl to help Alice in the summers when Mattie went home to her family in North Carolina. This year she once more drove to Alice's alma mater, Mount Holyoke College, in South Hadley, Massachusetts. As always the tiny town, no more than a crossroads, gave her a sense of peace as she remembered how Alice had enjoyed the quiet pleasures of learning in this former seminary from which Emily Dickinson had fled. She had been delighted when Alice had chosen the school, and she hoped that her grandaughters would become "MHC girls" as well, now that there was a trend of interest in all girls' schools again.

Miss Markle was still in the placement office, and they had a good chat before sorting out the applicants for the summer of 1976. It was a point of pride with Mrs. Arlen that Alice had always been pleased with the girls she'd chosen for her over the past sixteen years. Mrs. Markle was pleased that she had always had such a good selection for

Mrs. Arlen's choice. This year she sighed, for the job was getting harder and harder. Girls were so free these days, it was difficult to find the quiet type Mrs. Arlen preferred. The students were either busy tramping about Europe and California, or if they wanted to work, they wanted something lucrative and/or glamorous. Doing housework and taking charge of a five-year-old was apparently not high on the list of preferred occupations.

As they looked through the file of available juniors, Mrs. Markle pulled the application of Amy Cullum, a scholarship student from the town whose job preference stated simply "anything." Her résumé was neat and well written, and her references from clergy and faculty were excellent. Her major was drama, which should be good for entertaining a bright, lively, little girl like Lissie. Without a car it was difficult for her to find local area employment. Yes, Amy Cullum should be glad of the opportunity to live in a fine house and share the luxuries of the upper classes for three months.

When the girl came to the office, Mrs. Arlen was pleased with her quiet manner and her modest way of dressing and speaking. Yes, Amy would be delighted to work for the Bradleys in New York City and wherever they decided to summer; six hundred dollars would be satisfactory compensation, since she would have no expenses at all. "New York City!" she silently exulted, "at last!"

Part III

In all of her nineteen years Amy Cullum had rarely been out of the South Hadley area. As the daughter of the local ne'er-do-well handyman and his slatternly wife, she had neither the means nor the opportunity to do so. Ibram Cullum couldn't afford a car, and his neighbors would gladly tell you it was just as well, since he would be too drunk to maneuver the winding Berkshire roads without killing someone. His wife, Ida, earned his drinking money by cleaning or by doing laundry and ironing when she wasn't busy with her brood of six.

The next oldest after Amy was thirteen-year-old Harley, and the children ranged down to five-year-old Celia. Ida had to hide the Pill; her husband would have beaten her if he had discovered that she was depriving him of the fruit of his loins. The doctor at the college infirmary slipped her a supply each month when she cleaned the office. She had told her husband that she was in early menopause. Though she was only thirty-seven years old, she looked closer to fifty. Ibram grumbled that his mom had had fourteen kids and had looked a hell of a lot better in her coffin than Ida did walking around, but this never stopped him from asserting his conjugal rights almost every night. The roughly squeaking bedsprings were a constant noctural refrain in the crowded house. Amy would gladly have stabbed her father if for no other reason than to stop these noises and the contrapuntal groans, wheezes, and *ooffs* that accompanied his climaxes. If her mother forgot the obligatory *oohs* and *aahs,* the next sounds were blows, as he beat her for not appreciating his virility.

"Whassa matter, bitch? Not good enough for your fancy whore ways?"

Once (fired by a TV feature series on wife abuse) Amy had begged her mother to leave her father. Her mother had looked upon her lovingly with great, sad eyes.

"Nowhere to go, honey. We don't even have bus fare to Springfield for the seven of us. 'Sides, who would have us? At least he owns this property free and clear and he's never laid a hand on you kids. He knows I'd kill him if he did." This last was said so matter-of-factly that it did indeed seem a truism. "It'll be enough for me to see you get out and be a fine lady. That's all that matters—for you to get out."

Local rumor had it that Ida stayed with Ibram because he'd married her after she'd gotten knocked up in a gang bang and didn't even know which of the Amherst fraternity gentlemen was Amy's proud pappa. It had been considered great fun in the fifties to get a local girl drunk, or high, and rent her out for "initiations." In any case, Ibram had thus bought her loyalty, even though he'd started beating her regularly when it took her six years to start to produce his own kids. Between the beatings and the sex, she rarely had a chance to get out of the ramshackle, hundred-year-old house left to this scion of the Cullums.

Despite it all, Amy grew up to be a credit to her father. She looked like a lady, even in the cheapest hand-me-downs and Bargain Box finds; her intelligence was phenomenal. If the Cullums had nothing else, they had the smartest child that ever attended Holyoke High. Even Ibram shone in her reflected glory. She easily won one of the Mount Holyoke College scholarships set aside for local girls, and was even entitled to room and board at the college in return for waitressing and various light duties around the dorm. In the evenings she worked at the Snack Bar or Guest House to earn a few dollars for spending money. It was the best thing that had ever happened to her. She loved to walk through the peaceful campus, past the tennis courts, alongside the waterfall leading to the small lake—as a student, not as the cleaning woman's daughter. It was a dream her mother had given her from the time she was three years old and had been taken along to sit quietly in a chair while her mother did the cleaning on campus.

"Someday, baby, you'll be one of the young ladies here. Learning all that fancy stuff and going out with fine gentlemen. So you've got to remember to always be good and do everything the teachers say. They'll show you the way you can live like those swell people on the TV. How about that, sweetheart?"

And the child would nod gravely, as if comprehending everything her mother said between bursts of scrubbing.

Most of the girls were kind and always asking her if she could "use" some item of clothing. Taught early that "beggars can't be choosers," she gratefully accepted everything, but couldn't help resenting these girls who apparently, effortlessly, had everything. Stolidly, she saw them attempting not to be condescending as they tried to avoid noting her threadbare accouterments in the communal shower rooms. She always got dressed when her roommate was out, so no one could report on her raggedy underwear. Even though the style was worn jeans, theirs were carefully styled French imports with stitching and outer labels that proclaimed "fifty dollars and up." Their makeup alone cost more than she had ever earned in a year of after-school jobs baby-sitting and working at the drive-in restaurant.

From age eight her mother had warned her to never let a boy touch her anywhere.

"They're all after one thing, and once they have it, it's good-bye! You don't let no boy touch you until you've got that gold ring on this finger. Hear now, Amy? Promise Momma you'll always be good, then you can go to college and be a lady. Promise?"

"Yes, Momma," came the reply in the clear, sweet voice. "I promise."

She certainly had kept the promise, she thought. It was one thing for these fancy girls to screw around, but let her be seen once kissing someone's grandfather, and all those whispers about "bad blood" and "that Cullum family—our own Tobacco Road, you know," would be giggled about. As far as she was concerned, the school was still a seminary. Not a breath of scandal ever touched her.

The frustrations were overwhelming. All around her, especially on weekends, girls were getting laid. She was probably the only virgin on campus—probably the only one over age twelve in the whole goddamn state, she sighed. She wondered what it would be like—not the screwing she'd sometimes been privy to between her parents, but making love, like in the movies, or on TV, or in the hundreds of books she'd read. Once she had her diploma and a good job, she was certainly going to find out. For now, she could in no way jeopardize her scholarship. One more year to hang in, and then watch out world!

Amy ran down the main street, cut through the bank's tiny parking lot, and across the weeds around the shingled house. Her mother was on the sagging back porch hanging out vast quantities of laundry, clothespins in her mouth.

"Momma, guess what? I've got a job for the summer in New York City!"

Mrs. Cullum stared at her daughter. "But, baby, your daddy won't never let you go, you should know better than that."

"He's got to let me, Mom—you've got to make him let me!"

She poured out the story of a fairy tale job with a family in a Manhattan town house who would pay her fifty dollars a week, all expenses paid, to do light housework ("A cleaning woman comes in three times a week to do the heavy work, dear," Mrs. Arlen had explained) and watch over one five-year-old girl with a day and a half off each week.

". . . and they'll be going away to some resort or traveling somewhere and I get to go along free. I'll be an *au pair* girl—that's French for an equal member of the household. Mom, he's *got* to say yes!"

The hope in her clear eyes and the stubborn set of the cleft chin told Ida that this time her husband would have to agree, or else. As she listened to her firstborn, best-loved child chatter on, a plan formed in her mind. No—no way was Ibram going to keep Amy from having a chance at this job. Next year, she'd be starting a full-time job, and who knew if she'd ever have a glamorous summer like this again? Maybe she'd even make some contacts in the outside world through these rich people.

"Who is the family, Amy?"

"Mrs. Arlen interviewed me for her daughter, Mrs. Alice Bradley. She said she was an MHC grad and that she hoped her granddaughters would be coming here."

"Arlen—Arlen—wonder if that could be Alice Arlen. Used to clean her room when she was here. Real pretty girl with gorgeous blonde hair. What's the mother like?"

As Amy described Mrs. Arlen, Ida frowned in remembrance of the heavyset woman with hair that looked like she was trying to bleach it to her daughter's color and straighten it to match its texture. She and the husband used to come up and visit once, sometimes twice a week. Said they had to bring her special vitamins. Older couple, always very kind they were. Alice was always giving her stuff and the father would slip her a few dollars to take special care of his girl's room. Amazing how such ordinary people had had such a beautiful daughter. But then she knew people were always shocked to find out this glowing young lady was Ida Cullum's own. Well, in her day, she had been quite a looker, not classy like Amy, but she'd turned a few heads. Too bad Amy's real father couldn't see how she turned out. As always her heart swelled with pride as she gazed upon this marvelous creature she'd hatched under these circumstances.

"Yeah, think I remember the old lady. Married to a doctor, isn't she? From Connecticut? Foreign they were, had a funny accent. Daughter married a doctor too. Right out of college."

"Right, Mom. You *know* them? That's incredible!"

Beaming at having finally impressed her daughter, Ida nodded and chuckled, showing gaps in her teeth.

"Sure I remember. Was the last year I worked full time at the college—before—that is, before I got married."

"Only he's a psychiatrist—Dr. Bradley is. Wow. That's going to be exciting, to live in the same house with a shrink."

"Well I know one thing, we can't tell your father. He just won't let you go. So you just leave everything to me. When school ends you get all your stuff together and leave it at the dorm. When you're ready to go, leave from there and I'll take care of the rest. Leave me your address, but when you write don't put it on the envelope, that way he won't be able to find you. By September he'll have gotten over being mad and you'll only have nine months till you're finished here forever."

From a secret hoard, Ida gave her daughter a few dollars to buy a secondhand suitcase and a few summer things at the end-of-semester sales the girls always had out on the quadrangle lawn.

Amy left for Springfield to catch the New York City bus the day school ended. Ida told Ibram that her daughter had left for a New York City summer job, leaving no forwarding address. She told him as he was undressing for bed,

88

calculating that since beating her gave him a fine erection, he wouldn't beat her too long before he started screwing. She couldn't decide which she hated more.

Harley heard the blows, and the sound of his mother stifling her cries. He heard the rusty bedsprings creak interminably to the accompaniment of his father's animal groans and grunts. Sounded like the old man had a piss hard-on—could go all night like that. He clenched his fists and prayed for the strength to someday kill his father.

The bus ride to New York City took about two and a half hours, most of it through the ugly sprawls of a megalopolis, which Amy found majestic; her eyes were bored with rustic scenery. A mountain was just a mountain, but gaze upon what man hath wrought! Manhattan was the dazzling experience she'd expected, viewed through the window as the bus driver steered the huge vehicle toward its berth at the Port Authority Terminal on Forty-second Street. It looked exactly like a scene out of *Midnight Cowboy,* but she wasn't a bit nervous. It was what she'd been waiting for ever since she'd first heard about the Big Apple—where everything's at, where everything is happening, where she knew she belonged as surely as she knew that Ibram Cullum was not her real father.

Pretending she was before a camera, she walked through the teeming crowds as if it were a regular part of her routine, as she'd seen it done on the screen so many times. Beneath the cool exterior, her senses were being assaulted by the sights and sounds and smells of people of every description scurrying along—from blue-haired dowagers to men who could only be pimps on the lookout for additions to their stables. She looked so purposeful that though some glanced appraisingly in her direction, she was not, to her relief, approached. One tall black man, with an evil face, wearing a purple felt hat that matched his suit, was literally dragging a blonde girl behind him. She looked no more than thirteen, the vacant smile on her face a sign of drugs or retardation. No one even bothered to look at them.

Following Mrs. Arlen's written directions, sent along with her ticket and a thoughtful week's advance on her salary, she went up the escalator and straight ahead to the Eighth Avenue cab stand.

"Sixty-eight East Seventy-ninth Street, please—and take Fifty-seventh Street over to Park—it's the easiest way to get across."

Words by Mrs. Arlen, delivered perfectly by Ms. Amy Cullum. What would her stage name be? Having read enough about theater successes in her course work, she was positive that she was going to be a star. With a background like hers—practically out of O'Neill for godssake—how could she miss? She'd been pretending ever since she could remember; there were so many masks she had no idea of who the real Amy was. Better so. Stamp out reality, help others to do so, and you were rewarded with fame and fortune. One day she'd be living in this grand canyon called Park Avenue—yes, it looked just like it did in the movies, as did the street of brownstone town houses where the cabbie stopped. She grandly tipped him fifty cents above the meter and climbed the stone steps to the elegant Federal-style entry.

A pleasant-looking, middle-aged black woman opened the door to her ring, and greeted her warmly.

"Come right on in, honey. Miz Arlen called to tell us you should be here about two, and you're right on time. Family'll be back about four. You come in and rest awhile. Want something to eat or drink? You just call me Mattie now, and I hear you're Amy—right?"

90

As she talked, Mattie drew Amy along the hall and up the back staircase that ascended from the glass-walled garden entrance to the kitchen above. The girl's experiences in the elegant drawing rooms and public areas of the dormitories, and at the Guest House at school, helped her to act at ease in her new surroundings as she removed her floppy brimmed hat and shook out her hair.

"Where do I put my stuff?"

She was led up to another level of the house and shown into a delightful small study that apparently doubled as a guest room, with a private bath. Everything was color coordinated in a palette of blues set off by bold, beautifully framed posters.

Mattie told her to come down to the kitchen for a cool drink when she was "freshened up" and unpacked, then left her alone. Quickly, Amy stripped and, for the first time in her life, had a shower in a private bathroom. Luxuriating in the feel of the navy-blue velour bath sheet, she padded about on the thick carpeting and pulled on fresh, if not exactly new, clothes. There were three sets of pretty underwear in good condition; she had a sneaking suspicion her mother had carefully been swiping them from the laundry for her use on her great adventure. Three pairs of jeans purchased at the end-of-term sale all had the right labels and cut—even a pair of "Jags"—all for under fifteen dollars. Thank God these girls were crazy—and her size! Six tops carefully chosen for their labels and dye lots would give her enough changes and could be worn with the white slacks, denim skirt, the white skirt, or a long cotton wraparound Robyn Andrews had given her upon hearing she was probably going to work at a summer resort.

"White pants and a long skirt, and you're dressed for about anything," was her advice.

The pool attendant had given her a whole bunch of suits the girls were always leaving behind, and had even included a pink terry beach top that her mother had altered to fit her.

She had a lime-green slicker she'd gotten on sale the previous summer, her red MHC sweat shirt, and a good navy-blue cardigan her mother had given her for her birthday last July. Her prize bargain was a roomy Gucci bag used only for two years by Jane Irving, who sold it to her, complete with matching, slightly worn wallet, for only ten dollars. Her one extravagance was a brand-new pair of forty-dollar shoes from the best store in Northhampton. They were cloglike sandals that the clerk assured her would "go with everything." Amy had learned quickly from her fellow students of the importance of the "right" accessories. The Tretorn sneakers the gym assistant had found abandoned in her size were worn looking, but no one wore brand-new sneakers. The girl was pleased with her acquisitions; she had really learned a lot at school. Everything looked *comme il faut*. The zipped suitcase wasn't Vuitton, but a slightly battered Lark, perfectly O.K. and a steal at five dollars. The Cullum family fortune had been totally exhausted by her purchases, but she and her mother felt that they were making an investment in her future. The college had taught them the value of making a good impression. For jewelry Amy wore the only two "real" things she owned: an antique ring handed down in her mother's family and the gold medal she'd won for high school scholarship on a chain around her neck. Since she couldn't afford a good, i.e., Tank watch, she wore a campy plastic thing, which she knew was acceptable for a coed's casual wear.

As pleased as she was, she thought bitterly of the girls at school who wasted more in a casual hour's shopping than the cost of this, the most extensive, expensive wardrobe she'd ever owned. Carefully she'd watched how they dressed so that when she had the money, she'd know how to shop properly. One day she'd show them all. They'd be bragging about the fact that they'd gone to school with *the* Amy Cullum. Best not to change her name, she decided, this way everyone would recognize that it was the raggedy girl from the shack who had her name in lights.

"Coming down, honey?" The question intruded upon her reverie, and calling, "Coming," she quickly slipped into jeans, a blue-striped caftan shirt, and the blue leather clogs she'd worn on the bus. Amy clattered down the polished wooden stairs to the kitchen where Mattie waited with a pitcher of lemonade and a plate of freshly baked sugar cookies.

"Want to have it here or out on the terrace?" asked the maid, pointing to the deck that ran the length of the kitchen and overlooked a three-story terraced garden visible from all the public rooms in the house.

"This will be fine, Mattie, thank you so much," she replied in the gracious tones the girls used for the help at school.

Mattie proceeded to tell her about the family likes and dislikes and of what her responsibilities would be toward each member. There was a week to "break in" before Mattie left for the summer, but that was plenty of time because they were the best family in the world to work for, according to their employee. Her duties would be making beds, baby-sitting Lissie, some marketing, clearing and setting the table, emptying and loading the dishwasher, and doing some laundry each day. There'd be a daily to help out half a day, Mondays through Fridays.

As the housekeeper spelled out the duties, an enchanting little blonde, blue-eyed girl ran into the kitchen and plopped herself in Amy's lap, smiling up as if expecting instant love.

"I'm Lissie and my grandma says you'll love me and play with me. Right, Amy?"

She received a quick hug from the surprised girl who couldn't help contrasting this fairy creature with Celia at home. Poor snuffling little sister was glum, always scruffy looking and looked upon the world with rightful suspicion.

93

A true Cullum, her mother always sighed, and a little backward too.

The child was followed by her mother, who looked like a page out of the *Vogue* magazines Amy read at the school library. Cool and crisp in blue-and-white seersucker, she quickly put the girl at ease with questions about school and her bus trip, while gauging her potential helper. Her mother was usually right, she thought, but this girl was different from the others—a quality she couldn't as yet define. And definitely more mature than the others, in a strange way, also as yet undefinable. It was odd to say about this plain, thin girl, but she was somehow too sexy for a household with an adolescent boy—the apple of his mother's eye. Alice supposed she was becoming one of the neurotic mothers, but the girl made her vaguely uncomfortable.

Amy was instantly aware of it; for some reason, she made most women unsure of their own sexuality. Using her most disarmingly naïve manner, she saw Alice start to relax. Amy always found ways to practice her acting, and now she was putting Mrs. Bradley at ease.

"Would you like me to read Lissie a story or help her take a bath before dinner? I have a five-year-old sister of my own, so I'm pretty handy around kids. Or would you rather I helped Mattie here in the kitchen, Mrs. Bradley?"

"Goody, goody. Amy, you come to my room and play with me, please?"

With Mrs. Bradley's indulgent assent, Lissie pulled Amy along to a beautiful pink-and-white room, fit for a princess.

The *au pair* girl met her employer when he stopped by his baby's room to listen to the squeals of delight from the tub, where Amy was helping her play with an armada of rubber toys. At Lissie's shout of "Daddy!" Amy looked up into the face of one of the most attractive men she'd ever seen, the kind she knew her mother had in mind when she urged her to "save it for the right one—the one to marry." Perhaps a man like this was her real father? Imagine having a father like this instead of Ibram Cullum. Better yet, imagine him as a lover. Oh, God! He looked paternally amused at the admiring reaction in her eyes—eyes rarely left so naked.

Recouping quickly, she scrambled to her feet, hand outstretched.

"I'm Amy Cullum, Dr. Bradley. It's a pleasure to meet Lissie's father. She's an extraordinary child."

The clasp was warm and firm on both sides as the father evaluated the newcomer, now poised and smiling in her best "to the manor born" style. The girl he saw was tall and very slender, not a spare ounce of flesh on her, yet the effect was one of seductiveness. Her dark hair had a sheen that fine hair has when there is a great deal of it. The face raised to his was rather angular, but the full mouth and thickly lashed greenish eyes were the most sensuous he'd ever seen on a female of that age. Delicately shaped eyebrows lifted slightly under his scrutiny, as if recognizing that he liked what he saw.

"Welcome aboard, Amy. Hope you'll enjoy being part of the Bradley bunch until September. Alice says to please come to the kitchen now, I'll finish off in here."

As she went downstairs, Amy realized that she was resenting Lissie for having the attention of this gorgeous man, whose warm, resonant voice had made her ache with desire the instant she'd seen and heard him. Better get off cloud nine fast, she thought, blow your cool and you blow this job. His wife probably watches him like a hawk, she correctly assumed.

Alice, Mattie, and Stacey had the kitchen bustling with their preparations for the evening meal. Amy quickly noted that the table was set for six, defining her position as an *au pair* girl, not a servant.

"O.K., Amy," Alice sang out, "let's see you do your stuff with the salad—oh, sorry, you haven't met Stacey yet. Stacey this is Amy Cullum, she'll be with us for the summer. Perhaps she can convince you to apply to my alma mater in the fall. She seems to have survived successfully over the past three years."

During the brief exchange of "Hi's" the girls assesed each other instantly. Rich bitch, thought Amy. Stacey was wearing the full complement of status symbols—Gucci shoes, LaCoste shirt, Cardin pants, Cartier Tank; her face was carefully made up, her hair fresh from a cut at Kenneth's. She would have been a stunning-looking girl if overweight hadn't coarsened her figure and face. The effect of magnificent hazel eyes, aquiline nose, and oval chin were spoiled by a layer of fat, but Rubens would have loved painting her fleshy beauty. Unfortunately her looks were "out," while Amy's leanness was definitely "in"; the older girl was aware of the younger's instant resentment of the contrast between them.

"Calculating cunt" was Stacey's instant reaction as she smiled charmingly and drawled mechanical pleasantries to the hired help as they worked. Her parents were total fanatics about being nice to the lower classes. Probably a heritage from some Puritan ancestors that had skipped her, but this was one area where the spoiled daughter was not allowed to flout the rules. Those less fortunate must be treated with more courtesy than those more fortunate, like the Pope's washing of feet, for chrissakes, Stacey thought. Good thing her father's family was dead, they'd most likely be total bores from what she gathered from her father's reverential reference to them and to their ministry on Cape Cod.

This year's girl would be treated politely, casually, and forgotten as soon as school began, except by Lissie who talked about the "pears" for months afterward as her world changed with a piece removed to puzzle her. People were supposed to be forever, in her happily limited experience.

Richard had excused himself from dinner by phone, he was studying for his last exam with Benjie. At the dinner table the subtle cross-examination began, to ensure that Amy was indeed fit to share their summer and take charge of the youngest child. It was as much a ritual at the Bradley dinner table each June as was the Seder service for the Jews at Passover, Bert often joked, and just as serious. As a psychiatrist he was only too well aware of the damage that could be inflicted upon a young child by an emotionally unbalanced or unstable person in charge. He probed for the flaws that weren't obvious to the lay person, but his mother-in-law had an uncanny instinct for mental health. She'd never sent them anyone who couldn't meet his high standards, and it seemed Amy would also pass with flying colors. Her answers in his professional evaluation indicated an individual of remarkable ego strength and emotional stability. The doctor felt quite comfortable about leaving his little girl in her charge.

Like the quick study she was, Amy, on her part, had already decided on her characterizations. To the parents she would be demure and respectful, to Lissie lively and funny, to Mattie gracious, and to Stacey friendly, but slightly deferential as behooved their respective ranks. Just now she was doing a very creditable part of a perfect young lady, poor but proud. Yes, it would be easy to see her doing the Ann Baxter role in *All About Eve* as she explained why she had chosen to go to Mount Holyoke.

"It was really a matter of the school choosing me, Dr. Bradley. I'm on full scholarship, you know, and I don't even have the expense of traveling home, I just walk a few blocks down the road. This way I'm able to help my mom with the five kids when she needs me." Nicely done, she thought, honest, simple, unashamed of poverty. She sensed the parents' approval of her as she ate her meal with impeccable manners. Mother's years waiting table in the college dining rooms had paid off. She had taught all of them, even Celia, to eat with backs straight, one hand cupped in the lap, mouths firmly shut while chewing small bites of food. That—and a properly set table—were the only social amenities observed in the Cullum household. She wondered what these genteel people would think if they saw how she lived. Fiercely she wished she could get out of that hole forever.

The inquisition was over with the end of the meal. Amy was sure she'd passed. She'd never flunked anything in her life. As she helped Mattie to clear the table, Richard walked in to "view the latest victim," as he cheerfully phrased it.

"You must be Richard. I'm glad to meet you. Nice family you've got here," Amy greeted him breezily.

"Hi, Amy, nice to meet you. Think you can stand us for the summer?" he grinned as he gave her the once-over. Nope—he was finally old enough to think about making out with the hired help, and here they stick him with a girl built like a string bean. No ass, no tits, nose too big. Wondered if his mom did it on purpose. Probably noticed he was shaving now and didn't want to put temptation in his path. Hopefully he'd find a real built broad at the beach he could make out with, time he stopped jerking off.

On her part, Amy was glad to take the measure of the son of the house and find him unattractive and unattracted. Richard was too young and looked it; his glasses were heavy and thick and he was tall and gangly with bristly hair. It would be difficult to maintain pleasant relationships all around if the kid decided to slobber over her and she had to fend him off without hurting his feelings. For him she would play quintessential nice big sister.

By the weekend Amy was letter-perfect in her routines. Life seemed to be idyllic in the Bradley houshold as they prepared to move to the beach house, everyone in high spirits in anticipation of a totally new summer experience. The parents were going out for the first weekend to get the house ready, and to bring out some clothing and household paraphernalia. The following weekend would be the big move out.

Bert loaded the black Chrysler wagon with bag after bag of clothes, packed by Alice and Stacey, and boxes of toys Lissie "needed" to take so that they wouldn't be lonesome for her all summer. Most were stuffed animals, all named, and well loved as substitutes for the real pets to which Alice had an aversion. Richard had packed some books and microscopes, Bert some sports equipment; only Amy had nothing to send on ahead. When Bert asked about the arrival date of her trunks with the rest of her clothing, her simple "There isn't anything else" tore his heart. He'd forgotten that not all girls had wardrobes like Stacey's. The wagon was, as Bert teased, "bowlegged" as they started off that June weekend. They chatted gaily, like kids playing hooky from school for some wild adventure. On George's considered advice, Bert hadn't mentioned the clinic again. His friend had said that he'd start the campaign to change Alice's mind in July, in the meantime Bert was to devote all of his efforts toward making Alice totally happy, an order he was determined to carry out.

"I can't wait to see your face when you see this place. I know you'll forgive me completely for my nonconsultation act."

"You'd better be right, or there'll be a lot of commuting back to the city. Which reminds me, how are we going to work the six weeks until you're out with us full time? Shall we all go back and forth, should we leave the kids while I go back and forth with you, or should I stay out with them while you do the weekend husband bit? I really can't decide how to swing it."

In all their years of marriage, they'd rarely been apart. When the children were young, the Arlens had gladly "boarded" them all summer while the parents came up to Connecticut for the weekends. Bert had always taken August off (it seemed to be as built into his profession as Wednesday golf was for the M.D.'s) and they spent the month together. When the older two were in camp, their mother spent her time in her art studies in New York City. They enjoyed the peace of Manhattan summers together when everyone else had fled. Alice had always professed scorn for those wives who left their husbands alone all summer because "it's so good for the children." And here she was, a potential drop-in on that scene, feeling guilty for her past sarcasm on the issue, and even guiltier at the thought of joining the ranks of those despised wives. She was fair-minded enough to admit to herself that part of her refusal to be parted from her husband was due to the fact that he was so damned attractive that there was no point in leaving him open to temptation. These days females were so predatory that they propositioned him right in front of her, jokingly, of course, except that all concerned knew it wasn't a joke. Alice often wondered if Bert had ever been unfaithful. She never had been—out of choice of course, rather than from lack of invitations. She had a feeling he wouldn't tell her if he had.

"Well, I've given it a lot of thought, love. It's my considered professional opinion that we move out with the kids next week, and that you stay until it's time for them to get ready for school. We have the place until September thirtieth."

"But won't you miss me, Bert?"

"Of course I will, darling. But I'll feel terribly noble knowing I'm suffering for the sake of my own little family."

He smiled as she laughed at his imitation of pomposity.

"Besides, I've decided to take Fridays off, so I'll drive out late Thursday night, have a full three-day weekend, and leave either very late Sunday or by five-thirty Monday morning. That way you'll only have two full days without my august—or June or July—presence. How's that?"

100

Alice pondered his proposal. It certainly sounded a lot better than dragging back and forth every week and/or worrying about finding a responsible adult to supervise the household in her absence. It was her firm belief that mothers of teen-agers should be around, even more so than those of little ones. It was the older kids who got into the really serious mischief. She hated to even think of it, but their friends' kids had been through everything from abortion, rape, drugs, drunks, runaways, communes, sects, O.D.'ing—the list seemed endless. Yes, Bert was right, it would be best for her to be around to supervise the children—and Amy. Relieved that her husband had made the decision for her, she smiled gratefully.

"Sounds like an ideal solution. Just as long as you don't shack up with Sheila."

They laughed at that possibility. Poor Sheila, they all well knew of her unrequited love for her employer, but only she knew the intensity of her pain, as real as a knife wound.

Alice turned her attention to the scenery, her first experience with a shore area, and as Bert retraced the route George had taken, she was as entranced with the vista as he had been.

"My God! This is utterly glorious. My parents were crazy to keep me from this all of my life. What is wrong with them? It's the most beautiful setting I've ever seen," she raved.

Like Bert, she had a perfect day for her first view of the Hamptons, which deliberately seemed determined to seduce her, with a gently swelling sea reflecting an azure blue sky set off by a sun as yellow as a kindergartner's drawing. Beach plum and dune grass added color to velvety sand borders, while on the left as they drove east on Dune Road, three-hundred-year-old trees in full, perfect leaf waved protectively about the weathered shingled houses they'd been planted to shade. The estate section of Southampton impressed her, and Alice was not easily impressed. By the time Bert proudly pulled up the driveway of "their" house, she was excitedly chattering about getting her parents to sell their house in Connecticut and move to the Hamptons. It was about the same distance from New York City timewise, and she was sure they'd love a change of pace.

"Well, what do you think of it?"

"I love it!" came the instant response as she ran up the stairs to the gracious front porch with its embrasures. "Hurry and open up, I can't wait to see inside."

Bert opened the door and scooped her up to carry her over the threshold, his happiness intensified by hers. They were young lovers again, as cares and worries about kids dropped from them.

On a wild impulse he carried her up the stairs, despite her laughing squeals of protest, and unceremoniously dumped her on the bed where he proceeded to give her what he referred to as "a good old-fashioned kid-stuff go." He just unzipped his pants, tore her panties off, and had at it. They both had a good time and unscrambled themselves breathless and laughing like old times.

As Alice "repaired the damages" in the bathroom, Bert started unloading the car and bringing the bags to the rooms. On his last trip in, he found Alice in the living room, staring at the door next to the fireplace, oddly quiet.

"Peculiar thing, isn't it? We'll have to keep it locked. The stairs behind it are perpendicular," and he proceeded to explain its use to her.

"Lissie must never go near it, Bert. I want it nailed up and something put over it. I know it sounds crazy, but I could swear there's something evil behind it."

Her husband stared at her in disbelief. He hadn't breathed a word of the Desmond tragedy to her, and Alice was hardly the one to experience psychic phenomena. She was about the most level-headed person he'd known, with no patience for even listening to stories about ESP or anything in the area of parapsychology. What emanations could she be receiving? Suddenly, chillingly, the perfect day seemed less than perfect.

Part IV

With Mattie and Ms. Warren helping, the move the following Friday went off quite smoothly. The former was off for North Carolina on Saturday, while the latter would be in charge of the house and office until her own August vacation. They waved the family off amid hugs and kisses and promises to keep in touch. Sheila Warren was secretly thrilled at the thought of having the doctor to herself, as it were, for days at a time.

Bert drove the heavily loaded wagon, while Alice took the lead in the Mercedes, her son navigating with the aid of a road map. Stacey, who considered station wagons déclassé, chose to go with her mother, leaving Amy and Lissie to keep Bert company on the two-hour trip to their summer home. Bert couldn't help contrasting the quiet demeanor of the *au pair* girl with the constant squabbling and demands of his own children. He believed that deprivation had some positive aspects. This girl who came to spend twelve weeks with them, with only one small suitcase holding most of her possessions, was dignified, intelligent, sensitive, and perceptive. He was impressed by her capabilities and sense of responsibility. Perhaps Amy would be the key; he could show Alice how much better off their children might be if they, like Amy, had less when he started his new career. It might be to late for Richard and Stacey, but he'd like Lissie to grow up with many of Amy's apparent good qualities.

On her part, the young woman was in a state of euphoria. In her two weeks in Manhattan, with time and some money, she had explored the museums, walked the theater district, and had even seen a Broadway matinee—her first professional theater experience. It had left her more determined than ever to succeed in her chosen field. Now she was en route to one of the fabled vacation lands of the world. Even in South Hadley they had followed the doings of the rich in their summer playgrounds on Long Island's golden sands. She, Amy Cullum, would be part, albeit a tiny one, of that scene in the company of a family who treated her beautifully. except for that bitch Stacey, she thought, but she'd just keep out of her way. She amused her charge all the way out with songs and stories she invented, which made even her employer laugh at her ingenuity.

The occupants of both cars were duly impressed with the beach scenery, and Lissie tumbled out of the car whooping to get to the beach to play in the waves. Her enthusiasm was infectious, but Alice was firm. They were to get unpacked and settled in first; they had three months to enjoy the beach.

The young people roamed the house, excitedly exploring the large old-fashioned rooms, marveling at details never seen in modern quarters. Everywhere they looked there were architectural surprises—window seats, built-in cupboards, unexpected alcoves and cubbies. Amy's quarters were promptly dubbed "Amy's Attic," and though they were attractive, it did effectively establish her as apart from the family, and the attic was warmer than the rest of the house, which was cooled by the giant shade trees and porch overhangs. Still she did have her own apartment. Its dormered sitting room had a small fireplace, and off the pretty, flowery papered bedroom was a tiny bathroom. She unpacked quickly and then put away Lissie's clothes and toys to the child's satisfaction in the lovely yellow room set off with white batiste curtains and spread. Stacey appeared in the doorway to announce,

"Hurry up, Amy. My mother needs you in the kitchen."

Amy went quickly down the back stairs into the large-country kitchen to find Alice Bradley surrounded by cartons of groceries.

104

"Amy, you put away these staples while Dr. Bradley and I do the marketing for perishables. I want the same arrangement we have at home on the pantry shelves. When you're finished you can take Lissie for a walk around the grounds and acquaint yourself with the kitchen."

With a wave, she was off.

When she was finished with her chore, Amy took Lissie for a tour of the grounds, down to the playhouse at the end of the garden, surrounded by hedgerow. It was a delightful little place, obviously recently redone, like the rest of the house. There were three tiny rooms, perfect for a child Lissie's size. She waited outside, smiling at the child's exclamations of delight. Suddenly there was silence and the little girl emerged to beckon Amy to peer into the tiny bedroom. On the miniature bed lay a mother cat contentedly suckling four kittens. Lissie was wide-eyed and clasped Amy's hand tightly.

"It's a real cat and kittens, isn't it, Amy?"

"Of course they are, Lissie. Haven't you ever seen a cat before?"

Vigorously the little girl shook her head. "Mommy can't 'bide cats. Daddy says when I'm all grown up I can have some, but not while I live with Mommy. Oh, Amy, do you think she'll let them stay here when she finds out?"

The child's yearning love for the animals was so intense that Amy decided to try to let her have a summer of learning the pleasures of pet owning. Kneeling down, she put her arms around the child and looked into her eyes.

"Now, Lissie, do you want to keep the kitties and play with them while we're here?" She smiled at the eager nod of assent. "O.K. then. I'll ask your daddy, and if he says yes, then we won't tell Mommy anything. Whenever we have free time we'll come here and feed the kittens and play with them. If they come near the house I'll shoo them away. But they're wild, so I don't think they'll come near strangers. Do you think you can keep the secret? If you don't, your

105

mommy will be very angry and send me away. Promise?"

"Oh yes, Amy. I promise promise promise. Just you and me and Daddy. Now I have two secrets. The kittens and not telling Grandma about this house. That's hard, but I'm a big girl now." Her sweet voice was serious and determined. Amy would bet she wouldn't tell about the kittens under threat of torture.

Lissie had one secret less to worry about, much to her relief. Alice called her parents before dinner to gently break the news of their removal to the seashore. There was shocked silence at the other end of the phone, she reported to her husband, and she quickly put all three children on the phone to tell their grandmother how wonderful everything was and how happy they were. Alice signaled them to hang up without putting her back on, to avoid any argument with her mother concerning her mild deception.

"At least that's done," she announced with satisfaction. "It's a lot better to present her with it after the fact than to have agonized for weeks while she tried to convince me to change my mind."

"Why is Grandma so set against the beach, Mom?"

"Oh, she has all sorts of old-fashioned ideas about dampness and dangers of undertows, Richie. When I was a very little girl, about Lissie's age, we were staying at a beach resort somewhere and we got caught in a big hurricane. I remember some of it—crashing surf, a weird, scary noise, darkness and a lot of tension. My mother said I was terrified for years, but I think she was, and projected her fears onto me, to make sure we never went back to the shore again. My father said she was going to make sure never to be near

106

a beach again when a hurricane struck, and that the best way to do that was to never get near an ocean. Makes sense. O.K. gang—let's eat."

Dinner was simple; cold cuts and salads from Herbert's with Roberts' ice cream for dessert. The children were delighted with the picniclike atmosphere, being jaded by nightly gourmet meals. Amy was delighted because since there was no dishwasher, this meal meant no pots and pans to clean. Everyone helped to clear and scrape, but the rest of the job was hers.

When she was getting Lissie ready for bed, the doctor came in to say good-night to his daughter. The child looked at her "pear" significantly, and Amy plunged into the story of the cat and kittens, asking permission to engage in a loving deception to make the little girl happy.

"I know I don't have to explain to you, Dr. Bradley, what having a pet means to a child this age."

"I know, Amy, especially for Lissie. Her siblings are so much older than she that she's really an only child. My wife was frightened by a large dog when she was very young. She's obviously never recovered from the trauma."

The child looked gravely from one adult to the other. Unable to resist the hopeful pleading in those blue, blue eyes, her father grinned, and agreed to become a co-conspirator. He was rewarded by the child's joy and Amy's thanks.

"Thank *you* for caring so much about making my daughter happy, Amy. I appreciate that," he said, and with a nod and a smile he went downstairs.

They all went to bed early that first night. Alice had to go into Lissie twice, because the child cried out in her sleep. Bert said it was due to the excitement of the change of scene.

3

The next morning was perfect beach weather. After a quick breakfast, the entire household decamped for the confines of the beach club, temporary membership provided by Dr. Courtney as a professional courtesy to his colleague. After registering, they were provided with changing rooms and lockers and charging privileges at the lounge and restaurant. The steward showed them the facilities and introduced them to a few members around the huge pool overlooking the beach. Amy was instructed to take Lissie down to the water's edge and to watch her carefully. Holding the towels and the little girl's beach toys, she ran after her charge, who was frantic with impatience to jump into the surf. Dropping everything on the sand, she grabbed Lissie as the child flung herself fearlessly into the waves, laughing with glee, apparently in her element.

When the rest of the family came down for a swim, they found Amy instructing Lissie in the rudiments of the crawl near the shoreline. As they emerged from the ocean, the four Bradleys stared at the sight of Amy in a red string bikini. The girl had a perfect body, that clean, sexy look that Europeans identify with typical American good looks and appeal. She walked with unselfconscious pride. This was one place where Amy Cullum was more than equal to any other female, and she well knew it. Richard quickly raced into the water to hide his erection, and it took Bert's restraint to keep himself down. She was the most perfect thing he'd ever seen since he'd first set eyes on Alice twenty-five years before. Unbidden thoughts flashed through his mind of what it would be like to bed a young girl again. Instantly contrite, he started to chase Lissie into the water, while Alice coolly explained the beach procedures to Amy, in reference to length of time in sun and water, distance from shore, proximity to lifeguard, and a myriad of other details pertinent to her youngster's health and safety. Leaving Amy on shore, she and Stacey joined the others for their first experience in the sea.

Bert felt like a boy again, gamboling in the surf, showing off for his family, and, truth to be told, for Amy as well. As she sat on the sand watching them frolic, young men kept drifting by, stopping to introduce themselves, assuming she was a new club member. Unable to contain her jealousy, Stacey waded out to announce in her haughtiest tones that she'd appreciate Amy's getting her things from the locker room since she, Stacey, didn't feel like going back. Battle lines had been drawn. Amy followed the best strategy under the circumstances: She retreated to do the bidding of the daughter of the house, who briskly took over the pro-cedures to insinuate herself into the younger set's social whirl. Coming on strong with her flagrant sexuality, it didn't take her long—the boys recognized a good, easy lay when they saw one. Her parents beamed at their daughter's easy entry into the summer society and at her popularity. Richard was in no position to disillusion them, since his entire aim for the summer was to finally get laid himself, hopefully with the girls he might meet through his sister's good offices. He was starting to fill out, and with contact lenses he wouldn't be at all bad looking, he thought. With a tan and one of those fancy haircuts his mother was always urging, he might even be sexually attractive. People were always saying he was going to look like his dad.

His parents seemed to be having a good time, they'd already met some friends of friends. It seemed as if the summer was going to be a good one for all concerned.

4

Within a week, routines had been established; tennis in the mornings, beach in the afternoon. A genial woman in her fifties, a Mrs. Hanks came in three times a week to do the housework and laundry, while Amy tended to Lissie or did minor chores around the place. Every day they managed to visit the kittens, secretly bringing them scraps of food and milk. On weekends, Bert managed to go with them, and the three marveled at the beauty and antics of the kittens, and at the solicitude of the mother cat. Amy cherished these moments together, fantasizing the three of them as a happy family. Was it her imagination or did Bert's hands actually linger on hers as they passed the kittens back and forth? Was it his imagination or did Amy press against him deliberately, lingeringly, as they played games with Lissie?

Bert found himself looking forward to the time he spent with Amy. Her gratitude for the simplest kindness or consideration was touching; she made him feel so—well, masculine and protective. Her youth and energy was so refreshing—what would she be like in bed? Alice was practiced and expert, but he sensed she felt sex was a wifely duty. Would Amy be eager, inventive, innovative? From her looks he felt she'd be all that and more. Each weekend he found excuses to spend more time with Lissie when Amy was in charge. No one seemed to look askance. Alice was busily involved in a consciousness-raising group made up of local and visiting feminists who were planning a series of workshops to promote C.R., and with her work sculpting in her airy studio. Richard was absorbed in either books or buxom girls, as far as his father could tell, while Stacey was rarely to be seen. When she was home she was engaged in series of mysterious phone calls. It seemed that only Lissie still regarded him as the center of her universe—and Amy? The signals in body language seemed unmistakable.

On her part, Amy found herself merely existing all the days when her employer was in New York City. She recognized her total infatuation with his looks, his voice; the very smell of him made her dizzingly happy. It was time, she felt, to get rid of her virginity. Despite her deep emotions, she was calculating as always. He would probably be gentle, expert, and grateful for her youth. He would also be discreet and possibly helpful to her in her future in New York City. Succumbing to fantasies, she envisioned him leaving his wife to make her Mrs. Dr. Bertram Bradley, with Lissie coming to visit them, always young and adorable.

Lissie was delighted to have two adults to share her playtime and her secret pets. She made a perfect chaperone. Her nights, however, grew increasingly restless. Alice complained that she rarely had a night's unbroken sleep since their arrival. The child would cry out in her sleep or wake screaming in the middle of the night, apparently in wild-eyed terror. Yet in the mornings she woke up fresh and happy, while Alice was tired from having her sleep interrupted. Since Lissie rarely woke when Bert was there, he ascribed her night-terrors to feelings of insecurity due to her father's absence, explaining to Alice that it was part of the Oedipal problem, which would be resolved with patience. It further justified the increasing amount of time he spent with her—and with the *au pair* girl whose presence made Bert act boyish and carefree. He felt younger and gayer than he had in years; the almost thirty-year difference between them meant nothing when the man was affluent and in good shape. The fact that Amy and Stacey were close in age concerned him, but after careful reflection, he felt assured that his sexual longings for Amy had no tinge of incest

111

syndrome. It was a healthy lust for a highly attractive young woman who exuded sensuality and whose interest in him was an ego booster.

It was Amy as "predatory female" who made the first overt move in the courtship pavane.

"Mrs. Bradley, would it be O.K. if I took my day and a half together this week?"

"Why, Amy, and when?"

"I had a letter from my mother asking me to visit her sister in Brooklyn. It's her only sister and she hasn't been well. I thought I'd leave Wednesday after lunch, and Thursday is my regular day. I'll be back in time for breakfast on Friday morning. I'd be most grateful, Mrs. Bradley."

Alice frowned. It wouldn't be that convenient. Wednesday night was her C.R. group, but Stacey or Richard could baby-sit. Amy *had* been performing her duties perfectly and quietly. In all fairness, she deserved some consideration. Her only diversion was browsing in the well-stocked Bookhampton South store. Its pleasant ambience and the classical music playing in the background made it a "cultural oasis" on the touristy Main Street. She rarely took her time off, since she had nowhere to go, and no friends in the area; she'd spend a few hours at the beach, or in town, both within walking distance, then be back early, much to Lissie's delight.

"O.K., Amy. There's a one-oh-five train daily, I'll have Stacey or Richard take you to the station. If you know exactly when you'll be back, we can pick you up."

"Thanks awfully. I really appreciate this. My uncle may

be able to drive me out to Brookhaven—I can catch an early morning bus from there. He works in a factory somewhere in that area. I promise I'll be making breakfast by the time you get up."

Amy had planned everything perfectly, as usual. By 4 P.M. that Wednesday in late June, she was at East Seventy-ninth Street, waiting for Ms. Warren to leave at 4:30. While waiting, she went into the drugstore on the corner of Lexington Avenue and bought some Delfin Foam and some contraceptive gel. She'd get the Pill as soon as possible. Theater training was always helpful; she now psyched herself up for her new role as ingenue seductress.

Five minutes after Ms. Warren left, Amy was ringing the bell. The look on Bert's face was a kaleidoscope of emotions, the last being one that might be described as stunned, if wary, pleasure.

"Hey, Amy! To what do I owe this unexpected, if most welcome, pleasure? Come on in."

"I hope I'm not bothering you, Dr. Bradley, but when I called my aunt's house in Brooklyn to tell her I was on my way, there was no answer. I got tired of waiting around Penn Station, so I took the bus here to wait. Is it O.K.?"

"Sure thing, but this isn't your day off. I hope it wasn't an emergency visit."

"Not exactly. My mother said Aunt Rose wasn't feeling well, and that she was worried about her. I thought it would ease her mind if I could tell her everything was O.K. She can't come down because she has Dad and the kids to take care of, and quite frankly, she can't spare the bus fare. Mrs. Bradley was so kind, she said I could put my day and a half together so that I could stay with my aunt overnight. Now that there's no answer, I can't imagine what's happened."

As always, Bert's ready sympathies were touched by references to her poverty and her familial devotion. Now that she was troubled to boot, his gallantry knew no bounds.

"Do you want me to drive you to their house? I can try to get your uncle at his place of employment, or do you want to call your mother? How can I help you, Amy. Just say the word."

"That's awfully generous of you, Dr. Bradley, but if you don't mind, I think I'll wait until six, then try to call again. If there's no answer, I'll have to go over there. I don't want to call home and scare my mother."

"Sensible girl, Amy. Just make yourself at home. I have some work to clear up here, then I'm supposed to meet George Webber for dinner at seven-thirty. That'll give me time to drive you to Brooklyn if necessary."

With a wave, he stepped into his study. Amy considered carefully. She had an hour to make a definite move.

Going upstairs to "her" room, she shaved her legs and underarms before taking a long shower and shampooing her hair. She rubbed oils into her sun-dried skin and brushed her hair into a magazine sheen. No makeup except some no-run mascara to accentuate her striking eyes. A dab of Bal à Versailles from a tiny sample bottle one of the girls at school had given her at Christmas, and saved for a special occasion, completed her toilette. Wrapping herself in the blue bathsheet, she padded barefooted down the stairs to knock timidly at Bert's study.

"Come in, Amy—I'm almost finished here. What's the word from your relatives?"

"I just wanted to ask if it was O.K. to use the phone."

"Of course—you know there's no need to ask."

"Well, my mom always says it never hurt to be super-polite, most people prefer it to being taken for granted." Flashing a smile at Bert's laugh, she went into the adjoining office to do her act.

Bert had a good view of her great legs as she sat on the edge of the desk pretending to make her call.

"Uncle Al—Amy, how's Aunt Rose?—Oh, that's great!—When? Did she call my mom?—Good. Gee that's

114

really good news. Tell her I send my love.—Yes, I'll drop her a card.—Thanks a lot. Hope to see you soon.—Bye now.

"Gosh that's a relief! My aunt is at her sister-in-law's house upstate for a rest, and she called my mom before she left yesterday. Guess my trip was a waste of time."

"At least everything's all right. You can have a day in town and I'll drive you back tomorrow night."

"That leaves me with tonight. Guess I'll have a TV dinner, if that's O.K.," she said forlornly.

Bradley gazed at her thoughtfully. Deciding quickly, he said, "Tell you what. I'll call George and cancel our date, and I'll take you out to dinner. Would you like that?"

He laughed at her reaction.

"You look like a Christmas tree that's just been plugged in."

"I feel like one. Wow, I'm glad I brought a skirt to wear to see Aunt Rose. She always hates to see girls in pants."

She ran up to change as Bert called George to cancel their weekly dinner date.

They walked to the Sign of the Dove where Bert, at his most impressive, ordered an extravagant meal accompanied by the finest wines. He loved the way her eyes widened at everything that he and his entire family, even Lissie, had come to accept as their due. It was fun to show her how to eat *escargots,* and to explain how to choose proper wines. He enjoyed the envious glances cast his way for his being with a woman who glowed with youth and verve. It was like being on a date—it *was* a date, he realized. After dessert and cheese and fruit, he suggested they walk off the effects of overeating. Guiding her through his turf and pointing out landmarks, they were both high on good wines and everything seemed delightful. On an impulse he took her to Le Club, and scored more points.

"Isn't this the really exclusive disco? I've read about it in magazines. It's famous."

"A friend of mine is one of the owners, a former patient, as a matter of fact. He gave me a charter membership in appreciation of my services."

Amy danced the way she looked, sexy but classy. Completely absorbed by the music, she moved to the persistent beat with eyes half-closed, silken hair tossed to the demanding rhythms. In her simple white cotton skirt and black T top, she outshone all the sophisticates in their designer clothes and elegant jewels. Again it was an ego trip for Bert to be envied as her escort. When the D.J. changed the pace to a medley from the forties, Bert laughed at Amy's dismay.

"But I never learned these dances."

"My pleasure to teach you, young lady."

After a few stiff moments, her sure instinct for movement took over, and she relaxed in his arms as if she belonged there. Humming the familiar tunes to himself, he was carried back in time. Eyes closed, he wrapped both arms around her, his chin resting on her perfumed hair, as Frank Sinatra sang "The Things We Did Last Summer (I'll Remember All Winter Long)." Unconsciously his arms tightened around her as she pressed against him, Bert pulled away, embarrassed by the past intimacy, but Amy gazed at him with the clear eyes of an innocent child.

"Better get back, Amy. I've got a ten A.M. appointment," he said briskly, trying to break the spell.

As they walked back to the town house, Amy trustingly slipped her hand into his as she chatted about her plans for Thursday. When they got inside, Bert bade her a short but courteous "good-night," then disappeared into the master bedroom.

Amy used the contraceptive jelly, then the foam, as directed on the boxes. She pulled on an old white T-shirt that barely covered her bottom and left her flowered bikini underpants on. Swiftly brushing her hair to a center part, she padded silently to Bert's room, to tap at his door and

116

enter before he responded. Her employer was sitting on the edge of the bed wearing only his "sexy" jockey shorts, as Alice called the hip-hugger style he preferred.

Standing in front of him, her body tense with desire, Amy smiled at the surprise in his eyes.

"I'm sorry to burst in on you this way, but I just had to tell you what this evening has meant to me."

Kneeling at the bed, looking into his eyes, she explained,

"I have never been to a restaurant in my whole life, I've never been on a real date, and aside from school dances in the gym, I've never been dancing. What you did for me tonight was to make me feel that I'm a real person, not just a servant or someone everyone pities because her father is a drunk and her mother cleans houses. Tonight for the first time you made me feel real. Thank you."

And putting her face to his trustingly, she pressed her lips on his and wound her arms around his neck. Bert gave up trying to resist. She felt so good, smelled so wonderfully of youth and sex and perfume. For a long time they just lay on the bed, bodies pressed together. Their tongues explored each other's mouths as Bert's hands stroked firmly against Amy's back and buttocks. He slipped off his shorts and pressed his hardness against her, rubbing against the thin nylon of her panties. As in dancing, she followed him perfectly. He helped her pull her T-shirt over her head and lingeringly kissed her small, firm breasts with their surprisingly long nipples.

Slipping his hand into her panties, he lovingly caressed her, then pulled her atop of him, letting her rest between his legs to feel him throbbing before he rolled over to pull the wisp of nylon off her. Her hips arched up to meet him as he entered her, her hands firm on his hard buttocks as he thrust into her, pushing down on him as she pushed up so that he wouldn't pull back when he met the resistance of her membrane. The penetration was over in a few seconds as Bert climaxed in a series of gasping breaths. After a few minutes of rest, he wordlessly brought her to climax with practiced fingers and lips. Those waves of pleasure she'd read so much about washed over her. She thought she'd gladly drown in the intensity of such physical sensation. If nothing else in her life had ever been right, her defloration had been perfect. Kissing Bert passionately, she rolled over into a fetal position and promptly fell asleep.

Waking refreshed, she was amazed that the luminous dial on the clock indicated it was only 2 A.M. Her lover, she quivered at the thought, was sitting up against the pillows staring into space and smoking a cigarette.

"Hi, Dr. Bradley," she called softly.

He smiled at her. "I guess you could call me Bert now, or do you think we ought to wait until we know each other better?"

She laughed and snuggled up to rest her head against his shoulder. "One more thing to thank you for. It was so perfect for me, just as I knew it would be. I'm so glad I waited until I found you."

The sincerity in her voice was unmistakable, and touching to Bert.

"I've been thinking while you were sleeping, Amy, that I don't think what happened was wrong for either of us. It was a normal, healthy physical reaction between two people who do have good feelings about each other. And I'm flattered to be the first in your life because it means you'll never forget me. What an intimation of immortality!" he grinned self-deprecatingly.

She nudged against his shoulder waiting for him to continue. Gently he kissed the top of her head.

"I don't like the idea of being unfaithful to Alice, but I don't believe that I have to feel guilty—nor do you. Sexuality is a part of life—a good part of life, an affirmation of life. You make me feel young again, give me a new perspective. If we can work it out so that no one will ever find out and so no one will ever be hurt by our relation-ship—including you, Amy—there's no reason we can't see each other whenever possible for as long as it's a mutually beautiful experience."

How much was rationalization neither would ever know. All that they realized was that this couldn't be a one-night stand, they were both already aware of the depths of their feelings for each other.

"I'm perfectly willing to be fatalistic—*que sera, sera* and all that. I learned when I was a little girl, like Puff the Magic Dragon, 'nothing lasts for ever.' I'm mature for my age because I've had to be. I'm also an awfully good actress," Amy admitted, "so you don't have to worry about my giving anything away. I've always played every role to perfection. You can check my marks in acting."

"Well, you certainly did a good job of acting like a virgin. You could've fooled me!"

Amy laughed up at him. "I read every book on sex and sexuality I could lay my hands on preparing for that part."

"What about contraceptives, did you go on the Pill before the summer?"

When she explained her use of gel and foam, Bert groaned and told her to pray a lot. Her first appointment of the day would be to get the Pill with his prescription.

"Dr. Bradley—I want to call you that so that I won't slip up in front of other people—could we do something else I've always read about?"

"And that is?"

"Could we take a shower together?"

Bert pulled her up and in a few minutes they were laughing and soaping each other under the spray. Amy's exploring hands felt Bert grow hard and she slipped out to "pack herself." Delighted by her total openness and eagerness for him, Bert carried her back to the bed, and wet and slippery, they made love, this time he waited for her before giving himself release. Watching the bliss on her face and hearing her moans of pleasure, he realized he'd taken sex for granted for many years. Yes, this girl, *his* girl, presaged a whole new life for him. Exhausted, but happy, they finally slept, her leg flung over him so that they could touch in their slumbers.

The radio alarm woke them with a start at 7 A.M. Plans had to be made for the day, since Ms. Warren would be there at 9 A.M. Amy put together a quick breakfast while Bert showered and dressed. Carefully she removed all traces of her presence. She washed and dried the sheets and towels and put them back in place. Ditto for the breakfast dishes.

Bert insisted on pressing money into her hands as she left at 8:40, along with a prescription for the Pill.

"You have to have some cash to spend if you have to wander in town all day. I'll be finished by three and I'll find some pretext to get Ms. Warren to leave then. Be back here by three-thirty. *Ciao bambino.*" With a hug and a hard kiss he gently pushed her out the front door.

When she got to Fifth Avenue, Amy looked at the money, astonished to find a hundred-dollar bill. Impulsively, she walked to the nearest post office to send her mother a fifty-dollar money order, along with a silent prayer that her father wouldn't get it. She had a second breakfast, wandered the shops, went to the drugstore, then, after a hamburger lunch, to an exhibit at the Metropolitan Museum of Art. At three she called and got the O.K. to go back, taking a cab at Bert's urging.

"Hi," she breathed as he welcomed her by sweeping her into his arms and silently holding her close. Cupping her face in his hands, he gazed at her then kissed her with a passion that surprised them both. Wordlessly they climbed the stairs hand in hand to the big bedroom. While Amy disappeared to "spermicide myself," since the Pill wouldn't become effective for several weeks, Bert realized he was actually trembling with desire, like an adolescent on his first time out. Furthermore, he didn't want to analyze the feelings, he just wanted to enjoy them. He did for the next three hours, Amy's obvious joy and delight in their sexual performance spurring him to bring them both to even greater pleasures than either had thought possible.

He liked her quiet as they rested between lovemakings; her happiness at just being there with him was evident in the way her body touched his.

"Rightfully, my dear one, we must get up. I leave here at seven P.M. Time to go back to the real world."

"I hate it—the real world, that is. I guess that's why I'm so good in theater. 'Stamp Out Reality' would be my motto if I had a family crest."

"Are you trying out your act on me, Amy? If so, I must say you're destined for an Academy Award," he teased.

"Oh, no, you're the first and only real thing in my life. If I had designed us, and our time together, I couldn't have done a better job."

The sincerity in her voice was touching, she was grateful for so little—for him and a few hours in his bed. He'd forgotten females like this existed. He certainly never met them in either his professional or social world. Grimacing at the thought of the brittle, self-absorbed women he knew, he thought again of his plans for the clinic. While they dressed he told Amy about them.

". . . so for once in my life I'm going to do what I intended when I started my career, I'm going to help those who really need me. Call it a God-complex, if you will, but that's where I'm at right now."

"But won't Mrs. Bradley mind your not having an income?" asked the always practical girl as she brushed her hair.

"Aye, young lady—that is the exact rub. If I can't get Alice to accept a change in life-style, my plans will be all bollixed up, but good—but let's not talk about my problems, we'd better decide the logistics for Operation Return."

En route to Southampton, they stopped for dinner at the Coach Restaurant and discussed their plans. Bert would drop Amy at a rooming house on Hill Street, a ten-minute walk from Mulberry. They would practice scrupulous care to avoid being found out, and continue their relationship as long as it was mutually satisfactory. Either party's request to have it ended would be instantly honored, with no recriminations. It was understood that Bert would not consider destroying his family at this stage of his life, and that Amy was too young to consider planning her life around a man almost thirty years her senior.

"I've been through these situations with my patients for over twenty years now, Amy, and though it sounds awfully cold-blooded, you'll just have to trust my judgment—my professional judgment, in this case. It rarely works. As a matter of fact, in my personal experience, I've never seen a situation like ours survive happily. Much as we like to think that what we're experiencing is unique, I'm afraid we're just another cliché."

Bert was impressed by the maturity of Amy's reaction.

"I can accept that, Dr. Bradley, even though I don't think anyone can intellectualize an emotion, and I can project myself into the future and accept the truth of what you're saying. I trust you implicitly and I have no choice but to

122

take you on your terms or not at all. I can't imagine ever not wanting to be with you, but I recognize that you probably know best."

"Intellectually I know I am, but emotionally I'd like to spend the next few weeks or years in bed with you."

"And me with you, good doctor. When shall we two meet again?"

"I'll have to work that out. I'll probably drive out to meet you somewhere twice a week, but it needs a lot of thought. Call me on my private line from a phone whenever you have a chance, reverse the charges of course, or from the house if you're absolutely sure it's safe, and I'll give you a coded message along with my Jack Armstrong ring."

He laughed at her puzzled look. "It's an old radio days' joke. See, the generation gap is already taking its toll."

At 9:30 P.M. Bert dropped Amy at the Rose Cottage on Hill Street, which appeared to be deserted. Carrying her bag, he walked her to the gate and insisted that she take another fifty dollars "just in case." As he gave her a lingering, passionate kiss, they were observed from a window in the darkened convent across the street. Sister Theresa Immaculata shook her head. Always immorality, everywhere. The street lamp was bright, and it seemed to her that the people and the car were familiar to her.

Bert entered his summer home trying to be as natural as he could, remembering his usual routines. Richard and Stacey were apparently out, Lissie was asleep, and Alice met him looking tired and irritable. Just as well, he thought; he was dreading the thought of Alice in a seductive mood. After the past two days he didn't think he could get it up

123

again. Alice, he knew, expected him to come in horny on Thursday nights from a week away from her bed. He expected her to want him, and he realized suddenly that their sex life had become part of a routine that neither of them had the courage to question, a knee-jerk reaction.

"Thank God you finally got here Bert," his wife said as she raised her face for the automatic kiss, "It's been an absolutely hellish week."

"Mind if I take this sitting down, preferably with a drink? I've had a hard week too, and a long drive out."

"Sorry, Bert, I didn't mean to dump on you instantly, but without Amy for two days I've been more pressured than usual."

"Oh, what happened to our 'pear' girl?"

Alice briefly explained the circumstances while Bert made the appropriate noises and Alice made him a drink.

As they sat in the club chairs near the fireplace, Alice told of a week during which Richard had been rude, Stacey had stayed out twice until 4 A.M., and Lissie had wakened screaming one night.

"It's not getting better, Bert, it's getting worse. She kept screaming. 'Don't cry, Mommy, don't cry. I'm here with you.'"

Bert frowned, totally alert now, both as a parent and as a professional. Could Lissie be sensing tension between her parents that they were subconsciously trying to suppress? Or was it just a difficult adjustment to her first experience away from her own home, other than the Arlen estate?

Alice was, as always, impressed by his professionalism in trying to resolve a problem. His questions about Lissie, the family, the routines of the week were terse but telling. In answering, Alice became aware that it had been a week in which Lissie had been exposed to more than the usual family tensions. Yes, she admitted, she had argued violently with both Stacey and Richard, yes, Lissie had been upset by Amy's absence. Yes, Alice was feeling her usual pre-

124

menstrual tension. Yes, she was remembering to take her special pills.

"So you see, Alice, Lissie is a highly sensitive child living in a community of adults who are all working through tensions or resolving personality conflicts. Since she's already learned that we value a bright and sunny disposition, and she can't yet verbalize what's bothering her, her fears and tensions come out in these night-terrors. We'll just have to make a concerted effort to resolve or mitigate some of the problems, and to try to help Lissie express what's bothering her."

He went on in a slightly pedantic tone to deal with the subject of their children's sex drives. Richard must prove his manhood by denying parental authority—especially that of a female. Stacey had to assert her own femininity by challenging her mother.

"We both recognize that Stacey is still working through her Electra complex. She still resents you because you have me, she needs masculine approval and interest to move from her involvement with me to a healthy relationship with the opposite sex. So you see our supposed 'problems' with our kids are just a normal part of their breaking the apron strings. I guess because Daddy's a shrink we expect them to have their problems resolved by osmosis."

Alice sighed. Bert always made everything sound so easy to resolve. Sometimes, however, she felt that the adage about the shoemaker's children having no shoes was applicable to her own situation with Bert. She believed that her children needed more attention than their busy father had time to give them over all the years—or to give her, truth be told. Bert always seemed to expect her to be able to handle her problems and the kids as effortlessly as she handled the running of a household. Her C.R. group had helped her to see that her own supposedly enlightened family was as sexist as any blue-collar home. It was divided strictly on His or Hers responsibility lines, but it was too late to discuss that now. She felt totally drained by the week's tension; hopefully Bert wouldn't want sex tonight. She'd make it up to him on Friday, she thought. After all, if a man didn't get it at home, he'd find it elsewhere.

When they got into bed, the kids were still not home, but it was only 11. Bert waited for the signals from Alice, and she from him. The mutual relief was almost palpable when their tentative touchings met with an obvious lack of response.

"You're tired too?"

"Exhausted," sighed Bert, "it was an absolutely hectic week in town. Tell you all the details tomorrow."

A mutual obligatory peck, "good-night," and they both fell into an exhausted slumber, too deep for dreams.

Alice heard the noises first, her practiced mother's ear fine tuned even in sleep. They pulled her unwillingly back to consciousness. She lay in the stupor of half-sleep trying to sort out the meaning and source of the sounds. Be noble, she thought, no point in Bert losing sleep too. Going in to check on Lissie, she was startled to find an empty bed. Quickly she checked the other rooms. It was 3 A.M., the kids were still not home, and Lissie was not in Amy's Attic. Mustn't panic, pretend Bert isn't home, what would you do? She stood still in the now-silent house. Perhaps the child had gone to the kitchen to get food—she hadn't eaten much for dinner.

The full moon flooded the house with white light. The words from the Christmas poem "the luster of midday" ran through her mind as she quietly descended the broad stairs to the living room. She froze at the window-seated landing

126

where the moonlight filtering through the stained-glass window gave an eerie cast to the scene before her. Lissie was standing before the forbidden door next to the fireplace tugging at the knob with all her might and tapping at it with her little fist calling "Daddy, Daddy, I'm here, I'm coming to you, Daddy."

As Alice quietly, but quickly moved toward her little girl, she shrieked in terror as she saw the door start to open and caught a glimpse of a dark figure behind it.

Her shrieks woke Bert, who came bounding down the stairs. Lissie started to cry hysterically at the sudden noise and confusion about her as she was snatched first into her mother's, then into her father's arms. Bert assumed command of the situation instantly, carrying Lissie upstairs and guiding a sobbing Alice along. Once in the bedroom, the parents calmed the little girl, telling her she'd had a bad dream.

"But, Daddy, I went downstairs because I heard you calling me to open the door and let you in. I thought you got locked in, so I went down like a big girl to help you."

"No, sweetheart, it was all just a dream. Daddy was fast asleep right across the hall."

Alice told Lissie about all the nice things they would do the next day, reminding her that Amy would be back soon. The child brightened at once, Bert noted; he too would be glad of her presence.

Putting on his robe, he went downstairs to have a drink, automatically mixing one for Alice, who was singing Lissie a lullaby along with the music box whose sweet strains carried down into the living room. When Alice came down, Bert handed her her drink and chatted quietly.

"I don't remember hearing you sing that song before, Alice. It's pretty."

"Lissie found the music box in her room and I remembered the lullaby from way back—'Flow Gently Sweet Afton.' I think I used to play it on the piano as a child. She loves it."

When he felt his wife was composed, Bert gently started questioning her about the scene she'd observed. When Alice spoke of the door opening to Lissie's pressure, he raised his eyebrows and stared at her as she described seeing a dark figure behind it. Wordlessly he went to the door and tried to open it. It was as he'd last known it—locked by his own hands.

"I don't care, Bert. I know what I saw. Don't look at me as if I'm one of your patients in the psycho ward."

"Easy, Alice, we don't want to wake the baby again. We've had enough for tonight. Let's try to get some sleep."

Lowering her voice, Alice refused.

"You're just humoring me, Bert. You don't believe me," she retorted angrily.

Before Bert could remonstrate, the front door opened, and amid giggles and mutual shushings, their two older children stumbled in—blinking in the sudden glare of the light, surprised to find their parents awake and downstairs at 4 A.M.

Alice turned to vent her growing fury upon them before Bert could stop her. "Be quiet, you scum," she hissed venomously, "if you wake your baby sister, I'll let you go back to sleep in the gutter where you belong."

As tipsy as they were, her offspring gazed at their mother, stupefied by her reaction. Never had they heard or seen her this way. She turned to their father who was trying to reason with her.

"Look at them, the bastards. Reeking of liquor and sin and smelling of sex. Not even old enough to vote and damned already. May they rot in hell!"

Before she could continue with her tirade, Bert led her firmly to the couch and pulled her down beside him. Authoritatively, he addressed Stacey and Richard.

"You two have no excuse for your behavior. Your mother is obviously overreacting because we've had a bad shock. Lissie was sleepwalking and we were afraid she'd been hurt. Fortunately she's O.K., but as you can see, it's driven your mother to the verge of hysteria. Now get to your rooms. I'll deal with both of you in the morning," he added ominously.

Frightened into unquestioning obedience, Stacey and Richard moved quickly up the stairs, shock still evident in the expressions on their faces. Bert turned to his wife.

"Alice, I know how upset you are, and the kids were dead wrong coming home at this hour, in that state, but you really should have tried to restrain yourself."

This was said as gently as possible, but Bert too was totally stunned by his wife's reaction to her own children. He would never have believed she was capable of expressing such hatred for them. He gazed upon her wonderingly. It could be menopause, he thought, or perhaps she'd been under a strain she hadn't mentioned. Could she be having an affair that was putting more pressure on her than she could handle? She certainly had the time and opportunity out here, and she was still one of the most attractive women around. Realizing he was too tired to think anything through, he urged Alice to finish her drink, and they wearily clambered upstairs like an old Darby and Joan couple.

Listening to Alice's regular breathing, he watched the play of early dawn in the room and thought about Amy. Just before he fell asleep, he thought he heard a whisper of "Lissie—Lissie." It must be the wind in the trees, he decided, and dozed off before his mind could register the fact that *there was no wind that night.*

Part V

Sister Immaculata was at her window after morning
devotions in time to catch a glimpse of Amy Cullum as she
quietly slipped out of Rose Cottage at 6 A.M. She walked
briskly toward Mulberry—less than a ten-minute trek. The
morning light confirmed the nun's suspicion: The girl she
had seen last night *was* the same one she'd seen at the old
Desmond house, apparently employed to take care of the
lovely blonde child the Sister admired on her frequent
strolls near the place. Ever since the 1938 hurricane she had
taken an inordinate interest in the families who rented
Mulberry.

She had heard of the search for heirs to what was reputed
to be a vast fortune left by the Desmonds. As the years
went by and claimants were rejected after thorough investigation, she had thought of how wonderful it would be if
somehow the millions of dollars in the estate could come to
the Church to be used for God's work. In the evening talks
before bedtime, she had been heard to say that she was sure
that Evalynn Desmond would have wanted this. The latter's
will never having been found, and Evan's precluding the
estate leaving the family, the only one to benefit would be
the government.

The nun's fantasy was that somehow, some way, the
house and fortunes might someday be given to her convent
to be used for acts of charity for those in need. The other
nuns knew of her obsession and would sometimes gently
tease her about it. When would her dreams reach fruition?

"God will show me the way, Sisters. Has He not
performed even greater miracles?"

130

Cheerfully the others would agree. They thought her a bit peculiar, but eccentrics were hardly unknown to their calling. Her hard work and fanatical devotion more than made up for her oddities. She and her dreams were quite harmless.

As her eyes followed Amy's slender figure moving down Halsey Neck Lane, she calculated that the tall man she had seen kissing the girl with such passion last night could well have been her employer. The car in which the man had dropped her off was similar in type and color to the one she often saw parked in Mulberry's drive, and a tall dark man seemed to be the head of the household. Could the house yet again become the background for a scene of family tension and distress? She shuddered at the thought, wondering if it gave off evil emanations of that other tragic family. Remembering how in her youth she had envied the Desmonds their family life (despite some rumors from town, which had reached even the ears of the Sisters, about Evan's doings), she wondered if God had sent her there to be witness to the frailty and the intransigence of all things temporal. Certainly, after the massacre, she had become noticeably calmer and happier in the religious life to which her family had consigned her, half against her own volition. Families, it would seem, were not by definition enviable. Were the Bradleys to be another instance to prove the point?

As Sister Immaculata went about her morning tasks, George Webber was en route to visit the Bradleys for the weekend, a late appointment having precluded his original arrangements to make the trip with Bert. It was all for the best, he thought. This way he would be free to leave on

Sunday morning and have the day in town to work on plans for the clinic. Nedra, who was proving herself an invaluable assistant, would help him. Then too, truth be told, he could take only so much of Alice, whose charm and beauty could never make up for the uncomfortable feelings he had about the greedy, grasping child he sensed just below the surface of that elegant facade. Bert's total devotion to his wife had always struck him as a kind of enchantment, blinding him to all the flaws that George could note in their marital relationship—and in their children. He knew better than to point them out to Bert, realizing that it would mean the end of their personal and professional relationship. Having analzyed Bert, he knew what his friend could and could not accept. Criticism of his family, an extension of his ego, was a blind spot—a willful one George often thought, while accepting the fact that everyone must have them in order to adjust to less than perfect worlds.

Swinging off the highway to have breakfast at the diner in Hampton Bays, he thought of the clinic-to-be, and of Nedra's total commitment to the project. As he ate his greasy, but satisfying, meal, he acknowledged a sense of jealousy. Nedra would probably never have joined the venture with such alacrity had it not been for the attraction of working with Bert. He wondered how much of this she admitted to herself. The question was, would she stay on when she realized that Bert's interest in her was strictly professional? George had never known Bert to become involved with a woman, unless there had been a one-night stand here and there. His pious upbringing and his anguish over the deaths of his parents made him treat his wife and children as sacred beings, despite, or perhaps because of, his profession. No, Nedra didn't have a shot with Bert, and besides she was too voluptuous; a guy would need a snorkle lying between those breasts. Bert liked them lean, like Alice.

As he approached the house called Mulberry about

132

twenty-five minutes later, he noticed the figure of a nun limping along the road. Automatically he stopped to see if she required assistance. "No," she assured him with a gentle smile, "I was just taking a walk in the cool morning air." With a "God bless you, sir," she waved him on, leaving him to wonder how nuns survived the voluminous folds of their habits. He remembered, with a smile, that as a boy he had wondered if they had bodies under those long robes.

Standing near the driveway, Immaculata studied the Mercedes intently. Yes, she was sure that it was the same one that had dropped the young girl off last night. The father of the household was indeed involved with the young woman in charge of his little girl. Breathing heavily, she prayed for their souls and for those of everyone in that ill-fated house, past and present. Fingering her beads, so smooth after forty years of use, she remembered how a pang of envy had struck her again, after all those years, when she had seen yet another handsome, healthy family take over the unhappy place. Their little one had reminded her so much of poor Jessica Desmond. Families like the Bradleys made her realize and relive the barrenness of her existence from birth until she had fully accepted God after the hurricane of 1938.

Grace and John Ryan had prayed for a child for fifteen years, but He had not seen fit to answer their prayers. Obviously found wanting, they had redoubled their attentions to God's word; their devotion was remarkable even in that town of good folk near Springfield, Massachusetts. Father Alba's unannounced arrival on their doorstep one spring morning was God's tardy, but expected, welcome response to their faith and piety. His kindly face was beaming as he showed them the treasure, a bundle of soft, sleeping, baby girl. The good Father was gratified by their tears and cries of joy, but, he explained gravely, they had to accept one of God's wounded birds. Silently he showed them that the infant's foot was cruelly deformed.

"Perhaps He did it as a test to see how much you wanted a child."

"Oh, Father," Grace replied, "we gratefully accept God's will. If this is His test, then you will see that we shall pass it." Cuddling the baby in her arms, she sank into one of the wine-colored, antimacassared chairs to overcome her emotions; John broke out a bottle of whiskey to celebrate the great event.

"I've had my eye out for a likely Catholic baby for you for a long time, but they have been rare up here. Then as you got older, it became harder because agencies tend to want young parents for the rigors of raising an infant. When I heard about this little lass, I knew I could get her for you. Not too many people are willing to take on the burden of a crippled child."

The new parents winced at that word, but Father continued, "You have shown yourselves over and over again to be good Christians, and I knew the poor babe would be raised in the true faith—and in a manner that would prevent her from falling into the wicked ways of her poor mother."

"Yes," he answered to the question in their eyes, "she is born out of wedlock, but the mother, I was led to understand, is a devout Catholic who asked only that her child be raised by religious people who would keep her on the path of virtue and in a manner that would prevent her from falling into evil ways."

"Perhaps," Grace said softly, "that is why He crippled her, so that she could not stray from the path?"

"More likely it's a question of the sins of the parents being visited upon the children," reflected her husband.

134

"In any event," the priest concluded, "we can be sure that this daughter of the faith will not fall in sin as did her mother."

The three people knelt to pray that this child be saved from her mother's wicked ways and for the mother's return to the paths of righteousness.

Near age forty, the Ryans had not realized the demands of an infant on their time, patience, and stamina. They believed that the baby cried excessively and was too demanding. Determined not to "spoil" her, the baby was held to a rigid schedule, her cries for food or comfort ignored if it was not time. She was not "handled" unduly, and when she persisted in sucking her thumb, her elbows were encased in cardboard cuffs so that she couldn't reach the comfort she so needed. Her howls and screams convinced her parents that she would indeed grow up to be a willful and wayward child if not properly restrained. They were further convinced that the little girl had inherited evil ways from her parents, which if not curbed would bring shame upon the family and certain damnation upon herself.

To prevent these ends, the child was deprived of most normal pleasures. She had a minimum of toys and was kept on a rigid routine for eating, sleeping, and defecating. Grace Ryan was proud to announce that the baby was toilet trained by the age of nine months. This had been accomplished with the judicious use of suppositories and by waking the child from sleep several times a night to put her on the potty. To prevent her from the sin of vanity, her beautiful dark hair was kept cut above her ears and only dark, unbecoming clothing was considered suitable. Though she showed great talent in art and music in school, the teachers were told not to encourage her, as it would only lead to the sin of pride. The nuns understood; having been told of their charge's history, they knew she had to learn humility.

The girl had few friends, due to her handicap and to her shyness. The Ryans discouraged her from bringing friends into the antiseptic environment of their home, where children only felt uncomfortable anyway. If she did receive an invitation from a compassionate family, it was rejected on the grounds that she was needed at home, and that her time must not be taken from her studies. After-school time was to help her mother clean the immaculate house and to read Christian books.

When the girl was ten years old, Dr. Chauncey, their family physician, told them of a new operation, one that he felt could greatly alleviate her lameness.

"Of course it wouldn't be a total cure, but she'd have a good chance of an almost normal gait. It's been done quite a few times at Columbia Presbyterian Hospital in New York City and I'm sure I could arrange a consultation there for you with my friend Dr. Goldberg."

Chauncey was amazed at their reaction. Instead of the joy he'd expected, there was a total lack of response. As they hesitated he added, "Of course, if it's the cost you're worried about, I'm sure something could be arranged. The Church will provide funds and Dr. Goldberg often donates his services free of charge to those in need."

"No, doctor," came the stiff reply, "we're saving people, but we have to talk this over at home before we decide to put our little girl under the knife."

The child could hear their voices from her bedroom when they sat near the kitchen window, as they were now doing. She was sure that eavesdropping was a sin; it seemed as if everything were. As she heard them discussing the possibility that she might walk like other children, she thought her heart would stop for joy. Ever since prayer had been explained to her, she had prayed to wake up to find that ugly appendage gone, replaced by a foot as beautiful as her "good" one. She could be like other little girls—running, skipping, jumping rope—instead of being the "steady ender." Maybe she could even take dancing lessons! God was indeed good to answer her prayers at last, what with all the important things that He had to do.

136

"Even the name bodes no good—a Presbyterian hospital and a Jewish doctor! Grace, I think it's a sign from the Almighty that we should refuse this operation."

"I have the same feeling. Besides, I think it would be unnatural to change what God has done. If He had wanted the child to be normal, He would not have given her that clubbed foot. I'm afraid we would all be punished if we tamper with divine will."

The child froze in horror as she heard this exchange between her parents. Then she started to scream as she stumbled down the stairs and into the kitchen to beat at her parents with her fists, trying to kick them with the clumsy orthopedic boot that encased her twisted foot.

"I want the operation. Do you hear me! I want it! I WANT IT! I WANT IT!"

Quickly recovering from their surprise and shock, the parents dragged the child into the dark basement and locked her in. It was clear from her outburst that the sinfulness was still in that child, despite all their attempts to eradicate it. It was also a sign that should she have the operation, that she would indeed go bad. They left her in the cellar all of that night and most of the following day, ignoring her heartrending pleas for release as she screamed her terror of the dark. When they released her on Saturday morning, they finally had a child more to their liking. She seemed to be totally docile at least; never again did she defy them. The Ryans finally had the perfect child.

She chose the name Immaculata as if to erase the memory of her birth, the shame of which had been impressed upon her over and again from earliest recollections. When she reached puberty, she finally understood what the taunts of "bastard" meant. The Ryans explained that God had chosen them as the instruments of her salvation, and that of her true parents. If she would join the Church in Holy Orders, she could pray constantly for their souls and, in gratitude for their kindness, for the souls of her adoptive parents. Proudly they showed her the huge sum of money they had saved for her dowry for the Church, so that in her marriage to Jesus Christ, she need be second to none. She could enter any order of her choice and buy the finest trousseau. Glowingly, Grace described the wonderful life she would have in dedicating herself to God. Heaven would be a certainty, and she would escape the shame of being a spinster or, worse, the drudgery of being someone's wife— for what man would have her except the lowest? To escape the marriage bed, according to Grace, was the greatest blessing of all. She wouldn't have to have anything to do with "that"! The nuns in school added their urgings, as did Father Alba, who had always taken a special interest in her. He felt that she was a naturally morose child, which, coupled with her handicap, meant she had no place in the outside world. As he put it, she should either take the veil or plan to spend her life taking care of elderly parents. She chose God. As Immaculata, she could pretend to herself that her mother too had been a virgin, wrongfully scorned. And the habit would conceal her deformity.

Everyone was shocked when she chose a sequestered order in Vermont, but no amount of urging could make her change her mind. Mrs. Ryan wept as her dreams of visiting and being visited by her daughter the nun vanished. There would be no contact now between the novice and her former life—she had chosen to be cut off.

Shortly after the death of Sister Mary Joseffa, however, Sister Immaculata changed her mind. After a great deal of time and trouble, she managed to change to a different order. She claimed her true calling decreed a more active participation in the lives of others, the better to serve God,

138

as she had felt Him explain it to her. She also specifically requested, and was granted, the transfer to a convent in Southampton. With a dowry like hers, she was entitled to some consideration. The change did her parents little good. They were now in their sixties, and the trip was too arduous for their health. When they died within a few months of each other, she did not go to either funeral, explaining to the Mother Superior that bodies are just temporal; she'd rather just pray for their souls. She did; praying that they be consigned to purgatory where they rightfully belonged. When the lawyer was permitted to meet with her, she arranged that part of her parents' estate go to the Church. She concealed the fact that the major part of it was hidden away in a secret account under a secular name. The Sisters would have been shocked at the cunning and deception of the young Immaculata.

Bert could see the nun staring up at the house as he dressed to go down to breakfast. He heard Amy's voice ushering George into the kitchen.

"Is that nun always around, Alice? Or is it just when I'm here?"

Alice peered out of the window. "We seem to see her very often; must be her regular route for a walk. Can't tell if it's the same one, they do tend to look alike," she laughed, but continued soberly, "it's terrible to admit, but I've always hated the sight of them, like some great bird of prey about to swoop."

Surprised at her admission, Bert was equally surprised, but pleased, to note that she behaved as if last night had never happened. "She stopped Amy soon after we came to ask if we wanted to enroll Lissie for Sunday school. She said that the woman seemed surprised that we weren't Catholic. Mumbled something about this being a Catholic house and went off—as you see her doing right now. Let's go get breakfast."

With Amy around, Bert found it harder than he'd thought it would be to pretend that everything was normal. George's presence made it a bit easier, since Alice was busy doing her hostess number. He felt sure that Amy would have quite a career in the theater if she was as good an actress on stage as she was in the kitchen. No one could have guessed that there was anything between them, yet already he ached with longing for her. He watched as she busied herself at the stove in a blue shirt and white shorts, her clogs accentuating the long smooth line of her tanned legs, and tried to be as cool as she was being about what had passed between them. She was busy with Lissie, who seemed none the worse for her trauma of last night, thank God. Perhaps her joy in having Amy back had driven the memory of her terror out of her mind.

"And here's the rest of the brood," Alice called gaily as Richard and Stacey came clattering down the uncarpeted back stairs. From her tone of voice it was obvious that she had forgiven (forgotten?) them for last night. He could see the relief on their faces when they heard her friendly greeting.

Soon the kitchen was a cheerful bustle of eating, drinking, cooking, and clearing away as everyone, except Lissie, had self-service at breakfast. But Amy did have the washing up to do when everyone was finished. As he saw her attacking the huge pile of dishes, looking so young and vulnerable, he vowed to himself that he'd have a dishwasher installed that very day. As the family went their separate ways, he announced that he and George would go into town to buy some liquor, and the two men set off for the short walk into the village.

En route, Bert described the scene of the previous night to his companion, who gave a low whistle at the story.

"Whew! That is quite a happening! Sounds like the scene from *Gaslight* where the villain is trying to—you remember, trying to make the woman think she's going crazy."

"Yeah, except that I'm not Charles Boyer, and Alice isn't Ingrid Bergman. She's always been the most level-headed person I've known. I simply cannot account for the metamorphosis. It seems as if my whole family has slipped onto levels of emotions and behavior hitherto unknown to me. I guess it's a cheap shot, but do you think Alice could be menopausal?"

George sighed, "You sound like a typical husband coming to ask me why his wife wants a divorce. The fault lies not in us, dear Brutus, but in the female hormones. Of course it's a cheap shot, you asshole, and if you didn't look so strained, I'd tell you what I really think."

Bert stopped dead in his tracks and stared at his friend. Quietly he said, "I've had the feeling you'd really wanted to do that for a long time, George. I'm hardly insensitive or unaware, just resistant to the realities that I insist upon for others. You know how much I value your judgment, so give it to me. I have a feeling that I'm going to need a few months of therapy by the end of this summer anyway."

Motioning George to follow, he cut across the road to a hollow in the dunes where they could sit and watch the ocean while they talked.

"I think Lissie is picking up the tensions in the household from the energy discharged by the psychic conflicts. She would seem to be a sensitized receptor. You have two young women in the house who are jealous of each other. They look to be highly sexual beings and I have no doubt that these feelings are being beamed at you."

Bert nodded; he couldn't and wouldn't deny the Electra complex that he sensed in his daughter. It was also natural for George to assume that Amy would be interested in him;

most women were. It was not vanity on his part, simply a matter of fact that he'd lived with since he'd outgrown the gangly stage.

"Then you have Alice in a sort of competition with these girls. As gorgeous as she is, she *is* in her forties, so automatically she must lose out to youth eventually. Richard is your prototype of the Oedipal theory, preparing to challenge you on an emotional level, no doubt by embarking on sexual adventures of his own. Lissie is convinced that she is the center of the universe, a stage some never outgrow," he added parenthetically, "and she wants you all to herself. You come along now every weekend and charge this heavy atmosphere with your own subtle chemistry. On some level you invite the adulation and competition of the four females, and the envy of your son, who can't as yet measure up to you. Sexual energies are in a constant flux and I have a feeling that Stacey is the catalyst."

Bert looked startled, "Why Stacey?"

"Because as much as you and Alice try to compensate on a conscious level for her having been 'displaced' by Lissie's birth, you have never really convinced Stacey of that. Mommy has Richard, Daddy has Lissie, and what does Stacey have? Nothing—as far as she is concerned. We're all aware that she started gaining weight right after Lissie was born, which unfortunately coincided with her puberty. It's hard enough for a pubescent girl to accept the fact of her parents sexuality without her mother's belly screaming that they've been screwing. Very embarrassing to the peer group. Then to be 'replaced' as daughter by a charmer like Lissie—well, she's probably going to shove food into herself as a gesture of 'I love me.' She's perfect for sending hostile feelings into your environment."

Bert had been listening intently, nodding again and again at each telling point George ticked off. It was pretty much how he would have analyzed the situation had it not been his own. What would George have added if he'd known that

142

there was an affair with Amy to thicken the plot? Better left unsaid until the girl was back at school; it was her secret as much as his.

"You're right, of course," he said quietly. "Thanks partner, I needed that. In September I'll start coming to you for regular sessions—you're still the best shrink in the business. That is, if you'll have me?"

"Consider it my pleasure," George laughed. "I'll take you as a clinic patient, costs less that way."

Bert's face darkened at the mention of their project as they got up to continue their walk into town down a street lined with giant Dutch elms.

"I still haven't raised the issue with Alice. I thought she'd be so happy after the summer that she'd be willing to fall in with our plans, but lately she's been so tense that I wonder if she'll even consider listening to me by fall."

"I told you that we'd work something out by then, Bert. I have an idea in mind, not quite ready to discuss, of how we can convince your wife to untie the purse strings. Just keep her happy in bed and I'll do all the rest."

Bert laughed and glanced at him admiringly. "I can always count on you, George. I know the clinic means as much to you as it does to me."

"Even more," the older man said softly, "even more."

"That's hard to imagine since it's become my *raison d'être.*"

"Even so," George smiled oddly, "even more."

The dishwasher was delivered that afternoon as promised. It was a portable model that attached to the sink faucets and plugged into the electrical outlet. Alice was puzzled by the purchase, until Bert, smooth and convincing as always, explained. "Since Lissie has been having these sleep problems, I want Amy to be with her as much as possible, instead of spending hours over the dishes. This way she can put Lissie to bed and stay in the room next to hers when we're out, in case she should cry or get out of bed. And then too, you don't do dishes at home, so why should you have to do them here when Amy is off?"

"You are one terrific husband, Bert. Remind me that I said that the next time we have an argument. I guess we can sell it back to the estate when we leave."

"Why not? It's a good attraction for the next year's tenants," and with a hug and a kiss he left her to join Amy and Lissie at the end of the garden. They were exactly where he knew they'd be—feeding the cats with the scraps Amy hid for them each day. He wondered if part of Lissie's tensions could be the fact that she had to keep this a secret from the rest of the family. He'd have to ask George if he had any solution to that problem, but he knew if Alice got wind of a cat, the ASPCA would be at the door within the hour. Sometimes he thought her fear of animals bordered on the pathological, but her father had firmly advised against attempting behavior modification, and she always followed his advice.

His heart leaped shamefully when he saw Amy playing with his daughter and the kittens. It was an idyllic scene that he wished he could capture somehow. He scooped Lissie into his arms as she ran toward him squealing for joy, and tossed her into the air, delighted with her happiness. Gravely he listened to her happy chatter, then sat next to Amy on a bench behind the playhouse safely screened from the main house by its own mass of hedgerow and trees. They talked quietly as the child played with her toys, singing to herself and the world at large. Briefly he told her that there had been some problems with the "kids" that had upset Alice, so they'd have to be even more circumspect than they'd planned to be.

144

"I've worked it out fairly well, I think. I should have been a con man," he grinned ruefully. "On your day off, catch the eight A.M. bus for Riverhead. No one we know ever goes there. Get off the bus in front of the Howard Johnson's and I'll be there waiting for you. There's a Quality Court nearby, and they have phones in every room. The calls don't go through the switchboard, but are direct, which is necessary to the plan. I've told Sheila to switch my schedule so that I can take Thursdays off by starting earlier and working later the rest of the week. Ostensibly I'll be working with George on clinic plans, which Sheila knows is anathema to Alice, so it must be kept secret. I'll have to let George in on part of it because in case of an urgent message, he'll have to relay it to the motel room. Sheila will call his number, and he'll call the motel room. I'll arrange to have the same room every week and George won't know where I am—or who I'm with."

"How did you manage to work it all out so quickly?" the girl breathed. "I'm overwhelmed."

Softly he assured her, "I've thought of nothing else except how to be with you since the first moment I held you in my arms and danced with you." He wondered if it was as hard for her as it was for him to sit so closely without touching.

As if reading his thoughts she whispered, "I think one of us had better leave because I don't think I can sit here much longer without kissing you."

"I know," he said. "If there were comic-strip balloons over my head to show my thoughts, we'd be banned in Boston."

She laughed in spite of herself, and its musicality delighted him. Heroically resisting the impulse to hug her, he ran to play games with Lissie and carried her giggling into the house for her bath.

7

The entire family had been invited to the ubiquitous Saturday cocktail party, this one given by Dr. Courtney on the grounds of his estate on Little Plains Road.

"Now this is the man in charge of the hospital here who got us the guest membership in the club. I want you all on your best behavior tonight."

"Yes, sir," his children chorused. He looked at them with a rush of affection; spoiled as they might be, they were his and they were great. His wife looked more radiant than ever with that tan that only blondes in the Hamptons seem to achieve, set off by an understated, but wickedly expensive, white frock from the Elizabeth Arden Salon in South-ampton. Even Lissie had been included in the invitation, which meant that Amy had to come along to watch her in order to leave the family free to socialize without being concerned about her whereabouts.

As Amy led her downstairs in her party dress, the little girl glowed in the admiration that she evoked. She was wearing a cornflower-blue, dotted-swiss pinafore that reached to the tips of her white patent leather Mary Janes. Her hair was piled atop her head and she wore tiny white gloves. As for Amy, she was dressed in her usual simple style; a long black print wraparound skirt with a bold red halter top and her "good" sandals. Her dark hair fell smoothly to her shoulders with that particular sheen that seemed to be exclusively hers. Aside from mascara to emphasize those fabulous eyes, she was totally without makeup or adornment of any kind. Her clean sexuality almost broke Bert's heart with longing to hold her. He felt a

146

rush of guilt for his betrayal of everyone, and yet everyone he held dear was together in this one room.

It was a large party. A policeman was on hand to direct traffic and young men were on duty to park the guest's cars away from the scrupulously tended lawns. Alice signaled her approval; this was real wealth—the house a replica of a Newport mansion with a pool and tennis courts lost in the vast expanse of grounds sloping gently to the small lake. About one hundred people were enjoying the drinks and hors-d'oeuvres set up under yellow-and-white-striped awnings, while white gloved, uniformed servants circulated with food and champagne. It was the Courtneys' annual summer bash to which local and visiting gentry were invited to mingle, except that they rarely did. The Bradleys sought out their hosts and found that Mrs. Courtney was as gracious and as aristocratic as was her husband. The party was greeted warmly; the woman seemed entranced by Lissie, as indeed most people were.

"Goodness, I don't think I've seen eyes that blue since—well, that is, for many years."

"Usually people question us as to how all we brown-eyed types came up with a blue-eyed child," Alice smiled.

"Oh, I'm up on my genetics," replied the older woman. "Blue eyes are a recessive gene that brown-eyed people may carry, so two recessives can produce a blue-eyed child, but the reverse is impossible, since the blues are 'pure.' You can see that I learned my Mendelian theory well."

"You certainly did, Mrs. Courtney," George said admiringly, and stayed behind to chat while the Bradleys circulated. Bert saw his two older children with the young set and went over to warn them away from the alcoholic beverages.

"Remember that scene your mother played last night? I'm sure none of us wants a repeat."

He was gratified to see them immediately reach for the soft drinks. Feeling certain that they'd watch it for tonight at least, he walked away. Seeing Alice in animated discussion with some club cronies, he went over to check on Amy and Lissie. They were seated away from the action, near the pool, where Lissie was excitedly taking everything in, asking innumerable questions, which Amy answered patiently and with good humor. People drifted by to admire the little girl, and Bert noted, with a pang, the number of males trying to pay unobtrusive court to his girl. In a few years he would be too old to vie successfully for her affections and that knowledge filled him with a quiet sense of despair. Recognizing its futility, he determined to live for the joy of the moment, as he had so often advised his clients to do.

As he knelt to talk to his daughter, he pressed against Amy and was rewarded by the pressure of her thigh against his shoulder. What would become of them? Pulling himself away he walked over to talk to Michael Carleton.

"Hi, Mike. We're really enjoying the house."

"Glad to hear that, doctor. Sometimes people are angry at me for not telling them about the tragedy of the house before renting. Courtney said he'd told you about it. No hard feelings?"

"Why should there be? There aren't any resident ghosts, are there?"

"No," laughed Carleton, "it's just that some folks get upset about being on the scene of the crime. Glad you're not one of those sensitive souls."

"I'd just appreciate your not mentioning it to my family, though, they apparently haven't heard any gossip about the place yet."

"They probably won't. Most people have forgotten about it—or don't care. It's been almost forty years now after all. Then too it's something not usually discussed with 'outsiders,' if you'll pardon such a designation."

"Anyone else here who could fill me in on the details? I'm interested in forensic medicine. I'd like to get some background."

"Sure thing, doctor, anything for the profession, and for a good client. Maybe next year you'll come back to buy a place of your own. Most folks do."

Bert was led over to a cluster of gray-haired gentlemen who were earnestly discussing local politics, within easy reach of the bar. They were interested in meeting the most recent occupant of the Desmond house. The massacre there had been the worst since the Indians had wiped out the Osborne family in 1643 on Halsey Lane.

The details of the estate's imbroglio were supplied by its attorney, Tom Skidmore, who explained that Evan Desmond's will had been foolproof; the money could go to no one outside the family. With five healthy children he could not have considered the possibility of no direct descendants. The bodies of Drew and Edward Desmond had never been found, and the courts had been busy for years investigating the claims of a number of men who purported to be one or the other of the brothers. Each stated that he had suffered amnesia after the storm and one day awoke to realize that he was the heir being sought, with little or no memory of the intervening years, due to "traumas." There were also innumerable people claiming to be Desmond's illegitimate children. Much of the interest from the estate was used to investigate all of these would-be instant millionaires, and thus far, no claimant had been successful. According to law, if no one had been recognized as an heir by 1980, the money would go to the state and federal governments. So far, however, not even their voracious experts had triumphed over Evan. Even in death he was managing to have his own way. The bank got its fees for managing the principal and used the rental monies from Mulberry to keep the house in mint condition, should an owner be acknowledged.

The other men in the group added their memories of Evan Desmond. If even *some* of the stories were half true, it sounded as if the man were a certifiable psycho. His wife, too, was peculiar, according to their gossip, but that would hardly be surprising in view of the man with whom she had to live. Yet all agreed that the five kids had been nice youngsters. There were still many of their classmates around who could testify to that. The Desmonds, it appeared, had been good parents—if nothing else. But as for the exact nature of the crimes, only Tom Doyle knew them, and he had stubbornly refused to divulge them to the public, even after all these years.

"Perhaps it was just gossip that accounted for the grisly stories," ventured Bradley.

"Nobody's damn business," the former police chief stated flatly, still an imposing authority figure in his seventies.

His attitude intrigued Bert. "But why, sir?" he asked the burly, silver-haired man.

"Because, young man, even the dead have the right to their privacy. Don't do them nor nobody else a damn bit of good to know the gory details. 'Sides I always figured that if that poor little girl had got better, or if her brothers was ever found, they'd never be able to hold up their heads for the shame of that dastardly crime. Bad enough without having them know all those horrible things that there bastard done 'fore he killed hisself. I pray every night that he is roasting in hell!"

Seeing the look in Bert's eyes, he continued, "You would too, had you had to see that house full of blood and death, and things that never should be—that poor little girl singing away to her dead mother with a dead kitty in her arms." Overcome with emotion, his voice choking, the big man moved away, leaving an embarrassed silence in the group to be filled by Skidmore's apology.

"He's had a bit to drink tonight and I really believe that he never got over the shock. Seeing your little girl over there probably made it worse. If I didn't know better," he added, "I'd swear she was a Desmond—never saw blue eyes like those since they were alive."

150

8

The trip home was lively and noisy as they all exchanged observations about the party. Only Bert seemed withdrawn, not his usual weekend self. After dropping off the young people, the three adults switched to the Mercedes and drove the fifteen miles to Amagansett for dinner at Gordon's. It was a highly recommended storefront restaurant, which lived up to its reputation, jealously guarded by the two elderly gentlemen who tried to maintain standards in a world fast approaching none. Forewarned, they were still amazed and amused to see an elegant couple with reservations turned away because the man was tieless and the woman wore party pants.

After a marvelous meal, they sat contentedly under the glow of the Tiffany lamp over the round table near the window, companionably sharing gossip and sipping cognac. Bert became aware of his growing sense of frustration because Alice's presence precluded a serious professional conversation between himself and George, and he was sure the latter felt the same way. He reflected upon the hours adding up to years of meaningless chatter that dominated his life; the vapid self-pitying monologues of many of his patients, the self-centered talk of his family, the exchange of social banalities and pompous platitudes with the members of their "set." He recognized a growing sense of urgency in himself and in his impatience. If he didn't do something constructive soon, it would be too late. Alice had been right in her harangue, he realized bitterly; he did feel the need to expiate the sins of a hedonistic life to justify his existence.

Never would he be able to escape the influences of a church-dominated childhood and threats of damnation for a wasted life. How then, he mused, could he welcome Amy into his life? Probably by rationalization; they were each filling a need and he intended to help her in every way possible for as long as she needed him. Surely love could never lead to hellfire; what he felt for the girl was not simply lust, she needed him—it was right.

When they got into the car for the trip home, Bert was stunned to hear George calmly discussing the Desmond tragedy with Alice.

"I must say it was brave of you to agree to stay in a place with such a history, but your husband has always said you're the world's most level-headed person. Silly to be nervous about something that happened forty years ago, but still most women, er, people, that is, would be hesitant about staying in such surroundings."

Alice stared at him blankly, wondering if he'd had too much to drink, and brushed aside Bert's attempts to change the conversation.

"Just a minute, Bert. Exactly what is it that you're talking about, George? What history of what house?"

"God, I hope I haven't said anything wrong," George stammered as Bert glowered at him fiercely. "I just assumed that you knew the story of the place you're in. I figured someone would have mentioned it to you."

"And what, pray tell, is there to know?"

Casting an anguished look at Bert, George made as light of the events as possible. "It seems that the family that used to own the house was murdered by the father, who then took his own life, during the 1938 hurricane. According to what I heard, he was a heavy drinker and had a lot of problems with his wife, who was a little peculiar."

Although Alice probed for details, they were mercifully few, thanks to the reticence of Chief Doyle.

152

"And why was this kept from me, Bert?" came the steeliest tone imaginable.

Concentrating on his driving, Bert tried to be as offhanded as he could. "I honestly knew nothing about it until after I paid the money, and I don't see what difference it makes. We're hardly the type of people who worry about spirits or bad vibes—true?"

Reluctantly, Alice agreed. She felt too content to start an argument. Bert was relieved to see her relax, but his fury with George was mounting. Could it have been deliberate? If so, why? His friend's face was a professional blank. Angry, he decided to have it out with him at the earliest opportunity; after having told him of the trauma of the other night, it was a damn fool thing to do! In the meantime he'd have to use all of his efforts and charm to keep Alice mollified or God alone would know the consequences if she decided to fly into another rage like the last two. Despite George's jeer, he still thought she might be starting menopause, which personality disorders he'd witnessed often enough to be concerned about. Women's Lib or no, the phenomenon existed.

George at least cooperated by keeping the conversation light and funny all the way home, so by the time they reached home, she was no longer upset. He was relieved to find his older children at home, and apparently on their best behavior. Perhaps Alice's outburst had had a salutary effect; they needed something to keep them in line every so often. They had both been given perhaps too much freedom in order to make them feel trusted and therefore trustworthy. It was possible that too much had been given too soon. They might be too immature to handle the responsibilities that went with the freedom. Raising kids was like walking a tightrope, he had often told his patients, the delicate balance could so easily be destroyed by a slip in either direction; too liberal or too strict and you had kids in trouble. Sometimes it seemed that the only philosophy he could accept was that whatever you did was wrong. He made a mental note to talk to his offspring the following weekend.

Alice was really happy now with her brood about her. Amy reported that Lissie had gone to sleep without any problems. Without even a glance in his direction, the *au pair* girl said her good-nights and went up to her attic. The adults sat around with a few drinks, while the kids had Cokes, and talked until after midnight. Bert had hoped to get Alice too tired to want sex, but she seemed wide-awake as they all parted for the night. She preceded him into their room with that gleam in her eyes that meant she'd had enough to drink to really relish the idea of sexual activity. Normally he would have been delighted at the thought of not having to spend time arousing her, but tonight he dreaded the "anything goes" scene he knew she would play.

Slightly tipsy and therefore aggressive, Alice quickly stripped and paraded around in her high heels, pearls, and perfume. Laughing at his slow response, she unzipped his trousers and pulled them off him along with his shorts. Kneeling in front of him, she tried to arouse him, but her efforts left him limp. Kicking away his clothing, he carried her to their bed. With agile fingers he tried to bring her to climax, but though he could feel her throbbing, she insisted on having him for release. Sitting astride him, she moved above him with expert strokes until she gave herself satisfaction. He felt that he had been raped, taken totally against his will and left in a state of arousal. That was remedied as soon as Alice noted that his member was still erect and pulled him atop of her to "finish off." Pretending it was Amy beneath him, he managed a creditable performance, while praying he could satisfy Alice enough so that she'd fall asleep without waking him for another "go-round."

Apparently satiated, she fell into a deep slumber, leaving

him to stare at the ceiling and to listen to the creakings of the old house around him. When he heard the clock strike three, he could restrain himself no longer and, on an insane impulse, pulled on his pajama bottoms, crept out of the room and up to Amy's Attic. He told himself that he would just watch her sleep in the moonlight, but instead he slipped in beside her and into her before she was fully awake. Pressing his lips against hers, he felt her body welcoming his as if she had been waiting for him. The sense of urgency brought them to a quick climax.

"It was so hard to be up here knowing you were down there with her," she whispered.

"It was even harder being down there," came his murmured response. "I know this is crazy and we must never do it again, but aren't you glad we did?" At her smiling nod, he left.

As Bert opened the attic door and stealthily moved down the hall, a pair of eyes followed his seminude figure, then Stacey closed her door. Her father would have been horrified if he had seen the play of emotions upon his daughter's face. They were expressions he had seen often enough upon the rounds of the mental wards—eyes rolling, skin suffused with a rush of blood, teeth gnashing, and mouth close to frothing. She was actually tearing at her hair and screaming silently, already plotting her revenge for her father's treachery.

Sunday morning was Amy's half-day. The family was expected to sleep as long as they liked, allowing Amy the same privilege; everyone prepared his or her own breakfast, even Lissie. Bert awoke at noon, feeling sinfully refreshed, and went downstairs to find George and Lissie engaged in a grave conversation about whether or not animals went to heaven when they died.

"Morning, Bert. Glad you got down here before I left. I have an appointment with Nedra about setting up clinic programming for the fall. Just wanted to say good-bye and thanks."

"I have a feeling that you're trying to avoid a discussion I want to have with you, but I'll see you on Monday. Lissie, you finish your cereal while I walk Uncle George to the car."

En route to the driveway Bert said, "That was a stupid, dangerous thing for you to drop on Alice last night. How could you have done such a thing when I told you I was worried about her stability lately?"

"Bert, I honestly couldn't believe that Alice hadn't heard the story. My most humble apologies, and truly, there is nothing to discuss."

Regarding his colleague with narrowed eyes, Bert shrugged and decided it wasn't worth getting into a hassle with his best friend over something it might be better to disregard. Pragmatically, there was no point in rehashing the incident. He had enough problems already.

"O.K., George, but I'll see you at dinner Monday night anyway. I have some personal matters to talk over with you, if you have the time."

"Fine, Bert—say, isn't that the nun I saw the other day when I was driving up here? Are you part of her rounds?"

"Guess so. Alice says she hangs around here a lot. Maybe we ought to start locking the doors, she could be a burglar in disguise."

Laughing at the incongruity of the idea, Bert waved his friend off and went back into the house, ignoring the nun's stare in his direction.

They had a pleasant family day; Alice seemed happy, thank heaven, and Stacey, though distracted, was polite.

"What's the matter, baby," asked her father sympathetically, "you want to talk to your old man about some problem? Having trouble with your boyfriend?"

Giving her father a queer smile, Stacey shook her head. "No, Dad, nothing like that. I guess I'm just growing up and getting more serious about life. If I may be excused now, I have to make some phone calls about the party at Dana's house tonight."

"You won't be late, dear, will you?" queried her mother. "Your father may decide to go back tonight, and I don't like to be here without a car."

"No, Mom, it's an early party. Richie and I should be home by midnight. It's a barbeque, so we won't be here for dinner." With a wave, she disappeared into the house, leaving her parents on the shaded porch.

Bert and his wife discussed how nice it was that the kids seemed to be becoming friends at last, and what they might be up to sexually. They both assumed that though Stacey was probably indulging in petting, she was still a virgin. She understood enough about sex from their serious discussions to understand that it was nothing to be indulged in lightly or meaninglessly, and that promiscuity was an illness. On the other hand, both hoped that "poor Richard" was getting it from some nice, sweet girl, who would be kind and gentle in initiating him into the mysteries of intercourse. With all their "modernity" and education they realized that they couldn't seem to escape the sexism of their respective backgrounds. Virginity for their daughter, healthy sex for their son, at the expense of the virginity of someone else's daughter. Recognizing the hopelessness of this dichotomy in their thinking, they started to make plans for dinner.

As a treat, Bert suggested that they take Lissie and Amy out to dinner with them to Villa Paul's restaurant in Hampton Bays. Alice agreed, and they had a fine Italian meal on the converted old house's flagstone terrace. Much to Lissie's delight, there was a birthday party at the next table, with the restaurant supplying a candlelit cake. She sang "Happy Birthday" so lustily that she was rewarded with a piece of cake by the sixty-year-old gentleman whose celebration it was. He beamed at her radiance.

The talk turning to birthdays, they found out that Amy's was the following week. Lissie was thrilled, parties being her favorite thing in the world, and her indulgent parents agreed to her plan to have one for Amy. "Will Grandma and Grandpa be back so that they can come too?"

"No, darling, they're still in Europe, but they'll be back soon and then they'll come to see us."

"Are they enjoying themselves, Alice? I haven't even had a chance to read their letters."

"So it would seem. It's the first vacation they've taken for just the two of them since I can't remember when. When I announced that we weren't parking on them this summer, Daddy surprised Mom with the tickets."

What Alice didn't know was that her father had almost canceled the trip until Bert had assured him that Alice loved the shore and was exhibiting absolutely no symptoms of unease. Knowing how good a psychiatrist his son-in-law was, the old man had reluctantly agreed to go, more because his wife would think there was something to worry about if they didn't, rather than from conviction, Bert had thought.

It had been such a pleasant day that Alice felt very affectionate and kept her hand on her husband's inner thigh all the way home, while Amy amused Lissie in the back seat of the car. He sighed inwardly, knowing Alice would insist on an early bedtime so as she put it, "to get in a week's worth of loving in advance."

Stacey was the main course at her dinner party. Knowing what was going on between her father and the *au pair* girl had helped her to make the decision to be initiated into the "Kinky Klique," as this group of college kids was called. She had hesitated because of their reputation for alcohol and drugs, but now she didn't give a damn anymore; this was her revenge on Daddy. Richard was ready to agree to anything to get laid; all he'd gotten so far this summer was some dry-humping of teeny boppers. The older girls who were promiscuous rejected him as too young, and the younger ones were holding on to that membrane for dear life. Seems that they were a part of a new age; just his luck, thought Richard sadly.

The group had been delighted by Stacey's phone call agreeing to be initiated. They had gotten together an hour earlier to plan the details; they'd had no new members in weeks and were getting bored with one another. Everett Soles was whoremaster, and he was anxious to show his virtuosity; it should be a night to be long remembered. Stacey was a cunt who was blasé about everything he'd tried with her; he'd teach her to respect him. His grandfather, now a spry octogenarian, always told him there was only one thing girls wanted, and regaled him with tales of the many ways he had given it to many girls in his lifetime, leeringly insinuating he was still doing it. Everett wouldn't doubt it, the old geezer was quite a character, and an inspiration to his grandson. He had taken him to his first stag-film party, followed by his first visit to a brothel. He had also assured him that there was no such thing as rape, for if a girl didn't want it, she wouldn't be with a guy who did, under circumstances which would permit it to happen. He'd found it sound advice; like Grandpa, he was totally without conscience.

By 5 P.M. the group was satisfied with the scenario, and the servants were given the night off; Dana's parents were not out that weekend. The Bradleys were greeted with true enthusiasm. There was a lavish steak barbeque and the siblings were plied with Scotch and pot, which they couldn't refuse under terms of the club rules. After a snort of coke, Everett signaled readiness and the girls took Stacey into a large guest bedroom where they gently disrobed her and pushed her down on the bed. Expecting to experience her first gang bang, Stacey watched bright eyed; she'd show them she could take whatever they had to dish out. Richard had been placed in the sitting room next door where he could hear but not view the proceedings. He prayed he'd get a turn at Lu Ann, who was almost as well endowed as his sister.

The latter was lying back watching as everyone stripped. She was surprised and repelled to find the girls mounting her, while the boys called directions and encouragement to cheer the girls on in their exploration of that lush body on the bed. Stacey fought to get away, but was held down as the girls took turns at her. Against her will her cries of protest changed to moans of delight as they skillfully brought her to climax while the boys waited their turns at that incredible body. After the "warm-up," Stacey was moved down to the edge of the bed, and the boys caressed her to the point of frenzy, till she begged them to take her before she went crazy. They all did.

It was Stacey's first group experience and Everett was merciless as he directed the scene. Inspired by *Last Tango in Paris,* he brought in butter, and after much initial difficulty and protests on Stacey's part, she lost her last vestige of virginity.

160

Richard had been allowed to watch for a few minutes as the young gentlemen swarmed about his sister, and then was led away for his part of the night's festivities. Blindfolded he was told he could have any girl he could identify from touching her breasts. Disappointed that Lu Ann obviously wasn't in the lineup, he lucked in on Doreen by the feel of those conical breasts he had often admired in their cloth bikini cups at the club. When he undressed for action, the girls gave murmurs of pleased surprise. He was, they assured him, "built to pleasure a woman," and proceeded to show him how, with Doreen as his first guide. She was a good teacher, showing him how to hold back, and to move in her rhythm to prolong his own pleasure. His parents would have been pleased to know how much he'd enjoyed his first sexual experience. He was insatiable, and the girls were amazed at his fund of sex lore.

"I'm a great reader," he boasted and they laughed delightedly as he insisted that he have a turn at Lu Ann. They told him to rest up first, so he could go all the way with a pro like Lu Ann. At 10 P.M. he was brought into a pitch-black room and led to the bed. Happily he clambered atop the voluptuous body and, though a bit put off by the lack of active response, reveled in the feelings of sinking into flesh, plunging between soft full thighs over and over again. An abrupt flash of light interrupted his pleasure, then the overhead lights were put onto reveal Richard and Stacey locked in incestuous embrace, the latter still groggy from drugs and liquor. The look of shock on both their faces was recorded for posterity by another flash of light from Everett's camera, as he accepted the plaudits of the group for yet another work of "genius."

"Well, kiddies," he called cheerfully, "your folks probably expect you back early. Better wash up and go home now. You'll be contacted about future meetings soon."

Silently the siblings separated, each to stand for a long

time under a sobering shower, trying to untangle their emotions.

11

Richard drove home, since Stacey's muscles were screaming in protest over the misuse they'd been given that night. She'd have to sit in hot tubs for two days, she thought, before she could appear in public with a normal gait. Luckily her mother didn't fuss over her, and Dad would be gone in the morning.

After an initial stunned silence, she had had to reassure her brother, "Look, Richie, I've read all the books and so have you. There's a thirty percent incest factor in this country and now we're just part of that statistic. Let's not make a big deal about it, or the folks will find out."

"O.K.," her brother sighed, "after all, the pharaohs had to have sex with their sisters, and my anthro teacher said that taboos were just cultural. But I don't think I want to have any more to do with that gang. They're too far out and that drug scene scares me."

His sister's response was even scarier. "Sorry, baby brother, but we're in this for good. They film everything, and if you back out, they send pictures to your folks, and then they sell the stag movies to kids in your school. Keeps one from squealing should an attack of conscience occur."

Richard was understandably aghast. "How long does this go on?"

"Until Everett gets tired of you. Doreen said that last year he had some of the girls come up to his school to hustle for the frat boys on weekends when his parents wouldn't give him money to get his car fixed. So you see, unless you want to lose your family and friends, you just play along. Can you imagine our folks seeing what went on tonight?"

162

Shuddering at the thought, they drove the rest of the way home in total silence and went to bed without exchanging another word. Their father, hearing them come in as the clock struck midnight, thought, "Good kids," and fell back into dreamless slumber, Alice pressed closely against his side.

It was Alice who again heard Lissie's whimpers, the sounds pulling her out of a satisfying dream. About to wake her husband, she decided against it; he had to leave at dawn. Slipping on her robe, she quietly went to her baby's room. As she pushed the door ajar, she froze, unbelieving, at the scene that met her eyes. Her vocal chords paralyzed by fear, her screams could be heard reverberating only in her own brain, as she saw a handsome, blonde man bent over her child. She could hear his pleasant baritone crooning the lullaby of the music box they had found in the room, the song that Lissie had made her own, "Flow Gently Sweet Afton." Gently he stroked the sleeping child's golden hair, while blood from a horrifying chest wound dripped onto her pillow. As the stranger raised his head to smile at her, she had an impression of the bluest eyes she'd ever seen, before she fell into a dead faint in the doorway of the room.

Unaware that his wife had left, Bert was irritated when he found himself swimming into consciousness in pitch-darkness. Alice's hands were on him, tense and probing, moving over his chest, then down to cradle his sex. Her body was against him, breasts and thighs pressing with increasing excitement. Irritation gave way to desire as he grew hard under her ministrations. Her body was naked, but as he slid over to press it beneath him, he had a sudden sense of dislocation. Even in the darkness, he had the feeling that something was wrong, out of place. The body of his wife, as familiar to himself as his own in many ways, had changed, had become the body of a stranger; the breasts somehow smaller, the legs and thighs around his heavier, the scent altered.

But his mind was still groggy from sleep, caught in a

halfway world between consciousness and sweet oblivion, and his body could not resist the heaving, jerking, pulsating demands of the body beneath his. Long fingernails were digging fiercely into his back and buttocks, demanding deeper and deeper penetration. He was being swept into a torrent of need that was close enough to pain to make him unaware of anything but the urge to fulfill the moist fulcrum of sexuality that was sucking him down into dizziness.

A hoarse cry exploded in his ears when the climax finally arrived, and he was writhing in a tangle of sheets. Sweat oiled his body. He was breathing heavily, Alice's pillow clutched in his arms. A wet coldness was congealing between his legs, stiffening the sheets. The bed was empty. He shot bolt upright. After a few seconds, the situation began to sink in. He almost laughed aloud. It had been a dream, nothing but a wet dream! He turned to tell Alice, but the earlier realization returned; she was gone. The vividness of the dream clung to him, and he could swear that his back and buttocks still ached from those insistent nails.

Shaking his head at such foolishness, he rose to seek out Alice in the bathroom, which proved empty as he switched on the light. The pain in his back had not relented. He twisted to look at himself in the mirror. Long jagged scratches caked by drying blood, ran down his back. Grasping the sink for support, he thought, this cannot happen, it did not happen, and yet the images in the mirror and the pain were real. Back in the bedroom, he switched on the light and studied the bed. Something on the pillow caught his eye. There were several strands of long black hair, still smelling of that foreign scent.

Like a man caught in a maze, he stumbled from the room and went down the corridor. I have to find Alice, he thought to himself, like a child. She will explain it and everything will be all right again. But he almost stumbled over her where she lay in a heap on the hall floor,

164

unconscious, and yet breathing with soothing regularity, as if asleep. His thoughts immediately flew to his daughter. Panic-stricken, he fled from his wife's still form and rushed to Lissie's side.

Bending over the child, he was relieved to see her sleeping, serene as a princess in the soft light from the hall. Only a tiny frown marred the curved ivory planes of her beautiful face. Tension ebbed from him in a rush, and he bent to kiss her. It was then that he saw the dry black circles on her pillow. He looked closer to see if she had had a nose bleed, but there was no sign of one. His hand moved instinctively to touch the circles; the blood was not yet completely dry. After switching on the light, he examined the spots more closely, careful not to disturb his still-sleeping daughter. Years of medical training came to his aid, as he realized, with a shock, that the blood was arterial.

Always a practical man, a man of reason and logic, Bert could not accept the madness of what had occurred. Confronted by illogic, his mind simply retreated into the rationale of the scientist: What seems beyond explanation is merely as yet undiscovered. The strange dream, his wife's fainting fit, the blood on his sleeping daughter's pillow, they were only puzzling because he had not found the key. In his dealings with the human mind, he knew that its power to deceive even itself was enormous, and he refused to be deceived. The important thing was that everyone was all right.

To give himself something to do, to reassert the normalcy that was essential to his new perspective, he left his daughter to her dreams, and after carrying Alice back to bed, walked downstairs to inspect the house. He felt solid and purposeful as he went from room to room, switching lights on and off with decisive authority. Nothing disturbed or moved. As part of the normal, daylight world, the house was unaltered by whatever psychological forces had unhinged his own equilibrium.

Then he saw the cellar door. It was open. Again, however, the fact of it was not mysterious in and of itself. Someone had left it unlocked, ajar, despite his warnings, but that could be cleared up in the morning. Now, he did the sensible thing and closed it, locked it, and put away the key.

Bert tried to make his voice brisk when he called Sheila Warren at her home at 7 A.M. to tell her to cancel his appointments for the entire week.

"Just some minor matter," he told her with false cheeriness. "Please reschedule everyone for next week with my profound apologies." And as shaken as he was, he still remembered to tell her the story he'd concocted to leave Thursdays free for Amy. Such is the power of love, he thought wryly, remembering that he had thought his patients demented when they described their longings to be with the new love in their lives, to the exclusion and destruction of everything in their previous experiences. Here he was, his world trembling about his ears and he couldn't wait to be with that bewitching young girl asleep under his roof. Indeed everyone beneath his roof was still asleep. He'd been awake since 3 A.M. patrolling the house, and no one had stirred. Alice continued to sleep normally with no sign of shock, and the last time he had checked, Lissie was smiling in her sleep. He checked all of his impressions; the scratches were still on his body, and the strange odor still clung to his skin. He put the strands of black hair into an envelope and sealed it carefully. What next? He'd have to research the history of the house or he'd

166

end up believing in ghosts and/or being taken away in a straitjacket.

He stayed awake, carefully watching Alice sleep. When she stretched awake in the morning light, she smiled in glad surprise to see him still there.

"Hey, what are you doing here? I thought you were leaving with the dawn's early light."

"Just a surprise, darling. I arranged to take a few extra days to make up for the rough time you had last week. How are you feeling?"

"Great. I want a huge breakfast. Sex is great for the appetite."

Relieved that she seemed to have no memory of whatever had transpired, he was suddenly totally exhausted.

"You eat, I sleep," he smiled at her, and safe in the sunshine pouring through the windows, he slept for hours as if drugged.

He woke to find himself alone in the house. The family schedule would call for spending the day at the club, including lunch there, so that they could practice for the tennis tourneys in their respective divisions, while Amy amused Lissie at the beach and pool. After a sketchy breakfast, he drove to the Roger's Library on Job's Lane, where he carefully studied the back issues of the local paper for news of the Desmond tragedy. The details were indeed few, and knowing Doyle would refuse to be of any assistance, he drove to the hospital, hoping Dr. Courtney would help him.

While waiting for the director, he prevailed upon his secretary, who remembered him from the May conference, to look at the autopsy files for 1938. His charm always worked. Quickly turning to the D's, he read a Dr. Johns's meticulously detailed report on the state of the murdered bodies. It was no wonder that Doyle was still too upset to discuss the case. Even with the passage of thirty-eight years, it was truly horrendous. Despite the dry scientific detachment with which they were described, he found himself dazed by the details of gratuitous brutality. Desmond must have indeed been a monster to have perpetrated such insane mutilations upon the bodies of his own family, and upon the poor maid with whom it was rumored he'd been having an affair.

Dr. Courtney was curious about Bert's interest in the case. "I think I mentioned to you, Dr. Courtney, that forensic medicine has always been a specialty of mine. It's intriguing to be inhabiting the same space once occupied by a psycho like Desmond. I'd like to try to establish a sort of profile of such a criminally insane personality; perhaps even give a paper on him at the next national convention."

"Fascinating idea. How can I be of assistance?"

And under Bert's skillful questioning, a picture of Evan Desmond, as the town had known him, began to emerge. A war hero, a heavy drinker, a lecher, a seducer of young girls (at this Bert inwardly winced, but recalled that actually Amy had seduced him), an indifferent husband, but a devoted father; a man of enormous wealth, of great charm with the looks and physique of a much younger man. The doctor recalled envious contemporaries who had likened him to Dorian Gray. His wife was quite the opposite, a quiet, dowdy woman who looked years older than she was, who only went out to go to church.

"Why would he have married such a woman? Was she wealthy?"

"Good Lord, no! My parents were friends of the Ambroses, and I remember hearing stories of how lucky they were to have gotten bailed out of bankruptcy by their daughter landing such a 'catch.' My mother said that Evalynn was the proverbial ugly duckling who became a swan and captured the heart of the most eligible bachelor around. I heard stories of that fairy tale wedding for years at my mother's teas. They said she was the most beautiful

168

bride imaginable and had been coaxed into marrying Desmond. For a while they seemed to have gotten along quite well."

"Obviously they never got to live happily ever after. Anyone know what happened?"

"Afraid not, the assumption was that it had been too late for Evan to change his wicked ways and that in despair his wife just turned to having kids and eating. For such a strictly reared convent-bred girl, living with Evan must have been like living in hell."

"Convent-reared and married right out of school? And there were six children?"

"No, there were five children; the two found dead, the two who have never been found, and poor Jessica who died at the Payne Whitney."

"Only five! But—O.K. tell me about Jessica."

"She was an exquisite child, everyone always stopped to talk to her—very much like your Lissie as a matter of fact. Funny though," the doctor reflected, "Lissie looks more like a Desmond than Jessica did."

"How so?" asked her father.

"Jessica was the only Desmond with the Ambrose eyes, great dark velvety ones, almost black. In that delicate pink-and-white face with her platinum hair all in curls, she was a true beauty. I'll never forget my shock when she was brought in, covered with blood, the dead kitten grasped in her tiny hands. Those beautiful eyes were staring in the classic catatonic way. I had an almost instant impression that she was doomed. You know that feeling, don't you, Bert?"

The younger man nodded soberly. He knew exactly what he meant. Some sixth sense in a pro seemed to zero in on the possibilities for cure almost instantly. He nodded again as the older man described the month of treatment the child had received at this very hospital. Even by modern standards, except for newly discovered drug therapies, everything possible had been tried. The move to the Payne Whitney Clinic had made no difference, although all reports indicated that Dr. Barakian had devoted himself to the case.

"Did she have any relatives who visited her?"

"No, every attempt to turn up any family on either side failed. For the first few months, people here in town visited, but it was a five-hour car trip to New York City in those days, and there was never any change, she just stared. The only one I recall who went regularly, until the very end, was a nun from the local convent, who said she felt it her duty to the child's mother. Her prayers didn't work any more than did Barakian's skill."

"How did Jessica die?"

"I don't recall the exact details, but there seemed to have been a total lack of will to live, which was hardly surprising under the circumstances, and of course the support and feeding systems were not as sophisticated as ours are today. I believe that she finally succumbed to pneumonia."

"God! that's tragic."

"From what Barakian told me, it would have been more tragic had she lived. He said that if by some miracle they had been able to break through to her, she probably would have become a violent schizophrenic in view of her trauma."

"One more question, sir, how good a coroner was this Johns?"

"The best," came the unhesitating reply. "Harvard Medical graduate, retired out here in his fifties, liked to keep his hand in, as it were. I'd match his conclusions against any of these miracle gadget machines they're using today. The man was a genius."

He rose and stretched out his hand. "And now, young man, I have to get back to my patients. Be sure to let me know when you have the paper ready for the seminar, I'd enjoy reading it."

170

Bert walked out of the hospital slowly, totally absorbed and puzzled by the interview. If Dr. Johns was an infallible genius, how was it that the report on Evalynn Desmond stated that she had given birth to six children, and not five?

His next stop was at Tom Skidmore's office on Windmill Lane, just across the street from the police station, where he got a picture of the financial entanglements of the estate.

"And how much would the estate be worth today, Tom?"

The answer staggered him.

"Oh, about ten million dollars."

"Sweet Jesus! No wonder the list of claimants is endless!"

"Yep. Uncle Sam figures he can wait them all out and get it for the IRS, with a few bucks for local, county, and state taxes. That Desmond really knew his stocks and bonds. Everything he owned has increased incredibly—IBM, ATT, ITT, Coca-Cola, Standard Oil—you name it, he'd bought it."

Skidmore sighed at Evan's wisdom. "There's no one whose claim has checked out in thirty-eight years, so the government expects to dispose of the last two or three cases by 1980, and grab the loot."

"Who is still claiming, do you know?"

"You'd have to check that with the state attorney general's office. Is there anything else I can do for you, Bert?"

"Yes, I want a copy of the police report on the Desmond murders," and Bert persuasively explained his need in such a way that to have denied him would have been a roadblock in the path of science, as well as preventing a possible breakthrough in the cure of psychopathic personalities, thus thwarting the improvement of society. Dazzled by the verbal pyrotechnics and by the impressive vocabulary, Skidmore agreed. Within an hour, Bert was walking out of the police station with a Xeroxed copy of the report. The chief had agreed that after all these years, it couldn't hurt anyone, and that since Bert, like a priest, was sworn to confidentiality, there would be no chance of Doyle ever finding out that his orders had been countermanded.

Sitting in Monument Square Park to read the document, Bert felt drawn back in time and space. The sunny day seemed to darken, the sound of an insane wind whirled through his head, and the cries of the happy children on the swings became the shrieks of the victims of the foul and loathsome deeds committed at the height of the storm. Like Barakian, he could only feel grateful that the child had died. Who would want to live after experiencing in childhood's reality that which chilled the very marrow of his adult bones? Detached from the act by almost forty years, and sitting in a park on a lovely summer's day, he still felt cold. Poor Jessica, ten million dollars couldn't have put her world back together again. Bemused, he started to think of the good such money could do in the projected clinic. With that kind of funding, a foundation could be established to treat the mentally ill indigents of the entire city. With the new techniques he and George had been developing, they could show a cure rate that would have the rest of the world beating a path to their door to learn how to care for emotional and personality disorders. "The Bradley-Webber institute for Mental Health." Ten million dollars!

"Fifty dollars! Where in hell did your slut daughter get that kind of money to send home? Must be up to her old ma's tricks. Answer me, woman!"

Amy's devoted father was drunkenly slapping her mother all around the living room, ignoring her pathetic pleas for him to stop. She insisted that she knew neither how the money had been obtained, nor her daughter's whereabouts. Ibram had become worse by the day since Amy had escaped the house. There was a dim awareness in his brain that beating and screwing her mother had lost a great deal of its savor when the girl wasn't around to hear it. How badly his wanting the body under him to be Amy's was a sensation he'd been repressing since she had turned twelve—and for what? She was no kin of his. Here he'd let her grow up decent, and she just ran off to New York City to sell her body on the streets. As proof he had the money order she'd sent. In his mad search for traces of her whereabouts, he had also unearthed his wife's birth control pills, which had led to a week of violent beatings and rapings.

"Here you whore," he ranted as he rammed into her over and over again, his foul breath almost suffocating her, "this is all you was ever good for. Trying not to have my kids, would you? Not good enough for you, huh?"

Rage as always was his aphrodisiac and he'd drag her off to the bedroom whenever it engorged his cock. The terror in her eyes made him feel like a real man again. She'd never known him to be so brutal. She'd always managed a degree of control over him, but with Amy gone his fury knew no bounds. He stopped going out of the house and swore not to let her out until she was pregnant with his kid; he'd keep her barefoot and pregnant winter and summer, he'd never let her out of his sight again.

"All these years since Celia you've been on that infernal pill so's you could whore around like you did in the old days and not get caught. That money you been bringing in—you must have earned it lying on your back, you whore of Babylon! Making me out no man in front of the whole town by not having my kids! I was ashamed to go into the bar with everyone wanting to know how come I'd run out of steam. 'Whassamatter, Ibram,' they'd say, 'can't you get it up no more?'"

The children were frightened into silent shadows, locked out of the house most of the day while their father sat in the house with the shades drawn drinking beer with the welfare money and studying Amy's money order. He hid all of Ida's clothes and shoes, except for an old cotton wrapper, so she wouldn't dare go into the street. It was also faster to get at her when the notion took him; he just pulled up the dress and had her anywhere he'd a mind to—the more discomfort it caused her, the more time he took to finish.

"Now, woman, you tell me when you had a man who could pleasure you as long and as hard as this—eh? Who?"

"Nobody, Ibram, I swear I was never even with nobody but you, except that time those boys got me drunk," she gasped as he kept pounding into her. "Please, Ibram, let me up now," she pleaded.

He had forced her down on the sisal mat on the living-room floor and the fibers were tearing into her flesh.

"I ain't getting up until we're both finished, woman. I'm a gentleman, I ain't going to leave you unsatisfied, and 'sides, I'm a long way from finished—what with you not doin' your part," he leered down at her, eyes glinting wickedly.

Despite the pain it caused her, she had to writhe under him, wriggling and grinding to force him to climax while pretending to moan in ecstasy at his "performance." With

174

all the liquor in him, he seemed to be able to go forever. When he finally released her, he was grimly delighted to see her scratched buttocks as she limped away from him. He'd wait it out. Sooner or later he'd find out where that fancy brat of hers was whoring around. He'd get back all the money he'd invested in her care over the years. Added up to a pretty penny. Anybody wanted to have her would have to pay her daddy for his expenses. But when he caught up with her, he'd show her first what it was like to be with a *real* man. After a couple of days with the old man she'd see what she'd been missing all of these years, probably wouldn't be able to keep her away from him. Maybe he'd get them both knocked up at the same time. Then everyone in town would know that Ibram Cullum was still as good a man as ever he was.

His firstborn, Harley, sat on the back porch keeping his eyes on the younger kids. He could hear his mother moving haltingly about the kitchen, trying to stifle her sobs as she put supper together for them. Her bravery tore at his heart as she pretended that things were no worse than usual. He had to do something. It seemed that there were only three choices. He could try to find Amy, he could try to move them away from his loving father, or he could resort to the only real solution—he had to kill the old bastard before he killed Ma.

Bert dressed quietly in the early dawn on Tuesday morning. He'd managed a successful family evening on Monday playing husband and father to the hilt, treating Amy casually and being generally charming, while solicitous about the Charley horse Stacey had developed after she'd gone riding. The only disconcerting news had been Alice's amused announcement that Astrid Newsome had been at the club. She was in town for two weeks as Marge Walker's houseguest, and she'd specifically asked for him. Bert had groaned at the thought of having to see that woman on the invariable round of social activities. He'd jokingly suggested that he leave town for two weeks, but Lissie anxiously reminded him that he had to come to Amy's party. He'd given Alice an extra fifty dollars, suggesting that she choose something for Amy from each of them so that the girl would have many gifts to "please Lissie." Alice had agreed, complimenting him on his thoughtfulness, and making him feel guilty as hell.

Bradley cast a longing glance at the attic door as he slipped into the hall, but cheered himself by remembering that Thursday was the day after tomorrow. He'd have a busy time before then. The strand of black hair was in an envlope in his attaché case, along with the police report and the blood-stained pillow case from Lissie's bed. He stopped by his little girl's room to check on her before he left. The first pink glow was just lighting her room as he crept soundlessly to the bed. He stifled an involuntary outcry of horror. On the cotton patchwork quilt was the child's favorite kitten, the calico, its wide innocent eyes glinting at him in the first rays of the sun—quite rigid in death.

176

George must have sensed the urgency in Bert's voice, for he instantly agreed to change his afternoon schedule and come to the latter's office. It took about an hour until the older man had the picture, while the "evidence" was laid out on the beautiful antique desk that Alice had chosen so carefully for the room.

"Let me play devil's advocate. I've listened to everything you've said, now you try not to interrupt while I react to your recitation of the 'facts.' First of all, the strands of dark hair on the pillow; your *au pair* girl and Stacey both have dark hair. One or the other could have been napping, or who knows? even fooling around on your bed when everyone was out—no let me finish, I didn't interrupt you," George said in his most authoritative tone.

"Next we have a bloody pillow case, and you say that Lissie did not have a nose bleed. The stains could have been on the case and not have come out in the wash. Then we have this poor little creature in the plastic bag. The child could have smuggled it into her room and accidentally smothered it in her sleep while hiding it under the covers. All your other instances of peculiar doings seem pretty flimsy, Alice claiming to have seen a spook, Lissie hearing voices, your finding a supposedly locked door open—who should know better than yourself the tricks the mind plays?"

"And finding Alice in a dead faint at Lissie's door in the middle of the night?"

"Who knows what hysterical episodes she may be experi-

encing? You've told me you think she is becoming menopausal or even that she's under the strain of an illicit affair.
Perhaps she's become a victim of narcolepsy, or she's taking
drugs."

"You know damn well that Alice takes nothing except
those vitamin pills that her father gives her; and how do you
explain away the scratches on my back and ass?" Bert made
a move to drop his trousers, furious at the casual dismissal
of incidents that had so upset him.

"Spare me," laughed George. "I believe that the marks
are there and that you did have a wet dream, which is a
common enough phenomenon. I'd say that the scratches
were made by Alice and that in the heat of passion you
didn't feel them—or by some other lady with whom you've
been having the pleasure?"

George stared sharply at the look on his friend's face,
"Shot home, eh? I wondered if you were projecting your
own illicit liaisons onto Alice. Anyone I know?"

Blurting out the story of his affair with Amy, Bert saw the
look of surprise and disapproval on his colleague's normally
imperturbable expression. No nonjudgmental facade they all
cultivated so assiduously in their profession. Bert felt
ashamed, as if his father were taking measure of him.

"Jesus, Bert, the male climacteric is hitting you early.
Pardon my lack of professionalism, but you are a nut case!
A girl young enough to be your daughter—and under your
own roof to boot! No wonder you're seeing and hearing
things! You're under an overwhelming strain, especially for
a minister's son—or are you subconsciously trying to wreck
Alice?" And with a piercing glance added softly, "Or is it
conscious?"

They both recalled their joking conversation about
Gaslight.

"George, you can't possibly think that of me!" came the
anguished reply.

"Why not? Haven't you told me time and again that our

178

clinic is the most important thing in your life? Your way to redeem the waste of your talent?"

"Don't say those things to me. You know I'd never hurt my family."

"What do you call what you're doing now?" George shot back. "What would you say, my esteemed colleague, if one of your patients came to you with the story you just repeated to me?" Forestalling the attempted response, he added, "and don't give me that shit that 'this is different, if you could only understand,'" he savagely mimicked the words they had both heard hundreds of times from men their own ages, over their years in practice.

Bert looked at his friend aghast, finally understanding the frustration of being on the other side of the desk. How could he make George understand the wonder, the joy, the sense of being young and alive on seven levels at once? He recalled his own condescending tolerance when his patients tried to explain why they were willing to give up everything in order to continue a relationship they were having with a young girl. He'd felt so smug and superior, knowing that such a thing couldn't touch him. And here he was, a therapist, acting as adolescent as they had. No wonder George was being so savage. Quietly he tried to explain.

"O.K., but I started this affair with the idea of 'what the hell, why shouldn't I try it?' It was going to be a purely physical thing, encapsulated from the rest of my life and no regrets when it was over. I even rationalized that it would help me to better understand my patients, and that I was good for Amy as the first man in her life because I would be kind, and be able to handle any problems she might have with it."

"And now?"

"Now," he sighed, "I know nothing except that being with her is the center of my life."

"You'd destroy your family, your way of life? You'd sacrifice your goal to build the clinic to help the destitute just to get between a girl's legs?" came the incredulous query.

"No, to each of those. I recognize on one level that this affair will end. My training can't keep me from this form of insanity, but it does preclude that I'd destroy my world. Clinically I'd say that in a few months I'll be a 'burned-out case,' and go back to what we call 'normal.' Right now I find that thought depressing, but this too shall pass." He smiled and weakly asked George to forgive all of the clichés.

Visibly relaxing, George looked at him intently. There was no doubting his sincerity, nor his perceptions of the realities of the situation. "Good, my friend, I feel a bit relieved. You do sound fairly rational."

"If you agree that I'm rational, then will you help me to get to the bottom of whatever the hell is going on at the house?"

"I'll do what I can to humor you, but my original reaction still stands. There is a perfectly reasonable explanation for everything, but your inner turmoil is too intense for you to recognize this. The only point I'll grant is that a household so full of tensions can create an ambience conducive to the experiencing of strange sensations."

"But will you help me?"

"Just tell me how. I'm anxious to disprove all of your imaginings."

"Yet you've always shared my interest in parapsychology. Why become a cynic now?"

"Because I do not believe that evil emanations from forty years ago are surfacing now to torment you and yours. It's as I told you on the dunes that day, your house is too full of an emotionally charged atmosphere—only now, from what you've told me, I'd say that Amy, rather than Stacey, is the catalyst."

Unable to budge George from his position, Bert finally gave up trying. George, however, did agree to try to trace Dr. Barakian and to have Nedra investigate the last claimants of the Desmond estate. He also promised to read the police and autopsy reports of the case that Bert gave him, but asked of what use that would be to Bert.

"I've got a hunch that Desmond did not kill his family."

"Based on what, Sherlock?"

"It doesn't fit the pattern of everything I learned about him, and from what people who knew him have said. I'd say that he would be incapable of killing his kids, unless he were perhaps drunk or drugged—and the autopsy shows that at the time of his death he was neither."

"And Mrs. Desmond, was he capable of killing her?"

"I'd speculate yes to that, but not within this pattern of carnage and not in that manner. I'd say his cruelty was of a much more subtle nature. For instance, the report shows that the wife had been sodomized. Can you imagine what that would have been like for a devout convent-schooled Catholic who believed that sex was only for procreation? It also said that she showed no signs of having had intercourse since the birth of her last child. Desmond apparently flaunted his illicit liaisons, but wouldn't go near his wife."

"That's in the report too?"

"Yes, this Johns was the most thorough coroner I've ever come across. He also noted that she had her period at the time of her death."

"Signifying what?"

"Not too elementary, dear Watson, but that is the detail, among others, that makes me think it is *'Cherchez la femme.'* I think she killed them all, and then fell downstairs on her knife while in pursuit of that poor little girl."

A low whistle greeted this statement as Geroge looked at him in amazement.

"You see her as a total fruitcake? And all of this from these reports?"

"I've also talked to many people who knew her. The picture that emerges is one of a religious fanatic in a sadomasochistic relationship with definite psychotic overtones. She may have even caught the insanity."

"Psychosis association?"

"Exactly!"

"Do you think their kids were involved in the delusions?"

"It's a possibility, because at their ages it would not have manifested itself strongly enough to have been noted by a nonexpert."

"I wonder," mused George, "if it could have been a hereditary factor for the kids and an association for the mother. Perhaps it's just as well that they're all dead; might have had a slew of crazies running around otherwise."

"If it was the communicative form of the psychosis association, it would almost be the same as heredity, except that the kids probably would have gotten worse. I'd have to check on Evan's parentage to see if there was any madness in the family, but there would be no way to tell for sure whether theirs was genetic or not after all these years. If the etiology was organic or psychogenic, the results were the same."

"What about syphilis? The father could have had it—or even inherited it—and passed along a form of syphilopsychosis, which wouldn't have shown up until well into the adult lives of the kids."

Bert smiled as George became excited about trying to pin down syndromes; he was an excellent diagnostician with a passion for the hunt.

"Yes, I agree it's a possibility, but that isn't our problem now. I hate to bring you back to present realities, but I have to find out what's causing the spooks in the house."

George looked sheepish at having been carried away with his theories. "Sorry. I think you were about to tell me why

182

you thought the mother was the murderer and what her menstrual cycle had to do with it."

"Right. The picture that emerged of the woman was one of a repressed personality with a fanatic religious devotion. Somewhere along the line she is missing a kid. Her husband had sodomized her, which is a sin, and if she enjoyed it, the sin was even worse. She became dumpier and frowzier as her husband stayed remarkably young and, according to all accounts, remarkably virile, while he assiduously avoided her bed for the five years after the birth of the last child. There was no sign of any penetration since the last healing of the laceration of the perineum. She had to endure the gossip of all his liaisons with beautiful women while knowing people regarded her as a pathetic figure to be laughed at behind her back."

"So you say Evalynn Desmond turned into a psychotic killer of her entire family due to sexual envy and repression?" The tone was skeptical.

"Possibly. According to Courtney's sister, the last rumor in town was that he was banging the sixteen-year-old housemaid under his own roof."

Bert had the grace to blush as George shot him a sardonic glance. Defensively he went on, "She also said that my cleaning woman, Ellen Hanks, is the younger sister of Nancy Chester, so she might be able to supply me with more details. It was her understanding that while Evan carefully hid everything from his kids, he'd make sure his wife always knew of his sexual exploits, so she'd certainly have known he was screwing the maid."

By now his listener seemed to have become engrossed with the story. "I see, you feel she had the motive and the psychotic rage needed to commit acts of such insanity. What do you think was the trigger?"

George listened intently as Bert persuasively built the picture of this half-crazed woman on her last night on earth.

"The barometer was dropping steadily and she had her

period. Like most of us she had to be affected by the air pressure, which, combined with tension, might have made her mood unbearable. The sounds of the storm are frightening, giving her a feeling of terror and desperation. Her husband comes home, and she thinks she hears him going up to the attic to fuck the sixteen-year-old maid, a girl younger than his older daughter, which has an incestuous overtone in her mind. This lends a sexual excitement to the catastrophic excitement pervading the atmosphere. Remember all the stories of people desperately engaging in intercourse during bombing raids?" George nodded.

"A storm of that proportion would have the same affect, it made Evalynn want someone inside of her. Instead, she believed her husband was pumping away at the maid. Imagining his sexual frenzy increasing with the frenzy of the storm, she probably snapped at this point, and while the kids were in their rooms, she goes upstairs to kill her husband. The meat knife from the kitchen is in one hand and a lantern to light the way up the attic stairs in the other. Seeing figures writhing on the bed in the light of a nightstand candle, she starts slashing and stabbing. She castrates the man's body and shoves the genitalia in Nancy's face as she opens up the poor girl's belly. When she picks up her lantern to view her triumph, she sees to her horror that the body is not Evan's but that of her firstborn and best beloved child, her son Garrick."

"Sweet Jesus," murmured George prayerfully, "that would have triggered off a rampage all right. The shock of realizing that her son had engaged in mortal sin and that she had killed him before he could confess and receive absolution, meant that she had not only been responsible for his death, but guaranteed that he would burn in hell for eternity! That would be enough to send her on a massacre. Probably started to feel like an avenging angel and wanted to wipe out evil by starting with her own household."

"That's how I read it. According to the police report, she

184

next went into the older girl's room. Diedre sat in front of her dressing table lighted with candles, and her mother severed her head from her neck before she even turned around. The head was found staring at itself in the mirror and the body had slid to the floor."

"What incredible force!" gasped the listener.

"Well, we know that adage has been proved scientifically. Mad people *do* indeed have the strength of ten men. After a stop in the kitchen to dispatch and behead some cats and kittens for some reason, she seems to have caught her husband off guard in the living room. Between the surprise and the fury of the attack, she managed to plunge the knife right through him. The police speculated that the little girl had witnessed either the results of and/or the actual murders, and had tried to hide in the basement. From the position of the body, they believed that Evan had killed his wife and thrown her body down into the cellar before plunging the knife into his chest; but, in my opinion, it would seem that the woman fell down the stairs, onto her knife, as she tried to find the child. She bled to death slowly, and there were too many broken bones for her to have moved from where she'd fallen. She apparently lived until the next day."

Total silence greeted this recitation as George allowed himself the rare luxury of giving into feelings of grief and horror for the plight of the five-year-old Jessica Desmond— who had had to witness carnage as overwhelming as that of Hitler's camps. Worse, in the sense that it was her own mother who had committed the atrocities. What greater betrayal could a child suffer than to have the one person in the world who represented love and trust turn into a blood-crazed monster? And all of this to the contrapuntal fury of the elements venting their wrath upon the earth. It *was* better that she had died. The alternatives were terrible to contemplate.

His friend's voice brought him back to the present. "So

you can understand now why I'm convinced that there is paranormal activity at Mulberry?"

"Not necessarily. I see that as you find out more about the tragedy, you're becoming more sensitized to believing in evil emanations, which hardly befits your training. And I don't see why, if you're convinced these exist, you don't get the hell out of that place."

"Fair enough question. I think it's because as a man of science, I have to refuse to acknowledge the existence, and my fear of the supernatural. I also wouldn't know how to begin to explain to my family why we're leaving. They'd probably consign me to the loony bin and ascribe my fears to overwork. How do you tell your family that you think there are ghosts in the house?"

"I'm almost ready to have you committed myself, Bert. Better get some sleep now. I promise that I'll try to get the information you want, if for no other reason than to try to preserve what sanity you have left. I'm convinced that there is a perfectly reasonable explanation for anything that you think has happened." And before Bert could once more remonstrate about the "evidence," George said "goodnight" and left.

Bert tried to get to sleep, but his mind kept replaying the horror of the slaughter he'd just described to George. It was a Technicolor movie with a full sound track of the sounds of erotic encounters and of a violent storm. The faces in the movie, however, were those of himself, his family, and of Amy.

The next morning, over coffee, Bert explained the details of her part in the "innocent" Thursday deception to Sheila, who could see no wrong in lying for her boss. Poor, good man, trying to help the world, and all he gets for it is trouble from that wife. Having to sneak away to work on the clinic. Sheila was to contact Dr. Webber if Mrs. Arlen called on a Thursday, and stall her. Dr. Webber would get in touch with Dr. Bradley. The latter would then return his wife's call. Fortunately for Bert, his loyal secretary never thought to ask why she couldn't relay the message to him herself—but she would never dream of questioning anything he asked. Dr. Bradley, on his part, didn't want Sheila to know he was at an out-of-town exchange when he was supposedly working with Nedra downtown. What would she have thought if she'd known it was all to provide her employer with the opportunity to sleep with his girl friend?

Bert drove quickly to the Whitney Clinic, where, as a staff member, he had ready access to the files of Jessica Desmond, October 1938–August 1939. It was as Courtney had described it, each entry meticulously detailing treatment and total lack of response. The listing of visitors showed that indeed Sister Theresa Immaculata had been the most faithful to the very end. He made a note to interview the Sister that very next weekend, presuming that she had remained in the local convent and was still alive. He also found the records of the names of attendants assigned to Jessica's case, and was surprised and delighted to note that two of them were still there, both now in supervisory capacities. Jane Arkin was in her office checking on files of incoming patients. An attractive woman in her late fifties, she had a gentle, unhurried manner, much appreciated by the staff on their hectic rounds.

"Yes, Dr. Bradley, I certainly do remember the child. I was eighteen and it was my first case. I can tell you that it was quite an honor to be working with Dr. Barakian," Jane reminisced, "and the child, Lord she was a beauty. We were all taken by those looks. It's a terrible admission to make, but I think we all tried just a bit harder because she was so exquisite."

Bert nodded, recognizing the truth of her statement.

Even in a madhouse beauty was given its due. Looks discrimination knew no bounds.

"Do you happen to recall anything about the treatment?"

"No, not really. All I can tell you is that the experimental programs that Barakian tried out on Jessica when all else failed have since become standard procedures here. I don't think I've ever seen anyone work harder with a patient in all my years here. When I had the night shift, I'd find him near her bed, talking, reading her stories, trying to feed her. He'd had her room fixed up like a normal bedroom for a five-year-old, and he even had the three of us who worked with her wear regular clothing rather than uniforms."

"Were you on round-the-clock duty?"

"Yes, eight-hour-shifts, we spelled one another on days off, so her routine wouldn't be disrupted, and there would be no strange faces around her."

"Did you notice any changes or reactions in the child to anything at all?"

"Not that I recall. If there was, it would probably be in the files."

"How did she die?"

"I really don't know. She seemed somehow weaker and Dr. Barakian said that her lungs were congested, but in her state, changes were difficult to detect. She was rigid and staring all the time I saw her. One morning when I reported for duty I was told that she had died sometime during the night." And after the passing of all these years, her eyes misted at the memory.

"Did you see the body or attend the funeral?"

"No to both. Her body had already been placed in a casket and sealed for the burial in the family mausoleum in Southampton. Dr. Barakian said there was no point in a wake, since he'd arranged for a Catholic service for the repose of the poor baby's soul. We all sent flowers, that was all we could do."

"And the good doctor, did you ever find out why he left, or where he went?"

188

"I seem to be giving you a lot of nos, but I have no idea what happened to him. The war began in Europe just after Jessica died, and I know he was very upset about that, he talked about it all the time, and before the New Year, he'd resigned. No one ever mentioned hearing from him, although we talked about him for a long time afterward. He had one close friend, another Armenian, but he dropped out of sight too— No," she smiled, forestalling his query, "I don't remember his name."

An interview with Mabel Phipps, now in personnel, confirmed the account he'd just heard. In her early sixties, she'd had a few years of experience before being assigned to the case.

"It's difficult to explain, but there were some changes in the child despite the cataleptic state. It was a sensation I had, rather than being able to see anything happening."

Bert nodded. There were hypersensitive people who sensed nuances that were physically indiscernible. Barakian had obviously chosen his people well.

"Do you recall when these changes occurred?"

"When we played a music box that the nun had brought, or gave her stuffed toys in the shape of animals—or whenever the nun came to visit. When I noted this for the doctor, he said I was very perceptive and had chosen the right field, even though I had to admit I couldn't tell whether the changes were positive or negative." She still preened at the memory of the great man's praise.

According to her account, she had been assigned to the 4 P.M. to midnight shift, as the records ascertained, for August 22, 1939, and when she'd gone off duty, the child, though weak, was still alive. Angela Terbell had not come in that night. It was her birthday—and the doctor, considerate as always, had told her that he would cover her shift himself.

"That's the kind of person he was. I still remember when Angela found out the child had died, she was as distraught as if it had been her fault."

"These records show that Jessica died at three A.M. Did anyone you know see the body?"

"No one except the doctor. He said she looked at peace at last, the look of terror finally gone from that haunted, hunted face. He cried too."

"One last thing, Mabel, why isn't there a photo on her file?"

"There was, I put it on myself. Look here, you can see where it had been glued. It must have slipped off and gotten lost," she said with a puzzled look.

But it obviously hadn't worked itself loose, for Bert could see where someone had peeled it off, leaving remnants of the backing on the file.

"Curioser and curioser," George intoned as he and Bert compared notes on the results of their respective research. They were conferring at the former's West Side apartment, after having shared an excellent meal prepared by the Chinese houseman. "As much as I hate to admit it, I'm beginning to think there might be something strange about this case; not necessarily paranormal, but the pieces don't fit, and I'm enough of an obsessive not to rest content until they do."

"That's a relief," sighed his friend. "I'd hoped you'd work with me rather than try to persuade me that I was crazy."

"Let's not get paranoid, old buddy. I'd never work against you, just for your best interests. I couldn't get a lead on Barakian, but the wheels have been set in motion by a friend of mine who had access to a computer at the Institute for Mental Health. Nedra, marvelous as always in your service," he mockingly bowed to Bert, "has already found that there are only three claims left for the Desmond estate. There are two men who claim to be the brothers who were lost in the storm, Drew and Edward. Seems they *were* orphaned by the storm, but nothing else matches after years of checking their claims. They said they were so traumatized by seeing their grandparents, the Ambroses, swept away in the hurricane, plus their own exposure to the elements, that they had collective amnesia for years afterward."

"Until they heard of a ten-million-dollar estate?"

"That's about it. At any rate, their dental records don't check with those finally found in the files of the old dentist in Southampton, so that's the end for them. The only claimant left in the ball park is one of a Margaret Soles, who has sworn an affadavit that she is the illegitimate daughter of Evalynn Ambrose Desmond, born in Vermont on April 21, 1916."

"The sixth child! I told you that Johns couldn't be wrong!" and Bert jumped out of his chair with excitement.

"So it would seem. She claims that since there are no descendants of Evan's side, and that all of her mother's other children and family are dead, the estate should be hers. Her mother was the last to die, and therefore was the sole inheritor of the Desmond fortune."

"What proof did she present?"

"Nedra couldn't get that, everything she's gotten so far has been off the cuff. Apparently the guy in charge of the files couldn't resist the story she gave him, or the boobs she waggled in his face." George was aware of the disapproving look. "Well, it's true. The guy gave her all the info over drinks and dinner. I don't know if he doesn't know any more or is waiting for her to surrender her virtue to give her the rest. She'd even do that for you," he added, rather bitterly, Bert thought, and decided it would be best to ignore the remark.

"From what I know about the law, this Soles woman

should be able to get fifty percent of the estate, at least, and the government the rest, unless she actually gets to walk off with the ten million. Why don't we find this woman and then you can marry her, George?" Bert teased. "We could sure use the money for the clinic."

The ploy was ignored. "We'll have to go elsewhere for funding. Have you mentioned it to Alice lately?"

"No, but the Arlens will be out next week. When they see how happy she is, I'll hit my father-in-law for the money. You know he's one of the great humanitarians of all times. If he only weren't so obsessed about his little girl's security, I never would have gotten into this bind. But right now, man, as we say in the vernacular, I've got a piece of heavy news for you from the rest of my day's research. Hold on to your teeth for this one!"

"What now," sighed his friend, "another vision of Christmas past?"

"No," Bert announced almost triumphantly, "I had the stains on the pillow analyzed at the forensic lab. The blood is not venal, but arterial and the type is rare, A negative, which from the autopsy report, you will recognize is Evan Desmond's blood type!"

On his drive out to Riverhead the next morning, Bert recalled with satisfaction the look on George's face when he'd dropped his bombshell. His jaw had actually sagged and he'd sputtered trying to come up with a logical explanation for the facts. When they had wearily parted at midnight, George had told him that he was sure he could find some reasonable explanation. Bert was tired of trying to think of any; all he wanted to do was to enjoy his day with Amy. He saw her sitting at the counter at Howard Johnson's as he pulled into the parking lot, wearing the floppy hat that was her trademark. A joyous smile rewarded him as he slipped onto the stool next to hers.

"Hiya, honey, wanna get into the movies?"

She giggled delightedly and he felt like a carefree boy again. Suddenly ravenous, he ate an enormous breakfast and insisted that Amy do the same.

"Just want to fatten you up for the kill, little girl. You're too bony—eat up now."

The town was hot and muggy, set as it is in a valley, but they walked off their breakfast exploring the river's route that gave the town its name, marveling over the juxtaposition of beautiful old houses next to tawdry business enterprises. It was a relief to get into the air-conditioned darkness of the motel room, where Bert made love to Amy so sweetly and slowly that time seemed to stop for both of them. He could actually feel her fluttering with desire for him as he finally pressed into her, and with all the skills he had learned over the past thirty years, he brought her to climax again and again, before allowing himself release. The look of rapture on her face was one well worth the earning. He felt so grateful for her youth and freshness; she made him feel as if his life were still before him. He loved her smoothness and her smell, and the fact that she was as intoxicated by being with him as he was with her. Despite Alice's great sexual performances, he always had the nagging feeling that she was "giving it to him" so that he wouldn't have the time, inclination, or energy to seek elsewhere. Some of his patients had verbalized this. With Amy he had no doubt that she was giving because she wanted him.

After they'd showered, he took her for a drive and then for lunch at the Henry Perkins Hotel. When they returned to the room for the few hours they had left, he took a package from his attaché case.

193

"This came for you yesterday, I'm sorry I forgot to give it to you before, but I got carried away by other thoughts."

"But that's impossible. Who could be sending me a package?"

Eagerly she unwrapped it and gasped as a Cartier box was revealed. Almost unbelievingly, she slowly opened it to find therein the most expensive model of the Tank watch. Wordlessly Bert turned it over in her hands so that she could read the inscription on the back.

FOR AMY
FOR ALL TIME
8/1/76

He was rewarded with an absolute torrent of tears that he had difficulty in stemming.

"Hey, if I knew the reaction," he teased, "I would have gotten you a Mickey Mouse instead."

"I just can't believe how good you are to me. No one in my whole life has ever done anything like this. Why did you do it?"

"Because you make me so happy just by existing that I want to share my happiness with you in every way possible. You've given me a new lease on life; it's like being on a high, everything is so much sharper, clearer, more meaningful. No wonder people always want to be in love; it's cheaper and healthier than pot, liquor, or drugs—and a lot more fun."

So they made love again and marveled that each time was better than the last, though neither of them would have thought that possible.

On the drive to the bus stop, where he would have to leave her to avoid suspicion, he told Amy that one of the kittens had met with an accident, and asked if Lissie had noticed that it was missing.

"Funny, I noticed, but since Lissie didn't seem to, I thought it best not to say anything."

194

"Good girl. Should she ask, tell her that I took it to give to a friend who needed company. She'll understand, she's a very generous little girl. And now we'd better rehearse the scenario for the presentation of the watch at your birthday party."

It was slipped back into the wrappings to be resealed by Bert, who would give it to her on Saturday, by explaining that it had been mailed to the town house. Amy picked up from there.

"I'll be absolutely ecstatic and show it off in a total daze. I'll explain that it's from my very wealthy beau from Amherst who wants to marry me after graduation. We're testing our love by remaining incommunicado for the summer."

"You certainly put that together fast," said Bert admiringly.

"Theater majors all have to be good liars," came the matter-of-fact reply, "it seems to go with the territory." And with a wave she was gone.

Bert drove back to the motel and slept soundly until his 8 P.M. call. Thoroughly refreshed he drove to Mulberry, hoping he could pull off another weekend of deceit. His prayers were answered—Alice still had her period and never felt sexy then. The gossip was mostly about Astrid and the swathe she was cutting sleeping around. Amy had greeted him with her usual casual public smile and nod, and then retired to her quarters so as not to intrude upon the family get-together. It had been done so coolly that his heart had almost stopped. Was she that consummate an actress at her tender age? Was it possible that she was just playing a role when they were together? *Theater majors are all good liars, it seems to go with the territory*, rang in his ears. Deciding it was counterproductive to torture himself in this way, he fell asleep while trying to devise schemes to see her during her school year.

An unearthly, inhuman moan crept into his sleep, forcing

him into consciousness. The room was dark, and Alice was not beside him. The eerie sounds were coming from their bathroom, and as he walked into the room, he saw Alice shrunk up against the wall. She was actually foaming at the mouth, as she stared hypnotically into the light emanating from a phosphorescent glow in the mirror. Putting his arm around her, he followed her gaze. Instead of their reflections, what was given back was the image of the severed head of what appeared to be a young girl with long, black, curling hair. Her blue eyes stared at them sightlessly, her nostrils flared widely as blood spurted from her nose and from the arteries in her neck. As the mouth opened as if to speak, the apparition faded.

"The head," Alice jabbered, "the head the head the head blood blood blood blood," and finally fainted in his arms.

Staring at the mirror, while frozen against the wall for what seemed to be an eternity, Bert finally gathered Alice up in his arms and carried her to their bed. Once more he was astounded to find no sign of shock as she fell into a peaceful slumber. Going back into the bathroom, there was no trace of what had frightened them; all he found was a strand of black curly hair on the sink, and a trace of what could be blood on the floor. Tucking the hair into a drawer, he wiped up the stain on the floor with a handkerchief and put that away with it. He listened to all the night noise of the house until the reassuring sounds of dawn could be recognized. Creeping back into bed next to his wife, he finally fell into a troubled sleep. The next thing he knew, Alice was shaking him awake, cheerfully calling,

196

"Hey sleepy head—we've got a tennis date in thirty minutes. Up and at 'em!"

Bewilderedly he stared up into her smiling face. There was no sign of strain, no sign that she had undergone that terrible experience of last night. She looked totally refreshed and happy. Cautiously he questioned her. No, she had had a good night's sleep, she hadn't gotten up at all, he might have heard the kids, but she'd slept like a log. Looking at her bustling around the room, Bert began to consider seriously if he was in the process of losing his mind due to the guilt he felt about his affair. George must be right after all.

Alice had laid on such a hectic schedule that he, fortunately, had little time to worry about his sanity or lack of it. He drank too much that night at the Clausens' party so that when he awoke the following morning it was with a raging hangover. Pleading excruciating pain, he was allowed to stay home while the others toped off to the club. After a few cups of black coffee, he got up his courage and opened the drawer where he thought he had placed the evidence of that night of horror. He didn't know whether or not he was relieved to find it there. It proved to him that he was not crazy, but it also proved that the experience he didn't want to believe had actually occurred. How was it that Alice was completely free of any effects? A chilling thought struck him. Could she be trying to *Gaslight* him? God, now he was getting paranoid!

Determined to find some clue, he started to go over every inch of the bedroom and bath meticulously. His search was finally rewarded when the bottom panel in the walk-in closet yielded to the pressure of his fingers, and he found a secret cubby. In it was an old-fashioned canvas zipper bag, the kind he'd used for gym clothes when he was in high school. He spread its contents on the bed and started to examine articles that someone had packed many years ago,

197

as evidenced by the newspaper, dated September 28, 1938, which had been used to wrap a little girl's shoes. It was a weird assortment: boys' and girls' items in a range of sizes along with various toilet articles. Under this jumble was a leather-bound photo album and an envelope of what appeared to be legal documents. Eagerly opening the album, he was startled, because the first picture he found was one labeled "Diedre," whose looks resembled the face he'd seen in the mirror. Evan was indeed handsome, according to his photo, as were the other children, but Jessica, as they'd all assured him, *was* a beauty. She did bear an uncanny resemblance to Lissie, except for the eyes. The only picture of Evalynn was one taken on her wedding day. It was hard to reconcile the descriptions he'd heard of a dowdy frump with the lovely young bride looking at the camera with a tremulous half smile. Too excited to absorb all the details of the find, he remembered the hiding place in these bags, and swiftly he reached inside to pry up the cardboard at the bottom.

His hunch was rewarded, for in his hands he now held what seemed to be a diary written in a composition notebook. The writing was minute, and the author seemed to have used some kind of code. He'd leave that to Sheila to transcribe; she was good at that sort of thing. The notebook, envelope, and the album were transferred to his case. Samples of the hair from each woman's hairbrush found in the bag were placed in envelopes labeled A and B. Envelope C contained the hair he'd found in the bathroom that night of terror and D the handkerchief with the stain he'd wiped from the floor. His mind racing with possibilities, he finally decided to wait to explore them with George. Lying back on the bed after hiding his cache, he napped until the family returned from the club.

The birthday party went off beautifully, just as Lissie had planned it. The local Saks had been having a sale, so for the fifty dollars Alice had gotten Amy a nice assortment of summer tops, one from each of them. On cue Bert presented Amy with the package that he said had arrived for her in town, claiming he had assumed it was a birthday gift, and had kept it until the party. All went as rehearsed, and Lissie asked if she could be the flower girl when Amy married her admirer. Busy clearing away the debris, no one noticed Stacey slip the mailing wrapper from the watch into the pocket of her denim skirt. Going up to her room, she studied it carefully. Just as she'd suspected: The stamps weren't canceled and the handwriting was unquestionably her father's. Seething, she remembered how adamant he'd been when she wanted the "good" Tank for Christmas, chiding her for extravagant desires and preaching a sermon on waiting until "you earn your own money." She'd gotten the two-hundred-dollar model. Now that dirty old man had up and given that little tart the fifteen-hundred-dollar watch he'd denied to his own flesh and blood. How good in bed could that whore be to earn that kind of gift? Anguish and rage boiled in her as she plotted a just revenge for this heinous crime of adultery.

Somehow Bert had gotten through the weekend, leaving early on Sunday by claiming the press of unfinished work in the office. It had been a good weekend in terms of the kids; they seemed to be maturing and getting along better with one another. Had he not been so absorbed in his love and in his searching, he might have professionally noted that his offspring were superpolite lately, a sure sign that something explosive was brewing.

Letting himself into the house, he did something he rarely allowed himself, and took a sleeping pill. Mercifully it worked until Sheila Warren shook him awake on Monday morning. Giving her the diary, he asked her to concentrate on the deciphering and to hire an office temporary to do her clerical work, which she refused.

"Don't be silly, Dr. Bradley, I'll just take this home with me and work on it at night." Bridling with pleasure at his effusive thanks, she went off to start her day's work.

Before he got started with his patients, Bert called a messenger service and had the envelopes delivered to the forensic lab, with a note requesting that the analysis be expedited. Fortunately he was so busy all day with his rearranged schedule that he hadn't a spare moment to agonize over the possible lab findings. Leaving Thursdays free meant a killing pace for the remaining days in the office. Despite Ms. Warren's objections, he didn't even allow himself a lunch break. It was 9 P.M. when he wearily locked his office and went upstairs to the soothing comfort of the small family room. Flipping on the TV set for company, he sprawled in the big leather chair with a large Scotch and water, giving himself a half-hour respite before opening the lab envelope awaiting him on the coffee table where Sheila had placed it, along with his personal mail. After reading its contents he went to the phone and asked George to please come at once.

Bert let him into the house and silently led him upstairs. Concerned by his friend's unnatural pallor, George listened quietly to his recitation of the scene of a severed head in the mirror, and of his subsequent finds of "evidence." His reaction was one of disbelief and a gentle suggestion that Bert start therapy with him the next evening.

"But you don't understand," came the response, "the lab report proves that all of these things have been happening."

George looked at him askance. He either *had* experienced paranormal phenomena or he was as mad as the Hatter; either alternative being equally unacceptable to his listener's sense of reason, he listened with professional mien, pretending Bert was a patient.

"The hair I found on the pillow after what you called a 'ghost screw,' matches the hair from one of the brushes I found in what has to be Evalynn Desmond's bag. The hair I found on the bathroom sink is a match with the hair on the other brush in the bag. The first match would be from Evalynn's head, since there is gray mixed in, and the darker hair must be her daughter's." Taking out the photo album, he showed George the picture of Diedre with long, dark, curling hair.

Leafing through the album, George demanded, "How is it that these apparitions keep leaving signs behind for you to trace? First you had Desmond's arterial blood on Lissie's pillow, which you claimed came from the mortal wound made by his loving wife, and now you present me with strands of hair conveniently left behind. Don't you find this rather odd?"

"No, not at all."

"Why not?"

"Because when I studied psychical research, I learned that a place where great violence has taken place contains charged particles in the ether that are measurable by sensitive equipment. This tension makes things happen, draws attention to whatever occurred that was left unresolved."

"If you recall, I took that course with you. I found it fascinating, but you're taking it seriously?" George seemed incredulous.

"Yes, anger and hate are strong enough to reach out from beyond the grave."

"And you're perfectly serious?"

"Perfectly. You've read the reports by the Society for Psychical Research. There is no other way to explain away the enormous wealth of material concerning supernatural phenomena that has actually been documented over the years. We know that strong emotions are sent into the atmosphere by a sort of ionic electrical charge. I simply submit to you that when the intensity is overwhelming, these particles do not dissipate. I'd also add that I think you're exhibiting an ego insecurity in refusing to admit that there are things on earth we cannot as yet scientifically define, and that we may never be able to do so. Why are you so resistant to that theory? It's as valid as many others."

It was George's turn to be on the defensive. It was true that he had always been interested in parapsychology, and was aware of the respect the Psychical Society had earned. Like the Church's attitude toward miracles, their thrust was to disprove. Yet there were still enough cases all over the world each year that defied their expert scientific research to fill a small volume. Was his assumption that what he didn't believe in, didn't exist, due to arrogance on his part? He listened as Bert continued.

"The energies in that house are in a state of growing frenzy and excitation. The manifestations get stronger every week. There is an unhappiness there that wants comfort and an evil that wants exorcising."

George snapped to attention. "I think I saw that movie. Are you going to do the Father Damien bit?" he asked ironically.

"Never thought about a priest, though they were a Catholic family. I thought I might borrow the equipment from the Society and try to measure the electron pressure in the areas of the murders to see if they were more heavily charged."

"How would that help you rid the place of the unhappy spirits? Why don't you just leave them tickets for Palm Beach and let them haunt a different resort area?"

202

Bert smiled at this feeble attempt at humor. "No, I realize now that these energies will only dissolve when the truth is revealed. I think the problem exists because there is a great anger that the true murderer has never been revealed."

"So you think Evan might be up to all these shennanigans to get his wife acknowledged as the perpetrator of the foul deeds?"

"That's one possibility, but I'd like to propose two alternatives for your esteemed consideration. One is that that they were murdered by an outsider, because it's difficult for me to imagine that as sick as they were, they would murder their children in such a way."

"Although we both well know it's been done many times," murmured George thinking of some of the cases he knew from personal experience. "And the other possibility?"

"That if it was Evalynn, her spirit might be unquiet because she'd left her baby behind; she'd want to bring it back into the family—as it were."

"But if the child is dead, she would have contact with it— whoa there," George exclaimed as he realized what Bert was driving at, "you mean you think there's a possibility that the child is still alive?"

"Either that or—more likely and plausible—Jessica did *not* die from natural causes in the hospital, and her mother is trying to avenge her."

Refusing to discuss the matter any further in his state of bone deep fatigue, George left over his host's objections, promising to fill him in over dinner at his place the next night at 8 P.M. on the promising lead that Nedra had uncovered on Barakian.

Sheila came in the morning with apologies for not having been able to complete the transcription of the diary.

"The woman used a kind of speed writing, so that wasn't too hard to figure out, but the writing was so minute that by the time I had it all down in shorthand, I was too tired to type it up. I'll have it finished for you by the end of the day if you don't mind my putting off the other work."

Her face showed the signs of fatigue. She must have stayed up all night to have finished the transcription.

"Sheila, there's not a day that goes by that I don't realize how fortunate I am to have you in my employ. Please do finish today, and tomorrow you're to take the day off and buy yourself something with this," and over her protestations, he forced two fifty-dollar bills into her hand. Then he went into the office to deal with the problems of one Mr. Norbert Kelsh.

The latter was delighted to find the doctor so sympathetic to his desire to throw away everything and run off with his daughter's college roommate. He really seemed to be listening intently.

When Bert arrived at George's apartment, the diary's translation was under his arm, hot off the typewriter. After the meal, they sat in the worn leather club chairs over cognac while George indulged in his evening cigar. Feeling more relaxed than he had in weeks, Bert realized that it was because of his friend's tacit acceptance to help him find an answer to the problems in Mulberry. Like a father surrogate, he felt that the older man could fix everything and make it better.

"I haven't had a chance to read the diary. I thought we could do so together and see if there were any clues. But first I'd like to hear the news about Barakian."

He listened intently as Nedra's hunt for clues was described. "You know how fantastically logical she is.

204

When I repeated the comment about his being upset about the war, and that he'd dropped out of sight in 1939, she assumed that he must have gone to Europe to help in the war effort, and she was right on the button! He served with the British army, first as a field doctor and later as a psychiatrist when the emotionally wounded started pouring in. According to his records, he was there when the concentration camps were liberated, and volunteered to stay until the victims were placed. The last heard of him was that he had been talking of going to Israel because the experience had made a Jew of him."

Bert nodded soberly, recognizing what that compassionate man must have felt. "How old is he now?"

"Just past seventy. Remember he was a *wunderkind* at the time he was treating Jessica Desmond; he was one of the youngest chiefs of pediatrics the hospital had ever had."

"If he's in Israel it shouldn't be too hard to trace him—it's such a small country."

"That's exactly what Nedra is doing now," retorted George. "We should have a lead on his whereabouts in a day or two."

The men then busied themselves with Evalynn's diary, passing each page along as they finished. It certainly seemed to verify the claim of whoever Margaret Soles was. If she was indeed Evalynn's offspring as the result of the rape by John Soles, she would be entitled to at least part of the estate. But what proof could she have? The mother hadn't even a clue to the sex of her child, let alone its whereabouts, and she had chronicled her despair at the death of the nun who had participated at the birth, and who had placed the child for adoption.

George was the first to break their ruminative silence when they had finished the pathetic chronicle.

"At least we've gotten a better picture of that poor tormented soul. She admits she'd rather see her children dead by her own hand than leave them in her husband's clutches. If half of what she writes of him is true, it would be hard to blame her. What a despicable excuse for a human being that bastard was!"

"No professional detachment? After all he too was the product of his environment. Imagine what sort of tortures of the damned must have been inflicted upon him as a child for him to have become the kind of depraved person she describes."

"True, but I get the feeling that Evan found it easier to follow the route to damnation rather than to seek the path to salvation. I also must admit that you did a thoroughly admirable job of deduction with the facts you had before this came to light. Congratulations, doctor."

The praise was sincere and Bert accepted it gratefully.

"Thanks, but now we have to get down to basics. Do you think this account is true or the imaginings of a sick, repressed psyche?"

"I'd say it was basically true. It sounds to me as if Evan might have been the offspring of a demented family, first cousins to boot. The insanity might well have been heredi-tary, in which case, as you speculated, it's better that they're all dead."

"Whom do you think killed them—him or her?"

"I don't know, I just have a gut feeling that at this particular stage of their respective psychoses, neither was ready for this kind of act."

"Do you think that the atmosphere of the storm could have brought about a strong enough change in their emotional levels to have caused one or the other to have made that psychotic break?"

"Interesting point," responded George. "I guess you've been reading the new studies on atmospheric pressure and mental instability. It's like the correlation of the increase in tension in a mentally disturbed person with the full moon. So many of these things that we contemptuously dismissed as old wives' tales now are sporting scientific verification that it's embarrassing. Yes, that's a possibility, especially in view of the fact that the mother had her period at the time, which would definitely have caused an increase in psychological and physiological tension."

"Don't say that in front of the feminists, George, they'll tear you limb from limb."

"Truth has no gender," George intoned a bit pompously. "We all know that it's true for most women, if through no other research than by the drug sales for medication said to relieve premenstrual tension. And the amount of water pressure on the brain increase is a fact. But all that taken into account, I still don't have the profile of a woman who could commit these unspeakable acts. Were they merely murdered, perhaps; but the manner in which it was done would indicate that the killer was someone who hated these victims with an overwhelming passion. No, it would take a schizophrenic paranoid to castrate the boy, tear up the maid's uterus, decapitate the girl, and then stop to chop up the animals before stabbing the husband. I just don't see this woman in that role—nor the father either for that matter."

Both men were silent as they contemplated once again the enormity of the horror, set as it was against the background of nature's own violence, which they had both admitted to having had enjoyed.

Bert was first to break the silence. "So then, we are agreed that it was murder by an unknown third party?"

"I'd guess it was a man from the strength and fury of the attacks, but of course it's possible for a woman in a schizoid rage to do just as effective a job."

"Damn straight," replied Bert vigorously. "Last week it took five very husky male attendants to pull Mrs. Kowalski off of her husband. I'd warned Brenner that it was too soon to let her see her family, but the fool wouldn't listen. She half-killed the poor bastard, and he's a stocky six-footer. Doubt he'll be too anxious to see her soon." He shook his head at the memory of their colleague's error in judgment.

"O.K., now let's get on to the sleuthing. I'll list possibilities, you cull.

"One, someone who hated one of the Desmonds enough to kill them all; two, someone whom Evan had cuckolded so badly he had to get his balls back in this way; three, an accidental thing—perhaps some crazy took shelter with them from the storm and the hurricane shook his/her hinges loose; or four, someone who stood to inherit the estate if the family was wiped out, and was crazy enough to chance it."

"Or clever enough, knowing it would be assumed that Evan had finally flipped his lid. Or maybe he *did* when he found out that the kid was screwing the maid he considered his property." Bert injected excitedly.

"O great Freud, father of us all," mocked George, pretending piety. "Yes, that is another possibility. Now all you'll have to do is to ask your spooks who did it, the next time one shows up to consult you."

"Come off it, George, you know damn well that I'm convinced of the validity of what I've told you about." His tone was angry at the teasing.

"I'll either be forced to agree with you or think that there is some lunatic going around the house pulling weird tricks. Since both ideas seem incredible, I don't know what to opt for at this point."

They bade each other good-night after agreeing to continue the research. What explanations would they have offered had they known that as they were parting, Alice dreamed that she was being mounted by a handsome blond man with eyes as blue as Lissie's?—the image of Evan Desmond in the photo album Bert had found. After they'd made love, he sang the lullaby to her before vanishing, leaving her with no memory of the dream, but with semen stains on the sheets that had been changed that morning.

208

Their mounting excitement got the Baker Street irregulars, as they'd dubbed themselves, through another grueling professional day. Since George worked the full week, he had had time to interview the people who had worked with Barakian at the clinic. He was to discuss his findings with his colleague over supper at the latter's home that evening.

Bert had put together what he described as a "bachelor dinner" and plied him with an enormous variety of cold cuts he'd had sent in from Zabar's, George's favorite "deli."

"You've got enough here for the Last Supper," he joked as he filled his plate for the second time.

"And I'm not even a Jewish mother," responded his host. "Eat, eat, you're a growing boy."

By tacit agreement they never discussed business while they ate. It was when they had moved into the airy beige living room, still light in the summer's glow, that George explained what his "cross-examination" had revealed.

"I had the advantage of your report, so I was able to tune in on another level. What seems to have escaped your normally astute perceptions is the significance of the fact that no one ever saw Jessica dying or dead."

Bert stared at him with a dawning sense of malaise. "How the hell did I miss that!"

As George explained it, he had read all the reports and there was no indication that anyone had handled the body, just Barakian's signature on the certificate, and his release of the body to Brockett's Funeral Parlor in Southampton. Their records, as a phone call had ascertained, showed that they had picked up a sealed casket and had interred it in the Desmond mausoleum after a funeral mass celebrated at the local church on Hill Street. The executors had given their approval after having been notified of the death by the hospital.

"I wonder why they showed so little interest, after all she was the sole heir to a major fortune," mused Bert.

"If it was anyone but Barakian, I'd suspect foul play to get part of the funds, but a man of his ilk wouldn't stoop to such tactics. I do believe, however, that he did have reason to try to conceal the circumstances of her death."

"Euthanasia?"

"Exactly. I'd venture to guess that he saw no sense in prolonging a life that was a death in life, so he probably dispatched her quickly and painlessly. Perhaps joining the war effort was his way of expiating the sin of violating his Hippocratic oath."

"Sounds like good logic to me, I think the next step is to exhume the body."

"What good would that do, Bert? All you want to do is to get rid of the spooks. How will examining the body help you in that?"

"Call it intuition, but I think that the key to this whole insanity is the almost subliminal message I keep getting that there is a need to find the murderer. Since we feel fairly confident that it wasn't either of the Desmond parents, we've got to pursue every avenue to find the solution. I think it lies with Jessica, since her consciousness on some level was grappling with it, keeping the memory alive."

"What makes you think that the murderer is still alive after thirty-eight years? And waiting for you to find him or her?"

"Just another hunch. I don't think the emanations would be as strong if he or she was dead. Psychical research studies have shown an incredible persistence in paranormal phe-nomena when there is an unresolved crime—which fades when, as it were, the ghosts are laid to rest by the evidence of the true facts of the crime being brought to light. The last case I read was of a 'haunting' in England that ended after *three hundred years* when an investigator published findings showing that the mother had not killed the baby, as she had been accused of doing, but that the father's mistress had done so."

George strained to try not to show the incredulity he felt. Bert was going a bit overboard.

"Have you considered just leaving that anguished house and finishing your vacation elsewhere?"

"As I said, I have, but I simply can't come up with a feasible reason. And then too, I have this gut feeling that if I don't resolve this situation, it's going to follow me wherever I go."

Before George had a chance to tell his friend that he was now carrying things too far, they were interrupted by a phone call. It was Nedra triumphantly announcing receipt of a Telex confirming the whereabouts of Dr. Barakian—in the U.S.A.!

The combination of the good news and the fact that he was en route to see Amy made Bert feel manic that Thursday morning. It seemed that some of the pieces of the puzzle might actually come together, and George had promised to spend the weekend finding their quarry's exact location. He was so happy when he pulled into the Howard Johnson's parking lot that he failed to see Astrid Newsome waving to him. On her way to the county courthouse to try to beat a fine for speeding, she couldn't imagine what Bert would be doing in Riverhead. She watched with great interest as he entered the coffee shop and sat down next to a young girl in a floppy hat, who, in turning to greet him with a beatific grin, proved to be none other than that sexy little *au pair* girl she'd seen at the beach taking care of Lissie. She sat in her car until they had left together, then followed them at a discreet distance until they pulled into the motel lot. Musing about the best way to pass on this bombshell of gossip, she turned and went to plead "not guilty" to the charges against her.

Totally unaware that their relationship was in jeopardy, the lovers spent a beautiful day in bed doing all the things they'd dreamed of doing all week long. When Amy's treasured watch showed it was time to leave, they agreed that it was harder to part each time they were together. En route to the bus stop Bert explained:

"We mustn't be too greedy, Amy, or we *will* be found out. I don't speak so much from personal experience," he said in answer to her glance, "but from worldly knowledge and the tales my patients tell. Those who are cautious have had relationships lasting for years. One woman has been seeing her boyfriend every Tuesday afternoon for twenty years, and no one is the wiser. For most people it's a truism that you only get caught if you want to destroy your marriage."

"Is that what happened to you that night you sneaked into my room to make love to me with your wife in the room below?"

"Possibly. Sometimes, just like everyone else, I'd like to kick over the traces and do exactly what I feel like doing, rather than doing what I know is right. But I also know that the twenty-eight-year age difference between us pretty well precludes our living happily ever after. I also know that I would never be able to shake a sense of loss and guilt, should I leave my family, which would poison any chance we'd have for happiness."

"So what is the solution?"

212

"To go on exactly as we are for as long as you want to see me. One day when you're all grown up, you'll gently tell me that there is someone else in your life, someone with whom you want to share a future that I'm too old to give you."

Soberly considering this, Amy knew he was right, but it was impossible to envision the time that she would not want to be with this man. She kissed him good-bye with a passion that made him wonder how he could ever let her go as he watched her board the bus back to town.

When Ida Cullum hesitantly announced to her husband that her period was late, he insisted that they go for the "new fangled" tests he'd heard about, and waited for confirmation at the clinic a short bus ride from home. When the frog decreed that he was indeed to be a father once more, he grinned delightedly. After five years of doubting his virility, he was vindicated. Take away those infernal pills and he'd see to it that the lying bitch was knocked up regularly from now on. Now all he had to do was to find that girl, but the sense of urgency was gone. He knew she'd be back for school in September, nothing could keep her from that. He'd enjoy the look on her face when she found out that her ma was pregnant again. He'd enjoy the look on her face even more when he would get her down in the basement and rape her all night.

He'd worked it all out, preparing a corner of the basement with an old mattress, some clothesline and cloth to use as a gag. He'd go down to the cellar once a day to gaze upon the set, playing the scene in his mind over and over again, with endless variations adapted from the porn books his cronies in the bar passed around. When he would have finally finished with her, he wouldn't have to tie her up when he next wanted her; his prick, that rod from heaven, would have tamed her into the acceptance of man's supremacy on earth. Anticipating the look of sick fear that he'd see in her eyes made him feel positively God-like.

The fantasies made him so happy that when his wife timidly said that the doctor had advised no further intercourse for the remainder of her pregnancy due to her age, he had magnanimously agreed. He'd show her other ways to pleasure him until it was time for the next pregnancy—which would be a month after this one was finished.

Part VII

It was a busy weekend at Mulberry, which meant that Bert and Amy scarcely even had time for longing glances as the household prepared for the Arlens' visit. Needed for a hundred last-minute errands, Bert had to postpone his planned "research" on the Desmond case. Everything was in gleaming readiness when the powder-blue Continental drove up the circular driveway on Saturday. Even the weather had cooperated to give the Arlens their first look at the Hamptons at their best.

Amy had stayed in the kitchen to put the finishing touches on lunch, and to keep out of a family reunion. She was deeply touched when Mrs. Arlen came into the kitchen to present her with a lovely green Shetland sweater she had purchased in England.

"I really don't know how to thank you. First you give me this wonderful job and now you remember me along with your family. I'll never forget your kindness."

"You're most welcome, my dear. When my daughter wrote to say what a treasure you've proved yourself to be, and how much Lissie adored you, my husband and I wanted to give you some token of our appreciation."

Looking at the woman's face, beaming with kindness, Amy felt a severe pang of conscience. How happy would she be if she knew about her relationship with the father of these grandchildren she absolutely doted upon, the husband of her adored daughter? Bert was right, she realized, he could never break with this family. Their relationship would have to be a temporary, albeit beautiful part of her life.

Wishing she had a heritage such as the Bradleys', she busied herself with her duties.

That night she opted to stay alone in the house rather than to impose on what was, after all, a family dinner at John Duck's restaurant. Lissie had taken a long afternoon nap so that she could stay up for the occasion, which did not begin until 8 P.M., usually her bedtime. As they drove off, Amy was aware that this was the first time in her life she'd ever been in a house alone. Every ordinary sound seemed to magnify into something ominous as she turned down the beds and prepared the kitchen for Sunday's brunch. Deciding it would be a good chance to get some extra sleep for a very busy week ahead, she was in bed by 9:30. She was asleep when some sensation seemed to pull her into a semiconscious state. In the light of a half-moon she was startled to see a good-looking young man near the window, looking down at her with what appeared to be great interest.

In a quasi-stupor, Amy decided that this must be a part of a dream. As if from a far-off place, she watched as he soundlessly approached the bed and stretched out next to her with a familiarity that suggested he was quite used to doing so. Hungrily he pressed his mouth upon hers and forced his tongue deep into her throat as she lay there, unable to move or to cry out, convinced that it was all part of a nightmare about rape. Deftly he pulled the covers off of her and his hands explored her body lovingly, stroking her until her nipples were rock hard and she throbbed with longing for release; but his mouth never left hers, so that she felt faint. When he finally stood up to take his clothing off, she stretched her arms out to him with an urgency pulsing throughout her body. His torso gleamed in the moonlight as he stripped, his eyes never leaving hers; she felt hypnotized. As he slipped out of his shoes and pushed off his trousers and shorts together, her eyes moved

216

downward, eagerly anticipating the bulge of his lust. Screams of horror tore through her throat as she saw that where his genitals should have been, there was nothing but a huge gaping wound—dripping blood!

Her screams could be heard as the family got out of the car, and without hesitation, Bert ran to the attic, terrified of what he might find. A quick glance showed the room to be empty, as he tried to shake her awake from what he assumed was a nightmare. He called down to the others, who were anxiously grouped at the foot of the attic stairs, that all was O.K., but the screams didn't lessen.

Quickly Dr. Arlen got his medical bag from the guest room and went upstairs to help, while Alice shooed the children to their rooms, explaining that their father would take care of the problem.

Amy was so hysterical that with a nod of assent from his son-in-law, the doctor gave her a tranquilizing shot. Within minutes, she was asleep. As they gazed down at her, Bert had a longing to take her in his arms and cradle her to protect her from whatever her subconscious had tormented her with.

"No need to stay now, Bert, she'll sleep soundly till morning, and with the Pentothal she won't even remember too much about whatever it was that upset her. Is she the hysterical type?"

"Far from it, she's about the strongest young woman I've met." It took all of his professional detachment to leave the sleeping girl and discuss the problems of bad dreams with Arlen, who was an expert in that area in his pediatric practice. It was even harder to lie at Alice's side all night when every fiber of his being cried out to be beside his beloved. He was so distracted that his conscious failed to register the fact that Lissie's music box seemed to be playing all night long.

When he awoke at his usual 5:30 A.M., Dr. Arlen did not

think it worthy of mention that he'd found the cellar door ajar, with the key in the lock. He'd merely locked it and put the key on the mantelpiece, where he assumed it belonged.

Everyone was happy with the Arlen visit except for Richard. Though he loved his grandparents, their presence made it impossible to go to the club meetings. His mother forbade the children to leave the house for the week, except as part of a family group. Stacey was delighted, since she loathed group sex and the sense of shame and degradation she felt in her enforced participation under Everett's ministrations. Every time they went she felt more like an object and less like a person, thus achieving Everett's aims. But Richard, despite his own humiliations at the hands, and pricks, of the group, missed the sexual outlet it provided. All day long he walked around in a constant state of arousal feeling like a character out of *Portnoy's Complaint,* trying to hide it and taking cold showers. On Sunday night he could take it no longer; when the house was quiet, he slipped into his sister's room. She woke as he sat down on her bed and put his hand between her legs. Flinging it off, she ordered him out of her room in a furious whisper.

"Come on now, Stace," he pleaded, "what difference does it make now? Look at me, I'm ready to burst."

His sister started to tell him to "go jerk off," when she suddenly had a better idea. "Not now, Richie, I'm not in the mood. *But*—if you promise that you'll do me one favor, I'll promise you one."

"What do you want me to do?" he asked, suddenly suspicious.

"Nothing serious, but if you do it, I'll let you do anything you want to me, whenever you want to, for as long as you like." Stacey calculated that this was a prospect her brother could not refuse. She was right.

"It's a deal. I swear a solemn oath to do whatever you want if you swear to keep that promise."

"I swear," came the grim, determined response.

Satisfied that she'd keep the bargain, Richard again demanded to know what was expected of him before he could collect his reward—and when.

"Don't worry, little brother, it won't take you long to collect." It didn't.

3

It was a serious Bert who met with George on Monday night to discuss the latest details in the case.

"When I managed to see Amy for a few minutes alone on Sunday she told me a few details of her 'nightmare.'" And he went on to repeat her story of dreaming that an emasculated young man had tried to make love to her, and her horror at the sight of the wound. "You explain to me how her description of that man tallies almost exactly with that of this picture of Garrick Desmond in the photo album! How would she know of his mutilation? And I swear to you on my most sacred honor, on the heads of my wife and children, that I have never mentioned a word of any of this to that girl and she has never seen this album!"

"Try to calm down now, Bert, it *is* an incredible story, but the answer might lie in telesthesia. Someone could be projecting images of what they saw in that house so strongly that even those *not* sensitized to the situation can actually visualize them. I don't know who that someone might be, but it's either that or real ghosts *do* exist."

This last was said with such resignation that Bert was startled, suddenly realizing that all along he had hoped that George would be able to come up with a totally rational explanation based upon science. There now seemed nowhere to go but to the Society for Psychical Research, which they agreed to call the next day.

"Oh, and one more odd thing. Lissie told me that her friend says that she is very happy with the calico kitten. She whispered it to me just before I left last night, I don't even know what she is talking about."

"Could be her way of making up a situation she wants to be true rather than accepting the reality of the creature's absence. She may even have been aware of accidentally suffocating it in her bed before you removed the poor thing."

Bert nodded, that at least had some sound psychoanalytical theory behind it, especially for a child his daughter's age.

"Possible, now let's get on to Barakian. How's that hunt going?"

Delightedly, he received the news that the man had been found, a fifty-minute flight away, in Boston, Massachusetts, traced there by the indefatigable Nedra.

"Has he left Israel for good?"

"No, he had changed his name to Abba ben Shalom, but when he came back to the States, she traced him through the Passport Bureau, since he had to give his previous name. He's registered for a six-week course at the psycho-pharmaceutical center of the Lahey Clinic."

Bert immediately called information to get the phone number, and tried to trace Barakian through the hospital, which refused to divulge his phone listing. As a professional courtesy they agreed to leave a message with the director that Doctor Bradley was most anxious to make contact with the doctor also known as Dr. Shalom.

"Suppose he refuses to see you?"

"I'm going up there anyway. I can't see Amy on Thursday, since Alice insists she needs her for the week, what with her parents being there, so I'll just fly up on the shuttle Wednesday night and haunt the clinic until I get in to see him. I'm convinced that he holds the key to much of this mystery."

Watching Bert pace with excitement, George turned the subject to the Arlens, whom he knew and liked. He'd never been able to understand why they hadn't done a better job on Alice, but perhaps it was only natural that they'd spoiled her so rotten, what with her being an only child born so late in their lives.

"How are your in-laws enjoying their stay? Have they noticed anything peculiar in the atmosphere?"

"Apparently not. I watched them watching Alice intently for the first day, but they seemed to visibly relax after a while at seeing no signs of whatever it was that they were worried about."

"Do you think that Alice's peculiar 'fits' could be the result of whatever that original seashore trauma had been, being stirred by another seaside setting?"

"I thought about that, but I rejected the idea because the catalyst for the original trauma was that hurricane, from which she's had thirty-eight years to recover. Merely being near an ocean isn't going to cause psychic disturbance. Then too, I've had the paranormal experiences, and so have Lissie and Amy, and they were far from even having been conceived at the time of that blow."

"True, but there might be a sensitivity in Alice, because of her fright, that makes things happen in the space she's in near the beach."

"But you know how steady Alice always is, she never gets upset, or at least never used to."

George nodded in agreement, keeping to himself the fact that he had always viewed her detachment as abnormal. "What exactly did happen to her during the hurricane?"

"As far as I remember, her parents were vacationing on the Jersey Shore and left Alice in the hotel with a maid while they visited some friends for the day. They were trapped by the storm and couldn't get back until the next day. When they finally did return, they found that the maid had locked their child in the room and gone off with her boyfriend; so she'd spent the entire time of terror alone in that room, unable to get out, her cries for help drowned out by the noise of the winds. Her father said it was years before she slept or reacted normally. They even moved to a new town to try to make her feel that she was starting a new life, free of the fears that had haunted her. I guess that's why she had so few early memories of her life before the hurricane."

"That *is* a bad scene," admitted George. "You can't blame them for being so overprotective—they must still feel guilty as hell."

"They do, especially with a previous trauma, also maid induced, when a cat or a dog bit her when she was very little. You know she's actually phobic about animals."

"For such overly concerned parents they certainly showed poor judgment in their choice of help!"

"They're aware of that, that's why they insist on choosing the people who care for our kids; as if they're trying to make it up to Alice as well as ensure that their grandchildren don't get messed up unduly."

"How do they like the house, incidentally?"

"Seem to be very happy about everything—which reminds me, why don't you come out for the weekend? Alice is giving a gala cocktail party for her folks. We may be able to put in a word about the clinic with her father."

"I just might do that. In the meantime you check out Barakian and I'll continue with the Soles thing and we'll compare notes. I'll also call the Society for Psychical Research and see how they react to the tale."

After George had left, Bert made his usual bedtime call to see if all was well at the house. Stacey answered explaining that "the old folks" were out for the evening but that all was well. She sounded cheerful; had her father known the reason why, he would have been agonized beyond endurance—yet it was but a prelude of what was to come.

Amy put Lissie to bed at 8 P.M. and went to her room, rather than spend the time with Richard and Stacey, in whose company she felt increasingly uncomfortable. She couldn't decide whether it was from a guilt feeling on her part due to her relations with their father or from an insidious change she thought she sensed in them.

Disappointed in not being able to see her lover the next day, she thought how wonderful the "make-up" time Mrs. Bradley had promised her would be, for Bert said they'd take the two full days "on the town" in Manhattan. Amy took a long shower, shaving her legs and underarms and shampooing and conditioning her hair. Wrapping the bath sheet around herself, she emerged into the pretty bedroom to find Stacey and Richard sitting on the bed. Startled, she automatically pulled the towel more tightly around her slim body and tried to make her voice sound casual as she asked.

"Is there anything wrong? Did Lissie have a bad dream? Does she need me?"

"No, Lissie is sound asleep and the others won't be home till about midnight, so that leaves us with plenty of playtime with Amy."

Chilled by the ominous tone, Amy mustered all the dignity she could, feeling vulnerable standing there in her towel, "Look, Stacey, I've had a long day and I'd like to get to bed now. These are my quarters, so you're off limits.

You know your mother expects you both to respect my privacy."

"My mother also expects her privacy to be respected, Miss Smart Ass," spat out Stacey, "and your fucking my father is an invasion of her right to his privates!"

Richard snickered and took another swig from the whiskey bottle he'd carried upstairs. Leave it to his sister to always have a good put-down.

Her acting skills taking over, Amy tried to brazen it out, but Stacey had apparently done her research well. "O.K., I can't convince you that you're fantasizing. Do you want me to tell your mother that I have to resign and go back home?"

"By no means, I wouldn't deprive my Daddy of his piece of tail. You're an *au pair* girl, so you'll just have to pair up with my baby brother here." And with a sudden lunge, Stacey whipped the towel off the startled girl, leaving her naked to their lascivious stares as they circled her as if she were on display at a stock fair, commenting upon her physical attributes.

On the verge of tears, the girl vainly tried to cover herself. "I warn you, don't touch me or I'll report you both to the police," she choked out.

"Really? And your school will get a letter from my mother about your adultery with my father and your attempts to corrupt her sweet little son. Mother always believes her baby boy, doesn't she?" cooed Stacey.

Her brother nodded eager agreement, whiskey dripping down his chin. Stacey always had the best ideas. That bitch had a hell of a nerve screwing his dad and trying to break up their happy home, leaving them fatherless and his mom unhappy. After a few drinks, it made perfect sense that it was up to him to redeem the family honor. He'd objected at first because Amy wasn't his type at all—too scrawny he'd argued with Stacey—but she had held him to his promise. This was the favor she had demanded in return for

224

promising him her favors the other night, and the two of them held promises as sacred, as they'd been brought up to believe them to be. Reluctantly, he'd agreed.

Amy had frozen at Stacey's threats; she had no doubt that the girl would do exactly what she said, and not only would Bert not be able to help her, she would have destroyed his life as well. A film clip played in her head—of her life repeating her mother's pattern.

"You win, not because anything you've said is true, but because your lies could destroy me and your father." Resignedly she lay on the bed and stared at the ceiling.

Richard stripped quickly; this was his first rape, and he relished new experiences. It was also titillating to go where his father had been. Happily he clambered atop his conquest and forced her knees up and apart, swarming all over her ecstatically. Turning her head away, Amy was horrified to find Stacey crouching by the bed to witness the event, her eyes glinting and her breath panting as she started coaching her brother as if it were a sporting event.

"Atta boy, Richie, give it to the lying bitch, show her you're as good as your old man any day!"

The boy's stamina seemed endless as he drove into her stiffened, resisting body over and over again with a driving force she wouldn't have believe possible in the so-called act of love. He was actually pounding the breath out of her so that she had to gasp for air. Desperately she tried to pretend that it wasn't happening, that it was another bad dream, but his body was too insistent. His long hard fingers lifted her in rhythm to his thrusts to accentuate the visciousness of the assault. After an eternity, he gave a cry and was done. For a long time after the siblings had clattered downstairs, laughing as they left her, Amy lay there staring at the light. She heard the phone ring and knew it was Bert; she could never tell him what had happened. After the clock struck midnight, she heard the others come in from the theater in East Hampton and heard the cheery family good-nights. What would become of her? The night noises of the house were no comfort, they sounded as if they were laughing at her plight in ghostly cackles.

5

It would have been of no comfort to Amy to know that Stacey was getting an even worse time of it than she had. Baby brother had come to collect on his promise as soon as his relatives were asleep. He wasn't worried about the noise, since the walls were so thick; sound only traveled if the doors were left open. Carefully locking Stacey's door behind him, Richard told her in his best "lord of the manor" tone, to get out of bed and strip. Grudgingly she did as she was bid; in an hour or so it would all be over and then they'd be quits. Hopefully after this summer she'd never have to look at the little shit again, except in passing.

"Now, woman," he commanded, "kneel at my feet and honor me."

Grimly she stared up at him—it was going to be one of those nights. She'd gotten through the others, she'd get through this one. Gingerly she did as she was told, but was forced to repeat the "honor" until it was done with proper "reverence." She was then directed to lie back on the bed with her legs apart, but, surprisingly, her brother made no leap upon her body. Instead he told her to caress herself as he watched intently under the bright glow of her reading lamp. "Play with yourself, spread your legs wide so I can see what goes on there."

Unable to take any more humiliation, Stacey tried to climb out of bed, but her brother grabbed her. "A promise is a promise, sis, keep going."

"Get your hands off me, I'll be goddamned if I'm going to

masturbate while you watch as if I'm an experimental animal. Go get your jollies somewhere else!" she hissed venomously.

As she wrapped the sheet around herself, Richard went to get his robe, but instead of leaving, he pulled a photo from the pocket. It was one of the two of them Everett had taken on their first night as club members when they'd found themselves in that first incestuous embrace.

"You either keep your promise tonight or I'll see that Mom and Dad find this tomorrow. Mom never blames me for anything. I'll explain that my big sister led me astray, and be repentant. They'll forgive me because I'm a boy and the victim of my sex urges, but imagine how they'll feel about you?"

Staring at him with total hate, she recognized the truth in what he'd said. Wearily she unwrapped the sheet and let him watch, as in spite of herself she had orgasm after orgasm as her fingers played herself at his instruction. Finally satisfied, he mounted the body he relished most, giving her no more mercy than she had allowed for Amy. It was so good to have her at his command, instead of the other way around, as it had been all their lives. If he'd thought of showing her mercy, the memory of her laughter and pleasure when he'd been gang-raped at the club kept him from doing so. The bitch deserved all that she was getting and more. All those years of patronizing him were over now forever. He was boss and she'd best not forget it; he'd learned a lot from Everett Soles.

When he'd finally left, Stacey staggered to the bathroom and turned on the light. Her body was a mass of bruises and she was painfully sore. She'd have to figure out an excuse for not going to the beach until they'd faded. As she soaked in a hot tub to relieve her aches, she tried to plot a fitting revenge. She hated them all for having forced her into a pattern that had led to this final indignity: her parents for not loving her enough, Amy for taking Daddy, Richard for

227

the rape—and even Lissie for stealing affections that were *hers*. Brooding, she planned vengeance; the guilty *must* be punished.

Feeling that this was the message of the house, that the murderer *must* be punished, Bert was desperately trying to unravel what he felt were clues in the strange happenings at Mulberry. A call from Dr. Barakian's office in Boston said that the doctor would consider seeing Bradley after receipt of a note explaining the urgency of his visit. Bert had responded immediately, stressing that he felt that only Barakian could help him with a problem concerning a child suffering from severe psychosis. Feeling guilty about the deception, he justified himself with the thought that Jessica was still in pain, even though she was dead, or the psychic disturbances at the house wouldn't have been manifest. It seemed somehow fitting to bring it full circle back to the doctor who had originally tried to help her, or was he losing his mind, as he knew George suspected?

On Thursday, Bert decided to continue his research in the Hamptons. Since he couldn't see Amy, and Alice didn't expect him until evening, it seemed a perfect opportunity to check on the convent. Should he be spotted in town, he would say he had found himself free unexpectedly and was coming to surprise the family. But luckily, he met no one who knew him. After parking in the lot behind the convent on Hill Street, he asked for and received permission to speak with Sister Immaculata on a "professional" matter. Surprised that it had been so easy, he was ushered into a cool, austere office, simply but elegantly furnished. Since he was not family, a chaperon sat unobtrusively in the corner reading her missal during the visit.

The Sister's eyes widened in surprise at the sight of him, obviously in recognition; he knew she must have noticed him on her daily rounds past the house. He wondered whom she had been expecting.

"I see you recognized me, Sister. I've often seen you walking by Mulberry."

"Oh, yes, it's one of my favorite rambles, such a lovely view of the sea." Her voice was surprisingly lovely, low and musical in contrast to the homely face redeemed only by lustrous black eyes. "How may I be of help to you, sir? Is it possible you come in search of the true faith?"

Irritated by the terminology, he quickly explained that he came in search of whatever information she could give him about the last owners of the house. Having become intrigued by its sad history, he had been doing some research and had found she was the only one in town to remain faithful to poor Jessica, visiting her regularly at the clinic. He saw her noticeably stiffen as he explained his own connection to the hospital.

"Indeed, sir, there is very little to tell. On my monthly visits I never noted any change in her condition. In fact, there was no reaction whatsoever, but since her mother had been so devout and such a true friend of the Church, I felt it my duty to do what I could for her child. I have said many prayers for the repose of the souls of the entire family, even for their murderer, may God forgive him."

"The hospital records indicated that you brought Jessica a music box. What happened to it when Dr. Barakian returned it to you?"

"I gave it back to the caretaker who had been kind enough to give it to me when I explained that it might somehow cheer the child. But I don't understand these questions, Dr. Bradley. What purpose do they serve? Is it merely for your own curiosity?"

"A bit more than that, Sister. I am a scientist in pursuit of knowledge about personalities that could perpetrate such horror upon their own children. The more I know, the better a psychiatrist I'll be. Could you venture a guess as to how the child escaped the slaughter?"

"One can only assume she had found a hiding place. A house of that sort provided innumerable possibilities for a small child." And rising, she signaled the end of the interview with a gracious nod, before limping quickly out of the room.

Mrs. Hanks lived on the North Sea Road leading away from the village. He was lucky to have found her home, she explained, inviting him into her small, neat house. Her Thursday A.M. had canceled, so she was taking the opportunity to catch up on her own work. Settling him on her couch, she seemed unsurprised by his visit.

"Guess you've come to ask me about poor Nancy," she ventured. "I heard you were asking around about the tragedy and I reckoned you'd find out about me soon enough. What can I tell you, doctor?"

A bit taken aback by her forthright attitude, his first question was obvious: Why would she work in a place that must hold such unhappy memories for her about her slaughtered sister?

"Well, for one, I've never been superstitious, and work isn't that easy to come by, especially at the rates your wife is willing to pay. She was highly recommended by a good customer of mine and, truth be known, I was curious as to what the place was like after all these years. I finished grieving for my sister a long time ago, may God grant her peace," she added crossing her chest. Under Bert's questioning, she admitted that she'd visited the house many times when Nancy had worked there. Mrs. Desmond was described as "right peculiar," but a pleasant woman. The children were all good looking and fun. As for Mr. Desmond, she actually blushed describing how handsome and fascinating he was. As Bert continued to probe, and with his assurance that talking to him was like talking to a

230

priest, she confessed that she'd had an affair with him, as it seemed had every girl in town. He could tell it was something she was still a bit proud of forty years later. She had been but sixteen when "he'd had his way with her" but had discontinued the relations when he had suggested doing "shocking things," of which she firmly refused to reveal the details.

But Nancy had no interest in her employer according to her sister, though she didn't understand how anyone could resist him. It was Garrick the poor girl was in love with, dreaming of a Cinderella romance replete with church wedding and all. "I had begged my parents not to let Nancy stay in the house, but she wanted to something fierce, and 'sides, money was real hard to come by. She always said she could take care of herself, and then too, she was crazy about that little Lissie."

"Lissie?" asked her startled father.

"I mean Jessica of course, but the names are similar, and they do look a lot alike, except for the eyes, what with being the same age as she was then."

There it was again, the resemblance between Jessica and Lissie. Perhaps his baby *was* the catalyst for the strange happenings. Jessica feeling another child was in her place? He had been taking the kids to see too many movies about possession; it was rattling his scientific detachment. It was a known fact that many children of the same age tended to bear a resemblance that faded as they matured.

"Do you know how the child escaped injury?"

"I don't know for sure, but I think I remember Nancy saying something about her playing hide-and-seek in a cubby in the pantry that Nancy had found by accident. It was supposed to be their special secret. Guess she just homed in on it when the trouble started." Truth be known, Mrs. Hanks had sought for and found that very cubby when she had started to work at Mulberry. When Lissie had found her on her hands and knees in the pantry, she had showed her the place inaccessible to anyone but a child, and unable to be seen unless one knew it was there. At Lissie's urging, they had made it their own special secret, but she had now told the father.

"One last question, do you know for sure which of her kittens Jessica was holding when she was taken to the hospital?"

"Of course, I was there when they broke in. I had come to see about Nancy. I watched as they carried the poor lamb out holding that Missy Boo, her favorite kitty. It was a colorful thing, the kind they call a calico."

When Bert pulled into the driveway of Mulberry at 5 P.M., his wife was delighted by his early arrival, but the three adolescents were noncommittal. He was instantly aware of extreme tensions among them; something had transpired of which the other adults seemed unaware, probably because they weren't walking into it cold, as he was doing. He'd have to try to get at the root of the problem when the Arlens were gone. He reflected that he always seemed to be postponing the investigation of family problems for one reason or another; perhaps it was just as well, eventually things always seemed to straighten themselves out.

Alice's news, that George had phoned to say that he would attend the party, delighted him; she had been pleased with his thoughtfulness in arranging to stay at a motel, despite her protests to the contrary. Another houseguest would be difficult with the party plans under way, and George had never been one of her favorites in spite of, or because of, his close relationship with her husband. George was one of the few who refused to worship at her shrine, treating her like an ordinary mortal.

After a fine family dinner, Bert asked Arlen to come into the library for some "professional advice." Settling down with brandy and a cigar, his father-in-law waited for him to begin. On a wild impulse Bert was about to ask whether the older man had known Barakian, since they were of the same generation, but at the last second thought better of it. Bringing up the name would mean discussing the Desmond case; should anyone at the party mention that Mulberry was the Desmond house, Alice's father would be aghast at his son-in-law's having brought his family onto the scene of such carnage, albeit forty years removed. Bert could still recall the Arlens' insistence that he be sure to protect their daughter from any "unpleasantness," before giving their reluctant consent to his suit. They had explained that she had been a hypersensitive child since her trauma, refusing to watch horror movies, or indeed to even read monster comics, preferring instead "Little Lulu." They wished him to continue this compensatory, protective shield. Against his better professional judgment, he had agreed and, as always, had kept his word. He'd felt, and continued to feel for many years, that having Alice was the most important thing in the world. Telling the old man that he'd brought the adored and cosseted girl into this charnel house would hardly endear him in the father's eyes; it would at the very least be considered a major error in judgment.

Skillfully he brought the topic around to the issue of free clinics and was gratified to find that Dr. Arlen was still totally committed to the idea of helping the indigent mentally ill to receive the kind of treatment they so desperately needed and which they almost never received. This accounted for their abnormally and appallingly high rate of institutionalization. He even said that if such a clinic was to be established, he would drive into New York City one or two days a week to offer his services as a pediatric health expert.

"You see, sir, this clinic is not yet a reality, and the major reason is that the money necessary to establish it is tied up in the trust fund you insisted that I set up for Alice as part of a prenuptial contract. Your fears that the marriage might not last were groundless, and I need your permission to regain the monies that are now in Alice's name. I hardly need to tell you that the family, while having to cut back, will hardly suffer." And with an impassioned plea that was worthy of his late father's skill in the pulpit, Bert then asked Arlen's cooperation.

The latter was duly impressed by the missionary zeal of the younger man, but still hesitant. "You don't think that a change in her life-style would be too much of a strain on Alice?"

"No, sir," denied her husband vehemently, "I do not! With your support I'm sure we can get her to agree that one's most important ideal in life is to help those less fortunate than oneself."

"True," murmured her father, "it's something most of us tend to lose sight of as we get older, and I must admit that we always have spoiled our daughter, but she's a good person. I'll speak to my wife, and if she agrees, we'll convince Alice to go along with the project. She's always listened to us. She should be proud to be married to a man who cares for others," and standing up, he shook Bert's hand warmly.

Glowing with the praise, Bert led the way back to the living room to rejoin the family, feeling more confident than he had in months. Alice, at Lissie's insistence, was singing the lullaby "Sweet Afton." As always, she replaced the name Mary with Lissie, which delighted the child—

"My Lissie's asleep by
Thy murmuring stream

234

Flow gently sweet Afton—
Disturb not her dream."

"What a pretty song, my dear, when did you learn it?"

"I don't know, Mother, when I heard the music it seemed that I had always known it. Did you sing it to me when I was a baby?"

Bert didn't catch the uneasy look between her parents. "No, not that I can recall, but perhaps you learned it at school or for one of your piano pieces?"

"Probably, and now, young lady, say good-night to your grandparents, it's past your bedtime! Tomorrow is the big party and you don't want to be too tired to enjoy it."

By 11 P.M. the entire household was quiet. Amy slept fitfully behind a bolted door, while Stacey tried to find a comfortable position for her aching muscles and bruises. Their tormentor slept peacefully dreaming of new conquests of the flesh. His grandparents stayed awake discussing the lullaby, finally deciding that there was nothing ominous about Alice's "remembering" something they were unaware she'd known, but all night long the strains of "Flow Gently Sweet Afton" seemed to weave through their dreams.

The Saturday afternoon cocktail party on the lawn seemed to be a huge success. Despite all the extra help hired for the occasion, Amy was still too busy to spend enough time with Lissie. With her father's assurance that George could be trusted, the little girl took him by the hand and, after an expert glance to make sure that no one was watching, slipped through the hedge to show him the marvels of her animal kingdom. It must have been very hard for such a young child to hold this secret for all these weeks, the man marveled, wondering if it would explain the tensions that he felt accounted for her sleep disturbances— most likely so, was his considered professional opinion.

He enjoyed the antics of the felines as much as Lissie did, promising her in the meantime that good homes would be found for all of them before they had to leave the house, and seriously contemplated taking one or two for himself to cheer his lonely bachelor existence. It was sad for the child to have to part with them, but it was a common enough pattern; many parents refused to allow their children to have pets, or just had them for a summer.

"She took the prettiest one, the one with all the colors, but she promised to take good care of her."

"Who did?" he demanded sharply, suddenly on edge, looking up to see the child's stricken face, both hands pressed over the offending mouth.

"What is it, sweetheart?" he prodded gently, only to be greeted by a wail from the little girl.

"I promised, I promised, it was a secret and I promised that I would never tell. I said 'Cross my heart and hope to die!'" She sobbed, totally distraught.

Pulling her onto his lap, George tried to soothe her, explaining that since he was not a part of the household, the promise did not extend to himself, so that she had actually not broken her promise at all.

"Are you sure, Uncle George? Are you sure that I won't have to die? I would miss my mommy and daddy so much if I had to go to heaven."

"Of course I'm sure," came the response to her tearful query, and the full weight of the majesty of his profession was in that assurance as he calmed the five-year-old. As he held her in the peaceful enclosure, feeling her relax against his chest, a slight sound made him look up in time to catch a glimpse of a little girl just going through the hedge into the field he knew lay beyond it. She turned, as if sensing his gaze, and he saw a beautiful blonde child whose velvet black eyes met his with a sad longing before she seemed to melt into the thicket.

Forcing himself to a calm he did not feel, he put Lissie on the grass to play with her beloved kittens as he strode toward the hedge. Peering through its gaps, he saw nothing on the other side except the mother cat, stalking some movement in the field. Far in the distance he could see a black-robed figure standing and gazing fixedly toward the house.

Thoroughly shaken, George had to wait until almost midnight to see Bert alone. They met in the library, where Bert heard a quick recital of the events in the garden in tense silence, his face visibly paling.

"It was Jessica Desmond, wasn't it, George?" praying that the answer would be negative, but knowing that prayer was in vain.

"I just caught a glimpse of her, but it looked like her photo in the album. She was even wearing what seemed to be the same gingham checked dress, the kind they called a Kate Greenaway in my day."

Breaking the numb silence, Bert asked, "Do you think it's catching, or are you now beginning to believe there's something paranormal going on here?"

"I think I've been converted."

"Did Lissie say anything else?" her father asked.

"No, she was too upset to talk about it, and I certainly wasn't going to pry with the state that she was in. You know how kids that age regard a secret as almost sacred magic. If I hadn't been tuned in, I would probably have thought that she was talking about one of those imaginary friends so many kids have."

"Well, George, I'm getting nervous. What the hell should I do?" came an anguished plea.

"I feel it's O.K. to hang in until you've seen Barakian. There's no point in blowing anything now that Arlen says he's going to back us to get the clinic funds. No harm has come to anyone here and there's no reason why it should. I think your first instincts were sound; it's a way to direct your attention to something that went wrong here that must be righted, so don't panic. We'll get an exhumation order and have a look at the bodies with some sophisticated modern equipment and see if we can play medical detective. If Josephine Tey could find out who killed the princes in the tower four hundred years ago, forty years should be a breeze!"

Buoyed up by his friend's reassurance, Bert felt an excitement that they could indeed fight the forces of whatever evil there might be. "Except for one thing, George—we're not going to wait for an exhumation order and have to explain why to incredulous clerks."

"Why not? What's the alternative?"

"We're going to break into the mausoleum tomorrow night and open that poor, tormented child's coffin ourselves."

The next day everything seemed to go according to their hastily arranged plan of the night before. The Arlens were seen off after breakfast, and Bert told his wife that he would leave late that same evening. George bought the necessary tools for their "caper" at the hardware store on Main Street, which was open until 1 P.M. on summer Sundays to accommodate the well-known vagaries of the summer folk.

The hard part was to tell Amy that their "honeymoon" in the city would have to be postponed until the following week. Despite all the tension he was experiencing, Bert was hurt to sense that she seemed almost relieved by the news. Sensitive as always to his moods, she lied effortlessly,

238

"Oh, that's so much better, I would have had my period then and what sort of honeymoon would that have been?" Her smile as she said this made him want to forget everything and drag her off with him somewhere to a tropical island where they would live on coconuts and let the world go by. Sighing, he resisted his impulses, as always, or as almost always, and went off to be devoted husband and father for the rest of the day. With Arlen in his camp now, he couldn't take a chance on upsetting Alice.

Amy had indeed been relieved by the postponement; she felt it a reprieve, giving her the extra week to decide what to do about Stacey and Richard. The former ignored her completely, but the latter leered at her every time no one was around. She had an uncomfortable feeling, sometimes reaching panic proportions, that he would try to rape her again with the threat of blackmail. She knew that no matter what, she could never again submit; somehow she'd have to find a way out of the situation.

Mrs. Bradley was delighted when her *au pair* girl said she would not be taking her time off that week, since there was nothing she wanted to do. She was oblivious to the looks her two eldest exchanged, but Amy wasn't. They were obviously puzzled. Good, let them chew on that awhile, it might give her the breathing space that she needed.

By prearrangement, Bert and George parked at opposite ends of the old Catholic cemetery behind the church. It had been "cased" during a morning walk, so they were able to go directly to the Desmond mausoleum. The lock was a simple matter to force with the tools George had brought, and once inside, they used his other purchase, a powerful flashlight. They stood this on end as they worked to pull out the drawer marked "Jessica," the brass plaque noting the pitifully brief years of her life on earth. They were surprised to note a vase of fresh flowers in a wall niche—pink roses. Their shadows played on the walls and ceiling of the tomb as they went about their grim task to the accompaniment of Bert's muttered prayers. It took all their combined strength to finally wrest the coffin free from its shelf, even with the tools. Twenty minutes later, after the application of much oil, it slid free. Looking at each other, wordlessly they lifted the lid. The light trembled, played within; they opened a canvas body bag to find a desiccated little body, pathetically and grotesquely revealed in its child's finery of four decades ago—hand-smocked, pink-checked frock, long white silk socks, and white kid Mary Jane shoes. A beautiful pink ribbon lay amid the long, silken, black curls. Bert clipped a lock of that hair, and the two men gently slid the coffin back into place. They pulled the heavy door of the mausoleum shut behind them and went to their separate cars. Too shaken for speech, they wanted only to get away, to escape that sunken, blackened parody of a human face and body. They'd be discussing this at length later.

A few minutes after the cars had left, a figure swathed in black emerged from behind a large tombstone and tentatively pushed against the Desmond door, surprised that the men had not sealed it again. Once inside, it lighted a candle, those used in memory of the dead, and studied the drawers. Jessica's was easy to slide out now and once more the lid was pried up. A sharp hissing sound could have been heard, followed by an inhuman growl as the flickering light revealed what the men had seen. The corpse was unrecognizable, but Jessica Desmond's short platinum curls could not have turned into that thick head of long black curls— not even after forty years in the grave.

Part **VIII**

The forty-five-minute shuttle flight from La Guardia to Boston carried Bertram Bradley to his Wednesday afternoon appointment with Dr. Barakian, whose confirmation of that meeting had arrived on Monday morning. Any guilt he might have felt about the deception he had played was completely overcome by his determination to get to the bottom of whatever ghoulish deception the good doctor had played in 1939. He carried with him an envelope with the lock of hair taken from the corpse in Jessica Desmond's coffin; how pathetic to be buried all these years in someone else's designated resting place! Where was Jessica? Who was in her coffin? Who was sending fresh flowers to the mausoleum every week? This latter fact had been ascertained by a phone call to the cemetery's caretaker, who said that they arrived every Friday and he placed them in the niche. It had been a custom for the thirty years of his tenure, and he didn't know for how long before. Given the name of the florist in Southampton, the woman proved to have no information. Cash arrived every month and, according to the records, had been arriving since Jessica's "death." There was no return address and the canceled postmark was the General Post Office in Manhattan. The amount of money had increased over the years to meet the rising price of fresh roses. Could Barakian be sending them? Bert had to lay the ghosts and quiet his own increasing unease of soul and spirit.

He felt somewhat like the avenging angel his father used

to describe from his pulpit as he gazed on the landscape of his native Cape Cod below. As always he was amazed at how the aerial view faithfully replicated the maps he'd studied in school, maps made long before the air age. How had the cartographers been able to do it? Momentarily distracted, he started to recall his school days as the plane began the descent to Logan Airport. During the cab ride to the hospital, Bert tried to order his thoughts, to choose the exact phrasing he would use when confronting Barakian with his crimes, which might include murder or, to put it more kindly, euthanasia. Whose little girl was in that coffin? Had her parents been aware or part of the deception? His brooding reverie was jolted as the cab came to a halt at the clinic. Shaking himself back into the present, he gathered up his belongings and went inside to confront the long-sought-for quarry.

Dr. Shalom, as he said he preferred to be called, was a stocky, white-haired gentleman of medium height. Dark eyes sparked with youth and intelligence from a tanned, seamed countenance. The proffered handshake was strong and warm, and Bert found it difficult not to respond instantly to the charisma, despite the wary antagonism with which he'd entered the room. It was easy to see how the man had become a legend in his brief tenure at the Payne Whitney.

The accented voice was charming as he led Bert into a comfortable modern office that had been reserved for their use. "I am curious as to how you found me, Dr. Bradley, and more curious as to why you searched so diligently, but since my time, and I'm sure yours, is quite limited, I shall

242

have to repress that natural curiosity and concentrate on the case you said was a matter of such great urgency. I find it almost impossible to refuse to help a child in such distress as you described in your note, as you apparently already know."

Settling into the large leather armchair, he waited for Bert to begin. At the evident hesitancy he prompted, "The child is a female, age five years, and in a severe schizophrenic state that you believe is chronic."

Taking his best diver's breath, Bert made the plunge, "Her name is Jessica Desmond and I would like to know exactly what happened to her in August of 1939, Dr. Barakian," he continued as the other man froze in his chair, "and I'd also like to know whose body is in Jessica's coffin in her family mausoleum in Southampton." As he spoke he took the lock of black hair and placed it on the desk between them, where it gleamed with a baby fine luster as Barakian's gaze riveted upon it.

Pulling himself together, but with a visible effort, the doctor looked at Bert intently. "I do not know what game it is that you think you have come here to play. I was kind enough to take time from a very busy schedule to help a child in distress, and here you come to question me about a child long dead. Since there is no cause for blackmail, I would appreciate your stating your business as quickly as possible and going on your way."

Impressed by the man's composure Bert pressed on. "Sir, I have the utmost respect for you and for the work you have done, but if Jessica Desmond is dead, why is her body not in the family crypt?"

"My dear young man, that is something of which I have no knowledge. The last I saw of that unfortunate child, she was in a coffin that was being taken to its final resting place. It is of course possible that the funeral parlor was remiss, or that they are involved in this mystery that is so deeply troubling you that you would go to such lengths to find and confront me in this manner. Whatever the case, I can simply tell you that I know nothing more of this matter, so I must ask you to leave and allow me to go about my business of helping the living. There are many little children in Israel who are waiting for my return. I have come here to find new ways of helping to relieve their bad dreams; I must leave you to yours." With a brief, but courteous nod, he stood up and walked quickly out of the room, firmly closing the door behind him.

The accuser was too stunned by the rapid dismissal to move or to try to stop him from leaving. He knew it would be useless; this was a man who would brook no opposition. Staring at the chair the doctor had vacated, Bert wondered if he could possibly have been lying to him. He had spoken with such firmness and authority, yet with kindness. Could the solution have been as simple as the funeral parlor mixing up coffins? But that still would not explain the mystery of the delivery of fresh pink roses every week. He had finally found the person whom he was certain could solve the problem of the strange occurrences at Mulberry, only to find himself dismissed like a schoolboy.

It was, as Bert explained to an anxious George that evening, as if he had been excused from the presence of royalty; there was no discussion or rebuttal permitted. As his friend gazed at him skeptically, he continued, "I sensed that it would be fruitless to pursue him. I know that you're thinking that *you* would have pinned him down and gotten the details out of him, but I assure you that is not the case, though you'll just have to take my word for it. I have a very strong feeling that he'll be incommunicado for the rest of his stay in the United States."

"You could have threatened him with going to the police."

"And how would I have explained our illegal and unlawful entry? Besides, a man who has done so much to alleviate the sufferings of humanity deserves better treatment than that."

George apparently agreed, since he changed the topic. "Do you think his story of a body switch could be true?"

"It might be, but I don't see how it could be possible. How many white children's coffins would a small establishment be handling in a day? And I fail to see how such a switch could be of benefit to anyone. In the final analysis, I would have to conclude that the man is lying, not for any venal purpose, but to protect someone else."

"The one man in the world who could solve the mystery and he refuses to talk. Well, Bert, where do you suggest we go from here?"

Deciding to approach the problem scientifically, the men started trying to devise an algebraic formula that might help them isolate some of the unknowns. A phone call at midnight disturbed them at their work in Bert's office. Praying that it wasn't bad news from the house, Bert answered at the first strident ring that shattered the stillness of his home. It was a boy's voice, asking to speak to his sister, Amy Cullum. When Bert offered to take a message, the flat tone stated, "Tell her that she's got to come home first thing she can. Our pa is dead and I got to call the cops now."

Before Bert could pose any questions, he hung up.

At 8 A.M. Bert walked into the kitchen of his summer home to find Lissie and Amy breakfasting together while the rest of the household apparently slept. His daughter's exuberant shout of welcome gave Amy a chance to pull herself together at the surprise of seeing her lover. She

245

sensed something was amiss as Bert asked the little girl to go upstairs to tell her mother that he was there.

Quickly he told Amy that there was bad news, but it was a relief to her to hear of her father's death. She had been afraid that he was going to tell her that they could no longer see one another or, worse, that they'd been found out. Since Bert had no details and the Cullums no phone, the girl went upstairs at once to pack her bag, accepting her employer's offer to drive her to La Guardia Airport to catch a plane for Springfield.

When Alice came down sleep-eyed, but happy to see him, Bert told her of Amy's plight and of his decision to drive her to the airport. He could see her struggling with her emotions. Of course it was a shame for the girl to suffer such a shock, but uppermost he could see that she was annoyed at having her summer so inconveniently interrupted. Sighing inwardly at her inherent selfishness, he explained that he'd be back on Friday morning. His wife nodded her assent, her mind busily at work planning on how she would get an *au pair* replacement so late in the summer.

When Amy came down, pale but composed, Alice made all the proper noises and kissed her good-bye. Lissie cried as much in sadness over parting with Amy as in worry about her beloved cats. Despite the turmoil of her own emotions, Amy recognized this and managed to whisper to the child that she could leave food in the usual place each day. The kittens were old enough now to hunt for food, as the mother cat had been teaching them to do, and added that her Daddy would take care of everything when he got back. Brightening at once, Lissie nodded and hugged Amy as if she'd never let her go.

Assuring the little girl that he'd be back the next day, Bert drove off with Amy, as his wife and daughter waved good-bye from the front porch. They were all too distracted to notice that Sister Teresa Immaculata was standing in the

246

shadow of a huge elm, staring at them intently, as if trying to puzzle out this latest change in the Bradley household's pattern.

En route to the airport, Amy explained that there would be no possibility of her getting back to the Hamptons; she was her mother's sole support in this time of trouble. Her relief at having escaped from Richard and Stacey even outweighed her sadness at leaving Bert. As for her so-called father, his death was a longed-for deliverance. Before she boarded the shuttle, Bert insisted that she take not only her week's wages, but an additional one hundred dollars, "Just in case." Neither one realized that Ibram Cullum's death could be attributed to that first hundred dollars that Bert had given Amy, half of which she had so generously sent home to her mother in that money order at the beginning of the summer.

Harley had decided to do it all by himself—less chance of getting caught that way, as the TV explained it. His pa was terrorizing the kids; they were used to his being drunk, but now he rarely left the house. The little ones were scared of him and his ma looked worse every day. He could hear her crying at night when she thought they were all asleep. Stealthily he followed his father around the house trying to determine the when, where, and how of the operation. Seemed the old bastard went down to the cellar every day to stare at that old mattress he'd put down in the corner, then he'd go up to the bedroom and do things that made Ma cry out in pain as he laughed and said to her over and over, "My pa always said, 'If you don't use it, you lose it,' and I got no intention of losing this, so keep on working at it, woman!"

The day the welfare check next arrived was when—he got drunker than usual then; the how was a mighty push from his firstborn son; and the where was the cellar steps. By the time Harley "found" him at midnight, he was quite dead of a broken neck. He called the phone number Ma had memorized, to tell Amy, and then he'd called the police. They were very nice; no one seemed a bit surprised. People wondered how he'd lasted this long. By the time Amy arrived, the townspeople were helping the family and planning a decent funeral out of respect for the widow. Fortunately Ibram had been a veteran, so the army buried him free of charge at the cemetery in Springfield. By the end of the week, the Cullums found themselves in relative luxury. The house was unmortgaged, and they were now eligible for Social Security payments as well as a ten-thousand-dollar V.A. insurance policy. They had never been so well off financially, so Amy had a phone installed with her last week's wages.

Arrangements were truly finalized, she felt, only when the abortion her mother had agreed to was over. They told the kids that their mother had made a mistake, she hadn't really been pregnant after all. They couldn't have cared less, but Harley gave them a glance wise beyond his years. He was now the man of the house and he'd have to take care of them all.

Thursday evening found George and Bert continuing with their algebraic quest for the solution to the mysterious happenings at Mulberry. They had shifted the emphasis to the search for Margaret Soles, the only possible winner in this insane sweepstakes. George's hunt for the source of the money for the roses had come up against a solid brick wall. There was no way to check cash sent from the Manhattan General Post Office on West Thirty-fourth Street in a small business envelope with a typed address. If Margaret Soles wasn't behind all of the weird occurrences, then they *were* supernatural, caused by unquiet spirits. George was willing to go back to the original hypothesis, that since Evan hadn't been the murderer, he had enough energy from beyond the grave to point up the fact that his wife had been responsible for the acts for which he'd been blamed.

"Why not?" said George. "We saw from the poor woman's diary that he refused to forgive her for having been raped and bearing an illegitimate child. He'd be a lot madder for a lot longer for being labeled as a killer of his family."

"That's the easiest out, and I agree that first hunches are usually correct," responded his partner, "but that still wouldn't account for the disappearance of Jessica and/or her body, or for the rose money coming in every week for thirty-seven years."

"Then perhaps it's a combination of the natural and paranormal?" Though throwing this out as a casual possibility, George had unwittingly hit it on the nose. Too tired to pursue the topic any longer, the two men broke for the evening. When Bert fell asleep it was to dream he'd found Amy dancing with a toothless old man whom upon closer inspection had proved to be himself!

Arriving back at Mulberry on Friday morning as promised, he was determined to try to put aside his hunt and just enjoy his family for the weekend. He certainly owed them his undivided attention for once, but thoughts of Amy kept betraying his good intentions. Before she'd left, she'd reminded him how upset Lissie would be worrying about her kittens. Just like her, he mused fondly, her father dead and she still thought about her responsibility to his little girl, so despite his own problems he'd worked out a solution, which he explained to her in the garden. George had agreed to take two of them, and Ms. Warren had volunteered to take the mother cat. That would leave Lissie with one kitten until the week before they left, one had been promised to Nedra, who as always found it impossible to deny any request her future employer made of her. The best part was that Lissie would be able to visit all of them when she got back to the city, and her mother need never know about the deception they'd practiced the whole summer. The child's delight was so palpable that Bert decided that all of the effort had been worthwhile. Neither one of them mentioned the missing calico. Remembering George's description of his encounter with an apparition in the garden enclosure, Bert shuddered despite the bright August sunshine, and scooped up his child to get ready for a day at the beach.

The day at the club was pleasant but uneventful, except for Astrid being her usual loathsome self. Her innuendos to Bert were of a nature to be patently obscene; sometimes it sounded as if she were trying to blackmail him into sleeping with her—another scalp for her belt. He avoided her as much as possible, to Alice's amusement. It was Alice's smug reaction to her attempts to entice Bert into an affair that enraged Astrid; that bitch would get her comeuppance— thinking that she was so great her husband wouldn't leave her bed. Wait till she found out that he was rejecting Astrid because he preferred girls of his older daughter's age. And that was another tale she could tell; from what she'd heard from her hostesses' children, the Bradley kids were involved with the most unsavory crowd in the country. That Stacey wasn't with her family today; she must be whoring somewhere else, or perhaps that brother of hers was pimping for her.

Mercifully oblivious to the woman's savage wrath, Alice was delighted to find someone at the club who knew of a possible *au pair* girl to care for Lissie for the few remaining weeks of the season. Richard, listening to the conversation, fervently hoped she'd be stacked, not a bag of bones like the last one. His prayers were more than answered when Vanessa Hodges showed up to be interviewed the next morning. She was built! Though she was not the type Alice would normally think of hiring, she seemed sweet and her references were excellent in praising her honesty and dependability. The family she had been working for had had to leave early, so she was unexpectedly available at once, which, after all, was a major consideration. The only objections were her age, she was only fifteen, and the fact that she seemed a bit slow, but she was immediately taken with Lissie who seemed to like her, so she was told to report for work on Monday morning. Hearing her husband and son joshing about the girl's obvious physical attributes, Alice wondered if she hadn't been too hasty. She was knowingly bringing a blatant sexual temptation into the household, but she consoled herself with the thought that it couldn't do any damage in the few weeks left before they went home. The two men, however, did not escape a scathing lecture on their male chauvinist piggishness for discussing Vanessa as a sex object. Duly chastened, they apologized, assuring Alice that it was just a hangover from preenlightenment days. Mollified, she forgave them, "this time."

After a rather strained family dinner due to the fact that the two older children were obviously at odds, Bert tried to talk to them in his capacity as a father as well as a counselor, but they just admitted that they had quarreled over something that probably "wasn't very important," but would prefer "if you don't mind, Dad," to work it out themselves. Alice agreed, saying it was hardly the first time, and wouldn't be the last, that the two were on bad terms.

"We were both only children, Bert," his wife reminded him, "so we find it difficult to understand their emotions within the family. Your profession makes you hypersensitive to these situations," and she couldn't help the snide aside, "that is when you find time to spend with your own family."

Deciding not to chance another quarrel, Bert changed the

subject and they spent a pleasant enough evening. It was a few days before Alice's period, the time when she was always at her most amorous. Bert's very creditable performance was as much due to his need to compensate for his feeling of guilt for not wanting to be there, as it was to his natural desire to flaunt the fact that his sexual prowess was not waning with the years, something Alice sometimes teased him with. Both finally physically satisfied, they slept deeply. It was Bert who first heard noises downstairs this time. At first he thought the kids were still up, but a look at the luminous dial on the clock showed that it was 3 A.M. Listening carefully, he was filled with a sense of dread as he realized that it was a child's voice he was hearing; Lissie must be sleepwalking again. Pulling on his pajama bottoms, he strode downstairs in bare feet as the sounds of the song from Lissie's music box grew louder in his ears in the otherwise silent house.

He could see her at the cellar door now, tugging at it as Alice had described the act to him weeks ago, when he thought she was hallucinating. The child was calling in a frightened, pleading tone.

"Here I am, Mommy, please come upstairs now, I'm scared!" But a voice from the blackness that yawned as the door opened called, "My baby, my poor baby."

The tableau could have taken no more than a few seconds as Bert froze at the realization of what he was seeing: It must be a reenactment of what had taken place the night of the storm. He made a mad dash to grab his daughter before she tumbled down those treacherous steps into the chasm of horror below, and as his hand brushed her nightgown, she turned toward him, teetering on the edge of that void. He saw that she was carrying a calico kitten and he also saw, as those velvety brown eyes streaming with tears gazed at him in surprise and misery, that it was Jessica Desmond who literally melted into the darkness as his fingers touched her pathetic form.

252

He sat on the stair landing for a long time, breathing deeply and trying to sort out his thoughts, pretending he was discussing the situation with George. But this was the proverbial last straw; he'd have to bring psychic investigators into the house to help to interpret these messages from the past. Trying to behave normally, he made the rounds of the house; all seemed in order. When he went into Lissie's room, she was sleeping soundly, her music box in its usual place near her bed. As he moved to cover her, he smiled at the sight of the teddy bear sitting on her pillow. When he picked it up to put it on her toy shelf, the head rolled off. It had been severed from the body with such surgical precision that the cut hadn't been noticeable.

True to his word, despite his problems, Bert delivered two kittens and a cat to their new owners in Manhattan, and one teddy bear to the forensic lab at the hospital. The lab could find nothing except a set of child's fingerprints; they did not match those on Lissie's picture book, which he'd brought for possible identification. As he told George that evening,

"If I could find Jessica Desmond's fingerprints, I'd be willing to bet we'd have a match."

They were in George's apartment watching the kittens gambol as they adjusted to their new home. He nodded, "You're probably right. I've already contacted the Society for Psychical Research—I have an appointment with them tomorrow. I told them they could see you on Thursday morning; I know you can't disrupt your schedule any more. You should have heard their interest when I said that we were both psychiatrists—they almost fell through the telephone."

"I can well imagine," replied Bert wryly. "They probably figure we're ready for the funny farm after catching something from our clientele."

"But," he continued on a sobering note, "I have a terrible feeling that time is running short—that if this situation isn't resolved before summer's end it will move back to the city with us, and the psychic manifestations will get worse, or even dangerous."

"Do you have any reason you could think of to explain this feeling, or is it one of your male intuitions?"

"You can call it that," he replied as George looked at him sharply. "I'm convinced that whatever it is has somehow become entwined with my family, and will stay with us until the forces at work are satisfied." After a brief but brooding silence, the men returned to their work, concentrating upon the Soles investigation.

Despite all of their connections and Nedra's hard work, all they had so far was the woman's deposition in her claim for the Desmond estate. She refused to answer letters addressed to her box number, and her attorney refused to answer their calls or letters requesting an interview. Sorting through Nedra's painstaking notes, George suddenly jumped to his feet scattering two startled kittens who had been curled up on his ample lap for a nap.

"Eureka! Hey, I never in my life thought I'd have occasion to use that word!"

"What is it, what clue did you find?"

"The one that's been here all along—the woman has no Social Security number!"

"That's the problem, you idiot, not the solution, that's why we haven't been able to get a trace on her."

"Some Sherlock you are. We've been stymied because we've been unable to recognize that a lack of a clue is a clue in itself. Think about it, what categories of people do *not* have Social Security numbers?" George looked on, smugly superior as he watched Bert's puzzled face.

The latter started a mumbled enumeration and as he got to "nuns," he stopped, mouth agape. "Sister Teresa Immaculata is Margaret Soles!"

"You got it, Bert. That would account for all of her visits to Jessica in the hospital—the child was her half sister; Evalynn Desmond was mother to them both. It would also account for the watch she keeps on your house; there may be documents she's searching for, like the ones you found detailing the events of her birth, which she needs for her case."

Catching the mounting excitement, Bert leaped to his feet, "She may have been the one who switched bodies, or perhaps she killed Jessica—or," he added more thoughtfully, "maybe she stashed her away somewhere. Any of those would be reason enough for the unquiet spirits in that house trying to make contact; perhaps Jessica's spirit is the moving force."

Quickly the men decided upon a plan of action. Before confronting the nun, George would get the dossier on her religious career from his friend at the Catholic diocese. Bert would work with the psychic investigators, and with luck, in a week they should be well on their way to at least part of the solution to the problem at Mulberry. When Bert left to return home in time to receive Amy's phone call, he felt better than he had in weeks. Once this situation was solved he'd work out a plan to get up to South Hadley to see his beloved.

While he was listening to her dulcet tones, there was an equally anxious phone call being completed to a home in Connecticut.

"Melkonian, is that you? Barakian here."

The stunned silence fanned over the phone lines. The soft voice continued, switching over to Armenian. "I have been

255

trying to reach you for days. Luckily I was able to avail myself of a computer center here in Cambridge and the services of a master technician who traced you through your change in registry number." This last was added as if to give the man on the other end time to pull himself together, and he did.

"What is it, Josef? Why after all these years? What has happened?" The hushed, anxious tone made it obvious that he did not wish to be overheard.

"It is imperative that we speak. When can you come here?"

It was agreed that they would meet on Friday, the earliest Gregory Arlen could get away without raising his wife's suspicions or disrupting his practice. "And please, should you have to call again, if Ilana answers, hang up. I'm sure that she too would instantly recognize your voice."

"I understand, Karakin. You of all people should remember that I am hardly the one to seek to cause distress."

"Of course, but I know that your call can bode nothing good, there is only one possible reason for it. Good-night then, till Friday."

Ilana Arlen was accustomed to calls at all times of the day and night in her fifty years as the wife of a conscientious doctor. She hadn't even glanced up from her favorite news program when he'd gone into the den to take the call, so as not to disturb her. He shook his head at her glance of inquiry as he reentered the living room; no, he would not have to go out now. But, he explained to his wife, he'd been called to Boston on Friday as a consultant in a very delicate pediatric cardiovascular case that might entail his spending the weekend there.

Cheerfully she accepted this disruption in their plans, proud as always that her husband's expertise was so widely sought after and so generously given. She wished for her child and grandchildren a marriage as wonderful as hers.

256

They had everything: love, respect, wealth, health, and happiness. Truly life was good.

Richard Bradley felt the same as he lay atop Vanessa Hodges in Amy's former quarters, where they were supposedly watching TV. She was hot stuff, he thought happily as he ran his hands over her heavy body. Not Rubenesque like Stacey, but a wide peasant's body, solid, with thick breasts. He felt her stiffen beneath him as he tried to work his hands under her shirt to get at them.

"Uh uh, Richie, none of that. I'm a nice girl and this is as far as I go."

This far was just being allowed to lie face-to-face on top of her, and to caress her above the waist through her clothing. She had explained to him that she took her virginity very seriously—it was to bring to her husband on their wedding night. Richard had other plans, but pretended to go along with her restrictions. Each night he'd gotten her just a bit more excited than the night before, after having started with a respectful good-night kiss and a whisper of how attracted he was by her beauty. He'd gotten her to the point now where she was getting pretty good at dry-humping; he could feel her mounting excitement as he rubbed his hardness against her crotch through the layers of her jeans and panties. He had even convinced her that French kissing was not a mortal sin. Pretty soon the bitch would have something besides his tongue rammed down her throat. He'd been taking lessons in seduction from that master, Everett Soles.

Having been prepped by George Webber, the psychic investigators listened to Bert's eyewitness accounts gravely and courteously. Ann and Martin Jenkins were a husband-and-wife team with twenty years of experience. They were impressed by the thoroughness of Bert's dossier on the case and especially by the laboratory reports. It was also exciting to be working with a man of science, the type who would so often be their adversary when they tried to attribute events to paranormal phenomena.

"No," he was saying, "the hospital did not have a record of Jessica's fingerprints, but I'm sure they would have matched those on the teddy bear."

"How about the door where you saw her apparition? There might have been a set there that matched."

"Mrs. Jenkins, do ghosts leave fingerprints?"

They smiled at the rising note of incredulity in his voice; it was common enough. "We have found cases where they actually did," answered her husband, "but don't ask me how. Unfortunately in our work we come up with few solutions, it's mostly a matter of verifying the questions. Yes, that an area we label supernatural or paranormal does exist. Most of the time, however, we seek and find rational explanations for what seem to be psychic phenomena."

"But you have found cases where the only answer is 'ghosts'?"

They nodded in unison as Bert stared at them. They were a pleasant-looking couple, hardly the weirdos he'd half expected. As a matter of fact they were nondescript; Martin looked like an accountant, and Ann could be your so-called average housewife. They were carefully dressed and groomed, well aware that the normalcy of the appearance had to balance what most people felt was the abnormality of their work.

"Yes," Ann picked up, "in the past ten years we have found three instances where despite rigorous, in-depth scientific research, there was no other explanation for our cases than ghosts—as opposed to poltergeists, telekinesis, astrophysical manifestations, psychokinesis, or any other quasi-scientific terminology with which the general public has become familiar due to the plethora of movies and TV shows on the topics."

As if in answer to Bert's as yet unspoken question, her husband added, "There is a theory that nothing is ever lost on the ether, that everything that has ever existed in the universe is permanently imprinted on the time-space continuum. For usually inexplicable reasons, there is sometimes a time warp and the past is unaccountably projected onto the present. In the case you've just related, the reason could be that a force from the past is actively seeking to get through—for justice or perhaps vengeance. It would be very strong and determined emotion to give the kind of manifestations you've been describing."

"Is there any other solution?"

"I think Dr. Webber said he'd mentioned telesthesia to you. That's another possibility where someone who had witnessed an event has the ability, usually on an unconscious or subconscious level, to project images of what they have seen that are so strong that they are visible to some sensitive people, almost as if they were watching a film clip. As for what makes some people sensitive to these images and others not—well, as of now we have no definite answers."

Much impressed with this team's logic and presentation of the facts, Bert felt relaxed as he went on. He'd been afraid he'd sound like an idiot, but these people treated the situation as he treated his cases. It was a profession with a discipline of its own. But how could anyone in his household project images of what they had never viewed? The answer had to lie elsewhere.

"Can you give me a clue as to why it's happening to my family? I managed to ascertain that no one else who ever rented the house had any 'sightings.' Everyone stayed the full time, and several even rented for consecutive years. According to the agent, most people ask if they can buy the place."

"There are innumerable reasons," (Ann Jenkins now took over,) "it could be a similarity of factors in combinations, such as weather, the ages of the people in the house, the stresses among or between them, the sexes of the people of specific ages—the permutations are considerable. From the information you've given us, you do have several similarities between your family and the Desmonds in terms of ages and sexes of the people in the house. The five-year-old could be the catalyst, since the unaccounted-for victim was that age when the horror took place. It could even be linked somehow to the cats. And to be perfectly honest, we may never find out. But I know that I speak for my husband too when I say we'd certainly like to have a crack at the investigation!"

Martin Jenkins nodded in vigorous agreement, but Bert was loathe to tell his family that he was bringing people into the house to look for ghosts, especially for Lissie's sake. He shuddered to think of the effects of that on her psyche, but the team explained that it would be impossible to get a proper "reading" unless all the factors were the same in the house as when the sightings had taken place.

Anxious to begin the investigation, but hesitant about the reaction of his family, Bert promised to call the Martins as soon as he and George had worked out an explanation that would seem plausible and nonthreatening. They left assuring him of how eager they were to get started, that

260

Mulberry sounded as if it would prove to be the most exciting case they had yet encountered. Being called in by two psychiatrists who had seen apparitions of the dead was hardly an everyday occurrence and would give them status in presenting the case to the public. What it would do for the careers of the doctors was a moot point.

When they left his office, Bert felt a tremendous sense of elation; help was on the way and he and George were *not* crazy. There was an entire scientific apparatus to deal with problems such as the ones they had been encountering, run by people as rigorously and scientifically trained as themselves.

In another office in Boston, however, a meeting was taking place that would have tempered his elation. Abba ben Shalom, aka Josef Barakian, sat facing Gregory Arlen, aka Karakin Melkonian. They regarded each other with great curiosity; it had been thirty-seven years since they had last met. Both had aged well and looked younger than the septuagenarians they were. In both minds was the same memory—their last meeting in October of 1939. Briefly, Barakian outlined the situation; a young psychiatrist had come to him to find out about the child they had saved so long ago, insisting that he had evidence that she was not dead.

"I told him that I had no knowledge of the so-called body switch and that Jessica Desmond was dead—which in a sense is absolutely true."

"Did he believe you?"

"I'm not sure. I think I convinced him that I had no knowledge of the body in the coffin, but I don't know if he is continuing the search. Even if he is, I don't see how he could find anything, we covered our tracks perfectly. There are no records left anywhere of the other child." A look of deep pain crossed Arlen's face at this, but paramount in the minds of both men was the need to continue to protect the

261

child they had miraculously saved all those years ago by a combination of luck, God, and genius.

"But why did he start the investigation? That makes no sense at all."

"I didn't even want to ask, I pretended that the matter was of no interest to me, but I am sure that he will not stop. He seemed to be a man of great determination. I've since checked his record in the field and found that he is highly respected."

"Who is he and where is he?" demanded Arlen intently.

"He's in New York City and his name is Bradley, he . . ." Barakian stopped at the look on his friend's face and at the involuntary cry of despair that issued from deep inside him. All was lost! Astounded, his colleague learned that Jessica Desmond was married to this Bradley, who was in fact none other than Arlen's son-in-law!

After the initial shock had worn off, the men got down to the business at hand: How were they going to continue to protect Jessica Desmond, aka Alice Arlen Bradley? Her father picked up the phone and first called his wife to explain that the case was more complex than anticipated, and, therefore, he would have to stay overnight. He saw no point in telling her the shocking news until the last possible moment. Let her happiness last until then. The next call was to Bert's answering service—he did not want to take the chance of calling Mulberry in case Alice should overhear what was going to be a cryptic phone call. He knew that Bert would understand when he checked with the service that it was a highly personal matter, and would telephone away from anyone's hearing. It was with a sense of dread that he awaited the return call.

262

7

It seemed to be a simple enough request from a man who had done so much for the organization, so the young clerk in the diocese office allowed George access to the personnel files of Sister Teresa Immaculata without consulting his superiors. After all, what harm could it do? It was all there, as Webber recounted his story to Bert that evening.

"Margaret Ryan, who calls herself Soles in her deposition for claim to the Desmond fortune, was an adopted child, parents unknown. Her birthplace and date exactly fit those mentioned in Evalynn Desmond's diary, where she describes the birth of her illegitimate child. On records for exclusive church information, a Sister Mary Joseffa is listed as the person responsible for bringing the nameless foundling to a local parish priest in Vermont. There is no doubt in my mind that Margaret Ryan Soles is Evalynn's daughter."

Ignoring Bert's quick intake of breath, George Webber continued. "It was just one of those strange, but unending quirks of fate that brought her to the very convent where Sister Joseffa was concluding her own life—the victim of cancer. As I would reconstruct the scene, the old nun was reminded of the clubfooted child she had secretly delivered when she noted the novice's heavy limp. In delirium brought on by pain, she may well have talked about Evalynn and the baby. I'm sure that as death approached, the incident and her deceptions preyed heavily upon her. What else would there have been to disturb her peace of mind in an otherwise tranquil, blameless life?"

"Until the very end, I would bet my professional reputation that she was unsure of the wisdom of her decision. She probably talked about it as her mind wandered, or she may even have made her last confession to the young nun in fear that the priest wouldn't reach her in time. At any rate, this

Margaret Soles is a very intelligent woman, according to her records, and she would have put the facts together. That she did is evidenced by her transferring to Southampton, where she had somehow been able to trace Evalynn Ambrose Desmond—which would not have been difficult. Both names had been in the Southampton directories since well before her birth and remained there until the hurricane of 1938. The Sister could very well have mentioned that was where Evalynn was living when she'd last heard from her, or she could have sneaked a look at the office files, which would show a regular pattern of letters received from Mrs. Desmond at Mulberry. I've seen their files, they're meticulously kept. So she came to seek her mother, but from Evalynn's diary there was no mention of her having announced herself. What she was waiting for, only Margaret herself knows, and that is what we have to find out. It seems that she is at the heart of the matter."

Bert gazed at his friend with frank awe. "Talk about historical detection! That sounds masterful to me. I'd venture that as Immaculata she was biding her time waiting for what she felt was the right moment—or who knows? for a sign from God. But the hurricane ended the possibly longed-for reunion. Next question: Did Margaret Soles have anything to do with Jessica's disappearance?"

"That's hard. I'd say that she was convinced that she was dead, or she wouldn't have risked applying as sole remaining heir to the estate, in lieu of all legitimate claims having been found invalid."

"But what would a nun want with money?"

"To donate it to the Church. She really is devout, and she might feel that being able to give the Church millions would justify her unhappy birth and life—as if God had done it as part of a plan so that she could help others through this money."

Bert nodded in agreement. George was right, he felt sure

264

of that. They would have to get to speak to Sister Immaculata as soon as possible. It wouldn't be easy, since his last
visit had probably made her shy of accepting visitors; she
might have been expecting her attorney the day he had
interviewed her. He and George spent the rest of the
evening debating the best way to get her to talk to them
without frightening her off. George felt they should tell her
that they had evidence she could use in her lawsuit to claim
the estate, but Bert was hesitant about using that approach
without being able to explain exactly why. Intuition again.
He decided he'd try to visit her at the convent on Saturday
and then decide on the next move in the game.

When he called his service on Friday and received a
message to call his father-in-law at a Boston exchange, Bert
understood that Alice was not meant to know of the call. As
soon as he could, he drove to the pay phone outside the
library and made the call on his charge card with a sense of
mounting excitement. There must be some contact between
Alice's father and Barakian—his intuition had been correct
when he'd thought of asking him about the man. He should
always play his hunches, he thought, as he waited impatiently for the connection to be completed. Arlen's voice
was straining for calm as he asked his son-in-law to drive up
to Connecticut the very next day.

"I have something of urgency to discuss with you, but you
are to tell Alice it is in the nature of a medical consultation.
Later I will telephone you at the house with this message
and speak with the family. I will apologize to my daughter

265

for calling you away and she will understand and not worry." Always there—Alice must never be worried or upset. He refused to tell Bert anything else despite his protestations.

It all went as arranged, and Bert made the 6 A.M. ferry from Orient Point to Connecticut. He enjoyed the novelty of the trip, while his mind raced busily trying to anticipate the connection between Barakian and Arlen, and what the latter would have to tell him upon his arrival in Sherman. As soon as he drove off the ferry, he called George to apprise him of the latest turn of events, and to explain that he would not be able to try to confront Sister Immaculata.

". . . but I've got another one of my hunches, that Alice's father is going to be able to clear up most of this case. The number I called him at was Barakian's at the hospital. He must have found out I was related to Arlen and called him. I'm sure they knew each other before the war—it might have been in context of the Desmond case. I think that by the next time I see you we'll know exactly what happened to Jessica Desmond!"

The day turned gray and cloudy as he drove, and when he switched on the radio, he was surprised to hear that there were severe storm warnings posted for the northeast coastal area. It was still three weeks to hurricane seson, he thought, probably just media hype to stir up some excitement in the dog days of August. According to the network meteorologist, the storm named Bella, would hit within the next forty-eight hours—if it was going to reach this far north at all—and it would either be devastating or just a heavy storm; there were still a multiplicity of factors to be monitored. References were already being made to the 1938 hurricane and he hoped Alice wouldn't get nervous. But forty-eight hours was plenty of time for him to get back and to move the family out, if necessary. Comforted by the thought, he concentrated on his driving and made good

266

time in getting to the Arlens' home. In the back of his mind was the idea that if the storm held off, and if he got out of his in-laws' house early enough, he might have a chance to scoot up to see Amy, less than an hour away now over the state boundary line. Perhaps it was just as well that he didn't know he would never see her again in this life.

Part IX

His in-laws greeted him solemnly, looking as if neither had slept that night; they looked aged and shrunken. The thought leaped into his mind that it was as if they had left their Shangri-la at last. Before he could express his concern, they motioned him to an easy chair in the lovely, flower-filled room.

"This is not going to be easy, Bert, so bear with us. Mother and I should have told you this a long time ago. Please accept my most abject apologies for the deception we have practiced toward you all these years. I, of all people, should have realized that it would be impossible to escape the consequences of our act. You must stop your search for Jessica Desmond."

"What on earth is this all about?" demanded the bewildered son-in-law. And suddenly he was filled with a sense of dread—he didn't really want to know. He felt as if he were being dragged back into a nightmare from which he had been struggling to escape, as the elderly couple at last disclosed the details of the lie they had been living for thirty-seven years.

Karakin and Ylene Melkonian had been married for ten years when their daughter was born. The little girl became even more precious to her parents, if that was possible, when it was medically determined that her mother could never have another child. Ava was just four years old when her father detected the early signs of leukemia. Desperately, he strove to save her life with all the resources available to him in Bulgaria in 1938. The most sophisticated treatment, however, was in New York City. As a pathologist, Dr. Melkonian had little difficulty in obtaining an immigration visa to the United States. It was just as well to get out of Europe, he had assured his wife, for he felt certain that war was inevitable.

Ava's remission, soon after beginning treatment at Children's Hospital convinced them of the wisdom of their move. Elated by the miracle, they took a small apartment near the hospital, and Melkonian, with his superb command of English, had little difficulty in passing the medical boards to be licensed to practice in New York State. Their happiness with their new life was shattered when the child's remission was followed by a severe relapse. For months they rode the emotional roller coaster familiar to all relatives of cancer patients, as the disease cruelly raised and dashed their hopes in its erratic progress. Miraculous remissions were inexorably followed by more brutal ravages of the disease. The grieving parents clung to every shred of hope—until Ava was readmitted to the hospital for what her father knew would be the last time.

It was during this last stay that Melkonian met Josef Barakian. Their common Armenian ancestry gave them a feeling of kinship, and they took an ethnic pride in their accomplishments in their respective fields. Now, both were hopeless in terms of cases closest to their hearts. When Barakian called in his colleague for a discussion of the Desmond child's deteriorating medical condition, the latter was immediately taken with her, as indeed was everyone who saw her. It was her large, dark eyes that captured his heart at once; they were Ava's eyes, though there was little other resemblance, except for their ages and terminal conditions. Bringing his wife to Jessica's bedside, her compassionate reaction to the child convinced him that Ylene would go along with the mad scheme his brain was frantically devising.

Melkonian realized that even should he and Barakian manage to save the little girl, she had no relatives. There would be no one capable of giving her both the constant professional care she required, along with the intense love she would need to dispel the effects of the incredible traumas she had suffered. Legally there was no way he could get the right to experiment on her, or to adopt her. He also knew that his own daughter would soon be dead. When the father broached his scheme to the psychiatrist, it was not rejected, as he had feared. After much soul searching, Barakian had agreed to the plan. The only alternative would be to leave Jessica to her dying. The chance to save her, however slight, must be risked. The plan was immediately put into effect.

Ava Melkonian was signed out of the hospital by her father, who explained that he wanted her to die in her own bed with her parents beside her. When the end was near, Barakian was notified to prepare his part of the plan. Upon receiving the latter's phone call, the father gave his child a final injection—one that ended her sufferings forever. After the grieving parents gave her a last kiss, they dressed the wasted little body in its Sunday best, wrapped what had been Ava in a sheet, and carried her to their car. They drove to the Payne Whitney Clinic to wait for Barakian.

His role in the drama had begun with Melkonian's call saying that Ava had no more than forty-eight hours to live. Arranging to take the next night shift, he had phoned his coconspiritor as soon as he was ready. Jessica had been placed under heavy sedation, and the midnight shift personnel were busy getting their instructions from those going off duty. No one would go near the Desmond child's room except if he called them. It was a simple matter to wrap the feather-light body in a blanket, quickly check the hall, then carry it down the nearby stairwell three flights to the delivery entrance, where the Melkonians awaited him. Karakin gave Josef his daughter's body, and then placed their new daughter in Ylene's arms.

The dead child was brought quickly to Jessica's room, where a screen hid the bed from sight. At 2 A.M., Barakian called the morgue to tell them to send a child's body bag to room 312. When it arrived, he told the attendant that he would take charge of the corpse. Glad to be relieved of the task, the man went back to his post to finish reading the *Daily News*. Quickly Ava was placed in the canvas bag, the straps tightly closed, the tags reading "Jessica Desmond— room 312" attached to the cord. It was during the next flurry of the change of shifts at the nursing desk that Dr. Barakian announced the death of Jessica Desmond. The 8 A.M. shift being the most hectic, there was little time or opportunity for expressions of mourning or grief. Her demise *had* been expected and the poor child, after all, was probably better off with God than continuing a life in death—or so ran the general consensus of opinion when the staff had a chance to discuss the event.

It surprised no one that Dr. Barakian himself took charge of all the details; everyone knew how much he had cared for the child and how hard he had worked to save her. Now he called the bank to tell them that their ward was dead, and that the body should be removed from the hospital at once. He also told them that he would have to insist upon a sealed coffin, since Jessica had died of a contagious disease—there was no point in taking a risk with the health of the living. The bank officials returned his phone call within the hour to say that all arrangements had been made, and that Brockett's Funeral Parlor was sending the most expensive model of a white child's coffin in which to pick up the body that very day. By 4 P.M., they had done so, and Barakian had watched them put the small bag into the satin-lined, tiny coffin and seal it at his direction. The death certificate was signed and delivered, and upon checking with the *Southampton Press*, the doctor was gratified to learn that the last of the Desmonds had been buried two days later, after a Catholic funeral mass at her home church. It was not until many years later that he found out that the body had been placed in a mausoleum, rather than six feet underground, and that was when Bert Bradley told him so. Before he could voice the question, Dr. Arlen told his son-in-law the answer. He and his wife had been sending flowers to their child's grave every week for thirty-seven years. His voice quavered and his wife's eyes brimmed with tears as they spoke of the beloved child whose final resting place they had never seen, in order to protect the living child whom they had literally made their own.

The real Jessica had, in the interim, been spirited away to a prearranged hideout, an old house in Brooklyn Heights that had been readied for her arrival weeks before. Ylene had started the legal procedures to Americanize their names. Henceforth the Melkonians would be known as Gregory, Ilana, and Alice Arlen. Ava's birth certificate was used for Jessica, who from then on celebrated the dead child's birthday as her own. The birthday parties for her had always been bittersweet occasions for the parents. The name *Alice* had been chosen to keep the *A* in memory of Ava, and to preserve a sibilant sound, which Barakian thought would be helpful in establishing Jessica's future responses. All traces of the Melkonian family were slowly eradicated. Along with their new names, they also changed their residence, their religion, and Ilana dyed her black hair to blonde so that it would seem that the little girl had her "mother's" coloring. Dr. Arlen eventually even received a new medical registry number when he changed his specialty to pediatrics, upon completing the required training. Their few friends and widely scattered relatives were informed that due to their grief over Ava's illness, the family was moving to Uraguay to try a new radical cancer treatment only available there. The outbreak of World War II, just a month after their plan was initiated, made everything much easier. There were too many major problems now for people to even remember the Melkonians and their brief stay in New York. The few family members in Europe who attempted to trace them after the war finally gave up trying. They seemed to have vanished.

As soon as everything was in order, the men began the extreme treatment they had carefully devised. The child Jessica was placed in a large, thin, rubber bag that was then filled with a solution exactly resembling amniotic fluids. She was pressed out in a semblance of birth contractions and held upside down to allow the fluids to drain from her lungs. The next step was to have the three adults spell one another in two-hour shifts to pattern her in the movements of a newborn and, later, those of a developing infant. Formally christened Alice, she was bottle-fed and given baby foods. In one year they had carried her through five years of the normal development of a child by carefully structured stages that included diapers, high chair, baby carriage, appropriate toys for each stage, increasingly complex language, even arranging the room's design to reflect the needs of a growing child. She was surrounded by films and photographs to resemble what would be a child's perspective of the world, and of her "parents," suited to each stage. Barakian left after six months, satisfied that the process of evolution was well under way. His parting advice had been that the Alice who had emerged from their womb of science must be kept from any unpleasantness in her new life. He was concerned that stress and tension could bring on a sense of dread, or morbidity, which could cause her to recall the trauma that had precipitated her mental illness. By a process of behavioral conditioning, she was accustomed to forget anything unhappy in her waking life during her sleep. Leaving little to chance, they also introduced a gentle relaxant, similar to modern Thorazine, which she was given each day in doses appropriate to her size, in the guise of her father's own special vitamins. When she reached adolescence, her father told her that she had a slight metabolism problem, which was to be controlled by a capsule he'd devised that contained a formula to prevent her from gaining weight. He counted on her feminine vanity to ensure that she would take them regularly until the day she died. Bert could never recall Alice ever forgetting to take her pill—so she wouldn't get fat.

Her life was one filled with gentle happy things, gay colors, constant reminders that she was an adored child by surprises and presents and trips, but never to the seashore. She was never left alone, and a night-light was always placed so that it shone into her room. In college she was encouraged to share a room with a girl her father had managed to screen, with the help of the college, to provide a compatible roommate. Alice was just an hour from home, so her parents continued the subliminal supervision. It was not unusual for an only child, especially a girl, to be so close to her parents. Most people thought it was lovely to see such a devoted family, and many were envious of the relationship the Arlens had with their daughter. The total result was a happy, hedonistic personality of great equanimity and self-assurance, which, coupled with the beauty that remained hers as Alice Arlen, so captivated the young Bert Bradley.

"I am married to Jessica Desmond?" gasped the incredulous husband.

His mind tried to absorb this incredible fact. On one level it was a relief to have an explanation of the phenomena at Mulberry; he'd been acquiring consciousness of matters held in his wife's memory. Before he could think of the ramifications of this improbable, yet possible process of telemnemonike, his in-laws were resuming their confession.

"Yes. We were afraid to tell you; the fewer people who know a secret, the less chance it has of being found out. If you were told, who knew what use you might make of it should you and Alice quarrel, or divorce?"

"We were glad that you were a psychiatrist, as well as being such a nice young man," Mrs. Arlen interjected. "We thought you'd be aware of nervous strain, and then too, your profession meant that you could have an office in the house, so Alice would be alone as little as possible."

"And that's why you concocted the story of her trauma in the storm on the Jersey Shore and about her fear of animals? And why you insisted that she have control of all the money?"

"Yes, my dear. After we die we want to be sure that there is always plenty of money for Alice in case, well should she . . ." her voice trailed off under Bert's frown.

Her husband completed the sentence ". . . in case the possibility arose that she might need institutional care at a future time. The only good care in these places costs many thousands of dollars weekly, as you well know."

"Are you aware," came Bert's strangled tones, "that your daughter is worth ten million dollars?"

"We'd heard mention of a large estate many years ago, but what good would it do her? The shock of remembering who she was, in proving she was entitled to it, would send her back into irretrievable madness."

"You are certain of that?"

"Beyond a doubt. Barakian and I discussed it at great length. He felt we were fortunate enough that she was in a seaside house without having it stir up memories. No, any triggering of the memory would send her back into some form of schizophrenia, worse than she was before, beyond anyone's skills to reclaim her."

"Good God! Dear sweet heaven!" Bert cried out as he leaped to his feet. "What have I done!"

"What is it?" cried his thoroughly alarmed in-laws.

"The house, the house we're in, Mulberry, it *is* the Desmond estate!" As they stared at him in speechless horror, he added more to torture them with, "And according to the radio, there's a storm coming!"

"Storm—what storm?"

"Haven't you heard the news?"

"No, we've been too distraught to listen to anything."

"There's a possible hurricane headed for the coast. I've got to get back and move Alice and the kids out as soon as possible. I'll call you as soon as I get them back to the city and settled." With this he flung out of the house, leaving his in-laws stunned and shaking and looking, if possible, worse than they had when he'd first entered their home.

Alice back in the Desmond house! The possibility had never occurred to them. They had been under the impression that the house had later been destroyed. During the time of Jessica's ordeal they had been busy with their own; the slow death of their Ava. They had payed little attention to any stories in the news, and at the time of the hurricane, there were so many terrible tragedies. It was easily buried away with others. Since the chief of police had never released any of the lurid details, it had just been a sad story of a father going berserk and killing his family during the stress of the storm. Barakian had given them few details, just that she had witnessed the killings and must be protected from being upset, and from storms. With Barakian gone, and the passage of so many years, they had given themselves up to the luxury of believing that Alice was Ava returned to them, and had entered into their own grand design quite willingly. It was a rude awakening.

"Perhaps it won't matter, Ilana," said her husband, always there to protect her and their child. "She has been there all summer and we saw how well she was getting on, she loved the shore, she was happy all the time. And she never forgets to take her pills, that alone could keep her from harm."

"Of course, and Bert will be there in time to have her back in the city before the storm even strikes." Thus these two gentle people tried to comfort each other as their fears mounted unbearably. It was well that they had never had time to find out from Bert the reason why he was in such a persistent pursuit of Jessica Desmond; there would have been no possibility of any comfort.

Turning on the radio, they listened with increasing tension to the constant, shrill broadcasts of impending disaster at the shore. The announcement that it might be a repeat of the hurricane of 1938 did little to assuage their fears.

". . . and should it strike at midnight, as it now seems likely, the combination of the high tides with the fury of the storm could swamp all coastal areas. Plans are now in progress to evacuate low-lying grounds."

Unable to stand the tension any longer, they tried to call Alice that afternoon to see if Bert had reached her, only to be told that trunk lines to the Hamptons were all tied up as people from all over the state, panicked by the radio and TV reports of imminent disaster, tried to reach loved ones. After the third unsuccessful attempt, they looked at each other and, without a word being exchanged, collected their rain gear and got into the big car. They had to try to reach their little girl, to protect her from the storm that was menacing her sanity, if not her life. They were responsible for having given her both, and that responsibility was forever.

They were both exhausted, and the wind driving the rain against the windshield made visibility difficult as they headed into the storm. In his desperate effort to bring comfort to his daughter, Dr. Arlen was speeding, as later reports would ascertain, but mercifully he and his wife were killed instantly as the Lincoln skidded off the road and into a ditch where it was not found until the next day. Better that they died than to have found out the end of the story of Jessica Desmond. It was equally merciful that he died without having imparted the worst of Barakian's news, that there was a chance that the psychosis in that doomed family was hereditary, as modern studies of that form of pathology now indicated.

2

It was better that Bert didn't know, because his mind was having enough trouble as it was trying to sort out the information he'd already heard. For whatever comfort it gave, he now at least knew the reason for the paranormal phenomena at Mulberry: Jessica Desmond was back home. Her spirit as a child might be trying to integrate with the woman who returned. Was she resentful that she had not died with the rest of the family? Was the family angry about that? Was she angry that the Arlens had stolen her life? Was she using telekinesis subconsciously to show that there was something to be solved about the murder of her family? Was he himself going crazy? He had to stop thinking about it and concentrate on his driving, or he'd be of no use to anyone.

When he was forced to stop for gas, he called George, the only other person in the world he could trust with the secret.

"George? Listen quickly and carefully. Alice is Jessica Desmond. I've got to get her out of that house before the storm hits. I can't get through, the lines from here are tied up. Keep trying till you get her, and tell her to have the family ready to go when I get there. Tell her I'm nervous about the storm and we'll go back in a day or two—which of course we won't, but I'll work out reasons for that later."

"Now you listen to me. I don't understand too much of what you're saying, but if you stop for a minute you'll realize that you are in no condition to keep driving all the way out to the Hamptons. You have to come through New York anyway, so just stop in front of your door and I'll come right out and share the driving with you. You can fill me in on the details in the car. I'm on my way to your place now." He hung up before his friend had a chance to reject the offer. As he continued his drive toward the city, Bert realized that it *was* a good idea. He didn't have the strength to keep going and then have to face the trip back to the city as soon as he got there. George was always a comfort. He needed someone with whom he could share this intolerable burden, and timewise it was just a matter of a few minutes to stop at his house.

Brief, fitful gusts of rain were just starting when he pulled up in front of his town house, but there was no sign of George. Impatiently he ran inside to find him waiting there. Despite his protestations of urgency, George insisted that he sit down for a moment and have the drink that was already prepared. "We'll be in Southampton in plenty of time, and back here well before the storm peaks. The last bulletin said the zenith would be at midnight. Just catch your breath and then I'll drive us out. I called Alice and told her we'd be there and that she's to be ready to leave for a few days."

"Did she ask why I was coming for them instead of asking her to drive in?"

"Yes, as a matter of fact she did. I told her you didn't want to take the chance of her hitting heavy rains with a car full of kids on her own."

"Thanks, George, you're a real friend. But let's go, I can't take a chance of her being there when the storm hits. Her father—that is, Dr. Arlen said it would be sure to send her into madness, permanently."

"She actually *is* Jessica Desmond?" At his friend's nod, "Then she is worth ten million dollars; the clinic is ours!"

Bert shook his head in disagreement. "No chance, George. If we have to tell her who she is her folks say there is no doubt that we lose her forever." His tone permitted no further discussion, as he rose to leave.

"Hold on one second," George left the room to return with "a short snort—have a quickie for the road," insisting that Bert down it before they left. It didn't take much urging, since Bert was becoming more and more shaken as the enormities of the situation began to overwhelm him. Now that he had George to share the problem with, he could afford to fall apart a bit. For the first time in weeks he didn't even think of Amy Cullum.

George took the wheel of the Mercedes and Bert was grateful for that. He felt as if he couldn't keep himself together. His companion started to discuss the clinical aspects of the Jessica/Alice case to take his mind off the tension of the long drive, and what the end of that drive might bring. Filled with gnawing doubts, her husband pondered how the knowledge that he was married to the daughter of Evan Desmond would affect his relationship with his wife, who must never learn of her true parentage. At all costs, the conspiracy to protect Alice must continue, he explained to George.

"As you're my executor, I must fill you in on certain details. If anything happens to me you must see to it that Alice continues to get a supply of those vitamin cum 'metabolism' pills she takes for the rest of her life," and briefly he explained the deception. "The formula for them is in with Arlen's will, and will become part of my legal papers. Alice will take them forever—you know how terrified she is of gaining an ounce. I can't see her ever changing. They'll keep her from tension, or being unduly affected by stress." He also explained the behavioral conditioning that the doctors had used to train Alice to sleep off anything that she found disturbing, with no trace of residual memory. "And I thought she had the world's sweetest disposition," her husband said rather bitterly. The realization of how he'd been duped started to bother him, making him doubt himself as the professional he'd always prided himself on being.

280

Fascinated by the genius behind the restoration of an entire personality, George began to discuss the possibility of the application of some of these amazing techniques to their practice, though he doubted that it could work again. It had been a rare combination of the right mixture of people and events; genius, miracle, luck and Jessica herself. It was probably a once-in-a-lifetime shot, but at least some aspects could be studied for future use. Bert gave monosyllabic answers to his questions and by the time they were switching back onto the L.I.E., the drug George had slipped into his second drink started to take effect. Just before he fell into an unconscious state, as the powerful car swung into the expressway, he sat bolt upright and exclaimed,

"Jesus! Margaret Soles is Alice's half sister!" Then his head slumped back against the leather headrest, and he didn't stir once, not even when George pulled the car to a stop in a natural lea outside the village of Southampton to wait out the storm.

George pushed the seat all the way back so that they'd be more comfortable, and watched the storm gather. The spot had been carefully chosen; they couldn't be seen from the road and would be protected from the full brunt of the storm. It was one of the few places left untouched in the 1938 storm, but would provide a good view of the elements at work, an exciting prospect. He'd start up again just before Bert was due to wake and explain they'd had a breakdown en route while Bert slept. The drug would disorient both his memory and his sense of time.

He'd always hated Alice, cold bitch—never appreciated how wonderful Bert really was, or the importance of his work. Spent all of her time in self-indulgence and in being doted upon. When he'd gotten through to her, just before Bert had stumbled in, she'd told him in a steely voice that they could forget the clinic. "After what I just learned about that bastard and his whore, I'm not going to leave him enough for chewing gum! Wait until my parents find out!" That coupled with the knowledge that she was Jessica Desmond started a plan working in his brain. Bert had said that she must get out of Mulberry before the storm struck or she'd go round the bend permanently. All he had to do was to make sure they got there well *after* the storm, and with any luck at all she would be ready to be carried away, leaving Bert and the kids to inherit not only the Arlen estate, but the ten million bucks as well. The clinic would become a reality. It seemed simple enough; it would hurt no one but Alice, who was no good as far as he was concerned, and would help countless people needing psychiatric care. They'd make it up to the kids somehow, and now that she'd found out about Bert and Amy, Bert was certainly better off without her.

He frowned as he thought of Amy, that with Alice gone, she might win Bert's affections instead. No, that infatuation was past, with the tragedy of his wife's collapse, for which he'd inevitably blame himself. He felt confident that Bert would spend his life trying to make up for all those hedonistic years that Alice had led him into wasting. The clinic was his true mission. All those years of being a minister's son would tell. They would spend all their time together—lunches, dinners, conferences, working side by side every day. He was already a member of the family as far as the kids were concerned; now he'd spend free time with his friend and the kids, helping them to adjust to their new situation as a motherless family. Thinking of the pleasure and excitement they'd have in working together,

282

he watched the sky grow more ominous and the winds more enraged, and gently cradled his friend's head on his shoulder.

Lissie had been singing "Sweet Afton" all morning to the accompaniment of her music box, teaching Vanessa the words so that she could sing the lullaby on the nights that Alice wasn't home to do so. Her mother finally called to them to stop, that the repetition was becoming unbearable and that they were to get ready to go to the club.

They all went as usual, ignoring the gray skies and the slowly freshening winds. The ocean was too rough, but it was an oppressive day and they could enjoy a swim in the pool after practice for the tennis tourney. Despite the continuous storm warnings the club was crowded; there was little else to do during the day. No one seemed unduly disturbed about the radio's hysteria promising imminent Armageddon. This happened every year, according to the old-timers, and just as often as not, the storm either never materialized or veered off well before it was due to hit. The fact that it was so early in the season, said the experts, would indicate that it wouldn't pack the power of a more mature storm. Listening to their casual chatter helped Alice to relax. She wasn't sure if she should drive back to the city, but according to these knowing people, it seemed as if there were no danger at all. If there was, she was sure that either her parents or Bert would have called to tell her to leave. No one else showed any signs of doing so, so she assumed it was safe to stay. If Mulberry had survived the blow of 1938, there was certainly no cause for concern.

Relieving her tensions in a brilliant game of tennis, she

went into the locker room for her shower in a glow of physical well-being, admiring her body for its performance on the courts with a much younger opponent. As she toweled off in her cubicle, she recognized Astrid New-some's distinctive tones, *being catty as usual,* Alice smiled to herself. Though she knew it wasn't right, she eavesdropped forgetting her qualms about good manners. The smile soon froze, however, as Alice realized that it was her own family that Astrid was dissecting with her scalpel tongue.

"You'd better believe that he was dipping into that honeypot! I saw them together in Riverhead, that's why she was sent off." Murmurs of interest from the listener apparently encouraged her as she waspishly continued. "You'd think that someone like Alice would have more sense than to replace her with that *zoftig* broad. Probably thought she was safe in finding the antithesis of what she'd had, but have you seen her little Dickey-boy eyeing that dish? My niece says he's the horniest kid in the Hamptons."

The listener's laugh enraged Alice. How she would loved to have gone out there and confronted Astrid with her lies and then pull her hair out! Aside from the fact that that was not her style, she was also too humiliated and stunned by what she had just heard. The mere idea that she and her family were a topic for gossip was enough to unnerve her. She couldn't give anyone the satisfaction of knowing that the serene Alice Bradley had been hurt. As she waited for them to leave, a part of her was sick with fear that these were not lies. It was with a fascinated sense of horror that she heard the rest of the viper's tale. Lowering her voice Astrid confided.

"My niece knows this friend of Everett Solès and he had it on the best authority that the Bradley kids are in the clique—you know?—the one that's into kinky sex. Well of course I didn't mean to, but I happened to pick up the phone while Clare was on the phone with Alison and I couldn't help but overhear that Everett had told Franklin that he'd gotten Richard and Stacey into a sex scene together!"

Even Astrid seemed to have finally gone too far, as Alice through a frozen stupor could hear the listener remonstrate with the gossip-monger. Apparently, it was one thing to discuss adultery among one's friends, but incest was totally unacceptable, not at all in good form, Astrid was told in the iciest possible tones. From now on she would be assiduously avoided by the people she'd courted. Realizing she had stepped beyond the bounds of decency, Astrid followed her angry listener out of the locker room, apologizing for having repeated such vile information, plaintively explaining that it had simply been too heavy a burden to bear all by herself. How was she to help poor Alice with her problems when they inevitably came to light?

Poor Alice mechanically collected her things and left the locker room, too dazed to comprehend what she had just heard. Best not to think of unpleasant things, her parents had always said. She'd make believe that it had never happened. After a good night's sleep all troubles would be gone, her daddy had always promised her and he never lied, as that bitch Astrid was obviously doing. She was just a vicious person, jealous of Alice and her wonderful family, jealous because Bert wouldn't even look at her. How Alice would have enjoyed strangling her with bare hands!

Instead, she went to the bar and had a drink before joining Vanessa and her children for the club's Monday buffet luncheon. So distraught was she that, for the first time in thirty-one years, she neglected to take her daily tablet at lunchtime. Fortunately, the kids were so excited about the impending storm that they didn't even notice her unusual, distant behavior.

5

The Sisters at the convent were all atwitter too, as the radio gave bulletin after bulletin on Bella's progress up the eastern coast of the United States. After lunch they turned on the local TV news on channel six, which was showing film clips of the 1938 storm. Sister Teresa Immaculata seemed mesmerized as she sat in the common room staring at the scenes of carnage being offered the viewers.

". . . And eastern Long Island was one of the areas hardest hit by the hurricane. One tragedy was not wreaked by the havoc of nature, however, but by a local man. In this lovely Southampton home a man named Evan Desmond brutally murdered his wife, children, and young maid before taking his own life. It was speculated that Mr. Desmond, known to be a drinker and rather unstable, was affected by the rapidly falling barometric pressure and something, as they say, snapped. The one survivor, five-year-old Jessica, was tragically driven into psychosis by the trauma. She died one year later in a New York City hospital. Meanwhile in Rhode Island . . ." The research person had done a good job of putting this segment together; there were pictures of Mulberry and of the Desmonds flashed on the screen over a montage of the storm's furious activity. But Sister had stopped listening. She limped out of the room and into the lowering day, pulled by some inner force toward "her" house, toward Mulberry. She moved quickly despite her handicap, seemingly unaware of the fog that was starting to drift in wisps off the rolling ocean. Whitecaps could be seen even from the road as she went unerringly to the side door and slipped the catch with an expert movement. With her own key, she unlocked the cellar door and, closing it behind her, moved with practiced caution down the steep stairs until she was safely on the earthen floor of the basement. Her hands found the cache of candles, matches, and her lantern in their concealed space behind the stairs. Settling herself on the floor, she waited with awesome patience for whatever God would decree. His will be done. Amen.

When Alice drove up to the house, the young people scattered inside looking at the signs of the storm's activity from different vantage points. It was a new experience for all of them. According to the radio, they were about to become eyewitnesses to history. Alice stood in the driveway for a few moments watching the whitecaps spewing into the air in the distance. A strange hush had started to creep over the landscape as birds and small animals instinctively sought low ground for shelter from the brooding atmosphere. The sky was leaden and there were fitful gusts of wind that died down almost as soon as they started. Now and again there were a few scattered drops of rain, but the clouds seemed loathe to part with their burden, saving it perhaps for a torrential downpour. What was weird was the fact that though the treetops moved, there was little if any air stirring as yet, although the newscasts promised winds of up to ninety miles per hour. As she stood bemused by the sullen clouds, a small figure ran quickly out the back door and, unseen by anyone, down to the playhouse. Lissie took her tiger kitten to the kitchen via the back door. She was its mommy now and she had to save it from the storm, as well as to hide it from her mother.

Her agile brain had devised a plan: She would put it in the cubby Mrs. Hanks had showed her, with some food and a dish of milk. Tomorrow, very early, she would take it back to its home in the playhouse, she assured the kitten as she lovingly tucked it away on some soft rags. Delighted with her cleverness, of which she was sure her father would approve, she scampered upstairs to her room to change her clothes. No one had even noticed her departure.

Alice sat heavily in the big chair in the master bedroom, just staring straight ahead as the venomous conversation she had overheard ran through her mind, playing and replaying like a tape. It couldn't have an iota of truth in it! She had to talk to her parents, but though their phone rang interminably, there was no one to answer. Where could they be in this weather? She started to worry. It was unlike her father to forget to switch to the answering service. Hesitantly she dialed her husband's number only to have his answering service report that the doctor was "gone for the day." Perhaps he was on his way out to join them, knowing how afraid her parents were about her being alone in a storm. Starting to feel slightly comforted, she suddenly thought about Amy—perhaps her husband was with his paramour! She tried to nap. Sleep always made the bad things go away. When she awoke Bert would be there to take care of her and all the tension would be forgotten.

Stretching out on the big bed, she tried to find surcease from the film clips in her mind: Bert making passionate love to Amy Cullum; Richard pushing into Stacey writhing beneath him in ecstasy. It was no use (especially without her pill), so she went to the bathroom to wash up. At the sight of her own reflection she became startled. It was as if she were in a nightmare—she had suddenly aged! Her hair hung lank and dull around a face etched with lines around a sharp nose and bloodless mouth. Her eyes gazed back at her from sunken hollows. The shock gave her an actual pain in the pit of her stomach. When she went to the toilet, she found the menstrual blood had already clotted on her panties.

"So it's begun," she whispered to no one, "the blood has begun."

After George's phone call she moved heavily, lifelessly to the closet and from a box on the back shelf took out a shapeless housedress and a pair of steel-rimmed spectacles. Brushing her hair back into an unbecoming knot, she fastened it with an old barrette from the drawer in the vanity. She replaced her tennis sneakers with a pair of old scuffs and sat down to wait. She would know when the time had come.

At five, the children came into their mother's bedroom to ask about plans for dinner. They could barely make out her form in the gathering gloom, but she insisted that she wanted no light, claiming that her head hurt. Telling them to put together some supper for themselves, she refused their offers to bring her a tray, and ignored their teasing questions about her new "specs." She stared at some point over their heads, gently rocking her body and humming Lissie's lullaby. Feeling slightly uncomfortable, they left her with wishes that she'd be better in the morning.

Richard was feeling a sexual excitement as the storm heightened—just as his father and George had discussed it often happening many weeks before. A worthy offshoot of his grandfather, Evan Desmond, he had been coaxing Vanessa into slowly relinquishing her virginity. Each night he had been slipping into her bed to introduce her to a new delight of the flesh. She was now at the point where she actually allowed his nakedness against her own, permitting

him to kiss and fondle her breasts while he rubbed himself
against her triangle. Her thighs, however, remained firmly
clenched. Richard might be able to convince her that all of
her other "inhibitions" were "chicken" or even unhealthy
or small-town stuff, but one thing she knew was that once a
boy got that thing between her legs she was no longer a
virgin and *that* was a mortal sin. It was this thought that
kept her legs glued together despite the fact that Richard's
fondling brought her to a fever pitch of longing to go "all
the way." Watching the trees tossing in the gathering wind,
Richard knew that this would be the ultimate night, the
night that he deflowered his first virgin. The sounds of the
storm would cover any noise the girl might make, and his
mother seemed out of it for the rest of the evening. He
couldn't wait for it to get dark!

He hadn't too much longer to wait. The phones went
dead about 6 P.M. and the electricity went at 7. After a
sandwich and milk supper they locked all the doors and
windows, and lighted all the candles and hurricane lanterns
that Alice must have brought up from the basement when
they were upstairs. The visibility was good, if a bit eerie
with dancing shadows making the familiar seem strange.
Alice had refused their offers of candles in a flat voice
intoning, "Please leave me alone until my headache is
gone." None of them could know it, but she sounded
exactly like her mother, Evalynn Desmond. All Lissie knew
was that Mommy didn't seem like Mommy anymore.
Nothing seemed right as she sat in her room wishing she had
her kitty with her. The candles made her room leap with the
light, and the sound of the wind was getting scarier by the

minute. All sorts of bangings could be heard as things were flung against the house, but Sister Immaculata could hear nothing as she sat six feet underground in the total darkness of the earth cellar.

When Alice stepped into the hall, she caught a glimpse of a man's figure going up the attic stairs. Astrid's voice hissed through her rapidly disintegrating brain, "Bert Bradley has been dipping into that little honeypot," Well then, so be it. She had things that must be done. The sight of the living room wavering in the shadows cast by the candles the children had lighted terrified her. It was as if a monstrous ogre were reaching out to envelop her, but that was her mission now—to slay the ogres, and she must. Passing through the kitchen, she thought she heard a kitten's soft mewing and a sense of shock almost made her heart stop. "It's the wind," she muttered to herself and went to her studio for her sculptor's tools, little used that summer. Slipping them into the pocket of the loose dress, she stalked up the back staircase and eased Stacey's door open.

Her eldest was sitting in front of the vanity table, the tapers on either side of the mirror reflecting and refracting their soft glow. She was nude from the waist up as she carefully inspected her breasts to see if the bruises her brother had inflicted were gone. A movement barely visible in the dim light of the mirror startled her, and she tried to cover her breasts with her hands as an amorphous shape seemed to move toward the mirror.

"Did Richard do this to you?" The voice was disembodied, vaguely reminiscent of her mother's. Too startled to dissemble, she stared at the wavering darkness before her.

"How did you know?" slipped out before she had time to think. Damn that Everett Soles to hell! She might have known that the prick would tell. But to her mother! She'd get even with the bastard if it was the last thing she did. Stacey never did learn of the distant bond between herself and her tormentor, for as she peered into the mirror, she noted how strange her mother looked. Catching her breath sharply, she turned to face Alice, but it was too late. Fingers like claws were on her shoulder, pinning her still, and the knife was in flight reaching for the ceiling, then swooping downward with impossible speed.

Pain and surprise, the surprise of a child, slammed into Stacey's throat, cutting off whatever she had been about to say. She struggled to free herself from the claws in her shoulder, from the silver sliver of steel striking at her neck. Blood gushed from her mouth and splattered against Alice's dress as the two forms became entwined and fell to the floor. The knife had a life of its own as it hacked at the cords of resistant flesh, broke through cartilage, began gnawing into bone.

The silence was soon complete again as the storm paused for another blow; Alice staggered to her feet, the knife wet in her hand. She was breathing hard, but her face remained impassive as she bent and pulled at her daughter's long hair, lifting the decapitated trophy above her like a warrior displaying a prize. Letting the blood trickle onto her face, she murmured, "Blood to blood. Blood of my blood."

A crack of thunder sent another current of rage careening through her veins. All must be as it once was. Carefully she placed the head on the table before the mirror, positioning it on its side before bending to gather up the headless corpse. The trunk was arranged to perch on the edge of the chair, arms around the severed head. Satisfied at last, the mother moved to the door, drawn by the thought of work undone. Above her in the attic a sin was being committed, a foul sin of lust that offended God's sight. She knew that naked bodies were twining in white sheets, were exploring each other's secret recesses in spasms of animalistic desire.

At the doorway, she hesitated and turned. It pleased her to see how peacefully her daughter was sleeping on the dressing table, the terrible wounds hidden by her soft, fleshy arms. Stacey could gaze at her reflection for eternity by the lovely gleam of the candles. Alice refused to recognize that a pool of blood from neck and nose had formed around the chin, or to note that the eyes were wide open in mute terror. The headless body was still gushing blood from the still pumping arteries as its mother softly closed the door and started down the long corridor to the attic stairs.

Tired of staying alone, and trying to be brave in the gathering gloom of the storm, Lissie took her lantern and went into the hall intending to join her big sister for company and solace. Mommy was acting funny, she'd better not bother her. When she spotted the flickering light from the other end of the corridor, she was drawn to it like a moth. It mounted the attic stairs and disappeared from view. Good, she thought, it must be Stacey going to Vanessa's room. She would go too. Maybe they'd let her bring the kitty; it would be like a party. Mommy would never go up there, she said that people who worked in the house must have their privacy respected.

The insistence of the storm had increased Richard's sexual excitement to the point where he would no longer be denied. Vanessa might have the build of a strapping wench, but his tensions made him more than a match for her as she desperately struggled to push him off. She was frightened as she realized that she would not be able to keep her thighs clamped shut against the persistence of his legs and hands while his body pinned hers with its long, lean, hard strength.

Piteously she wailed, "Oh, please, Richard, stop, don't do this to me. I am a virgin, truly I am. You have to respect that."

Grappling with her furiously, their bodies cast crazy pictures on the wall by the light of the candle he had placed on the bureau so that he could get a "good view." Grinning down at her maliciously he sneered,

"Fuck virgins, that's what I say. That's what they're made for."

"Don't! Oh, don't do that," she screamed as his fingers probed deep into her, until they met the resistance he wanted to overcome as prelude to guiding himself into that warm, wet opening. Damn the whore! If she'd only stay still for a few seconds he could get started instead of pitching like a ship on a stormy sea. Her whining enraged him as he panted to get inside of her, and he finally smacked her across the face. It shocked her so that she stayed still long enough for him to drive into her with all the force of his pent-up desire and his loathing for all womankind. The howling of the wind drowned out her scream as her virginity was brutally ended. Oblivious to her cries, he prolonged the pleasure he was taking in having his first virgin. This was one girl who would never forget her first man, he thought happily. Bet she'd never find one to measure up to the likes of Richard Bradley for the rest of her damn life.

He came, at last, with a great groan, pulling her against him with all of his might, then fell against the softness of her body fully content as she continued to sob beneath him. Deaf to her hysterical pleas for release, he found that her weeping made him feel even more contemptuous about her plight. Stupid female, just a hick kid, didn't even know what good was. Refusing to pull out of her, he toyed with her wide breasts. Ignoring her begging for mercy and relief from the pain she felt, he finally stopped her blubbering by a heavy smack to the head. That did it. Looking at the fear in her eyes made him feel macho, while her wrigglings of discomfort excited him. To the girl's horror, she felt that thing inside of her grow long and hard again, and the rubbings and thrusts against the soreness had to be borne all over again—until he exploded inside of her once more. Vanessa whimpered her anguish to a room full of shadows and the shrieks of the storm, like voices from God sent to protest what was being done to her. When after what seemed an eternity he finally rolled off of her with a grunt it took him only a few seconds to become aware of a lantern being held above the bed and then a few more seconds to distinguish the figure behind the light: A face full of hate and malice leered down at him.

"Mommy" he screamed, whether as a cry for help or of recognition would never be known, for the knife slammed into his chest with a solid thud, stopping his heart instantly while Vanessa screamed like a lunatic siren. In a frenzy to escape the madness that had entered the room, she tumbled to the floor and crawled to a corner of the room where she huddled in disbelief, eyes blinking rapidly as they focused on the bed. Alice was crooning to the body in the sudden lull of the storm's fury. Then it began again. The wind started gathering its power, whistling through cracks in the shutters while claps of thunder beat against the roof like huge hands.

"Blood of my blood," a new voice howled from its own dark depths as the knife swooped downward again, slashing at Richard's pelvic area. Only when Alice lifted the gory mass of flesh aloft did Vanessa begin to scream again.

"This is what you wanted, whore?" Alice came to tower over the terrified girl. "Take it then!"

Vanessa shrank from the warm flesh being thrust toward her, but a hand of steel clamped her collarbone. Her head hit the wall hard and she felt dizzy and disoriented. Her eyes became watery and remote as if from a great distance they watched that bright piece of metal diving toward her naked breasts, and felt a strange sensation when it struck

295

home. Unconsciousness was a relief when it claimed her, and she toppled over on her side.

Alice swayed above the girl's body while moans of joy alternated with deep sobs that heaved from the bottom of her stomach. Turning blindly, conscious of nothing but an urge to flee the carnage, she was shocked to see the figure of a little girl in the doorway, mouth agape in a silent scream, eyes glazed with tears too stunned to shed. Was this herself she was watching, was this Jessica Desmond? No, she realized, this was her little girl, her very own Lissie.

George Webber calculated carefully; the drug he had given Bert would wear off soon. With any luck at all, Alice should have had more than enough time to have gone mad, leaving her husband free to claim every single one of those millions. It was time to get started. He had less than a mile to go, but the storm was fast approaching its zenith, and it might take an hour to get through the flooded streets.

Lovingly he gazed at Bert, thinking of how much better it would be if he could reveal his true feelings. Perhaps one day it would happen. Time was on his side now; he started the car and began driving slowly through the wind-flapping sheets of rain, alert for falling trees and power lines. Bert awoke a few moments later.

"Was I asleep? Are we there yet? What time is it?" came the bewildered voice, harsh and masculine against the shrill scream of the increasing winds.

"Relax, Bert," came the answering shout. "We're just a few blocks from the house. We had an engine breakdown after you conked out in Westhampton, and it took hours until someone stopped to help me fix it. By then the damn storm had gotten worse, so we've been creeping along like this ever since."

Anguish ripped across the other man's face. "Christ! How could I have slept through all that when my family is in danger? What kind of man am I?"

"An exhausted one. You were so physically and emotionally drained that two stiff drinks were enough to knock you out for a couple of hours. It doesn't matter, Bert, honestly. There was nothing you could have done anyway. We'll be there in about fifteen minutes or so, unless some stupid tree hits us."

Vainly, Bert tried to peer through the windshield's blurred glass, but he could distinguish nothing, as wave after wave of gray rain was flung at the car by the wind. Thank God for a friend like George at his side in a time of trouble, was the thought that consoled him as he tried not to think about Alice and the house. George was a man of reason and sense, calm to the end. He drove with a cool dispassion through the deserted, black streets and seemed to know exactly which ones to use as detours when the huge limb of an old elm blocked the road. The car was vibrating and rocking from side to side under the impact of ninety-mile-an-hour winds, but George drove steadily through the hurricane, which seemed enraged that a moving thing could challenge its might.

He also tried to soothe his friend, whose tensions were almost palpable in the close leather confines of the Mercedes. "Just remember, Bert, that house withstood the 1938 hurricane without much damage, and according to the last reports I heard some miles back, this storm is nowhere near as bad. They've already scaled down the estimates of its severity, because the peak won't hit until high tide has passed. Fortunately, its progress was delayed off Cape Hatteras."

Bert quivered with suppressed frustration. "It's not the house, it's Alice who might not be able to stand up to it.

She's at the scene of her trauma with just the kids. Her father said that being there during this storm could send her back into permanent psychosis. Don't you see? She's too old now to be brought out of it again!"

"Arlen is good, but he's not God," George shook his head, his voice loud but steady. "There's no certainty in these things, ever. You'll see. They'll be fine when we get there. Having the kids to worry about will keep Alice busy enough so that she won't have time to remember."

When there was no answering shout, George glanced quickly at his passenger to find him praying aloud through clenched teeth, hands folded and eyes focused on some unknown space beyond the windshield's agitated surface. Snatches of the Twenty-third Psalm were audible, now and again, as the storm paused to take another breath before resuming its relentless assault upon everything in its path.

After the initial shock of mutual recognition, Lissie had broken and run from her mother, refusing to respond to the latter's attempt to hide the dripping knife behind her back and wheedle the little girl into coming to her with a false smile and honeyed tones. Despite the fact that she had dropped her candle in her flight, the child's little feet were sure as they flew down the attic stairs. She hesitated there for but a moment, her chest throbbing with fear and uncertainty; she could not really accept what she had seen, but an instinct much older than herself warned that she was in grave danger. Even the rattling of the hurricane seemed less important than the threat that seemed to emanate from the now strangely quiet attic. Her mind quickly lit on her big sister. Stacy would know what to do.

Guided by the soft glow of candlelight framing the outline of the door, she opened it cautiously, alert for the least sign of disorder. Relief coursed through her as she saw her sister asleep at the dressing table bathed by the aura of the two candles bracketing her slumped figure. The relief was so intense she did not notice the stains. Rushing to her sister, she began to tug at her.

"Stacey, Stacey, wake up! Mommy's doing bad things and you . . ." She never finished the sentence. As soon as Lissie had touched the bare arm, Stacey's body had begun to slide to the floor. Slowly, languidly, like a reluctant tree, the carefully balanced torso slipped from its perch and descended into a heap at Lissie's feet. The very oddness of her sister's headless body held the child in breathless wonderment for a few mute seconds as she tried to take in the jagged gash of violated muscle and flesh. When she turned to stare into the features of the head on the table, the spell was broken. The scream that was wrenched from her insides went on for a very long time.

Hearing the cries of wretched anguish in counterpoint to the winds battling to get into the locked and shuttered house, Alice knew that her work was not yet completed. All must be as it had been before. Unconsciously she wiped her knife against her dress, her mother's dress, and started to descend. "Lissie, darling, come to Mommy," she called softly, yet some unbidden part of her hoped that her baby would not hear, would not obey.

Lissie heard and saw. The sound of her mother's strange new voice made her race frantically for the back stairs, which led to the kitchen and her kitten. When she reached the bottom she looked back for a moment to see this strange monster, her mother, captured briefly in the light of her own lantern, the flash of the knife clearly visible in her fist. Lissie ran into the darkness ahead of her; her mother's inexorable tread could be heard on the uncarpeted wooden stairs.

Calmly, patiently, Alice searched every room on the first floor. "Come out, come out, wherever you are!" her voice followed the lamp's eerie glow from corner to corner, from the library through the dining room to the kitchen. No sign of her daughter. It was getting late. The storm's fury was achieving a fierce peak, shaking the house like a toy, shouting at her to hurry up and complete her task. Puzzled at the child's ingenuity in eluding her, Alice silently retraced her steps. Perhaps if Lissie did not hear her, she would unwittingly reveal her hiding place.

She was back in the kitchen. The arm that held the knife shook with barely repressed rage. How dare she? How dare she defy her mother? At that moment, the winds once more unexpectedly ceased, and in the unnatural silence that followed she heard it, a thin, piping sound. It was a kitten's cry of dismay, and it was coming from behind the closed pantry doors. *Of course, it had to be the pantry*. With a childlike eagerness, Alice opened the doors and reached inside the pantry, lifting the board from her daughter's hiding place.

Gently but firmly, her smile fixed in a grotesque grin, Alice pulled her rigid daughter from the hiding place she herself had used thirty-eight years earlier. Lissie said not a word as her mother cradled her in the hand holding the knife and began walking out of the kitchen. Her mind had retreated into the blank asylum of shock, remote from the tensed arm supporting her, unmindful of the knife handle cold against her thigh. Unerringly, Alice carried her human bundle to the cellar door, crooning "Sweet Afton" with monotonous persistence. The door was half-opened, and her foot pushed it back. She made her way down the treacherous stairs carefully, and did not hear the door swing shut behind her. Only when the dirt floor was solid beneath her feet did she lower the lamp and let the child slide from her arm to stand before her like a statue, the striped kitten quiet against her breast.

"You see, Lissie," she spoke gently to the silent, ashen, visage that confronted her, "Mommy has brought you to a safe place." The sounds of the storm's furious onslaught were muffled by the earth down here, and Alice found that her mind was wandering. The knife felt alien in her grip. "She was evil and wanted to kill me, I could *never* understand why. Why would she want to kill us all?"

"I'll tell you now, if you really want to know, Jessica." And Sister Teresa Immaculata emerged, materialized, from the darkness behind the lantern's bright arc.

Spinning around in panic, Alice dropped her knife. Her voice became a child's voice, that of the five-year-old Jessica Desmond she had been when she was last in this cellar. "Who's there? Who are you?"

"Don't you remember me, little sister? I am Margaret, the child that our whore mother abandoned at birth because I was born out of wedlock, seed of her sin of fornication."

The shape shuffling heavily on the crippled leg became larger, stepped into the circle of light where Alice and Lissie stood motionless. At the sound of the dragging leg Alice put her hands over her ears; her face and her beautiful velvety brown eyes mirrored the fear and tension of that night thirty-eight years before. It was that same sound that had pursued her through the house after she had witnessed the atrocities committed by this same black wraith. She had heard it pass her hiding place in the kitchen as the nun had sought her, until the sounds of the storm had ended, and in fear of discovery, she had finally left. She had heard it go into the living room where she had found her Daddy, and she had heard it descend into this cellar where she had found Mommy all bloody. The harsh, cruel memories struggled to reclaim her mind.

"You killed everybody and then you tried to kill me, but I hid in my cubby and when I came out you weren't here anymore."

"That's right, Jessica, that's right, my darling sister.

Everybody had to die because they were bad. God told me so, he sent the storm to tell me and now he sent the storm to tell you. I was with you upstairs, inside your mind, when you exacted his revenge." The nun smiled at her audience brightly, her eyes quite insane. "And now after I complete His plan, all of Evalynn Desmond's offspring will have joined her in the fires of hell and the money will be mine alone with which to do God's work here on earth." Her features twisted into a mask of rage. "All must be as it once was, blood of my blood, blood to blood."

Alice reeled under the blows of that voice and the alien mind that was trying to enter her own, to assert control over her. She fought back silently repelling the thoughts wriggling at the edge of her consciousness, like a swarm of snakes. A new cunning possessed her—she had to save Lissie, she had to save herself, the ending this time *must* be different. She stood looking at her sister Margaret with a docile, apologetic smile on her face as her mind raced to find a way out of this new nightmare.

Mollified by Alice's apparent fright and passivity, Sister Immaculata's fury abated to be replaced by an air of condescension.

"Our mother didn't know that God had sent me on my mission. I had hidden myself here and when the storm was at its height I went upstairs with this knife and I did what had to be done. One by one I dispatched the evil creatures and consigned them to the flames while your—my—*our* stupid mother hesitated in her room, hoping for a miracle, no doubt." She paused to laugh aloud, a laugh of maniacal mirth.

"Your father, that spawn of Satan, that despoiler of young girls, almost ruined everything. I was trying to find you, but this affliction," she tapped her leg impatiently, "prevented me from catching you. I was searching for you when I came across him in the parlor, about to come down here, probably to get more candles. He never realized what was happening. I had taken another knife from the kitchen and that I rammed home into his black heart. It stuck there and I watched as he vainly tried to pull it out until he fell to the floor, quite dead. That's why people thought he had killed his family and then had taken his own life. I left him there and tried to find you, Jessica. I wanted to destroy everyone who had stolen my own birthright, leaving me to a loveless, comfortless world. Most of all I wanted to destroy the mother who had given me that joyless life."

Sister Immaculata edged closer to Alice, who was now standing in front of the dazed Lissie, as if to shield her. Desperately she tried to keep the fear out of her voice. "I heard my mommy calling me, but I was afraid to come out of my place."

The nun was breathing heavily, her eyes glittered by the lantern light. "Yes, our mother came to look for her children, but she would find a child she was not looking for. I heard her moving above me when I came down here to search for you. I heard her footsteps, her voice calling her children to come to her. I heard her cry when she found the body of her husband and God gave me the wisdom to realize how I could get her to come to me finally. She was near the doorway up there and I called out to her in a small voice pretending to be you. 'Mommy, Mommy, please come help me. I'm scared down here. It's so dark.'"

Tears streamed down the woman's homely face as she remembered all those years without a mother's comfort. Perhaps she had even prayed these very words when her adoptive parents had locked her in the cellar for her rage at their refusal to fix her lame leg, sentencing her to a life of always being different, forever to be the outsider.

"Down these stairs she came, calling for you, for her baby, 'Jessica darling, Mommy's here. Where are you, my baby?' I lit my candle when she was quite near me. You should have seen her face when she saw me here! Her mouth was open in surprise and shock to see that ugly nun from her church in her cellar. But I was kind, I did not keep her in suspense. With God's voice roaring above us I told her who I was. She pretended to be overjoyed, but I told her of the life she had sentenced me to, and reminded her of how she had shrunk from me in revulsion when I tried to comfort her after I had told her of the death of Sister Mary Joseffa. It was that repugnance which had sealed her doom. I had dreamed that I could reveal myself to this woman, that we could have a clandestine relationship where she would give me a bit of that love she had denied me from birth. It was her sin that caused God to take vengeance on my leg. 'The sins of the father will be visited upon the children,'" she intoned, brushing away her tears impatiently. "And then I found that I was repulsive even in the eyes of the woman who had borne me.

"God's ache for justice festered in my heart until He finally gave the word for me to strike by sending the hurricane. I had watched her giving her love to you and to her other children when she brought you all to church, but I had waited for the Word silently, patiently. I told your—*our* mother all this, and she listened as dumbfounded as if she had been struck by lightning. I even told her how God must have directed me to go to the convent in Vermont, so that there I might minister to the nun who had attended my birth. In her last delirium Sister Mary Joseffa told me everything. It must have been the sight and sound of my affliction that reminded her of that babe she had taken from the womb with a twisted foot and had brought immediately to a priest to be placed for adoption. After I administered the pain-killers, I questioned her so skillfully that I soon had all the information I needed in order to know all the details of my conception and birth. It was then simple to track my long-lost mother here to Southampton, Mrs. Evan Desmond of Mulberry. Mrs. Desmond, who had never even once set eyes upon her firstborn, nor even once touched the hapless babe I had been." The nun glared at the child who *had* had her mother's love.

Alice stirred, aware that the woman confronting her was not satisfied with the bloodletting of the night, that the danger for herself and her child was increasing. From the corner of her eyes she spotted the blood-stained knife she had dropped on the floor, and imperceptibly began to edge toward it as she pushed Lissie aside. The nun fixed her with a malevolent look but continued with the story of how their mother had met her end.

"Our mother wept as I told her all this, and pretended she regretted her sins. I remember so well the surprise on her face when she attempted to take me in her arms and met the cold steel of this knife. Before one of her evil fingers could even touch my habit, I struck at her, struck again and again as God gave me the strength to do His will. When she fell to her knees, her eyes wide in shock and surprise, I kicked her with all my strength with this foot, this legacy that was the only thing she had left me. When I left her she was still alive, but I knew it was not for long. I didn't want to finish her off, I wanted her to have time to repent of her sins before she died. When I climbed back up these stairs she was crying out to me, 'my baby, my poor baby.'"

These words stirred an uneasiness in Alice; yes, she remembered them, remembered being down here with a woman who said them over and over again, until she spoke no more. "That was my mother, she said them to me over and over when I sat with her waiting for her to be better. I sang our song to her, but she didn't get up in the morning, and then I don't remember what happened."

Ignoring the bewildered comment, the Sister continued her recital of the fearful night. "I looked for you until dawn of the next day. I even played your music box, played it endlessly, hoping the familiar sounds would encourage you to abandon your hiding place, but the Devil had instructed you well. I had to leave to avoid being found here, but God was with me. He made you silent and covered your memory so that no one ever knew that it was I who destroyed your family. It was part of His design that is now revealed. You

305

must pay for your mother's sins for having abandoned me, as she was later forced to abandon you. A few weeks ago, when I found out that you were not dead, I realized that Mrs. Bradley must be Jessica Desmond, not only from your looks, but no one else could have given birth to a child that looks like your Lissie—a true Desmond. I waited for God's call again, and he has sent it to me now in this new storm."

Immaculata threw back her head and listened intently to the muffled sounds of the storm, now reaching its zenith. Arms stretched high above her, she closed her eyes and mumbled as if in answer to a conversation. Seemingly satisfied, she nodded her head and looked at the mother and daughter standing mutely before her, frozen in a tableau in the golden gleam of the lantern's light. "Yes, it is right. You of the Desmond blood stand in the way of the Church. The money must be used for God's work." Without warning, she flung herself at Alice, slashing at her throat with her knife, but Alice instinctively threw up her arm to ward off the blow. The knife cut a jagged gash along her arm, which she did not even feel as she thrust the nun away from her, causing her to fall backward. By the time she had regained her balance, her victim had retrieved her own tool for exacting vengeance. Lissie alone was immobile, her face blank and unconcerned as the two women crouched near her like primitive savages, knives upraised, prepared to fight to the death.

Before the car had pulled to a complete stop, Bert was racing for the front door of the house, key already in hand. While George struggled to free himself from the safety belt, Bert burst into the sealed house, the door swinging shut after him, automatically locking George outside. In vain the latter hammered against the unyielding wood, his voice lost in the howl of the winds. Realizing it was futile to try to attract his friend's attention, he retired miserably to the relative safety of the car. Bert would soon come to let him in, he thought. But he would have a very long wait.

Inside, Bradley raced wildly through the house, driven by guilt and fear, calling for his wife and children. His mind took refuge in the silence in the house. It could only mean that they were all fast asleep; they would laugh at his concern in the morning when they sat around the breakfast table together. As he mounted the front stairs, the sounds of Lissie's music box met his ears. How she loved that lullaby! Unconsciously, he started to hum the tune as he headed for her room first. Finding it empty, he assumed she was taking comfort in sleeping with someone in one of the other rooms. She was not in the master bedroom, nor was her mother. There was no one in Richard's room either. Hoping against hope that they were all safe together, he had but one room left, Stacey's. Entering her room gingerly, he caught sight of her headless corpse sprawled on the floor, the macabre head reflecting its now monstrous features in the mirror. Too stunned to scream his horror, he started to gag. Only panic, the urgent need to find the others, prevented him from vomiting up his terror. Instead, he spun on his heel and continued the frantic search for the rest of his family. This was something that Arlen had not expected, that Alice would reenact the carnage she had witnessed as a child in this house. Had Evalynn Desmond been the killer after all? Was Alice repeating what her own mother had done to her own children? Guilt nagged at the edges of his feverish mind. He had failed them all.

Grabbing a lantern from his room, he was about to continue the search in the lower regions when he remembered the attic. Sweating heavily he mounted the narrow staircase, not daring to call out. It was the very last time he would ever think of Amy, glad that she had not been here. The gory scene that greeted his arrival confirmed his worst fears. The murders were being done exactly as they had been during the hurricane of 1938. This time he had no control; he vomited violently, spewing up his anguish until he thought his stomach had been torn from him. Remembering the original police report, he realized that if Jessica had survived the original mayhem, Lissie might still be safe, hidden in the cubby that Mrs. Hanks had showed her.

Hurtling down the back stairs, he prayed that he might find her in the pantry, but the opened compartment indicated that someone had been there before him. What had his wife, Alice or Jessica, or whomever she thought she was, done with his little girl? He was now immersed in a state that George would have recognized instantly, a state of shock so profound that it formed a protective shield around his mind, refusing to allow it to confront the grim realities it had just witnessed in the upstairs rooms. His voice grew steady and calm as he sang out, "Lissie, Alice, I'm here—come out, come out, wherever you are!" He coaxed, he wheedled, he pleaded. But there were no responses.

Having left that which he feared most for last, Bert finally put his hand on the queerly placed door next to the stone fireplace. It yawned open to his pressure, but instead of the blackness he had anticipated, there was a dim but reassuring glow of light reaching up to him. Starting slowly down those precarious steps, his heart leaped for joy to see a tiny white-gowned figure sitting silently in the pool of light. The upturned face with those incredibly blue eyes revealed that it was truly his Lissie, no ghost child Jessica this!

"Daddy's here, sweetheart. I'm coming, baby," he cried out to her. Just as his feet touched the earthen floor and he was holding out his arms to his daughter, a banshee wail smashed into his senses. "Sinner!" came the inhuman voice, followed by a black-and-white swirl of fury. Sister Immaculata's knife was hacking into his chest, his face, his hands, while his ears were filled with the sound of his little girl's screams, which would ring through his soul for eternity.

Shreds of black robe and veil flew about the gruesome contortion of her face, as insanity gave Sister Immaculata the strength she needed to finish her work. Over and over, Lissie watched that silver speed into flesh, just as it had done to her mother, whose still warm and bleeding body was quite close by, just beyond the circle of light. Bleeding profusely, Bert tried to strangle the nun, but his strength was rapidly ebbing. Collapsing onto the cellar floor, his last few breaths came hard as he gazed mutely upon his silent little girl, who was staring at him with an indescribable expression of terror.

Just before his eyes dimmed, Sister Immaculata raised her lantern to view her triumph. He saw that Alice must have put up a mighty struggle, for the nun was bleeding heavily from all over her body—queer stigmata, these wounds were. As she started toward the rigid child, she swayed and fell atop the body of her sister, Jessica. It was there she breathed her last, her whispered prayers mingling strangely with the sounds of the song the child was now singing to the bodies of her parents.

By the time the storm had subsided enough for George to have organized a rescue team, it was 4 A.M. and he was frantic. As the others ran through the house crying out in horror and distress at what the early morning light revealed, George stood near that door to the cellar, afraid of what he would find. He stood there a long time gathering up his courage. Dr. Webber had never thought that murder would have resulted from his delaying Bert from getting to Mulberry. All he had wanted was to be rid of Alice by letting madness reclaim her in the storm. When he finally opened the door to reveal the depths of the blackness below his feet, he could hear a tiny, sweet voice, hoarse and cracking with strain. It was Lissie, singing the lullaby she had learned to love since she had been moved to Mulberry just three months before.

"Flow gently sweet Afton
Among thy green braes,
Flow gently I'll sing thee
A song in thy praise.
My mommy's asleep by
Thy murmuring stream,
Flow gently, sweet Afton—
Disturb not her dream."

Taking a flashlight from his coat pocket, George went down the steep stairs. The beam reflected off Lissie's madly glittering eyes as she sang her song to the quite still bodies of her mother, her father, and her aunt Margaret, a tiny, dead kitten clutched to her chest.